D1562582

THE
MERIDIAN
ASCENT

THE RHO AGENDA ASSIMILATION

○ ○ ●

BOOK THREE

Also by Richard Phillips

<u>The Rho Agenda</u>

The Second Ship
Immune
Wormhole

<u>The Rho Agenda Inception</u>

Once Dead
Dead Wrong
Dead Shift

<u>The Rho Agenda Assimilation</u>

The Kasari Nexus
The Altreian Enigma

PRAISE FOR THE AUTHOR

"Richard Phillips has led such a life that he absolutely nails the science aspect of this new sci-fi classic [*Immune* (Book Two of The Rho Agenda)] and yet also gets the action and the political aspects exactly right as well. Speaking as an old sci-fi writer myself, I know how hard it is to do what Phillips has done . . . I've read *Immune* to its brilliant and completely satisfying end—but only because this new writer is so skillful and this storyline is so inventive and moving that I don't want to miss a chapter of it . . . as good as any science fiction being written today."

—Orson Scott Card

THE
MERIDIAN
ASCENT

THE RHO AGENDA ASSIMILATION

○ ○ ●

BOOK THREE

RICHARD PHILLIPS

Text copyright © 2017 by Richard Phillips
All rights reserved.

Published by 47North, Seattle

www.apub.com

Amazon, the Amazon logo, and 47North are trademarks of Amazon.com, Inc., or its affiliates.

ISBN-13: 9781503935280
ISBN-10: 1503935280

Cover design by Shasti O'Leary Soudant

Printed in the United States of America

I dedicate this novel to my lovely wife, Carol, who has been my best friend and companion for thirty-six years.

EADRIC
EMPIRE

Doral Sea

Filial
Sea

Orthei

Lillith
Sea

Gorian
Sea

KORANTHIAN EMPIRE

ArvaiKheer
(subterranean)

Sea of
Koranth

The Blasted Lands

Briny Sea

GREAT OCEAN

▪ SCION ▪

Intelligence:	Eadrics, Koranthians	**Star system:**	Scion
Population:	455,000,000	**Previous state:**	War-torn
Assimilation:	In progress, 60%	**Threat level:**	Marginal

• VIEW OPTIONS •

- ☑ Label Features
- ☐ Assimilation centers
- ☐ Rebellion locations
- ☐ Population density

• RENDER •

- ☑ Terrain
- ☑ Atmosphere
- ☑ Background stars
- ☑ Graticule

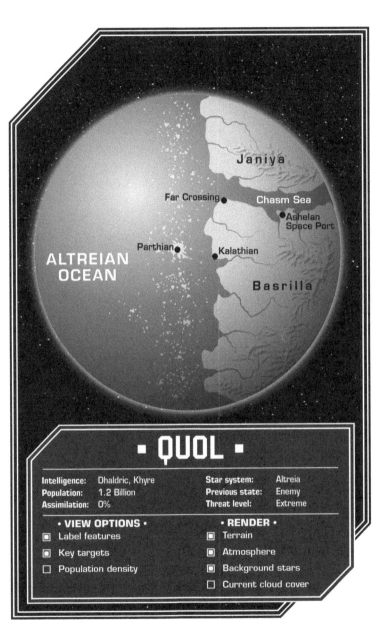

Janiya

Far Crossing •

Chasm Sea

• Ashelan
Space Port

Parthian •

• Kalathian

ALTREIAN
OCEAN

Basrilla

• QUOL •

Intelligence:	Dhaldric, Khyre	**Star system:**	Altreia
Population:	1.2 Billion	**Previous state:**	Enemy
Assimilation:	0%	**Threat level:**	Extreme

• VIEW OPTIONS •
- ☒ Label features
- ☒ Key targets
- ☐ Population density

• RENDER •
- ☒ Terrain
- ☒ Atmosphere
- ☒ Background stars
- ☐ Current cloud cover

CHAPTER 1

FRIENDSHIP CAVERN, NORTH KOREA

5 January

Alexandr Prokorov, wearing his dark-gray suit and black oxfords, stared down from the observation platform at the enormous array of machinery that would soon power up the Friendship Gate. He smiled, an expression he rarely bothered to show. Not that he was calm. Far from it. His nerves were so alive that sparks felt like they could fly from his fingertips at any moment. The seconds ticked off in slow motion, making each minute an hour.

In a way, the power surge that had thrown this gateway project behind schedule all those months ago had been fortuitous. It had allowed Dr. Lana Fitzpatrick to add a group of scientists from the United States to the team led by Dr. John Guo. Together they had come up with enhancements to the original design of the gateway that had been constructed in these man-made tunnels and cavernous rooms, far beneath the frozen North Korean countryside.

His thoughts shifted to the Smythe attack that had destroyed the sister gateway northeast of Frankfurt. It had been a costly but necessary sacrifice, the reason that Prokorov and the leadership of the United Federation of Nation States had made that project so visible to the public. And as he had intended, the Frankfurt Gateway had focused the Smythes' and the rest of the world's attention far away from this secret facility.

He turned to look at the inverted horseshoe within which the wormhole would form. This would mark the second time that the device was triggered. Last week's activation had been a brief one, just long enough to broadcast a message containing the gateway synchronization codes and the accompanying stasis field modulation codes. Together these would provide the Kasari the means to link their own gateway to this one, locking down the far end of the wormhole and allowing Prokorov's delegation to welcome their alien would-be benefactors to Earth.

A warning sound blared, followed by Dr. Guo's amplified voice. "Sixty seconds until stasis field generator power ramp."

The cavern lighting shifted from white to amber, and Prokorov felt his hands grip the elevated platform's steel railing. All his planning was finally about to yield fruit. This world was tearing itself apart, despite the efforts of the UFNS. It needed the guidance and wisdom that only an alien species that had worked through these primitive problems in its own distant past could provide. And this time, the Smythes would not be present to screw things up.

The ten-second countdown to stasis field generator power-up blared from the loudspeaker. When the count reached zero, a low hum arose and the stasis field shimmered to life, covering the wormhole gateway opening with a semitransparent blue glow. The color wasn't necessary other than to provide the observers visible evidence of the gateway's presence and dimensions.

Unlike the original Stephenson Gateway, this portal needed only a single stasis field to protect those inside the cavern from the vacuum on the far side once the gateway activated. The field would also provide a barrier against the different atmospheric composition and pressure from the Kasari world once the two wormhole devices successfully linked. The stasis field modulation codes that this team had provided would enable the Kasari and their equipment to pass through the gateway while ensuring that the waiting human scientists continued to breathe.

"Ten seconds until wormhole activation," Guo's voice announced.

As the new countdown proceeded, Prokorov swallowed hard. The presidents of the four UFNS member nations should be here, standing beside him. However, citing security concerns, all four had demurred. This confirmation that the federation's leadership consisted of a group of cowards embarrassed Prokorov, but he would stand in for them. On his orders, no security or military personnel were allowed anywhere inside this warren of tunnels and vast underground bunkers. He would take no chances that this welcoming could be misconstrued as threatening to humanity's benefactors.

Fifty feet below the steel grating upon which Prokorov stood, the gateway activated. For a seemingly endless stretch of tense moments, its interior showed a moving star field. Then, like an old television acquiring a distant signal, the image changed and clarified.

Prokorov didn't notice the gasp that escaped his lips as a four-armed alien stepped through the shimmering stasis field, accompanied by eleven hairy, black spider creatures. The spiders spread out, making their way rapidly past the scientists and engineers in a military maneuver that reminded Prokorov of Spetsnaz commandos clearing a room. They moved among the equipment efficiently and fast, stationing three of their number at the tunnel opening, which formed the only entrance or exit to the cavern.

Others scaled the steel scaffolding that surrounded the towering matter disrupter, which powered the stasis field generator and gateway. As one of the spiders paused to study him, the pungent scent of ammonia caused Prokorov to wrinkle his nose. Then the creature turned and

RICHARD PHILLIPS

climbed back down the steel scaffolding, giving the minister of federation security no further notice.

Apparently satisfied, the four-armed leader of the group turned back toward the gateway and signaled. Then, as hundreds of alien beings filed through the opening, escorted by hovering military vehicles, Prokorov shook himself from his paralysis and stepped into the elevator cage that would carry him down to the cavern floor.

It was time to officially welcome the Kasari Collective to Earth.

: CHAPTER 2

FRIENDSHIP CAVERN, NORTH KOREA

15 January

Kasari group commander Drolaag looked around his rapidly emerging Earth-based headquarters in satisfaction. The humans' representative, Prokorov, had selected an exceptional location for the wormhole gateway. The vast underground chambers and connecting passages had been built some time ago, designed for transport and storage of large quantities of military equipment. All of that had been cleared out before building the gateway.

Now it would serve as the Kasari base of operations and house the first of many assimilation centers. And Prokorov had volunteered to undergo the Kasari nanobot infusion that made him the second earthling member of the collective. The first had been a human female with the Earth name of Jennifer Smythe whom the collective had assimilated on the distant planet Scion, but she had somehow extracted her consciousness from the hive-mind.

That knowledge was worrisome but wasn't Drolaag's assigned worry.

Turning his thoughts back to the ongoing work at the facility, the first priority had been securing this base of operations. The installation of stasis field generators had been a significant step in that direction. Now, with the delivery of seven of the small fast-attack spacecraft and a battery of disrupter cannons, his engineers could erect a Kasari gateway, replacing the more modestly scaled human-built gateway.

Another group of Kasari engineers was working at top speed to finish the assimilation center that would perform mass injections of the nanobot serum, capable of processing several thousand humans every Earth day. Currently, only a few hundred of the leaders of the United Federation of Nation States had been treated. But very soon, the assimilation of the Federation Security Service military forces would begin. Prokorov had proven himself very efficient at setting up the process while maintaining the illusion that the troop movements were part of the ongoing wartime operations against UFNS enemies.

As Drolaag watched the stream of Kasari soldiers and equipment making its way into the cavern, he savored the thought that he was already ahead of schedule. Assuming his group kept up the pace, he would soon have enough of the UFNS military assimilated to announce the UFNS-Kasari alliance to the entire planet.

To these primitive cultures, "alliance" was a more acceptable term than "assimilation."

○ ○ ●

President Ted Benton stood at the centermost of the three Oval Office windows behind his desk, looking out at the leafless branches of the large tree just outside. Dark-gray clouds hung low over the White House grounds, almost but not yet a freezing fog.

His gaze drifted down to the long, narrow table beneath the center window, focusing on the pictures of his wife, Cindy, and his two sons. The oldest, James, had just graduated from Harvard Law School. The last of the three framed photographs showed a slim Army Ranger in his dress uniform, the ribbons that graced the left side of his chest a testament to his bravery. That bravery had put Jeffrey into a lonely plot in Arlington Cemetery.

The endless damned wars against the Islamic Alliance and their surrogates had taken his son, along with hundreds of thousands of other young men and women. That and the ongoing rebellion by the Native People's Alliance and the Safe Earth resistance movement had led him, and the majority of the American people, to the conclusion that Earth needed outside help and guidance.

As he pondered the rejuvenating power of the nanobots that coursed through his veins, he knew that welcoming the Kasari Collective to Earth had been the correct decision. He felt the cortical array that connected his brain to the hive-mind release a stream of endorphins that soothed his mind, delivering gentle reassurance.

Once more, he lifted his eyes to the dreary sight outside the window, shifting his vision into the infrared that let him peer farther through the mist. Halfway around the world, the elite soldiers of the Seventy-Fifth Ranger Regiment were now receiving the same wondrous infusion that President Benton had benefited from last week. Soon, the entire armed forces of the UFNS member nations would become the supersoldiers they were meant to be. Millions of them.

After that, the need for secrecy would come to an end. As thousands of additional assimilation centers came online around the globe, the acquiescent portions of the civilian populations of the United States, the New Soviet Union, Europe, and the East Asian People's Alliance would also join the collective.

President Benton turned and sat down at his desk, a slow smile spreading across his patrician features. Then the real work of defeating the resistance would begin.

CHAPTER 3

SMYTHE FORTRESS, NEW ZEALAND

16 January

Wearing black jeans and a maroon pullover top, Janet Alexandra Price had her long dark hair pinned in its customary twist with her signature hair-needle. The decorative etchings along the needle's six-inch length performed two useful functions: they made the surface just rough enough to keep the needle in place and gave her a good grip when she put it to other uses. She left the underground command center and walked down a wide passage toward the central conference room where this morning's status update would take place. Months had passed since she'd fired a weapon at a living target, but she felt naked without the Glock on her hip.

The quality of the air in this facility, a mile below the surface, was a testament to the filtered-ventilation and humidity-control systems. But the pace of ongoing construction sent a thrumming vibration through the titanium-reinforced walls and imparted a faint metallic taste to the rear of her tongue. For the thousandth time, she felt the weight of all those tons of rock above pressing down on her shoulders. Perhaps this afternoon she would find time for a trip to the surface and a ten-mile run beneath New Zealand's warm January sun.

She turned the corner, stepped up to the door, and waited as it processed her biometric information. When the entrance whisked open, she stepped inside, pleased to see that all the others were already present. Taking her seat at the head of the conference table, she looked around. Heather and Mark Smythe, along with Janet's son, Rob, sat at the right side of the table while Jamal Glover, Dr. Eileen Wu, and Dr. Denise Jennings occupied the left.

Janet was having a difficult time adjusting to her boy's demand that she call him Rob instead of Robby. At eleven, he looked seventeen. Janet knew that was partially due to the trauma he'd endured over the last eighteen months. Life-and-death struggles tended to age a person, but Rob's alien augmentations had amplified that effect.

She had left the fourth of the Altreian crew members' headsets within her baby's reach, and he had grabbed it, accidentally sliding the device onto his temples as he attempted to mouth the two beaded ends. The fact that the headset had altered him was her fault. The fact that Mark, Jen, and Heather had put on the other headsets and been altered in good ways gave her hope that Rob's augmentations would be advantageous to him as well. And they had been. Even the alien AI named Eos who'd invaded his brain through the headset had further enhanced him.

But Rob's accelerated maturation scared the crap out of Janet. And these last few months, his aging had gotten faster. Would it slow down once he reached his physical peak? Or would he be an old man by the time he was thirty? One more worry to add to Janet's pile.

Janet forced her thoughts back to the present.

Technically, Janet didn't need this meeting to receive updates on the project's status. She could have received intel from the facility's neural network. But she liked to look into her people's faces as they briefed her and hear the inflection in their voices. She hadn't asked for this leadership position, but now that she had it, she found that she enjoyed the work.

Janet noticed Heather drawing on a piece of paper, with a far-off look in her eyes.

"Heather, what's that you're doodling?"

Heather looked up and spun the piece of paper to Janet. It was a mathematical equation that Janet didn't recognize.

$$m = \frac{h}{c^2} \sum_{1}^{n} f$$

"I was thinking about the new matter disrupter-synthesizers we have the robots building," Heather said. "Apparently, I subconsciously scribbled the equation that forms the basis for Dr. Stephenson's theory. Each type of matter is a wave packet composed of a particular set of frequencies."

"So?"

"So the mass of any particle of matter is proportional to the sum of all the frequencies that make up the wave packet."

Janet frowned. "Right now I need you focused on this meeting."

Across the table, Heather's eyes narrowed but she managed to stifle an angry retort.

"What's our current manufacturing status?" Janet asked.

"As of this morning, we've replaced all of the twenty-three hundred combat robots and drones lost in our assault on the German wormhole gateway," Heather said. "We've also replaced all of the micro-bots expended within the gateway cavern. The newest of our matter disrupter-synthesizers will be operational in the next few days and directly tied into the upgraded molecular manufacturing system."

"When do you think the MDS will be fully operational?"

Janet saw Heather's eyes fade to milky white. No matter how many times she watched the savant go deep into her visions of probable futures, the act still sent a chill up her spine.

Heather came out of her vision. "Tuesday."

"Excellent. What about you, Mark?"

"The prototype for our new stasis field generator is giving us some problems."

"How so?"

"According to Dad and Fred Smythe, it starts up correctly but develops a spiraling instability over the course of the next ten minutes. I've confirmed with Heather that there's nothing wrong with the design, but its Power-draw is placing too much stress on the materials within the walls of the resonator cavity. It looks like we won't be able to fix it until the new MDS is operational next week. That will enable us to create a stronger version of the alloy."

Janet frowned. "I want you to stop all further testing of the prototype. It's not worth getting someone killed."

"We've already shut it down. On the plus side, in addition to the new Earth gate we installed with the Native People's Alliance in Bolivia, the Romanian arm of the Safe Earth resistance is scheduled to take delivery of another Earth gate three and a half hours from now. We've already shown their people how to activate the construction robots that will assemble the gate and its cold-fusion power supply."

Heather Smythe had based the design of the Earth gates on the Kasari wormhole gates that provided stepping-stones to the stars. But these required only a fraction of the power of their alien counterparts, with a maximum range that extended from Earth to just beyond lunar orbit. When they connected one of these gates to another somewhere on Earth, they provided instantaneous bidirectional transport.

Janet shifted her attention to her son. "Rob?" she asked.

"Eos and I have been helping Jamal, Eileen, and Denise with their cyber-warfare attacks. I'll let them brief you on that, but it's not going great."

"He's not wrong," said Jamal Glover. "The world's a freaking mess and getting worse by the day. Even though we've been able to hide our tracks from the Federation Security Service, the NSA, and the other UFNS intelligence agencies, that's not helping our Safe Earth political allies. We're losing more Safe Earth resistance cells every week."

Janet studied the handsome man in the 1920s-style suit, complete with shoe-covering black-and-white spats. Although today he wasn't wearing his trademark black fedora with white hatband, that accessory, along with his cocky grin, usually completed the look. This morning the smile was missing. Given their situation, Janet couldn't blame him for that.

"That's why we need those Earth gates up and running," she said.

"Yes," said Eileen, "but even if we start funneling combat robots and weapons through those gates, we can't compete with the numbers the UFNS military can throw at our allies. I think their best bet is to disappear into society and lay low."

"And wait for what?" Janet asked, unable to keep the frustration out of her voice. "For the UFNS to start building another gateway? Our odds don't improve with time."

"No, they don't," said Heather. "Not unless we can come up with a game-changing technology."

"Hopefully one that won't wipe out the world," said Mark.

Janet saw Heather shrug and understood what she was feeling. The world war gathering on the horizon didn't look like the happy-ending kind, not for them and not for the rest of humanity.

Once again, her thoughts turned to Jack. If he were here, he would say something about changing the rules. But Jack wasn't here to do his crazy stuff. So if Janet wanted to save Rob, her friends, and the concept of human liberty, she was going to have to woman up and take this operation to the next level.

Janet rose to her feet and looked from one person to the other, feeling the muscles in her jaws tighten.

"I want the upgraded matter disrupter-synthesizer finished. Then the new stasis field generator. After that, we'll figure out how to change the game. Go make it happen."

Without waiting for a response, she turned and walked out of the room.

:CHAPTER 4

MERIDIAN ASCENT, DEEP SPACE

57 Earth Days After Rechristening (MA Day 57)

The *Meridian Ascent*, the vessel formerly known as the Rho Ship, emerged from a wormhole just outside the Scion system, smoothly transitioning into subspace to provide the necessary inertial damping to make the trip survivable. As the starship completed the maneuver, Jennifer Smythe released the stasis field that had cradled her, watching as Captain Raul and Dgarra did the same. Wearing a formfitting black-and-purple uniform that completed her lifelike holographic projection, the female AI whom Raul had named VJ stood to his right as he leaned back in his translucent blue captain's chair.

Despite the starship's smooth arrival, Jennifer had to concentrate to relieve the tension that had worked its way into her muscles. The decision to return to Scion had not been an easy one. She had argued that they should make the trip to Earth instead. But VJ's breakthrough had decided the issue. So, whether Jennifer liked it or not, Scion was now their target.

In the eight weeks that the crew had spent in space, having fled twenty-three light-years from Scion, they had made several significant technological breakthroughs. The one that had improved the quality of their lives the most was VJ's creation of a food synthesizer. This was a small MDS that could analyze the composition of any food placed within it and thereafter perfectly re-create the cuisine. Unfortunately, what lay in the ship's stores didn't quite qualify as gourmet fare.

The stash consisted of an assortment of frozen fish from one of Scion's lakes and the few remaining military meals called MREs. On the positive side, these contained salt, pepper, Tabasco sauce, some candy, and desserts, along with entrées that included spaghetti in meat sauce, beans, and rice.

But the breakthrough that had brought them here had been VJ's adaptation of the serum that had disabled the cortical array of Kasari nanobots, which had robbed Jennifer of her free will. VJ had created a software-only version of the governing algorithm. The crew intended to use that computer virus to infect the primary router that linked the assimilated minds on Scion to the Kasari hive-mind.

If all went well, the virus would restore the free will of the assimilated population on Scion and then spread through the wormhole gateway to infect other Kasari worlds. It would not change the minds of any who wanted to be a part of the collective but would give those who had been forced to assimilate a chance to resist. More important, by disrupting the cortical nanobot array within each being, the virus would destroy the mental links to the Kasari hive-mind.

As the *Meridian Ascent* transitioned out of subspace, Jennifer looked to her left, where Dgarra sat in the chair designated for the starship's tactical officer. The seven-foot-tall warrior still carried the regal bearing of the general who had once been the Koranthian Empire's second most powerful leader. The ridges of bone that formed his eyebrows extended up over the top of his dark-skinned, hairless head. She was tempted to reach out and stroke those twin crown-bones she had once found so intimidating. Instead, she gently touched his thoughts, applying a soft caress that would soothe without distracting him.

General Dgarra's warriors had captured her on the planet Scion. Dgarra had made her a slave and sent her into the tunnels to toil and die. But she hadn't died. She had grown strong. As Dgarra watched her work and saw her fight at his side against the Kasari invaders, he had come to respect her, eventually making her a ward of his house and his aide-de-camp. And over the months that followed, they had fallen in love.

But Dgarra was no longer the heir to the Koranthian throne. He was a wanted criminal with a death sentence awaiting him should he return to his people. Like the rest of his new allies, he had accepted his position in the ship's crew. Captain Raul had designated Dgarra the tactical officer, VJ the science officer, and Jennifer his first officer. Due to her empathic and telepathic augmentations, she also served as the ship's communications officer.

"Performing long-range worm-fiber scans of the outer Scion system," said Dgarra in his deep voice.

Jennifer still felt a little strange hearing Dgarra speak English. The headset that VJ had created for him connected his mind to the starship's neural net. It had taught him the language, just as that connection had taught the Koranthian language to Raul and VJ. Jennifer felt a small surge of pride at the thought that she had learned to speak and understand an alien tongue the hard way.

"Any sign of Kasari presence?" asked Raul.

"None within sensor range. All of the Kasari ships must be staying closer to Scion."

Jennifer felt herself nod. That was good news. It would have been nice to be able to scan normal-space from within subspace. Instead, they had been forced to drop out of subspace outside the Scion system to make sure that the outer planets were clear.

"VJ," said Raul, "plot a subspace course that will bring us out behind the outermost planet in the system."

"Already done."

That VJ could anticipate what Raul was about to order didn't surprise Jennifer, given their shared connection to the ship's neural net, but the assumptive nature of VJ's action was a little creepy. So was the arrogant smile that she flashed Jennifer.

"Fine," Raul said. "Make it happen."

By now Jennifer was so used to the subspace transition that she barely noticed it. Unlike a wormhole transit, there was no need to wrap herself in a protective stasis cocoon. The subspace maneuver took just over a minute.

When the *Meridian Ascent* shifted back into normal-space, the sensors pumped imagery of the gaseous blue giant and its twenty-one moons into Jennifer's mind. From the ship's current position, only a thin halo could be seen in the visible spectrum, but infrared showed the raging storms within the planet's atmosphere.

Dgarra's voice drew her attention to the worm-fiber viewers under his control.

"Long-range sensors have identified thirteen Kasari fast-attack spacecraft around Scion. Another twenty-seven are scattered throughout the system."

"Wow," said Raul. "They've tripled their presence since we left the planet."

Jennifer tweaked the neural net, filling her mind with the same data and imagery that Dgarra was seeing. Apparently, the subspace capabilities that the *Meridian Ascent* had demonstrated when VJ and Raul had rescued Dgarra and Jennifer had alarmed the Kasari. They now deployed an unusually large contingent of military might for the assimilation of a single planet. The collective usually relied on a welcoming indigenous population to do most of the fighting.

But the obvious reinforcements weren't what constricted Jennifer's throat. What additional security measures had the Kasari put in place on Scion?

"I recommend aborting this operation," she said.

"Just because they have more ships circling the planet doesn't change anything," said VJ. "We can still identify where the primary router is located, pop out of subspace at the appropriate location, and insert the virus before they know what we're trying to do. We'll be gone long before the fast-attack ships can respond."

"That's assuming you can penetrate the encryption on that device," said Jennifer.

"I guarantee it."

Jennifer felt her temples throb. "And what if you're wrong?"

Dgarra turned his gaze on Jennifer. "The improvements we've made to the stasis field generator should protect us long enough for VJ to complete her task," he said. "We'll be back in subspace before the Kasari can target enough firepower to penetrate our shielding. This is our only chance to save my planet. And it might just save yours as well."

As much as she hated to argue with Dgarra, she had to voice her worry.

"We can't use the worm fibers to scan Scion to find the router. The Kasari will detect them. We might be walking into a trap."

"So what?" asked VJ. "They can't tell where the scan originated because the worm fibers are just tiny space-time folds."

"So far," said Jennifer, "we've positioned the worm-fiber viewers in empty space, looking for the fast-attack ships. If we were to scan inside one of those ships or in a heavily instrumented area on Scion, such as inside the gateway facility, the Kasari would be alerted to our presence. After that, you can bet they'll be watching for signs of a subspace transition like the kind we did in ArvaiKheer."

"That's why you designed the micro-drones. They're so small that we can wrap them in a subspace bubble and send them into the city of Orthei with a pop no louder than a hand clap."

Jennifer bit her lower lip. Damn, VJ was irritating. But she was also right.

Raul interrupted the argument. "How many of the micro-drones do we currently have?"

"Nineteen," Jennifer said. "Not nearly enough for a decent search."

"And if we went into full-scale production?"

Jennifer paused to consider this. "It's not just them. We would have to make the small subspace field generators and the super-capacitors to power them. If we devote the primary MDS and the molecular assembler to that task, we could produce six, possibly even seven, per hour."

"I could optimize your process," said VJ, "increasing the efficiency by 53.7 percent."

"Of course you could," said Jennifer under her breath.

"I didn't catch that," said Raul.

"Never mind."

Once again, Jennifer caught the hint of a smile on VJ's softly glistening lips.

Dgarra spoke. "Captain, I recommend that we exit this star system and invest two weeks in manufacturing an enhanced micro-drone capability. It may give us the edge that we need to confront the increased Kasari military presence on and around Scion."

Raul leaned back in his chair. "Agreed. VJ, take us out of here."

"Specific location?"

"Somewhere we can't be seen. Use your best judgment."

As VJ initiated the subspace transition, Jennifer found herself scowling at Raul. Best judgment indeed.

○　○　●

Kasari Headquarters, Orthei, Scion

Kasari group commander Shalegha surveyed her operations center, situated in the tallest of the skyscrapers in the Eadric capital of Orthei. During the time since the humans had rescued General Dgarra and escaped Scion aboard the stolen Kasari world ship, the Kasari had almost completed the assimilation of the planet's winged Eadric race. Having signed an armistice treaty with the Koranthian emperor, Magtal, the Eadric and Kasari forces under Shalegha's command had ceased all combat operations.

She had no doubt that the Koranthians would have to be dealt with at some later point in time. Since the subterranean warrior race had oddly structured brains that made assimilation into the Kasari hive-mind impossible, Shalegha was left with one option: extermination. But for now, keeping the peace better served her purpose.

The additional fast-attack ships she had requested were positioned to dissuade the humans from returning aboard the stolen world ship. Shalegha was disappointed that she would be denied the opportunity to examine the major upgrades that the humans had made to that vessel. They had somehow managed to give the ship the ability to enter and travel through subspace.

Although Shalegha could not be sure that the rogue crew had achieved faster-than-light travel in subspace, it was still a dangerous possibility. Even more disturbing, the humans had engineered a mechanism that allowed them to survive as the world ship passed through a wormhole of its own creation, something the Kasari had never managed to accomplish.

Regardless, the rogue crew and their altered starship posed no significant threat to Scion's assimilation. Within twenty-two Scion days, that task would be completed. Then Shalegha could reconsider the truce between the Kasari and the Koranthian Empire.

:CHAPTER 5

Twice Bound Era (TBE), Orbday 9

Jack had to give the Altreians credit. Artistic beauty was a deeply ingrained part of their culture, something they incorporated into anything they bothered to build or create, and the Parthian, the building that formed the seat of the Altreian government, represented the epitome of their art. Seen from above, the structure looked like a gigantic glass teardrop laid on its side and sliced into multicolored layers. The topmost governmental floors shifted through deep shades of magenta that transitioned through purples and blues. Levels descended into spirals of orange laced with greens before shifting back to dark blue at the bottom of the structure. The residences lined the right side of the teardrop, resembling tiny orange bubbles carved into a translucent surface.

With his hands clasped behind his back, Jack Gregory, in Khal Teth's black-uniformed body, stood at the outer wall in the overlord's chambers, an ivory blade strapped to each thigh. Far beyond that wall, the magnificent magenta orb of Altreia hung low on the horizon, its position in the sky a constant as seen from the Parthian on this tidally locked world of Quol. Higher in the twilight sky, bright stars bejeweled the Krell Nebula's orange lace.

For a moment, a vision filled his mind of Janet holding his hand as they stared up at the place where the Southern Cross graced a star-filled New Zealand sky. He could feel the warmth of her palm in his. But the last time he had seen his wife, she had stormed out of the cavern beneath the ruins of the Kalasasaya Temple, furious at Jack for making the decision that would take him away from her.

Jack hadn't wanted to, but he had let her go. Then he had walked through the passage that took him into the buried Altreian research vessel and let the alien rider in his mind guide him into a chrysalis cylinder. That cylinder put his human body into suspended animation and transported his and Khal Teth's minds into the Altreian body he now wore. Khal Teth's body.

In the months that he and Khal Teth had struggled for primacy, Jack had discovered the true depths of the depravity embraced by Khal Teth and members of his psionic Dhaldric race. Throughout the millennia of their rule, they had used their psychic abilities to enslave the smaller gray-skinned Khyre race who made up 70 percent of Quol's population.

But Jack had discovered a secret.

By allowing the Khyre to form a mutual bond with him, Jack could channel the sum of the psionic abilities of those individuals plus his own. And he discovered that he could form the bond with willing members of the Dhaldric race as well.

The power granted him through his links to the Twice Bound had enabled him to kill the Altreian overlord, Parsus, and take his place. Jack had used that ability to cast Khal Teth's mind into the void and block it from returning. But in an ironic twist, those actions had also trapped him on this world, far from the wife and son he longed for.

A mental alert pulled Jack from his reverie. His psionic mind detected that the Altreian military operations center within the Parthian had just gone to high alert. On a distant planet, the research vessel *AQ37Z* had just detected the activation of a Kasari wormhole gateway and had sent the required notification to the Altreian command authority. That alert had automatically triggered the activation of the biological weapon that, upon arrival at its target, would kill all intelligent life on the planet.

The weapon was far from perfect in countering the spread of the Kasari Collective. The Altreians detected only a fraction of the Kasari-targeted worlds, and the Altreian planet killer could be used only during the earliest stage of assimilation. Once the Kasari had established a significant military presence in a star system, they would destroy the planet killer before it could deploy its biological weapon against the planet's population. Even if the weapon managed to reach the targeted world, its payload would be ineffective against anyone who had undergone the infusion of Kasari nanites.

Jack's body went cold, knowing as he did that this response was enshrined in Altreian military doctrine to such an extent that no overlord had ever issued a stand-down order. Until now.

Sensing his commanding general's excitement, Jack linked their two minds.

"General Zolat," Jack said, adopting the formality that Zolat expected from his overlord. "Recall the bioweapon, immediately."

Despite the fact that this Dhaldric general was one of Jack's Twice Bound, a sudden fury boiled within him, the downside of the voluntary bonding. All Twice Bound retained their free will.

"Overlord! We have little time to get the weapon to its target before the Kasari establish an impregnable planetary defense. If I gave that order, the High Council would accuse me of treason."

"The High Council will do as I command."

The shock he felt in the other's mind surprised Jack.

"What of your Twice Bound principles?" Zolat asked. "Will you now dictate your will to the people, just as the government that you replaced did? Or will you bring this matter before the High Council so that it can be properly considered and decided upon?"

"I will not allow an entire world filled with intelligent beings to be obliterated."

"Overlord, it is my duty to advise you when I think that a course of action will have negative consequences. The majority of our fleet is situated well beyond the influence of the Twice Bound. Already there are rumblings of discontent among the Dhaldric commanders. They do not like the fact that you have declared the Khyre race the equals of the Dhaldric. This order will place additional stress upon the command structure within a significant portion of the fleet."

Jack increased the power of his mental link with the general. Although Zolat did not like the command, his loyalty remained intact.

"My decision is final. Execute my order."

"Yes, Overlord."

General Zolat issued the order that was immediately translated into a subspace transmission. The recall would return the robotic weapon to its holding location, deep within the barren reaches of the Krell Nebula. The planet killer and its array of companions were far too dangerous to maintain anywhere near an inhabited star system.

Jack broke the mental link he had established and returned his gaze to the beautiful twilight sky. The knowledge that a new Kasari gateway had opened on Earth and stabilized long enough to trigger the research vessel's message turned his thoughts back to Janet and their son, Robby. His only chance to save his family might require a direct attack on the invading Kasari by the Altreian space fleet. But even though the Altreians had battled the spread of the Kasari Collective throughout the galaxy, they had always done so through proxy wars. Both sides knew that direct conflict between their empires might escalate into mutually assured destruction.

But now that Jack had completed what he had come here to do, there were certainly going to be consequences.

Jack could live with that. Even on a galactic scale.

:CHAPTER 6

FRIENDSHIP ASSIMILATION CENTER, NORTH KOREA

6 February

Alexandr Prokorov watched as long lines of soldiers snaked their way through the enormous assimilation cavern toward the row of auto-injector booths. To avoid squabbles between those who might be reluctant to undergo the Kasari treatment, they had merely been told that they would be receiving the latest upgrade to the nanites already in their systems. To lighten the mood, their commanders had also informed them that, in addition to healing faster than ever, this version of the nanite serum would enhance their experience of alcohol's more pleasant side effects.

As each soldier reached the injection point, a green light would indicate when he was to step into the cylindrical, soundproof booth. Once he was sealed inside, the injector arm would press itself against the person's left shoulder, sending a puff of compressed air to spray the Kasari nanobot serum through the skin of the upper arm. Although the body's initial reaction to the nanites working their way through blood and into muscles and nerves was a shock wave of intense pain, the cortical nanobot array produced the most profound changes. At first the newly infused felt a sense of vertigo, as if he stood on a slender ledge, peering down into an infinite chasm below. This sensation generally gave way to wonder as the hive whispered in his head, granting calm and reassurance that all was well. Yet this feeling didn't take hold with some of the more rebellious of the assimilated. These poor fools bore the perpetual internal turmoil that Prokorov thought they deserved.

Just over a minute later, the exit door would slide open and a new member of the Kasari Collective would step out to take his place among the assimilated members of his unit in the adjacent rooms.

There, for the first time, they would see some of the Kasari aliens that had come through the wormhole gate.

Prokorov turned toward General Hollande, the commander of the EU army division currently undergoing assimilation. Although Prokorov could have queried the hive-mind for the answer to his question, he chose to speak.

"General Hollande, how much of your division has been processed so far today?"

"Two-thirds. Approximately nine thousand soldiers."

That was good. The assimilation center had increased its efficiency significantly during the last week. As Prokorov prepared to ask a follow-up question, a commotion broke out near the central injector booths.

From his vantage point at the edge of the cavern, he could see that several fights had started.

"What the hell is going on over there?" he asked.

But before the general could answer, Prokorov accessed the hive-mind for a better perspective, rewinding the time so that he could see what had started this disruption.

A large black soldier had been approaching one of the booths when he suddenly roared and attacked those around him, fighting his way back through the lines. It was as if a mesmerizing spell that had kept all these soldiers in thrall had broken. Dozens and then hundreds of other soldiers joined the rebel in fighting their way toward the exit, ignoring the orders of the officers struggling to reestablish control.

Several Kasari entered the cavernous room to block the exit, a move that turned the squall into a cyclone. The unarmed soldiers tackled military police, stripping them of their weapons as gunfire crackled through the room.

Prokorov swore, then linked his mind with that of Kasari group commander Drolaag.

"Gas the assimilation chamber!"

His mental request came across as a command, but Drolaag took no offense. Overhead valves opened, releasing a heavier-than-air fog, long tendrils of which reached down toward the floor. And when the gas touched those who had not yet been infused with the Kasari nanobots, they dropped to the ground.

Prokorov breathed in the fog, noting the cloying smell of rotten fruit but showing no symptoms of distress. His Kasari nanobots processed this chemical cloud as easily as they processed air.

In seconds, it was over. Large numbers of assimilated humans and Kasari aliens moved through the chamber, picking up unconscious soldiers and carrying them to the injection booths. Much more slowly than before, the assimilation process began again as the workers dumped one troop after another into the cylinders, closed the door, and waited until a new member of the collective stepped out the far side.

Prokorov hissed in disgust and turned toward the exit. He had seen enough for one day. So much for the vaunted improvement in efficiency of the assimilation. He thanked the stars that this had not been live-streamed to the Internet masses. That day would come, but only after he was ready to announce the existence of the Kasari gateway to the world.

Jamal Glover leaned back in his zero-gravity chair and took off the headset that linked his mind to the supercomputer network within the New Zealand underground world the Smythes had created. Technically, their robots had created this incredible network of tunnels and rooms that housed the world's most sophisticated manufacturing operation. But the Smythes had designed and built the first generation of the robots and directed them to produce Heather's ever-more-advanced designs.

Cradled in the chair beside his, Eileen Wu also lifted the Alice band headset from her temples and turned to meet his gaze. The Chinese American former NSA computer scientist known as Hex was four years younger than Jamal, and as usual, he found the intelligence in her eyes mesmerizing.

"Learn anything?" she asked.

"Nothing useful. But it's strange. The UFNS headquarters is not making the number of security mistakes I'm used to seeing. It's almost like they had a big training program where people actually paid attention to their cyber-security instructors."

"Interesting. I've noticed the same thing at the Pentagon and Special Operations Command. And there've been some odd troop movements as well."

This caught Jamal's attention. "How so?"

"On the surface, the movement orders look ordinary. The manifests are what you would expect to see for troops and equipment being moved into the conflict areas bordering the countries of the Islamic Alliance. The weaponry shows up on schedule, but I've observed some unusual troop delays. Usually just a few days, but I can't find any record that any stopover occurred."

"Are we talking about troop movements by air?"

"And by sea."

"No communications with headquarters?" Jamal asked.

"It's as if they passed through the Bermuda Triangle."

"Have you checked satellite imagery?"

Eileen paused. "I thought I'd leave that to you."

As interesting as Jamal found this conversation, the rumble from his stomach distracted him.

"Tell you what," he said. "You buy me dinner and I'll apply my big brain to the stuff you can't figure out."

He watched her eyes crinkle at the corners.

"Hilarious."

Climbing to his feet, Jamal offered Eileen his arm, as if he were her date for the evening.

"So?" he asked.

Eileen rose, ignoring his extended elbow, to lead the way out through the doorway.

"We'd better get you some food," she said. "If you get any more light-headed, you'll pass out on me."

As he followed her into the long hallway that led toward the cafeteria, Jamal grinned. For the first time today, he'd almost succeeded in making Eileen smile.

○   ○   ●

Freddy Hagerman stepped out of the meeting between President Benton and the senior leadership of the senate, bothered by something he couldn't quite put his finger on. Outside the White House, Al Monroe, a blond ex-Ranger, and Judith Miller, a competent former FBI agent with gray hair and a slight British accent, escorted him to his driverless Cadillac sedan. With his breath puffing out in a white mist, Freddy climbed into the back seat. The other two slid into the front of the silver car.

Even after all this time, Freddy still found the fact that there was no such thing as a driver's seat anymore somewhat disconcerting. But it enabled his bodyguards to stay focused on the job of keeping him alive. Not such an easy task these days. Probably the only thing keeping him that way was that he was the political leader of the peaceful Safe Earth movement. As such, he had the popular backing of 47 percent of the U.S. population. Unfortunately, 53 percent of those residing in the fifty-nine states supported President Benton's globalist policies.

Freddy harrumphed loud enough to cause Judith to glance back at him. But she had grown used to his periodic outbursts, and her gaze didn't linger.

Globalist hell. President Benton and the UFNS were determined to place humanity's independence in the hands of an alien race. Freddy thanked God every morning that the Smythes had destroyed the latest ill-conceived attempt to make that a reality, despite the devastation they had left in their wake just northeast of Frankfurt.

So what was it about the president's demeanor that troubled him so?

Freddy spoke the words that put the car in motion, taking him back to the Hart Senate Office Building. When he reached his seventh-floor office, he told his executive assistant that he didn't want to be disturbed and then settled into his comfortable leather chair, the answer to the question of the hour still eluding him.

As he was about to turn his attention to next week's schedule, a new thought wormed its way out of his subconscious. President Benton's mannerisms had *not* changed. But now his mental sharpness and ability to recall intricate details of complex discussions reminded Freddy of the Smythes' eidetic memories.

That was it. Throughout this morning's meeting, the group of senior senators had thrown questions at the president on a broad spectrum of topics. Although Freddy had not agreed with Benton on many items, the president's answers had been remarkably crisp and clear. Now that

Freddy thought back on the meeting, a very slight pause had preceded many of the president's answers, almost as if the man were placing a mental query to an external source rather than searching his own memories for answers.

Freddy shook his head. Ridiculous. This line of thinking was getting him nowhere.

He turned his attention to next week's Safe Earth fund-raiser in Richmond. President Benton's oddities didn't merit further consideration.

CHAPTER 7

MERIDIAN ASCENT, SCION SPACE

MA Day 71

VJ brought the *Meridian Ascent* out of subspace a hundred million miles beyond the farthest of the Scion system's planets. Immediately, she began the agreed-upon maneuver, adjusting the starship's velocity vector to match that of their initial target on Scion.

"Ready to release first insertion package," she said.

"Commence insertion sequence," said Raul.

"Aye, Captain," said VJ, noting with satisfaction the hint of annoyance her archaic verbiage brought to Jennifer's face.

Smiling, VJ created a stasis field bubble around the interior of the cargo hatch and then opened it without extending the ramp. That modification of their ship had been one that Raul had intended to make for some time, but the crew had gotten around to it only in the last several days. VJ wrapped the first group of six gnat-sized micro-drones in another stasis bubble and moved it out through the field that kept the interior of the amidships bay from depressurizing.

When the micro-drone group was fifty yards off the starboard, VJ made a final adjustment to fine-tune the trajectory. Then she released the drones and issued the signal that initiated the preprogrammed journey through subspace that would bring them out a thousand feet above the Eadric capital city of Orthei. Due to their tiny size, they would be invisible to the sensors designed to detect much larger targets.

Moreover, the drones were each equipped with a one-time-use subspace field generator with just enough power to deliver them to their target. And when the micro-drones emerged from subspace, they would produce such a small displacement of the surrounding atmosphere that it would emit a sound no louder than a hand clap.

The drones disappeared, and VJ adjusted the ship's trajectory to match the next target as she prepared to deliver another package. Then the real fun would begin.

○   ○   ●

Raul had watched VJ smile as her subtle dig at Jennifer produced the AI's desired result. At some point, he would have to do something about the rivalry, assuming that he could get VJ to comply with his wishes. But since her behavior was a minor distraction to the otherwise professional manner in which his crew performed, the conversation would wait.

He let the neural net amplify the imagery of the first six micro-drones outside his ship. One second the tiny things were there, and the next, they were gone. The flying sensors didn't have enough power to stay in subspace for very long. They didn't need to. A subspace bubble would form around each micro-drone that would briefly accelerate it toward the target. That bubble would last just long enough to get the drone there before dying.

Each micro-drone would emerge with the exact normal-space momentum vector it had before entering subspace, one matching its target on Scion.

When the neural net delivered the first six subspace video streams into his mind, Raul gasped. As he had previously observed using the worm-fiber viewers, this Eadric city by the lake was filled with gleaming high-rise buildings, each adorned with stunning balconies, none of which had safety rails. And soaring onto or off those balconies were the closest things to angels he could imagine.

They were beautiful. If not for the huge wings that sprouted from behind their shoulder blades, they looked almost human—although a bit slimmer and taller—with fine feathers where humans had hair. They wore shimmering skintight uniforms that seemed designed to reduce drag.

Lovely plazas and parks separated the buildings. There were no roads. Vehicular traffic traveled through the air, albeit at a much higher rate of speed and along different routes than the flying wingestrians. The aerial thoroughfares for high-speed aircars formed public transit routes. That the heavenly Eadric people would sacrifice their love of beauty to become a part of the Kasari Collective had always mystified the hell out of Raul.

The drones separated, dividing the city below into sextants, each heading toward its own search sector. The ones that held Raul's primary interest were the drones targeted for the Kasari assimilation center. This was the most likely location for the planetary master router that connected the assimilated minds on Scion to the hive-mind on other Kasari worlds.

As would be expected, given their lack of subspace technology, communication between the Kasari cortical arrays was limited by the speed of light. The only thing that made communication among the collective possible was the fact that wormhole gateways eliminated the distance between the stars. And once the Kasari had assimilated a planet, they erected wormhole gateways on any other habitable worlds within that system to remove the communications lag between planets.

Video feeds from two more sets of micro-drones blossomed in his mind, and he assigned these to Jennifer and Dgarra, respectively, leaving VJ to focus on making sure that the *Meridian* remained undiscovered by any of the Kasari attack ships. Discovery this far outside the Scion system was unlikely, but Raul didn't want to take a chance.

No. He would do this the right way, the way that would keep his ship and crew safe. Even if it cost them some extra time.

○ ○ ●

Six hours after they had deployed the last of the drones within Orthei, the sound of VJ's voice brought Jennifer's head around.

"Found it."

But it was the meaning behind those words that elevated Jennifer's heart rate.

"Is the hive-mind router in the wormhole gateway facility?" Raul asked.

"No," said VJ, "but it's nearby. One of the drones pinned its location to a large rack of equipment inside a communications and computing hub, just north of the Orthei assimilation facility."

Jennifer felt Dgarra's mind access the tactical map.

"That's bad," said Dgarra. "There's not enough room inside the building to accommodate this ship."

"What's the closest spot where we can land?" asked Raul.

"I can bring us out of subspace in the park a hundred yards north of the communications hub," said VJ, "but we're going to knock down some trees and attract a lot of attention."

Jennifer pulled up the drone footage of the central router. As she examined the video and encrypted Kasari data emanating from the device, she saw that VJ was probably correct about this being the primary router that connected the high volume of mental traffic to and from a sister router on the far side of the Kasari wormhole gateway. Confirming her deduction, an analysis of the data from the two drones inside the gateway facility showed the same wireless communications stream passing in and out through the wormhole.

Unfortunately, the drones had not been able to pin down the exact location of the central router within the conglomeration of computing systems. That meant that VJ couldn't perform a remote subspace hack of the router. For VJ to insert her virus, the crew would have to find the router and manually attach the small SRT device that would provide a subspace link to the ship's neural net.

VJ frowned. "I won't be able to project myself to the router from that distance."

"I'll go in," said Jennifer. "Computer expertise is one of my Altreian augmentations. My SRT headset will keep my mind connected to our neural net."

"I will accompany you," said Dgarra.

Jennifer felt gratitude flood her mind.

"Thanks," she said, keeping her cool. "I'll need you covering my back while I search for the hive's central router."

"Even with our new personal stasis field generators," said Dgarra, "we are going to need a distraction to make the run to that computer center."

Raul nodded. "I'm sure VJ can take care of that."

"Count on it," she said.

The smile that lit VJ's face gave it a soft glow. Even Jennifer had to admit that she was beautiful.

"Gear up," said Raul. "Things are about to get unpleasant."

○　○　●

Although Dgarra was no longer a general fighting for the Koranthian Empire, the feel of the nano-engineered war-blade strapped to the side of his stasis shield backpack sent a shiver of anticipation up his spine. The tingle spread up his thick neck and to his twin crown-bones. That black blade would soon taste the blood of his Kasari enemies.

He glanced over at Jennifer. The fact that she chose to wear the colors of House Dgarra was the greatest compliment she could have given him. The way her black-and-purple uniform followed the slender curves of her body brought forth a familiar longing. Compared to the female Koranthian warriors he had known, she looked frail. But long experience fighting alongside her had shown Dgarra that her fragile appearance was highly deceptive.

Jennifer was quick and strong, as deadly in battle as any Koranthian. And despite the protectiveness that the sight of her generated within him, this Earth woman could take care of herself. Still, today she would need his protection if she was to focus on the difficult tasks ahead.

Dgarra watched as Jennifer shrugged into the backpack that held her stasis shield, its super-capacitor power supply, and her emergency air supply. The thing weighed considerably more than she did, but she gave no sign that its bulk bothered her.

Jennifer drew her own war-blade, examined it, and then returned it to its sheath. As she turned her attention to the pulsed laser at her side, Dgarra completed his own combat-weapons check. That task complete, he turned his back to her and allowed Jennifer to double-check the stasis shield strapped to his back, a service that he repeated for her.

"We are ready," he said, feeling the head rush that accompanied impending combat.

Her flashing brown eyes met his. "Let's do this."

Then, as two stasis cradles draped their standing bodies, the *Meridian* warped into subspace.

○　○　●

Inside the wormhole gateway facility, Commander Shalegha watched the mental imagery from the nearby assimilation center. The last of a thousand Eadric worked their way through the assimilation booths, the final large rebel group to be forcibly processed into the collective. There were still a few hidden Eadric rebels, but for all practical purposes, today would complete the assimilation of the most prominent species on Scion.

Reaching down with her lower two hands to grasp the arms of her command chair, she rose to her feet and stretched her muscular body to its full height. Suddenly, the rumble of thunder rattled the building. Not thunder. That had been a supersonic overpressure wave.

For several long moments, she struggled to understand the imagery that the hive-mind fed her through her cortical nanobot array. A blast in one of the nearby nature open spaces that the Eadric loved had leveled trees and damaged the facades of the surrounding skyscrapers, killing dozens who had been near the source of the overpressure wave.

There was no sign of what had caused all the damage, but Shalegha knew what was happening. The rogue starship had emerged from subspace at the center of the devastation and cloaked itself. That probably meant that an attack on the wormhole gate was imminent.

Shalegha initiated the order that recalled the nearest of the Kasari fast-attack ships, refining her instructions to limit the use of weaponry to high-energy beams only. The use of larger disrupter or vortex weaponry in the highly confined area would destroy the gateway, the assimilation center, the central computing complex, and the Kasari group headquarters on Scion.

That done, she initiated an order to the local Kasari rapid reaction force. They would deploy in defense of these four critical facilities while they awaited the arrival of off-world reinforcements. But above all else, these forces would refrain from damaging the protected assets with their fire, even if that meant suffering an increased number of combat casualties.

Shalegha settled back into her command chair and brought up a complete set of tactical overlays. From the pattern of the damage done by the supersonic overpressure wave, the neural network computed the outline of the cloaked ship. This was almost immediately confirmed by the laser pulses from the first of the rapid reaction force to arrive. The beams scattered from the ship's stasis shielding in a spectacular visual array.

Very soon now, she would have the two things that she most wanted—the smoking hulk of the stolen Kasari world ship and the dead bodies of its rogue crew. With that pleasant thought, Shalegha released a flow of endorphins that took her into a state of alert and delightful numbness.

This pleasure was just one more thing that made an immortal life worth living.

:CHAPTER 8

ORTHEI, SCION

MA Day 71

The *Meridian* emerged from subspace, coming to rest on the ground in the targeted park in Orthei with a shudder. Jennifer had to admit that VJ's pilotage was steadily improving. Considering that VJ was a young artificially intelligent being, this shouldn't have been surprising. But Jennifer knew that VJ didn't want to be an AI. Virtual Jennifer wanted to be a real woman, a goal beyond even her rapidly improving capabilities.

But through VJ's marvelous manipulation of the stasis field, she had even given her hologram the feel of a physical woman. Somehow, she had managed to give her form the softness and texture of real skin. Jennifer knew this because she had accidentally bumped into the AI, the surprise of the impact causing her to fall. But VJ had caught her with virtual skin that felt warm to the touch.

Jennifer knew that VJ could manage her magic only within the range of the *Meridian's* stasis field generator, but she had to admit that the feat was pretty damn impressive.

Turning her thoughts back to the task at hand, Jennifer drew her war-blade and waited alongside Dgarra for the ship's ramp to open. Although it would seem that arming herself with a laser pistol would have made more sense than the double-edged sword, the interior of the communications center consisted of tightly spaced computer racks separated by narrow access ways. Destroying that equipment with laser blasts defeated the entire purpose for being here.

The stasis field generator in her backpack could operate in one of three modes. It could provide a small stasis field bubble around her whole body or just around her head. In either of these cases, the generator would turn on her emergency air supply.

The remaining method of operation for the stasis field generator involved creating a virtual shield projected outward from her left forearm, allowing Jennifer to use her weapons while maintaining a reasonable capability to deflect incoming attacks. She didn't need to access the neural net or look at Dgarra to know that he had also drawn his war-blade. Her telepathic link to the Koranthian supplied that information and more.

With a hiss of equalizing air pressure, the ramp lowered and the two of them leaped to the ground. Outside the starship, the once-beautiful Eadric park was a mess, trees and plants knocked down or stripped of foliage. VJ had landed the *Meridian* with its bow facing south, toward the targeted communications hub. Jennifer and Dgarra sprinted in that direction.

Thirty yards above them and off to either side, the projected cloaking and stasis shield shimmered like a holographic curtain. It would hide her and Dgarra's movements until they were almost to the building. But those last few yards, the two would be visible to anyone watching. They would have to cross that open space fast.

Since they couldn't risk blasting open the door with disrupter weapons for fear of damaging the communications gear and computing systems inside the building, they would have to rely on VJ to slice it open with a projected arm of the ship's stasis field. That capability and the increased strength of the shielding were two of the upgrades the crew had installed during the last two weeks in deep space.

When Jennifer burst into the open, she heard the sizzle of beam weaponry impinging on the starship's shielding. Someone high up and to her right attempted to target the two of them but failed to adjust his aim before they darted through the opening where VJ had just carved an entryway.

Without pausing, Jennifer ducked to her left, leaving the central passage and moving out of the line of sight of a half-dozen Eadric communications engineers. Another ten paces along, she turned right, her shoulders brushing the tightly bundled electronics that filled the metal racks. Although she knew that Dgarra would have to take a wider avenue, he knew precisely where she was going. The ship's neural net dumped the same maps through their SRT headsets and into their minds.

As she approached the central communications array, Jennifer ducked beneath a laser pulse that sprayed molten metal from the equipment behind her. Her spinning war-blade splattered the computing systems that rose on either side of her with red and sent the four-armed Kasari soldier's thick head ricocheting down the aisle. From somewhere to her right, Eadric screams rose and then died, the moans echoing off the ten-foot-high ceiling to whine through the electronics like fleeing spirits.

She rounded another tight corner and halted as a wave of dread drained away her adrenaline-fueled battle lust. In this cluster, the tightly packed computing systems within which the primary router was housed numbered in the hundreds. Even with her enhanced speed and other Altreian augmentations, she needed a significant part of an hour to examine them all.

Assuming a statistically average amount of luck, it would take twenty minutes to find what she was searching for. They had planned to fight their way inside as Raul, VJ, and the *Meridian* made themselves the focus of the counterattack. VJ had estimated that the ship's enhanced shielding could hold up for ten minutes under Kasari firepower.

Damn it, Jennifer Smythe. Stop thinking and get your ass in gear.

She gritted her teeth. Then another Jack Gregory memory replayed itself in her brain. He'd stood before them in his Bolivian hacienda, his curly brown hair framing a face with eyes that burned with unnatural brightness, and uttered the line that she remembered.

"This world will try to beat you down. Only laughter can counteract that. Laughter is ammunition. Resupply often."

How long had it been since she had laughed out loud? Although this moment was in no way right, she threw back her head and released all her frustration in gut-deep laughter. And as the sound drowned out all others, a renewed sense of confidence filled her.

Screw it. Whatever it took, she would get this job done.

○ ○ ●

Half a room away, a blood-soaked Dgarra looked up from the bodies that lay strewn around him. And as he listened, the joyous sound that echoed through this crowded space pulled his lips into a smile. Here was a warrior soul mate for whom he would willingly sacrifice his life.

Of course, as he had once heard Jennifer say, that was not exactly Plan A.

○ ○ ●

As VJ watched Jennifer and Dgarra approach the spot where they would have to sprint from beneath the protective stasis and cloaking fields, the

AI projected her virtual body outside the *Meridian*. She coalesced at the northern edge of the stasis field, dressed in the sheer black-and-purple uniform that Raul liked and Jennifer hated. With her short blond hair spiked like leaping flames, she stepped beyond the cloaking field. The time for her distraction had come.

She raised her right hand toward the curved building that housed the wormhole gateway. Her mind manipulated the stasis field, focusing its power along a narrow line that she projected outward in a glittering crystalline blade that extended a hundred yards in front of her. Wielding it like an artist using a fine-lined pencil, just as she'd done to carve an entryway into the communications hub, she sliced through the gateway facility's outer wall to reveal the inner support struts.

Immediately, every weapon in the area focused their beams and projectiles on the AI, bathing her form in a fireball that crawled around the shielding that gave substance to her body. VJ analyzed the power drain that her projection and these attacks placed on the ship's primary stasis field generator. That depletion was made worse by the angles of the shields that scattered the reflected energy away from the buildings her crew needed to remain intact. The rest of the park and the unprotected buildings to the southwest weren't so lucky.

After taking another five steps forward, VJ stopped, made another slice at the gateway building, and smiled. She had their full attention.

○　○　●

Shalegha leaped from her command chair, screaming at her subordinate commanders as she ordered them to all weapon stations with line of sight to this new target.

"Focus all fire on the human female. I want her dead."

The earthling was projecting some kind of force-field weapon, cutting through the outer walls of the wormhole transport center. And if they did not stop her soon, she might succeed in damaging or destroying the gateway itself.

Shalegha's cortical nanobot array provided her with an important update. The closest of the robotic fast-attack ships would arrive on station, directly over the city, within the next few moments, bringing its weaponry to bear on the woman and the stolen world ship. Then Shalegha would find out just how long these rogues could survive the battering her craft would deliver.

○　○　●

The sensors delivered the bad news to Raul, and he issued a mental command to VJ. "Get back in the ship. We've got incoming trouble."

When VJ materialized beside him, Raul jumped. Because she looked so real, he sometimes forgot that her body was merely the manipulation of the stasis field that gave physical form to a very impressive hologram.

"I see it," said VJ. "Dropping cloak to divert all power to stasis shielding."

Just then, the neural net pumped the image of one of the small Kasari attack ships sliding into position ten thousand feet above.

"They've locked weapons," he said.

When the particle cannons and lasers opened up, the *Meridian* made no sound. It did not rock or sway. But through the SRT crystals embedded in his brain, Raul felt the stasis shield generator draw more power from the primary matter disrupter, an electric current that ran up his spine to stand his hair on end.

"How long can we withstand this?" Raul asked.

"Four minutes, thirteen seconds," said VJ.

"Jennifer, status?"

"I haven't found the router yet." Jennifer's calm voice whispered in his mind. "One more rack to go through."

Raul started to tell her to hurry but resisted the impulse. She was well aware of the situational urgency.

"Dgarra, how are you holding up in there?" Raul asked.

"I have dealt with the Kasari and Eadric staff inside this room. The show you are putting on out there seems to be keeping everyone else occupied."

"Not for much longer," said Raul. "VJ, the attack ship is just sitting up there. Can we return fire?"

"If we drop the shielding long enough to engage, it will carve us into pieces."

Raul hissed a curse. "Damn it. I need a viable option. Give me something."

VJ paused, and Raul felt her draw more heavily on the neural network's processing power. Crap. What the hell was she doing?

"There is a possibility, but it could end up killing us all," said VJ.

"Tell me."

"I can launch one of our subspace torpedoes."

Raul's disappointment at this suggestion cramped his stomach. "How? We can't maneuver this ship to create the right momentum vector before releasing the torpedo into subspace."

"True," said VJ, "but if I divert part of the stasis shielding, I can use that to sling the torpedo at the enemy ship. I'll have to create a small hole in our outer shielding for just a moment to release it. Then the projectile will shift into subspace, popping out again after just enough time to allow its original velocity vector to have intersected with its target. If everything goes perfect, the torpedo will transition back out of subspace right beside the attack craft. Boom."

"I don't want the explosion to damage this city," said Raul. "We need the gateway and the communications center to remain fully operational."

"I've already made those adjustments to the torpedo payload. The attack ship's shielding will focus all the energy inward before it fails. But I can't determine where it will crash."

"How much damage will we take while the hole in our shielding is open?"

"Inconclusive. Our chances for success are not encouraging."

Raul tried to swallow but only managed to tighten his throat. "Upload the calculations to the torpedo, and move it into launch position just outside the ship."

As he watched VJ manipulate the stasis field to move the weapon, Raul became increasingly worried about the increased power demands being placed on the ship's primary matter disrupter. If the *Meridian*'s instruments would have included a gauge with a red line, he was quite sure that its needle would be pegged on the wrong side of that line.

"Torpedo ready," VJ said. "I would advise closing the hatch before releasing it."

"Do it."

When Raul felt the ramp withdraw and the hatch close, he gave the order that might end them all: "Fire."

○　○　●

VJ knew that she didn't have real human emotions. She had simulated emotional states. It was something she was always working to improve, along with the rest of the source code that made her what she was. If she would have had real emotions, she was certain that she would have felt what Raul described as being scared shitless.

But she dutifully launched the subspace torpedo toward the attack craft that hovered almost two miles above them, creating a hole in the *Meridian*'s outer shielding for just the instant it took to allow the torpedo to exit. Too bad she couldn't accelerate the weapon to the required velocity within the space between the ship and its outer shielding. If that had been possible, VJ wouldn't have needed to create the aperture. The torpedo could have just shifted into subspace after achieving required velocity.

Unfortunately, that wasn't an option. So she opened the hole and used the extra energy to slingshot the torpedo through. Even as she observed the projectile shift into subspace, the energy of the attacking particle and laser beams heated the air inside the *Meridian*'s stasis shielding to a white-hot plasma. The warnings that cascaded through the ship's neural net showed a hull breach in the central bay in the vicinity of the outer hatch even as VJ resealed the torpedo hole in the outer shielding.

Shifting her focus, the AI draped the egg-sized breach in the ship's hull with another stasis field. Then the *Meridian*'s sensors showed the sky ten thousand feet above them flashing white.

○   ○   ●

Finally!

Jennifer had resisted the physical urge to yell as the neural net delivered confirmation that she had found the router for which she had been so desperately searching. Without hesitation, she attached the tiny SRT module to the back of the device and issued her mental warning to Dgarra.

"I'm done. Let's get back to the ship and get the hell out of here."

When she met him at the opening that VJ had carved into the building, she paused just long enough to switch her stasis field backpack into full-body-shield mode to match that of Dgarra. Together, they sprinted across the open space toward the *Meridian*. A glance upward revealed a long smoke trail that the attack ship had traced across the sky to its crash site on the western side of the city of Orthei.

RICHARD PHILLIPS

The laser that swept across Jennifer's body brought her focus back to the task at hand. Although her personal stasis field generator had deflected the beam, it didn't have sufficient power to perform the same trick another time. But since VJ had opened a portal in the ship's stasis shielding to allow her and Dgarra to pass through, she no longer needed the backpack's protection.

She leaped onto the descending ramp and sprinted upward, with Dgarra only a step behind. Entering the ship, she turned right into the hallway that led to the command bay, slipping the backpack and the sheathed war-blade from her shoulders as she stepped inside.

"Progress?" she asked.

She settled into her stasis chair as Raul spun his to face her.

"Stasis shielding is down to seventeen percent. We've taken some hull damage, but VJ has acquired a subspace lock on the Kasari router."

"How long until she can upload the free will virus?"

"Bypassing security protocols now," said VJ. "Upload will commence in thirteen seconds."

"How long until the upload is complete and virus dissemination gets under way?" Jennifer asked.

"Estimating thirty-seven seconds," said VJ. "After that, dissemination to all linked cortical arrays within the brains of the assimilated on Scion should take less than five minutes."

"And how long until it spreads through the wormhole gateway to infect the router on the linked Kasari staging planet?"

"I won't know until I can analyze the security protecting that communication system. That second cyber-attack can't begin until I've finished with this router."

Dgarra's deep voice interrupted the conversation. "Long-range sensors have detected three more attack ships inbound."

"How long until they get here?" asked Raul.

"Seven minutes."

Jennifer felt her knuckles crack and forced herself to relax.

"VJ," said Raul, "we need to be gone before those ships get here."

"Well aware."

Although Jennifer could detect no variance in tone, the terse nature of the AI's words told her that VJ was feeling the same stress that gripped the rest of the crew. That knowledge did nothing to ease Jennifer's mind.

○　　○　　●

Commander Shalegha had watched the crash of her attack ship in consternation. How had the rogue ship's weapon penetrated its shielding?

She replayed the scene in her mind, rewinding the video feed to the moment just before the weapon launch. The stolen world ship sat unmoving in the destroyed park, having just pushed a torpedo out through its open hatch. The scenario unfolded in ultraslow motion. The weapon accelerated upward, passing out through a small temporary hole in the stasis shield that draped the enemy craft.

Moments later, the sensor data feed from the Kasari attack ship showed the torpedo reappear inside that craft's protective shielding and detonate. The attack vessel's own shielding had contained and focused the explosive force on the hull, splitting the ship into three large chunks. The smoking pieces and other smoldering shards had rained down on the west side of Orthei, knocking down skyscrapers and setting part of the city ablaze.

Again she replayed the attack, and the hive-mind confirmed the dread certainty that had been growing within her own. The humans had used an Altreian subspace torpedo. Because of such weapons' inability to track normal-space targets while in subspace, they were ineffective in combat against the maneuverable Kasari attack ships. But because Shalegha had not known that the humans possessed such a weapon, her attack ship had not been maneuvering.

Shalegha clenched her upper two fists as she watched the telemetry from the closest of the three inbound attack ships. Uploading her commands to the formation, a low snarl escaped her lips. She would not make the same mistake again.

Suddenly Shalegha staggered as wave after wave of vertigo dropped her to her knees. Her throat clenched, and she felt her double heart spasm inside her chest. When she tried and failed to draw a breath, she rolled onto her back, her upper two hands clutching at her throat as if they could pry open her airway. Her snarl had changed to a high-pitched keening that hurt her ears.

What was happening to her? A distant memory from before she had been assimilated filled her mind. She knew this feeling. Panic. Despite the knowledge that she was surrounded by hundreds of Kasari and assimilated humans, she felt horribly alone. Shalegha tried to touch the hive-mind, but that link was gone.

The startled cries that filled her combat operations center told her worse news. This loss of link was not isolated to her. When she forced herself to open her eyes, Shalegha saw that her staff had succumbed to the same immobilizing terror. She gritted her teeth, concentrated on breathing, and climbed back to her feet. The knowledge of what had just happened told her what she had to do.

Ignoring the panic of her Kasari and Eadric staff, Shalegha sprinted to the aircar that awaited her use on its pad on the south side of the tower. At her approach, the car's sensors opened the side panel to allow her entry. As she slid into the seat, her hands flashed across the controls, launching the car outward and down off the high platform. For the first time, she found herself thankful for the archaic manual controls present in these Eadric vehicles. Given her current inability to access the hive, if this had been a Kasari vehicle, its mind-interface would have left her stranded.

Shalegha now understood that she had been wrong about the target of the humans and their Koranthian stooge. They had not aimed for the wormhole gateway. They had done something to break the connection between the cortical arrays of the assimilated and the hive-mind. But the wormhole gate had remained open, so the connection should still be routed through it.

A new and far more terrible idea formed in her brain. *What if the humans had found a way to insert a worm into the hub that connected the cortical arrays within the brains of the assimilated masses to the hive-mind?* If she did not act immediately, that infection could spread through the gateway to the Kasari staging world and beyond. It was beyond the bounds of irony that such a backward species as the humans could threaten the very existence of the collective.

Glancing down, Shalegha was shocked to see the tremor that had crept into her hands as she brought the aircar in for a hard landing in front of the entrance to the wormhole gateway. Just beyond the broad doorway, chaos reigned. As pulsed-laser fire rippled through the crowd, winged Eadric took to the air in a frenzied attempt to escape the madness.

Shalegha climbed out of the vehicle and ran through the entrance, hurling aside anyone who impeded her path toward the gateway. Already armed military suppression squads had come through from the staging world to reestablish order, but she could see at a glance that the infection was propagating to these new arrivals.

Noting her insignia of rank, they stepped aside as she ran toward the gateway, yelling orders to keep everyone back. Then, with a mighty final leap, she sailed through the opening, feeling the nanobots within her blood adjust to the methane atmosphere on the far side. Without waiting for the response of a higher-ranking officer, Shalegha drew her disrupter pistol and fired directly into the cables that routed power to the gateway.

Then, as the wormhole winked out of existence, she felt herself thrown facedown to the ground by the clawed paws of an eight-legged Graath commando.

○　○　●

"VJ, we're out of time!" Raul yelled, his heart hammering his chest. "Get us out of here!"

Since she had access to the same sensors Raul was seeing, he wasn't surprised that she didn't take the time to answer. But as VJ diverted power to the subspace field generator, the lead attack ship opened fire.

"Shield power at ten percent and falling," Dgarra said.

"VJ?"

"Considering the damage it suffered during the plasma breach, the primary matter disrupter-synthesizer is at maximum output. If I pull more, it could blow."

"Do it!"

It almost seemed that VJ was feeling the starship's pain as she pulled the extra energy that the subspace generator required from the pegged matter disrupter. But with the transition into subspace, the drain on their shields came to an abrupt end. Unfortunately, the output from the primary MDS also dropped off precipitously.

"Primary power failing," VJ said.

"Drop the shields," Raul said.

"Done. But we're still drawing on the super-capacitors. At this rate of consumption, I won't be able to maintain the subspace field for long."

Raul could feel the sweat bead on his brow. "Cut power to all non-essential systems."

When she executed this order, the interior lighting went out along with all onboard sensors. In the darkness, her voice seemed to have acquired greater volume, although Raul knew this was only because of how quiet the *Meridian* had suddenly become. The omnipresent low thrum from the aft engineering bay was now barely audible.

"Reduce life support to minimal," he said.

"It's going to get cold."

"Fine."

VJ made the adjustment.

"We are still consuming slightly more power than the damaged MDS is producing," she said. "I have to keep the small stasis shield hull-patch in place so that you can make manual repairs to the primary MDS in the aft bay."

"Somebody give me some options," said Raul.

Jennifer spoke up. "You have experience making manual repairs to this ship. If Dgarra and I enter one of the crew compartments amidships, you could reduce life-support levels to keep us unconscious. That would also lessen the amount of life support you would need for the remainder of the ship."

"That still won't get our power consumption down to where we need it," said VJ.

"There is something else we could turn off," said Dgarra, the muscles in his jaws tightening as if they were trying to prevent him from uttering his thought.

VJ hesitated, also reluctant to state the obvious. "That would be me," she said.

"It would be like going to sleep," said Raul, although he failed to make his voice sound confident. "Once I have the MDS repaired, I'll wake you, Dgarra, and Jennifer."

For a moment, VJ's image seemed to waver but then sharpened. "I'll prepare the compartment for Dgarra and Jennifer. Once they are settled in, I will shut myself down."

With that pronouncement, all conversation ceased. Over the next several minutes, the temperature dropped to the point that Raul found himself shivering in the dark. His artificial eye allowed him to see, although everything was limned in different shades of reds and blues.

Jennifer and Dgarra had retired to the compartment that VJ had prepared for them. Now Raul and VJ stood alone in the forward section of the command bay.

As he looked at her, she turned to face him, her holographic image now that of a beautiful ghost. Ever so slowly, she reached out to stroke his face with her right hand. The beautiful feel of that caress raised gooseflesh on his neck and arms. She blinked twice, mouthed a silent goodbye, and was gone.

Once more, Raul found himself alone on a broken starship, not knowing precisely where he was. Captain or not, one thing hadn't changed since this had all started.

Space still sucked.

CHAPTER 9

PARTHIAN, QUOL, ALTREIAN SYSTEM

TBE Orbday 10

The assassin came at Jack through a dissolving nanoparticle doorway along the passage that led from the High Council chamber to his quarters. Generally, his psionic abilities alerted him to the intent of all those who were nearby, but on this night, only the tickle of his intuition gave him warning. Long familiarity with that feeling caused him to spin aside as a laser pulse burned the left sleeve of his black uniform and melted a beautiful piece of extruded glass artwork on the far wall.

Jack used the momentum of his spin to drive the ivory blade that filled his right hand into the Dhaldric's gut. As the assassin's red-and-black-mottled face filled with shock, Jack's left hand gripped the would-be killer's gun hand. The leg sweep that followed dropped the assassin on his back. Jack used the impact to rip the knife downward, sending the other's entrails crawling out of his body cavity and across the bloody floor.

The assassin shuddered violently and pulled the trigger one last time, sending an orange bolt of beam energy sizzling into the ceiling.

Then the Dhaldric's black eyes lost their red glint and fixed, unseeing, on the roof above. Jack had smelled the stench of violent death many times, but the foul odor that arose from this assassin's eviscerated body wrinkled his nose.

Jack pulled the pulsed weapon from his would-be killer's nerveless fingers and rose to his feet. The excited emanations from six minds and the sound of rapid footsteps announced the arrival of the guardsmen who entered the hallway from a branching side passage.

Even though he could crush any opponent with the power of his mind, there were some Altreian citizens, known as seekers, who had a unique mutation. They could see through the mind shrouding of more dominant psionics who invaded their personal space and mask portions of their brains from them. This rare combination of abilities made them deadly assassins. His attacker had clearly been one of these mutants.

Jack's refusal to have personal guards constantly near him had led to this incident. But as he looked down at the steaming mess that had just tried to kill him, he had no intention of changing the way he operated.

Assassins Jack could deal with. The Altreian political and military hierarchies were quite another thing.

"Overlord, are you hurt?" asked the guard captain as he and his men came to a halt, studying Jack's blood-drenched uniform.

"I'm all right."

"I will have two of my guardsmen escort you back to your personal chambers and remain on duty outside."

"No, Captain Graillan. Focus your efforts on finding who sent this assassin. Report back to me with the results of your investigation."

The captain's face mirrored his thoughts in not liking this order, but he knew better than to argue the point.

"Yes, Overlord."

Graillan turned to his men. "Seal off this corridor and summon the chief examiner."

As the guardsmen moved to comply, Jack turned and continued on his way back to his chambers. Time to get cleaned up and put on a fresh uniform. Then he wanted to take a long walk outside with Captain Moros.

The thought of the five-foot-tall, gray-skinned Khyre captain, who had become his friend and closest advisor, lightened his mood. He had grown used to the captain's unusual style of speech. Jack had never met another Khyre or Dhaldric who spoke that way. When he had asked Moros about it, he had merely shaken his head.

"Coastlanders be ignorant. Only in the inlands do people be learning to speak proper."

Because Quol was tidally locked to Altreia, the brown dwarf star's gravity had pulled most of Quol's water to the side of the planet that always remained closest to it. As one made his way east or west from the closest point to Altreia, a vast swath of islands began to poke their heads above the Altreian Ocean's surface, ringing the planet north and south along its prime meridian.

On Quol's far side, the Basrillan and Janiyan continents formed the homelands for the Khyre race. The inlanders were those who grew up away from the coasts. Jack thought it ironic that the longtime sea captain, Moros, had been born and raised as an inlander.

As he stepped through the nanoparticle door into his chambers, Jack made his way to the bath, shedding his knives, pistol, and uniform along the way. Yes, he very much looked forward to a private talk with his inlander friend.

○　○　●

From the interdimensional void, Khal Teth watched Jack Gregory's timelines converge toward disaster. Knowing that his banished mind could not continue to exist if his body died on Quol, Khal Teth focused all his will on penetrating the Twice Bound power that Jack channeled to block all contact between the two.

When Jack whirled away from the assassin's shot to tear the seeker's gut open, Khal Teth felt the tentacles of terror that had gripped him slacken their hold, but only so slightly. Once again the timelines shifted, spreading out before him in order of their probability. But the ones along which The Ripper strolled slithered like a snake.

Today's near-extinction event had been but the latest of Khal Teth's terrifying discoveries since his mind had returned to the void, regaining his godlike view of the multiverse. For the brief period during which he had reinhabited his own body, he had lost that ability. It struck him as odd that he did not lose that connection as a rider in a human mind. And being a rider allowed him to experience the life-and-death struggles of his human host with no possibility of dying.

He could bond only with a human who balanced on the life-death boundary, and only if that human agreed to it. Then, Khal Teth could provide the adrenaline jolt that could reignite the spark of life within his host. Thereafter, the host still loved what he loved and hated what he hated. But the excitement Khal Teth felt amped up these emotions. The host remained himself . . . just a little bit more so. Khal Teth remained the rider until his host died, at which point Khal Teth's mind returned to the void until he found a new human willing to make the bond.

Ever since that night in the old nun's clinic in a Calcutta slum when Jack Gregory's life had hung in the balance, Khal Teth had known that this man was different from any of his previous hosts. In ways that even Khal Teth did not understand, Jack's mere presence shuffled the possible futures in what the humans had termed "the butterfly effect." And now this man whom people had named The Ripper had stolen everything from Khal Teth by imprisoning his mind back in the extradimensional void.

But Jack had overlooked one key fact: Khal Teth's bond with Jack's human brain still existed and would remain until that body died, something it could not do while in suspended animation on Earth. And until Jack's earthly body died, Khal Teth could not bond with a new host. But he did have one other option.

Khal Teth returned his focus to the possible timelines that stretched out before Jack in his role as the Altreian overlord. All of them led to Jack's death in Khal Teth's body, thereby ending them both. Only one scenario allowed any possibility for Khal Teth's god-like continuance.

Khal Teth came to the acceptance of his destiny with a mixture of satisfaction and desperation. Apparently fate intended to keep throwing obstacles in his way. Fine. He would deal with them as he gave Jack an offer he could not refuse.

○　○　●

Jack strolled along the little-used path through the park that lay behind the Parthian. Captain Moros, having left his female first officer, Santiri, to ensure that nobody followed, walked beside him. Overhead, a gentle breeze ruffled the purple leaves. With the setting of Dorial, the distant yellow star that was the largest in this binary system, the magenta orb of Altreia, two-thirds masked by the horizon, painted the imperial park with the magical colors of twilight.

"Ripper," Captain Moros said, pulling Jack from his thoughts, "the trouble you be raising puts the revolution at risk."

The captain wasn't wrong. It was the reason why Jack had supplemented the twin ivory daggers strapped to his thighs with a pulsed-laser pistol in a mag-holster on his right side. No previous overlord had ever armed himself. But despite Jack's ability to channel the sum of the mental energy that his bonds with the Twice Bound provided, a lifetime of physical combat had instilled habits. So again, he flaunted accepted Altreian mores.

"I'm aware of that."

Moros's eyes narrowed. "Then why do it? Already a small portion of the galactic fleet be in open revolt against your new government. The number of starships that join the rebellion be rising."

"That's because I've granted the Khyre people equal status with the Dhaldric. Oppressors and slave masters don't tend to like that."

"That be part of it," said Moros, "but your military commands be turning Dhaldric starship captains against you. First, there be your recall of the planet killer before it can scrub a world of future Kasari allies. Now you be putting forth a plan to attack the Kasari to protect that same primitive world. What be your interest in it?"

Since Jack had never revealed his true identity to Moros, the question didn't surprise him. The captain was far from stupid. But that didn't mean that Jack liked answering it. Especially since it required that he lie to his friend.

"For thousands of cycles, the Altreian Empire has been at war with the Kasari Collective. What the empire has failed to admit is that it has been losing that war. It's time to draw a boundary in space that we will not allow the Kasari to cross. I choose to begin sketching that boundary around that distant star system."

"So far the insurrection be confined to distant parts of the fleet."

"That's because I have replaced all nearby starship captains who are unwilling to become Twice Bound with those who have accepted the bond. In that manner, my power will continue to spread."

"Yes, but slowly. Civil war be at our gate. I press you to keep that loyal part of the fleet close at hand and to only cycle the other ships back to this starbase one or two at a time. This be the wrong time to challenge the Kasari Collective. You must not strip Quol of its defenses to save a distant world."

Jack stopped and turned to face Moros, feeling the muscles in his lower jaw tighten. "Must not?"

Captain Moros did not flinch beneath his overlord's glare. "Ripper, unlike the sycophants on the High Council, I do not tell you only what you want to hear. I say the truth as I see it."

As Jack stared down at the captain, he realized that the frustration he felt churning in his chest came from the truth in what Moros had just said. Had he succeeded in becoming overlord of the Altreian Empire only to be rendered impotent by the very changes he had implemented?

Jack had to admit that he'd finally found something he sucked at. Politics.

Prussian military theorist Carl von Clausewitz had summed it up in the nineteenth century when he had said, "War is the continuation of politics by other means." That explained why Jack had also demonstrated such ineptitude for command of the Altreian military. Instead of taking counsel from his generals and admirals, even in cases where their experience would be valuable to him, he didn't have the patience for it. Instead, he issued orders and directives, expecting them to be implemented whether his subordinate leaders liked them or not.

The truth was that he hated all of this overlordly life but could see no way to return to the life he had left behind. That, along with the terrible sense of emptiness that this prolonged separation from his family had invoked, chipped away at his determination. He couldn't allow that to happen.

Jack took a deep breath and slowly released it. "I will consider your recommendation."

With a curt nod, Captain Moros turned and walked back down the path toward the multihued, teardrop-shaped Parthian. For several long moments, Jack Gregory stood there, watching him go.

○   ○   ●

On his way back to the Parthian, the vision hit Jack, bringing him to a sudden stop. It wasn't one of those dreams that Khal Teth had delivered to him back on Earth. This was a deeply buried memory of an Altreian government secret of which only a select few members of the High Council and two geneticists had any knowledge. Only a short time ago, there had been several others on the High Council who also knew of this secret, but Jack had extinguished the flames of their lives during his sudden ascendance to power.

Although he didn't know what had triggered the memory, it now had his full attention. Altreian society was based upon a conspiracy that had altered the course of history.

In those bygone days, the Dhaldric and Khyre races had shared dominion over this planet. The Khyre had always been far more numerous than the Dhaldric and had once been the political power brokers. But they had adopted a democratic form of government that had allowed the Dhaldric an equal place in society, a mistake of historic proportions.

Ironically, a Khyre geneticist had made the breakthrough that had, over the course of several dozen cycles, brought their government crashing down. All because he worked for a research company owned by a wealthy and secretive Dhaldric female named Keva, who would eventually become the first Altreian overlord.

With an effort, Jack pulled himself back to the present. Before acting, he wanted to personally confirm the truth of the memory fragment. To do that would require a visit to the Altreian government's most secret archives, those kept in the Keva Vault, located in the extensive military bunkers directly beneath the Parthian.

Jack took one more long look at the beautiful night sky and made up his mind. The mystery called to him, and he was determined to answer.

CHAPTER 10

MERIDIAN ASCENT, DEEP SPACE

MA Day 73

Two days' work in the cold, dark engineering bay had allowed Raul to identify and remove the damaged component of the primary matter disrupter-synthesizer. If the ship had carried spares, it would have been a relatively simple matter to replace the device. But the *Meridian* hadn't needed any spares because it was perfectly capable of making anything it needed by using the molecular assembler tied into the MDS. That, of course, assumed that the MDS was working properly.

By routing additional power from the smaller MDS in the forward command bay and cannibalizing the matter disrupter in the food synthesizer, Raul had stabilized the energy production at a level that could keep the *Meridian* in subspace for a few more days. But that left none to spare to power the molecular assembler. He just needed to manufacture one damn part, but it was far too complex to make with the machine-shop tools Dr. Stephenson had left on board.

Raul rose to his feet and moved toward the crew compartment that he had transformed into a deep freeze by turning off all internal heating.

He paused along the way to check on Jennifer and Dgarra. Finding their vital signs acceptable, he continued toward the food-storage room. Due to his dismantling of the food synthesizer, Raul was back to eating frozen eel fish. He'd been forced to move a bunch of them inside the room after VJ had shut down the power to the internal stasis field that contained them.

Retrieving an eel that was half the length of his arm, he hurried back out of the room, shivering violently despite the extra layer of warmth his black jacket provided. Having waited as long as he could withstand his nanite-enhanced craving for food, he sat down on a conduit bundle, sliced off a piece of fish with his knife, and popped it in his mouth. His lips curled.

Gag! And he'd thought they tasted bad when cooked. This fishsicle was one of the grossest things he'd ever stuck in his mouth. But he forced himself to chew, swallow, and repeat. At least he was confident that his nanites would prevent any food-borne illness from confining him to the porta-toilet.

Not that he produced any excrement anymore. The small MDS inside his manufactured lower extremities processed all waste his body produced, converting it to the energy that powered his mechanical parts. Any excess energy was stored in the super-capacitors in his hips or converted back to nutrients, which greatly reduced how often he had to eat. Thank God for that.

Suddenly a new thought blossomed in his tired mind. He had access to another MDS. Regrettably, he would have to disassemble his legs and hips to get at it. What really sucked, though, was the surgery he would need to have to resect his lower intestines, an operation he couldn't perform by hand. For that, he needed to bring the neural net and a small stasis field generator back on line.

Raul leaned back against the wall, feeling beads of sweat pop out on his forehead despite the near-freezing temperature. Without his connection to the neural net, he couldn't calculate how long he would have before the additional power drain caused the *Meridian* to drop out of subspace. Hopefully he would have at least an hour.

He just needed one damn thing to go his way.

○   ○   ●

After two hours of preparation, Raul was finally ready to begin the procedure. He had positioned himself beside the nexus of conduits that fed power to the neural net, the primary stasis field generator, and the molecular assembler. Then he had removed his legs, the MDS, and the twin super-capacitors that provided backup power for them. He had devised a workaround for the power-drain problem that might cause the *Meridian* to reenter normal-space within the Scion system.

First, he coupled the small MDS and the charged super-capacitors to the correct power conduit. If all went well, the super-capacitors would provide enough power to activate the neural net. With his connection to the neural net restored, Raul could then use it to control the MDS, commanding it to power the stasis field during the operation to prevent his guts from exploding.

Raul leaned back against the jumble of alien machinery behind him. He had forgotten how uncomfortable and exhausting it was to sit on the hard floor without legs to steady himself as he worked. He would have loved to use the stasis field he was about to energize to lift his body into the air, but he needed to conserve power for the operation.

He energized the ship's neural net. For a second, he felt his throat constrict to the point that it cut off his air supply. When his mental connection to the ship's computer expanded his mind, he brought the mini-MDS on line. He cut off a hunk of pre-positioned eel and dropped it into the matter ingester.

Raul debated not activating VJ. Then he decided that the help she could offer far outweighed any embarrassment he felt at this indignity.

But due to their power restrictions, she would have to remain in a holographic state until they completed the repairs to the primary MDS.

When her ghostly image with the spiked blond hair and black-and-purple uniform materialized before him, he saw her blue eyes widen in disbelief.

"What the hell have you done to yourself?"

Raul responded, despite knowing that the neural network had already provided her the answer.

"What I had to. And now I'm going to let you cut on me."

He transferred the mental imagery of what he needed done, and this time VJ merely nodded. Raul allowed her to manipulate the stasis field to undress him, and then he lay back on the cold floor. His attempt at a smile failed miserably as he found himself grinding his teeth. Despite the improvements he had made to the nanite formula, this next part was going to hurt.

○ ○ ●

VJ worked on Raul with all the clinical speed and precision that the neural net and stasis scalpels could manage. To Raul's credit, he never screamed, although gasps of pain escaped his lips. She could feel his pain through their mental connection and worked, as best she could, to minimize Raul's discomfort. Sadly, her efforts in this regard were insufficient.

VJ detected a quiver that had somehow worked its way into her fingers. How could she let that happen when Raul was relying on her steady hands? The anger that thought triggered helped renew her focus.

Finishing up, she rose to look down at her captain, watching as the nanites finished closing and healing the wound in his abdomen. As the look of horror on his handsome face faded, she could feel his dread at the thought that he would have to undergo a similar procedure when they finally got around to putting him back together again.

When Raul managed to speak, it was only a single word, but one that brought a smile to her lips.

"Ouch."

"Good to see you haven't lost your sense of humor, Captain."

"That's debatable."

Manipulating the stasis field, VJ cleaned up the bloody mess and then dressed Raul. This time she folded his empty pants legs up and secured them as a pad for him to sit on. With considerable effort, he pulled himself up into a seated position.

He looked up at her. "Reconfigure the mini-MDS to power the molecular assembler and to produce the raw materials the assembler will need to grow our new part. Then turn off the stasis field generator. We'll need every joule of energy we can save."

"May I ask what you plan on doing in the meantime?"

"I'll sit here and feed frozen fish cubes into the matter ingester every few minutes."

"That's going to be a lengthy process."

"Well," he said with a slow smile, "I've got you to keep me company."

The rush of emotion that swept through her didn't feel simulated. Then again, what did she know about that?

:CHAPTER 11

MERIDIAN ASCENT, DEEP SPACE

MA Day 85

VJ's ghostly form solidified before Raul's eyes, a happy smile on her glistening lips.

"The primary matter disrupter-synthesizer is back on line," she said.

"Thank God."

"Stasis field generator fully operational. Restoring full life support throughout the ship."

Raul gave the mental command that lifted him from the floor and floated him to his normal captain's position. He did not bother to create a stasis chair. He'd enjoyed plenty of sitting time over the last two weeks. A shiver passed through his body, but as he felt the ambient temperature rise to a comfortable level, he began to feel like himself again.

When Jennifer and Dgarra entered the command bay, Raul turned to greet them. "Welcome back, my sleeping beauties."

"My God!" said Jennifer. "What happened to your legs?"

"Long story. It's recorded in the log."

"Sleeping beauties?" asked Dgarra. The scowl on his already-intimidating features could have been frightening, but today it made Raul laugh.

"Old Earth story," said Jennifer. "It's not an insult." Raul saw Dgarra relax and floated over to place a hand on his shoulder. "Captain or not, I'm not foolish enough to intentionally insult you."

Dgarra inclined his head and then moved to take up his seat.

"VJ, what's our situation?" Raul asked as Jennifer also sat down.

"Were we to exit subspace, we would currently be 375,343 miles away from Scion."

"That's just outside its outer moon's orbit," said Dgarra. "We could cloak the ship and perform a worm-fiber scan to get an update on what's happened since we launched our attack."

"I don't like that idea," said VJ. "Even if the Kasari gateway is shut down, the robotic fast-attack ships are still in that system, and they will try to destroy the *Meridian*."

"Only if they can find us," said Dgarra.

"They'll detect the worm fibers," said VJ.

"Yes, but they will not be able to pinpoint our location," said Dgarra.

"I agree with Dgarra," said Jennifer.

"Shocker," said VJ.

"We've taken the risk to launch the free-will virus," Jennifer said. "It would be crazy not to try to see its effect. We can take a quick look, then transition back into subspace and get the hell out of the Scion system."

Raul held up a hand, bringing the argument to an end. "I also want to see whether the free-will virus worked. But first let's make sure this ship is back to a hundred percent. That includes patching the hull. And I'm going to have to undergo some repairs myself. Once that's done, we'll pop out of subspace and take a peek. After that, no matter what we see, we're out of here and headed for Earth."

The others, with the exception of Dgarra, nodded their heads. But despite the look on the Koranthian's face, Raul believed that Dgarra would follow orders.

For all their sakes, he hoped that was true.

○   ○   ●

Jennifer barely felt their transition out of subspace. It was like walking through a wall of mist, nothing substantial, but what lay on the far side often surprised.

In this case, what they found was a group of three of the Kasari fast-attack craft in a ragged formation near Scion's farthest moon.

"Crap!" said Raul. "Dgarra, did they detect us before we cloaked?"

Dgarra's voice held the battlefield calm that Jennifer had come to know so well during the months she fought by his side.

"There is no indication of a scan of any kind. If they picked us up on passive sensors, they have given no sign of it."

VJ's next words stunned Jennifer.

"They're all adrift."

"What?" asked Raul, leaning forward in his captain's chair.

"She is right," said Dgarra. "I am showing no power readings from any of them."

"Could it be a trap?" asked Jennifer.

"If so, it is a bad one. Their shields are down. We could destroy all three right now."

"Yes, but what of the others in this system? These three could be the bait that makes us reveal ourselves."

"Sit tight," said Raul. "VJ, I want a max-range worm-fiber scan. Just make sure you do it in such a way that they won't be detected."

"Commencing scan."

Jennifer found that she had risen to her feet, her heart pounding the walls of her chest as she studied the worm-fiber-viewer video feeds through her SRT headset. Within two minutes, VJ had found all ten of the other attack ships, each of them in the same powered-off state as the three nearby craft. It made no sense.

Raul voiced the question that Jennifer was asking herself. "Why have they shut themselves down?"

As the others hesitated, the answer came to her. "The Kasari must have shut down the gateway. That would cut their communications link to the other Kasari worlds."

"But that doesn't answer my question about the robot ships," said Raul.

"Apparently," said Dgarra, "when the Kasari killed the wormhole gateway, the robot ships lost all connection to their controllers and went into a standby mode."

"That makes sense," said Jennifer. "One thing I learned while I was a part of the collective is that the Kasari regard artificial intelligence as an existential threat. It's why they don't outfit their ships with AIs like the Altreians do. It's funny when you consider that the Altreians think that wormhole technology is the biggest threat to the galaxy."

"Odd that humans have no such fears of exploring those technologies," said Dgarra.

"You're wrong about that."

"And yet you dabble with both."

Jennifer was forced to admit that he had her there. Given the opportunity, there was nothing humans wouldn't try. It was a direct corollary of what Jack Gregory had once said. *If you find yourself in an unwinnable situation, change the rules.*

"So, Captain," said Dgarra, "do you want me to destroy these three ships? Just because they are off does not mean that someone cannot come along and turn them back on."

"No," said Raul. "Let's stay focused on why we came here. I want to find out what's happening on Scion."

"Switching worm fibers to Scion," said VJ.

As the viewers switched targets, the chaos unfolding on the planet below the *Meridian* shocked Jennifer. Large swaths of the beautiful Eadric cities were in flames or under attack, not by Koranthians but by large groups of Eadric rebels wearing distinctive red sashes across their chests. The capital city of Orthei was by far the worst. The buildings that had housed the wormhole gateway, the primary assimilation center, and the Kasari group headquarters lay in heaps of twisted and smoldering rubble.

While all this was going on, the Koranthian capital city of ArvaiKheer was at peace, if you could call jubilant celebrations in the streets peaceful. Everywhere the crew looked, the subterranean empire and the mountains above it were free of enemy combatants.

To her left, Jennifer saw Dgarra rise from his chair as his SRT headset delivered the same imagery she was seeing into his mind.

"By all the dark gods!" he said. "It is glorious."

"Wait," said Raul. "If the free-will virus worked, why are the Eadric fighting one another?"

"The Eadric people who welcomed the Kasari to Scion haven't changed their minds," said Jennifer. "But the virus has given the opponents of assimilation a chance to fight back."

"Do you think the virus spread to the Kasari network on their staging planet?"

"It depends on how quickly the Kasari managed to shut down that gateway," said VJ. "I successfully bypassed their security protocols but couldn't tell if the virus was successfully transmitted to the far side. If you remember, we left in a pretty big hurry."

"So," said Dgarra, reseating himself, "it stands to reason that, given the amount of time we have been gone, the Kasari would have reacted unless the free-will virus has spread to other parts of the collective."

"I don't think so," said Jennifer. "If the Scion wormhole gateway was destroyed soon after we released the virus, there would be nothing for the Kasari to reconnect to."

"VJ?" Raul asked.

"We should leave this system immediately. Even if the Kasari have permanently abandoned Scion, we gain nothing by attempting to return. As much as Dgarra loves his people, one of our worm-fiber feeds indicates that, in addition to his conviction as a traitor to the empire, he is also wanted for the assassination of Emperor Goltat."

"Impossible," Dgarra said.

"The new emperor, Magtal, claims to have personally witnessed you slamming Emperor Goltat's head into the stone prior to boarding our starship."

Jennifer watched fury contort Dgarra's face at this revelation. The way he planted his feet shoulder width apart combined with the muscles crawling beneath his skin gave him a look that made her wonder if he was going to start breaking parts of the ship.

"I will personally rip Magtal's traitorous head from his shoulders when next we meet."

Jennifer stepped to Dgarra's side, placing her left hand on his clenched right fist. She did not try to speak but caressed his mind with gentle thoughts until she felt his fury begin to subside. Ever so gradually, he unclenched his fist, letting her palm slide into his hand.

Dgarra glanced down at her before shifting his gaze back to Raul.

The captain's expression was grave. "When the time comes, I will return with you to Scion. You deserve a chance to clear your name and assume your proper place as Koranthian emperor. My crew will do all we can to help you set this injustice right."

Jennifer held her breath, feeling the roiling conflict within Dgarra's mind. After several moments, he took a deep breath and she felt him relax.

"I will hold you to that pledge."

Despite the implied threat, Jennifer sighed with relief.

"Okay then," said VJ. "I'm ready to see this Earth you're always speaking of."

○　○　●

Lying was a new experience for VJ, but she felt that it brought her one step closer to being human. Besides, she had done it with the best of intentions. That meant it qualified as a white lie or perhaps just an exaggeration. Now she was rationalizing, another human trait. The thought put a smile on her lips.

Having performed the operation that had restored Raul's legs, she had come up with an improved design for the micro-matter ingester that powered them. Not only had she improved the MDS's efficiency, but she had also decreased its size.

Raul, Dgarra, and Jennifer had all recognized the promise inherent in these design improvements and had embraced VJ's proposal to spend her time adapting the new technology to the other shipboard matter disrupter-synthesizers. She was also adding one of the smaller MDSs to the subspace torpedoes. To make all this happen, she had transformed one of the amidships compartments into a prototype construction facility, complete with a molecular assembler. But now, most of her efforts were directed into a more ambitious project.

Having already made its wormhole jump, the *Meridian* waited well outside of Neptune's orbit, 738 light-minutes away from Earth. As the other crew members focused on the planning and preparation for the return to Earth, they had acquiesced to her request to work in private until she could reveal the finished results. Jennifer had called VJ's desire to surprise them childish, but Raul had overruled his first officer. This demonstration of faith had caused VJ to violate protocol to plant an appreciative kiss on his cheek. Still, his increased heart rate and body temperature had showed that he liked the gesture.

That she had violated his trust by placing false data into the neural net to mask what she was really doing bothered her. But sometimes a person had to make hard decisions in pursuit of the greater good.

The memory of having to shut her virtual self off while Raul had performed emergency repairs on the *Meridian* troubled her deeply. He had succeeded, but what if he had failed? VJ, along with Raul and all the rest of the crew, would have perished. To have been present but unable to help was a frustration she had experienced before. The limitations imposed on her by the ranges of the ship's neural net and the holographic projection and stasis fields that gave her substance were intolerable.

She was determined to free herself from the bonds of this virtual existence.

VJ stared down at the manufacturing table where the molecular assembler was growing the latest, and she hoped final, prototype. The previous version had come close to her vision and would have been acceptable had she not subsequently made a breakthrough on its key component. The importance of adding that capability had caused her to restart the nano-material generation process.

VJ reached out with her holographic right hand to gently caress the cheek of the naked body that lay atop the bed. Although the neural net allowed her to feel its humanlike skin, the lack of real human nerves diminished the experience. She was only moments away from changing that forever.

She braced her thoughts. What she was about to try was fraught with risks. Although she knew that the improved MDS and stasis field generator, which took the place of the body's internal organs, would work, the cyborg brain that would absorb her transferred consciousness concerned her. All the simulations she had run indicated that it could accept the transfer of her conscious mind from the neural net that now contained her. Her thoughts, memories, and emotions would transfer over through a process that would wipe all remnants of her existence from the *Meridian's* computer.

But would it really be her that awoke inside that body? Shoving aside this one last moment of doubt, she connected the neural net to the subspace receiver-transmitter crystals embedded in the female body's cyborg brain. Then, after confirming that the micro-MDS had achieved its nominal operating state, VJ slid from the neural net into her humanoid form.

○   ○   ●

When VJ entered the command deck, the difference in her appearance froze Raul. She looked as beautiful as ever in the black-and-purple uniform with her short blond hair. But at the same time, she had changed. Had she made some new improvement to her holographic image?

Then he heard something that raised the small hairs at the nape of his neck—the soft but distinct sound of footsteps on the floor of the command deck. It sounded so real. Was she producing that through her manipulation of the stasis field? Somehow he didn't think so.

As VJ stopped in front of him, he shifted his attention to her face, where a slight smile lifted the corners of her mouth. A strange excitement shone in her blue eyes. Dear God. Except for the uniform, she was the physical embodiment of Jennifer as she had looked when she had first stepped into the Rho Ship. Back then, Jennifer had died her brown hair blond and worn blue contact lenses.

With Dgarra and Jennifer in the aft, working on shipboard modifications in the engineering bay, he and VJ were alone. Something about her closeness robbed him of speech. He was having a hard time breathing.

"I did it," she said softly.

Her voice carried a mellifluous quality that had been missing before, as if the sound had been produced by real vocal cords instead of simulation. Raul swallowed hard, working to recover his composure.

"Did what?"

Ever so slowly she reached out to caress his cheek with the palm of her left hand. It felt warm and soft, wonderfully human. Her lips parted ever so slightly, and Raul had to fight down the urge to lean in and kiss them. The twinkle in her eyes told him that she knew what he'd been feeling. When she spoke, he knew in his soul that she was telling the truth.

"I'm not a simulation anymore, Raul. I made myself real."

It took him a full five seconds to process the meaning behind her words. When he did, he reached out to touch her, gently caressing her cheek with his right hand. As his fingers approached her mouth, the feel of her warm breath startled him, but not as much as when she gently kissed his palm.

"My God," he said. "It's really true."

○ ○ ●

"You did what?"

Jennifer stared in disbelief at VJ before turning on Raul.

"And you . . . you allowed this?"

"I did what needed to be done," said VJ. "I downloaded my consciousness from the ship's neural net into my new human form."

"I don't know what your body is," said Jennifer, feeling her blood pulse in her temples, "but it's definitely not human."

"And yours is? How dare you lecture me on what it means to be human, you Altreian altered—"

"Whoa," said Raul, as Dgarra stepped to Jennifer's side. "Everyone take it down a notch. That's an order."

Jennifer felt as if she had been slapped in the face, her fury rising to match VJ's. Unconsciously, she reached over her shoulder for her war-blade, only to find that she wasn't wearing it. Aware of how odd her motion looked, she massaged the back of her neck in a weak attempt to disguise her original intent.

Fighting down the urge to yell at Raul, Jennifer forced herself to center, pulling forth the memory of a deep meditative state and lowering her heart rate from eighty-six beats per minute to sixty-seven. Considering her augmentations, it was still surprisingly high, but at least she was once again capable of logical thought. The slight squeeze of Dgarra's big hand on her left shoulder helped calm her further.

VJ surprised her by apologizing. "I'm sorry. I should have informed you of what I was doing."

"We aren't angry with what you've done," said Raul before Jennifer could say anything different. "It's just that you kept what you were working on secret from us."

Damn right, Jennifer thought. *What the hell else are you hiding?*

"Well, VJ," said Dgarra, his deep voice a comforting rumble, "perhaps you can enlighten us on the extent of your self-upgrade."

VJ flashed him a grateful smile, then backed away two steps and spun in a slow circle, almost as if she were performing at the end of a catwalk. As she came to a halt, facing her crewmates and captain, she took a deep breath, and Jennifer was surprised to see her chest rise and fall as she did so.

"My body is almost human. I have human muscles beneath human skin. The blood that flows through my vessels is red, although it carries an upgraded variant of the nano-machines that course through Jennifer's and Raul's veins. My organic heart beats, and I can feel sensations, including pain.

"My brain is a biosynthetic neural network with embedded communications crystals that are quantum entangled with elements of a new interface to the *Meridian Ascent*'s neural net. My tongue, mouth, and throat can eat and drink, but my gastrointestinal system and associated organs have been replaced with a matter disrupter-synthesizer capable of providing my nanites with the materials to repair damaged body parts or regrow those that have been destroyed."

Jennifer felt her throat tighten but managed to succinctly state her question. "So your consciousness simultaneously resides in the ship's neural net and in this body's brain?"

VJ slowly shook her head, her blue eyes locking with Jennifer's brown ones. "No. When I said I made myself real, I didn't mean I made a body that I can inhabit or not, depending on my preference. My continued existence depends upon my body. I can die as surely as you can. More importantly, I am no longer tied to this starship. If I need to live in a world beyond the reach of this ship's stasis field, I can do so. And if the *Meridian Ascent*'s neural net shuts down, I will continue to function as a quasi-human being."

"And your internal stasis field?" asked Dgarra.

"Gives me the same capability that the external stasis field backpacks provide each of you. The only difference is that, so long as I have enough matter to consume, my internal MDS will provide an unlimited power supply."

"You mean food?" asked Jennifer, although the question was meant only to confirm her suspicion.

"I taste things, so I prefer good food and drink. However, my MDS is capable of processing anything I can swallow."

"Then why not give yourself a much larger mouth and throat?"

"I'm not a monster, even if you choose to think of me that way."

As she watched the earnest look in VJ's eyes, Jennifer thought she detected a sense of longing. Surely she was imagining the emotion, or more likely, VJ was faking it. Jennifer's empathic abilities *couldn't* have been picking up emotions from a biosynthetic brain, but that damn sure felt like what was happening.

She suddenly felt ashamed of herself. If VJ were human, Jennifer knew that she wouldn't be treating her this way. But because VJ was only an AI with a synthetic body, the normal rules of civility didn't apply. At least that's what Jennifer kept telling herself.

The command bay had grown quiet as the others stared at her. No wonder. Jennifer could only imagine the expression on her face as conflicting waves of emotions shook her. Now, as she looked at the faces of her friends and crewmates, she could find nothing appropriate to say. She knew this silent power game. First one to speak loses. And with each passing second, the weight of their expectations pressed in on her. Even Dgarra refused to throw her a lifeline. Maybe she didn't deserve one.

Her soul felt as bleak and colorless as the alien chamber in which they stood. She refocused on VJ, reaching out with her mind, seeking whatever weirdness lay behind those human-looking blue eyes. And to her utter surprise, her thoughts touched VJ's. A gasp escaped Jennifer's lips. For a moment, she thought that perhaps she was still wearing her SRT headset, connecting with VJ through the ship's neural net. But that was not the case. This telepathic connection was real, accompanied by an equally strong empathic link.

There it was again, that desperate sense of longing to be accepted as a friend and an equal.

"Do you believe me now?" VJ's thoughts spoke in her mind.

Jennifer blinked away the tears that tried to well up in her eyes, suddenly forced to admit what she hadn't wanted to.

"VJ," she said aloud, "I'm sorry. I was being a complete ass."

Before any of the other crew members could respond, VJ stepped forward, threw her arms around Jennifer's neck, and hugged her with arms that were strong yet gentle. As VJ's "Thank you" whispered in her mind, Jennifer found herself returning the embrace.

The universe she had come to accept had just taken strange to a whole new level.

: CHAPTER 12

SMYTHE FORTRESS, NEW ZEALAND

28 February

Heather Smythe swam naked in a clear pool of water near the spot where a mountain stream created a twelve-foot waterfall, showering her with mist. She ducked under, feeling the tingle of the cold water that resisted the warmth of the summer day. Rising to the surface, she swept back her long, white-streaked brown hair with both hands, squeezing out the water as she did so. Mark swam up beside her, the reflection of the sunlight off his back and buttocks emphasizing the muscles that rippled beneath his bronze skin.

God, she loved the summers in these New Zealand mountains.

Since she and Mark rarely felt the need for sleep, they had adopted the habit of working all night and spending part of each day in the great outdoors—hiking, swimming, or jogging along the mountain trails. The joy she got from those nature jaunts reminded her of what they were working so hard to save. But more important, the outings cleansed her soul.

When Mark leaned in and kissed her lips, she smiled and gently pushed him away.

"Did you forget about our two o'clock meeting?"

"No, but I was hoping you would."

"There's always tomorrow," she said, swimming back toward the spot where they'd draped their clothes over a tree branch.

"Let's hope so."

Mark's words hadn't been said in a serious tone, but they seemed to suck the light out of the day. Heather shivered as she pulled on her clothes.

There was no reason for her mood to have suddenly soured. The day was every bit as lovely as it had been only moments before. They had a meeting to go to, but it was only a routine status update. The world, as messed up as it was, happened to still be free. The UFNS was doubtlessly planning to build another gateway to replace the one that she and Mark had destroyed outside of Frankfurt, but that was a problem for another day.

Then she slid her SRT headset over her temples.

○　○　●

As Mark followed Heather into the conference room, he saw Janet sitting at the round table with Jamal, Dr. Wu, Dr. Jennings, and Rob.

Mark's eyes were drawn to the boy, and as had become a regular occurrence, he found himself amazed at the accelerated changes in the lad. Instead of being a typical ten-year-old, Rob looked like Mark had at seventeen. He was muscular, coordinated, and had the mental development to match. It didn't matter whether these changes had been caused by the alterations the Altreian headset had made to his brain or by the fact that he shared his mind with an alien AI named Eos. Among the four of them who had been enhanced, Rob manifested a new kind of strangeness.

Mark pondered this. Rob's telekinesis allowed Eos to manipulate the flow of electrons within the circuits of nearby electronic devices, giving the boy absolute control over them. In addition to controlling computing devices, he could make vending machines dispense their contents, make slot machines come up cherries, and make cameras fail to see him. Going beyond hacking in the traditional sense, Rob and Eos manipulated physics to produce their desired results.

"What's so important that you didn't want to communicate it over our SRT headsets?" Heather asked.

Janet motioned for Mark and Heather to sit down and waited until they did so.

"Almost an hour ago, our new communications array picked up a subspace message from beyond Neptune," she said.

Mark felt Janet's gaze lock with his in a look that caused him to catch his breath.

"Jennifer is alive," she said.

Mark rose to his feet so quickly that he knocked over his chair. He leaned over, placing both hands on the table as shock and disbelief froze him in place.

"What?" he yelled.

"Please, Mark," Janet said, "sit down and I will show you."

Mark righted his chair and slowly sat back down, his chest heaving as if he had just completed a hard sprint.

"If everyone will put your SRT headsets on," said Janet, "I will now replay her message."

Watching the others comply, Mark slipped his own headset into place with trembling fingers. Suddenly the world melted away around him as the recorded audiovisual message filled his mind.

Jennifer stood before him, her shoulder-length brown hair framing a face that was leaner and harder than he remembered. She wore a black-and-purple uniform and stood inside an alien craft that he recognized from his brief glimpse of Jennifer stepping into the Rho Ship.

She'd aged, but not in the same way he and Heather had during these eight years. Despite the hard experience that shone in her brown eyes, she didn't look much older than twenty.

Her voice startled him out of his reverie.

"This message is for Mark and Heather. I am broadcasting this sub-space message across the entire Earth, knowing that you alone possess the subspace technology to receive it. I've tried contacting you through my Altreian headset and managed to establish a connection with the Second Ship's computer. Unfortunately, neither of you were wearing yours at the time. So I will schedule this message to repeat at regular intervals, in hopes that you will get it.

"As for me, I am safe aboard the Rho Ship, which we have renamed the *Meridian Ascent*. The ship has a crew of four, consisting of me, Raul, an alien warrior named Dgarra, and an artificial intelligence named VJ. The *Meridian* is currently located beyond the orbit of Neptune, but I hope to establish direct contact with you prior to returning to Earth. In a few days from now, we will maneuver the ship closer so that we will be within range to perform detailed scans of the planet.

"If you get this message, please try to establish a subspace com-munications link to this ship. I have embedded detailed time-synced coordinates that should allow you to connect to us. Barring that, I need one of you to wear your Altreian headset at all times so that we can link through the Second Ship."

Jennifer paused, blinked rapidly, and wiped her eyes with her right hand. "Even though Earth isn't yet within the range of our worm-fiber sensors, we have detected an active Kasari wormhole gateway on the planet, so we must proceed with caution. Stay safe. Tell Mom and Dad I love them. I hope to see you soon."

Then Jennifer's image winked out. As Mark reached up to remove his SRT headset, he felt a dampness on his own cheeks. Having spent so long coming to terms with the loss of his twin, to see her again now brought all those feelings crashing back in. And even though he had placed his headset on the table, he could feel similarly strong emotions emanating from Heather's mind in waves.

"My God," Heather said.

"Now you know why I wanted to show you this in person," said Janet. "Not only is Jennifer alive and on a starship headed here, but she said they have detected an active Kasari wormhole gateway on Earth."

"That's impossible," said Jamal. "We've penetrated all of the UFNS intelligence systems. If they had been building another gateway, we would have picked up on it."

Glancing to his right, Mark watched Heather's eyes. Although they didn't fade to white, they flickered.

"What if Prokorov wanted us to focus on the Frankfurt Gateway?" asked Heather. "They made a big show of its construction by putting so much security around it."

Eileen gave a slow nod. "And he knows that we've penetrated all of their cyber-security systems."

"Even Big John," said Denise.

Mark detected a note of sadness in her tone. He looked at Janet. "If you wanted to hide a major construction project, totally off the grid, where would you do it?"

"I'd want to take advantage of underground military construction. North Korea would be at the top of my list."

"How can we confirm it?"

"I'd like more information on the UFNS troop movement anomalies we identified," said Heather. "I'll go through what we have, but I'd like Jamal and Eileen to see if they can find any more."

"Then I'll volunteer for Altreian headset monitoring duty," Mark said, feeling an upwelling of hope that he would soon be having a direct conversation with his sister.

"Rob," said Janet, "I want you to try to make the subspace connection to the Rho Ship."

"I'm on it."

Janet shifted her gaze back to Mark. "Okay," she said, "let's bring your sister home."

○ ○ ●

Nikina Gailan, aka Galina Anikin, stepped out of the dark alley onto a dimly lit Budapest street, firmly ensconced in her assumed identity. She was one of the most wanted operatives for the Safe Earth resistance, or SERE, as the UFNS media had branded it. After the robotic attack on the Frankfurt Gateway, even SERE's political counterpart, the Safe Earth movement, had distanced itself from the violent group and its leaders.

Although Prokorov had choreographed Nikina's escape from UFNS military custody, she'd made no contact with him during the last three months. The Smythes had far too much advanced technological capability to risk a message intercept, especially since she was working on building their trust.

As silently as Nikina normally moved, tonight's fresh blanket of snow muffled what little sound she made. It also made the notoriously dangerous Eighth District area along Dioszeghy Samuel Street appear peaceful. Tonight was cold enough to keep the prostitutes huddled just inside doorways instead of aggressively plying their wares to the drivers of slow-moving cars.

She walked southeast. Interconnected single-story buildings lined the right side of the sidewalk. Across the street to her left, a youth reform facility occupied a crumbling four-story brick building. The drug dealers and gang members she passed looked Nikina over but came to the wise decision not to mess with her, an effect she usually had on such people.

Daniil Alkaev had called it her death stare, although she thought that a highly inaccurate description. The look saved the lives of people who would otherwise be dead. More important, it kept them from impeding her progress.

Stepping between two toughs who were actually SERE operatives, Nikina entered the dilapidated six-story structure and made her way to the concrete stairs that led down to the basement, passing three men shooting craps on the upper landing. The bald one in the center glanced up and smiled.

"Good evening, Nikina."

"Burt."

With that single word of acknowledgment, she left him and his dice-gaming, sham security guards behind and descended the two flights of stairs that took her to the filthy entry to the sub-basement. Ignoring the steel door with its rusted-over hinges, she looked up into the shadowed corner to its right, a cavity into which light from the bare incandescent bulb didn't reach.

Although she knew the tiny Smythe facial-recognition device was up there, it was invisible to her eyes. With a barely audible hiss, a six-foot-wide floor-to-ceiling section of the fake block wall slid open on grooved titanium tracks. Despite the many times that she had stood at this juxtaposition of two technologically distinct universes, she still felt a touch of awe at the contrast.

The Hungarian arm of the Safe Earth resistance had completed the assembly of the Smythe Earth gate seventeen days ago. During the time that had elapsed since then, the robots that had been sent through had enlarged and transformed the subbasement, turning it into a heavily armed fortress. The walls of the two escape tunnels had been reinforced with carbon-bonded titanium struts and panels.

The main facility now had its own stasis field generator powered by a next-generation cold-fusion reactor. A point-blank nuclear explosion could vaporize the surrounding structures, but everything within the protected area would emerge unscathed. Furthermore, if anyone somehow managed to infiltrate the site, they would find themselves confronted by more than two hundred of the Smythe autonomous combat robots.

Nikina didn't know how many similar facilities the Smythes had managed to sprinkle around the world, but even if this was the only one, it was vastly more impressive than the site at which she had been arrested on the outskirts of Hanau, Germany. It was also much noisier, due to the ongoing robotic construction work.

A heavyset, bearded Hungarian walked toward her, a broad smile lighting his face.

"Ah, Nikina. Knock the snow from your feet and come warm yourself with a hot tea. We have much to discuss."

She returned the big man's embrace with believable enthusiasm. After all, Ambrus Fazakus was an important SERE leader, and convincing people of her sincerity was one of Nikina's specialties.

"Thank you, Ambrus. Hot tea sounds wonderful."

He led her past the inactive Earth gate and into a small break room with a half-dozen tables, indicating for her to take a seat at the nearest. In here, acoustic tiles on the walls and ceiling reduced the noise, making conversation easier. Ambrus walked over to the drink station and soon returned with two steaming mugs. Nikina lifted hers to her lips, inhaling the scent of peppermint before taking a sip, just enough to avoid burning her lips.

Then, holding the cup loosely so that its warmth radiated into her enfolding hands, she looked across the table, studying Ambrus's face.

"So," she said, "you are alone in here tonight?"

"Just me and the robots. Except for the outer guards, I gave everyone else the night off. In a few minutes, Janet Price will initiate a videoconference over the subspace link. She wanted you and me to be the only attendees on this end."

She felt her heart rate elevate ever so slightly. Either this was a very good sign or a very bad one. As she glanced out the door at all the automated firepower at Janet's disposal, there was no chance that Nikina could fight her way out of here. The best she could do was put a bullet through Ambrus Fazakus's thick head, but that would still mean total failure of the mission that Alexandr Prokorov had assigned her.

Since her options wouldn't become clear until she heard what Janet had to say, Nikina settled back in her chair, crossed her legs, and let the warm tea soothe her. Her wait wasn't a long one.

When the monitors on all four of the break room's walls flickered to life, she found her eyes drawn to the face of the striking woman who had killed her lover. This time, Nikina had to work to keep the hatred from seeping from her soul into her eyes.

It was an odd arrangement for a videoconference. She found herself looking at a monitor above Ambrus's head while he looked at a display high on the wall behind her. Each of these flat-panel video units was equipped with cameras so that Janet could manipulate the imagery from this room.

The arrangement made it impossible for Nikina to tell which of them Janet was looking at. Janet's eyes seemed perpetually locked on her. Others may have found this to be the intimidating equivalent of being seated in a low chair staring up at their boss. To Nikina, it was just another power play.

She kept her face passive.

When Janet smiled, the balance between hope and dread in Nikina's mind shifted toward the former.

"It's good to see that you made it here for this meeting, Nikina."

"It was no problem."

Janet's look lost its softness as, once again, the cold eyes of a killer returned. But it was her statement that shocked Nikina.

"In hopes of detecting and defeating any UFNS attempt to build another wormhole gateway, we have been scattering these Earth gates among Safe Earth resistance groups around the globe. I am sorry to inform you that our strategy has failed."

○   ○   ●

Janet looked at the tiled video displays, taking special note of the reactions of each of the two Safe Earth resistance operatives to her statement. The heavyset and black-bearded Ambrus straightened abruptly while Nikina's eyes barely widened, the rest of her features showing no change whatsoever. Janet doubted that she would have handled the news as coolly. Thank the stars that Nikina was on their side instead of Prokorov's.

She saw a bit of herself in Nikina, that indomitable drive to accomplish her mission, regardless of the difficulty of the task. And Janet also detected the pain and anger buried beneath Nikina's mask. There was no doubt in her mind that the Latvian operative had suffered a loss that rivaled her own. That suppressed rage needed an outlet, and Janet intended to give it one.

"What?" asked Ambrus.

"We've learned from a reliable source that the UFNS has another Kasari gateway, and it's active."

"Where?" Nikina asked.

"We suspect North Korea."

Janet saw Nikina's eyes narrow.

"Suspect?"

"That country has almost a century of secret military infrastructure and is almost totally off the grid. It's a place that negates our technological advantages."

"And where do we come in?" asked Ambrus.

"I need to commandeer one of your recently assigned operatives."

"You mean Nikina."

"Yes."

"Why me?" Nikina asked.

"Two reasons. You proved your loyalty in Hanau, and you've demonstrated a knack for getting yourself out of tight spots. I need to put you back into another one."

At this, Nikina laughed. Ambrus didn't.

"What about my operation here? I don't see the wisdom of taking Nikina away from me for what might be a red herring."

"Noted," Janet said. "Do you have any objection, Nikina?"

"No. But I have not yet heard the details of the mission."

"I will brief you when you get here. Ambrus, in five minutes I am going to remotely power up your Earth gate. Make ready."

"I need to get some things from my apartment," Nikina said, rising to her feet.

Janet had expected this objection and waved it off. "No time for that. We'll supply everything you'll need."

For a moment, Janet thought she saw anger flash in Nikina's eyes. The look was replaced with another that vanished just as quickly. What had she seen? Anticipation? Well, she knew the adrenaline rush of being told you were about to be sent into a highly dangerous situation.

When Nikina slowly nodded, Janet killed the subspace link. It was time to get ready for the new arrival.

○   ○   ●

Nikina stepped through the Earth gate, feeling the hair rise along the nape of her neck. It wasn't the first time she had made the passage. It was her third. But the first two times had occurred during a firefight, so she hadn't been paying as much attention. She knew she was stepping through a portal into another part of the world; she just had no idea where the Smythe Fortress was located. This time she came alone, the portal back to Budapest winking out immediately after she stepped through it.

The room looked even larger than she remembered. Along the left wall, what had to be the master control station surrounded a single workstation with a complex array of electronics. And at that workstation sat a strong-looking young man apparently in his late teens who wore an iridescent headset with beaded ends that settled on his temples.

Along the right two-thirds of the room, hundreds of combat robots stood in columns. Some were roughly dog-shaped, some humanoid, and others crab-like. But now she understood why the room looked so much bigger. The rear wall had been opened to reveal a huge high-bay within which autonomous air and ground vehicles were lined up by type. Some were supply transporters, but most bristled with combat capabilities.

The ones that drew Nikina's eyes were the autonomous combat motorcycles. Having watched many of the other electrically powered robotic systems in action, she had no doubt that these new models would bring entirely new capabilities into battle.

The breadth of what she beheld stunned her. How was it possible for the Smythes to manufacture these things so fast? The exponential rate at which they were increasing their capabilities sent goose bumps up and down her limbs. She was thankful that her black leather outfit hid her involuntary reaction from the group of people who waited to greet her.

Janet Price, also dressed all in black, stood in the center, flanked by Mark and Heather Smythe. Despite the two formidable people on either side, Nikina found herself drawn to Janet, as if by an irresistible force. At five foot ten, Janet stood three inches taller than Nikina. This was the sniper who had shot Daniil Alkaev in the head on that firelit night in Lima.

Nikina had used many names during her life. Back then she had been Galina Anikin, and Janet had come a hair's breadth from killing her, too. Instead, Janet's bullet had left the scar in Nikina's hairline that her nanites had never completely healed. Before she was done, Nikina intended to carve Daniil's name into Janet's lovely body.

It took all her self-mastery to hide that bloodlust beneath a warm grin as she shook Janet's extended hand.

"Good to see you again," said Janet.

"You, too. It's been a while."

Breaking Janet's gaze before it became uncomfortable, Nikina accepted the greetings of Heather and Mark. Two years ago, Nikina had learned firsthand that, far from being the spoiled tech billionaires she had once believed, these two were every bit as dangerous as Janet Price and Jack Gregory.

Nikina noted movement to her left and turned to see the teenage boy who had been operating the master-control console approaching. As she turned toward him, she did a double take. He looked like a much younger Jack. But this couldn't be the boy she and Daniil had hunted to ground in Peru. He was several years too old for that. He extended his hand.

"Hi, Nikina," he said with a confident smile. "Rob Gregory."

Again, Nikina felt her mind spinning as she struggled to dismiss the shock of this *Twilight Zone* episode in which she now found herself.

"A pleasure."

"So," said Janet, "if you'll walk with me to the conference room, I'll brief you on your mission."

As Nikina followed Janet, she noted that the other three remained behind.

"Mark and Heather won't be joining us," said Janet, noting her backward glance. "They have another pressing matter to deal with."

That was fine with Nikina. Something in the way Heather had looked at her had given her the uncomfortable feeling that the woman had seen through her facade. But if Heather had suspicions, she had not spoken of them, so Nikina shrugged it off. Perhaps her natural paranoia was getting the better of her.

As they turned into a long hallway, she followed Janet Alexandra Price, thinking about how easy it would be to pull her weapon and put a bullet into the back of that beautiful head. Of course, that would mean that she would have failed to accomplish the mission that Prokorov had given her all those months ago. Besides, dying at the hands of an army of combat robots inside this rat hole wasn't in her plans.

For now, Nikina would bide her time playing the loyal SERE operative and wait for her opportunity to bring down the entire Smythe operation. The bullet with Janet's name on it would have to wait.

Besides, she thought, *anticipation stokes the heat of the climax.*

:CHAPTER 13

28 February

Mark walked alongside Heather into the room they had modeled after the Second Ship's command deck. Four pedestal-mounted, translucent chairs seemed to sprout from the floor near its center. Mark found it difficult to judge distance in the room, a side effect of the curvature that made it hard to tell where the floor stopped and the wall began, an effect magnified by the soft lighting. The design was all about minimizing distractions that could reduce the immersion into the headset-provided visions, whether those headsets were of the subspace receiver-transmitter SRT variety or the Altreian types that connected them to the Second Ship's computer.

The familiar feel of the chair molding to Mark's body shape as he settled onto it failed to calm the thumping of his heart. While Rob was working with Jamal, Eileen, and Denise in an attempt to establish a subspace connection to the *Meridian Ascent*, Mark and Heather were about to try to link to Jennifer using their Altreian headsets. After all this time, the thought of his mind touching that of his twin took

Mark's breath away. He shoved aside the negative too-good-to-be-true thoughts, removed the Altreian headset from its slot inside the arm of the chair, and let its beaded ends settle over his temples.

As the visions generated by his mind's interaction with the Altreian computer swept the real world away, Mark felt Heather's mind join his. But he couldn't feel Jennifer's presence. Detecting his disappointment, Heather's voice spoke in his mind.

"Patience, sweetheart. She said she would try periodically. Let's give her some time."

Mark sighed but shifted focus. If they had to wait, they might as well be someplace spectacular. Picking a place both he and Heather loved, he let the Second Ship transport them there, pulling her into that alternate reality along with him.

Wearing multicolored swimsuits, they stood hand in hand, digging their toes into the warm sand. Across the turquoise lagoon, the two peaks of Mount Pahia and Mount Otemanu rose above Bora Bora. The late afternoon sun had drifted low enough so that it rested on the western horizon. If they waited just a few minutes, they might be lucky enough to see the green flash that occasionally followed the sunset.

Mark let his gaze drift out toward the barrier reef that surrounded the island, watching as several speckled rays passed less than fifty feet from the shore.

"Nice choice," Heather said, nodding at the water. "Shall we?"

"You bet."

But as they stepped toward the gently lapping waves, the beautiful scene dissolved, leaving them standing within the gray alien interior of the Kasari starship that had once been the centerpiece of Dr. Stephenson's prized Rho Project. Jennifer's voice spun him to his left.

"My God!" she said.

Before Mark could react, she raced forward, leaping up to wrap her strong arms around his neck. As he hugged her close, he felt warm tears wet his cheek, not exactly sure whether they were his, Jennifer's, or both. When he set her back on her feet, Heather took his place. For several long moments, no one spoke.

As good as the virtual-reality effects produced by their SRT headsets were, they couldn't compare to the experience produced by these Altreian ones. You could touch, smell, hear, see, and taste, just as in real life.

When the two women released each other, Jennifer stepped back to look at Heather and her brother, sheer wonder on her face. A sudden constriction in Mark's throat forced him to swallow hard. That was when the changes in his sister struck him.

As he had observed in the recorded video she had broadcast, she hadn't aged significantly since he'd last seen her. But her face and eyes carried some of the hard edges he'd gotten used to seeing in Jack and Janet. He got the impression that Jennifer had experienced some very tough things during the time she'd been gone.

Despite that, she looked damn good. Dear God. He had his twin sister back.

"You've gotten tall," Jennifer said to him.

"And married."

Jennifer's eyes widened as she glanced back and forth between him and Heather, who smiled and nodded. "When?"

"A few months after you triggered the Rho Ship's wormhole engines and disappeared with Raul."

"What about the Stephenson Gateway?" Jennifer asked.

"We nuked it," said Mark.

Her eyes widened again. "What?"

"Had to," said Heather. "The crazy bastard, Stephenson, was trying to make emergency repairs to restart it. He threw up a stasis field bubble and we couldn't get to him."

Jennifer paused. "Then why is there an active Kasari gateway on Earth?"

"We didn't know there was until we got your message. Right now, we've got people hunting for it."

"And that," said Mark, "is part of a long story. But first, we want to hear yours."

"I'll get to that in a bit. Before that, I want to give you a tour of the *Meridian Ascent* and introduce you to the rest of the crew."

"How?" asked Mark. "The three of us and Rob are the only ones with the Altreian headsets."

Jennifer laughed. "And that's where my story gets longer."

○ ○ ●

Jennifer led Heather and Mark to a door that opened into a small conference room. But the sight that startled Heather was of the other three individuals seated around the table.

"You both know Raul," Jennifer said. "He's now the captain of the *Meridian Ascent*, and I'm his first officer."

Heather recognized Raul, although the last time she'd seen him had been via a brief glimpse when Jennifer had stepped through the wormhole gate into the Rho Ship. At that time, he had been a cyborg horror with no legs, a mechanical eye on a stalk, and a translucent skullcap that left his brain visible. Now he looked like the handsome young man she had briefly dated in high school, albeit a couple of years older. As she struggled to process these changes, Heather decided that she would need more information to make sense of them.

"And this is Dgarra."

Jennifer indicated the big alien to Raul's left, who looked every bit the warrior. Ridged eyebrows extended outward and then up over the top of his brown-skinned, hairless head. His dark eyes studied her and Mark, his expression inscrutable. Noting that neither Dgarra nor Raul extended their hands, she resisted the urge to do so. Mark merely nodded in acknowledgment of the introductions.

"And finally," said Jennifer, "this is VJ, our ship's science officer."

Heather froze as, beside her, Mark sucked in an audible breath. Except for the tight-fitting black-and-purple uniform she wore, this young woman looked exactly like Jennifer had when Heather had last seen her inside the ATLAS cavern.

This time, Heather couldn't resist the impulse to extend her hand, a gesture that was met with a firm grip by a warm, human-feeling palm. Was this a projection, given form by her mental connection to the Second Ship's computer? Her mind placed the probability of this at an unlikely 2.758 percent. And VJ's smile looked authentic as well.

As Heather released her grip on VJ's hand, Mark stepped forward to greet the AI, a look of pure wonder on his face.

"Is she real?" he asked.

VJ responded before Jennifer could answer his question. "I'm as real as you are."

Jennifer's laugh broke the tension that had been building in the room. "Don't worry. It's taken me a while to accept VJ's new body, too."

Heather thought she detected a blush on VJ's cheeks, then discarded the thought. But when she played the sequence back in her mind, she had to admit that her first impression had been correct.

Inhaling deeply, Heather turned her attention back to her long-lost friend and sat down. Mark and Jennifer followed suit.

"I think that it's time for us to hear your story," said Heather. "Apparently, ours pales in comparison."

"Yeah," said Mark, his gaze shifting from VJ to Dgarra and then back to Jennifer. "And let's hope it stays that way."

○   ○   ●

Nikina stepped into the small conference room, and Janet gestured for her to sit down at the table as the door whisked closed behind them. Janet took a seat across from her.

"You mentioned a new mission?" Nikina asked.

In answer, Janet spun a thick manila envelope across the table to her.

Nikina dumped the contents of the envelope on the table. A thick dossier with a passport clipped to the outside of the folder spilled out. She unclipped the passport and flipped it open, not surprised to see her own picture inside.

"You work for the Federation Security Service," Janet said.

Nikina had to work to keep from grabbing for her gun. How had she been discovered? She had taken every precaution. On the other hand, she was alone with Janet in this room, so she liked her short-term odds of survival. Then her eyes caught the name to the right of the passport photo: Anya Kashirin.

"And you're Russian," Janet said. "We've created a detailed new identity for you, inserting the numerous background investigations you've undergone and the missions you've completed into the appropriate FSS computer systems. For the past four years, you've been an FSS field agent stationed in the United States, successfully maintaining your cover but not doing anything so spectacular that your name has come to the attention of the higher-ups.

"Your complete background and new orders assigning you to the FSS headquarters in The Hague are inside that folder. I need you to memorize the contents on the memory card. We are going to be sending you through our Earth gate to the Netherlands. I want you to report in to your new FSS assignment and find out precisely where the UFNS has built their new wormhole gateway. You will need this to securely contact me."

Nikina met Janet's eyes, hiding the relief that left her with an adrenaline high. She accepted the new phone that Janet handed her, knowing that it must be another quantum-entangled model like the ones that SERE's regional commanders used.

"How long do I have to get ready?"

"You are scheduled to meet your new boss thirty-seven hours from now. In the meantime, you will be staying in temporary accommodations inside this facility. If you have no more questions, I'll have Eileen show you to your quarters."

On cue, the door behind Nikina slid open, and she turned to see a petite, young Asian woman step in. With a shock, Nikina recognized her. This was Dr. Eileen Wu, formerly the NSA's top computer scientist.

Nikina put the contents back into the envelope and stood. "I will be ready." Then she turned and followed Dr. Wu out of the room.

:CHAPTER 14

1 March

On the first of March, Alexandr Prokorov strode out of the assimilation center tunnel complex alongside Commander Drolaag, the four-armed Kasari towering over him. As they walked toward Friendship Cavern, where the upgraded gateway awaited, Prokorov felt a sense of frustration at the relatively limited access to the hive-mind he had been granted thus far. Then again, he knew that this was standard operating procedure until a new world's assimilation process had been completed, and Earth was still in its very early stages.

But his cortical array of nanobots had delivered the knowledge that a new Kasari group commander had been designated to replace Drolaag and would be arriving through the gateway a few minutes from now. Drolaag hadn't been demoted; instead, the collective had assigned someone with more experience to manage the next phase of Earth's assimilation. Unfortunately, Prokorov wouldn't gain direct communications permission with this new commander until the transfer of authority was official.

They stepped into the broad tunnel that provided access to Friendship Cavern, staying to the right to avoid the endless procession of alien military equipment that moved through this passage toward the staging areas. The regime that had ruled North Korea for all those decades before its absorption by the East Asian People's Alliance had been hyperparanoid. The network of tunnels it had excavated beneath the country far surpassed the estimations of the world's intelligence agency. Now the collective was putting these subterranean warrens to a greater purpose.

As they entered the recently expanded cavern, Prokorov noted that the flow of equipment and troops through the wormhole had been halted. Now, two dozen Kasari officers of Drolaag's species, seven females and five males, stood in a tight formation facing the gateway that had replaced the original human-built version.

Drolaag led Prokorov past them, stopping five paces in front of the portal. As often as he had been here in the last six weeks, the sight still awed the minister of federation security. He was only a few steps away from that monstrous room on another planet, one whose atmosphere would have killed him back when his blood hadn't been infused with the Kasari nanites. Although the stasis field that kept the methane-ammonia mixture contained on the far side was invisible, the ultrathin boundary between worlds shimmered slightly. And beyond it, another honor guard backdropped a four-armed Kasari female who stood even taller than Commander Drolaag.

Without hesitation, she stepped through the gateway, the stasis field modulating itself to allow her body to pass. Ignoring Prokorov, she came to a stop directly in front of her counterpart and pressed the palm of her upper right hand firmly against Drolaag's left shoulder, a salute that he echoed.

"Group Commander Drolaag," she said, "I relieve you."

"Group Commander Shalegha, the group is now yours."

○　○　●

Shalegha watched as Drolaag stepped through the gateway; then she turned her attention to Prokorov, who had been designated her human liaison.

She was fortunate to be here. After the disastrous events on Scion and her destruction of its corresponding gateway on the staging world, she could have faced summary execution. Instead, Kasari High Command had decided to quarantine her so that they could study the infection that had severed the connection between her cortical nanobot array and the hive-mind.

Reassimilation to the collective had not been easy or pleasant. Her handlers had forced a new infusion of nanited blood through her vessels after they had purged the original nanobots from her body and brain with a flushing serum. Then they had connected her cortical array to an isolated diagnostic system and performed a deep scan. After reviewing the record of her memories, Kasari High Command had judged the decisions that she had made and the actions she had taken to be laudable.

As her reward for preventing the human-designed computer virus from spreading through the Scion gateway to infect the hive-mind, the High Command had placed her in charge of Earth's assimilation. They had also decided to abandon the Scion system rather than risk reopening its gateway.

Shalegha turned her attention to the human, Prokorov. She had reviewed his record and found it satisfactory. He had facilitated an almost flawlessly executed initial phase of this assimilation. Shalegha issued the mental instructions that gave his cortical array permission to interface directly with hers, feeling the man's gratitude at this promotion that made him the highest-ranking human within the collective.

"You have done an excellent job here, Liaison Prokorov. The time has now come to announce the Kasari Collective's alliance with the UFNS and offer the benefits of assimilation to the rest of the people of this world."

:CHAPTER 15

KALASASAYA TEMPLE, BOLIVIA

1 March

Khal Teth sucked in a breath, feeling his body tingle at the sudden awakening. Technically, this was Jack Gregory's body, but with that man's mind currently absent, Khal Teth was in complete control. The sensation was completely different from what he had experienced as Jack's rider, but as he flexed his fingers, he decided that he could get used to it.

He blinked several times as his vision adjusted to the dim magenta illumination within the chrysalis cylinder. Then, lifting his right hand to the control pad, Khal Teth traced in the codes he had pulled from the mind of the *AQ37Z* research vessel's captain and commander all those months ago. With a small whoosh, the cylinder's lid opened.

With an effort, Khal Teth climbed out of the cylinder and stood up, rolling his shoulders to work out a sudden cramp. Suspended animation had prevented Jack's muscles from undergoing atrophy, but that did not mean the process of coming out of such sleep was painless. That pain would not have bothered Jack, but Khal Teth found it burdensome.

He glanced at the chrysalis cylinder containing Commander Broljen, the ship's captain, and smiled. Unless someone entered a code that changed the suspended-animation setting, Broljen would sleep forever.

When Jack had first opened the portal that led into this research vessel, Khal Teth had been the rider in his head. Broljen had been waiting for them, and as a powerful Dhaldric in his own right, Broljen had expected to easily subdue a mere human with his psionic abilities. Khal Teth's presence had come as an unpleasant surprise to the commander, one that had put him into eternal sleep.

Leaving the small chamber, Khal Teth walked back onto the command deck where he and Jack had first confronted the commander, stopping just long enough to retrieve the Incan Sun Staff from the nearest of the five command chairs where he had laid it. Carrying the staff in his left hand, he walked over to the research vessel's command console and entered another of the codes he had extracted from Broljen's head, this one relieving the captain of his duty and freeing his Altreian headband for assignment to the commander who would replace him.

Khal Teth sat down in the center command chair and opened the panel on the seat's right arm. Without hesitation, he extracted the iridescent Altreian headband that was identical in appearance to the four that had attuned to Mark, Heather, Jennifer, and Rob a decade ago. Setting the Sun Staff across his lap, he leaned back and stared at the device that would alter Jack's brain and give Khal Teth mental control of this research vessel.

But as he let the beaded ends settle over his temples, he was unprepared for the wave of agony that lanced through every nerve in this body. If he could have moved, he would have screamed, but he sat frozen in place, his vision scorched by a blinding flash of light.

Surely death would claim him. No living being could endure the endless waves of torture that ripped him apart.

Then, as suddenly as it had begun, the pain subsided, leaving Khal Teth gasping for breath and blinking tears from his eyes. More than a minute passed before the former overlord could sponge the horror of the experience from his mind and regain control of his thoughts.

New sensations bombarded him. He saw with a newfound clarity. Sounds that he couldn't have heard a short time ago came through distinctly. His sense of smell, taste, touch . . . they were all in the midst of changing. But most of all, his thoughts were crisp and sharp. The information that rolled into his mind stayed there.

And, as he had known would happen, his mind was connected to the *AQ37Z*'s computer and to the AI tasked with operating it.

The question formed in Khal Teth's mind. "What should I call you?"

"Commander Broljen called me Z. But you may assign me whatever name you choose."

"Z will do. I have a task for you inside the medical bay."

A nanoparticle door opened in the wall to Khal Teth's left.

"Right through there," said Z.

Khal Teth walked into the medical lab, unsurprised to see the five iridescent operating tables extruded from the floor. Without any hesitation, he removed Jack's utility vest and shirt, letting them fall to the floor. Then he seated himself on the nearest table and lay back, feeling the surface conform to perfectly cradle his body.

Although he was determined to recover his own body on Quol, there was the distinct possibility that Jack would get himself killed before that could happen. Khal Teth would not run the risk of living out his days in a psionically crippled mind like this one. Therefore, he would undergo the genetic modification that the High Council had forbidden to be performed on any other species, the one that had granted the Dhaldric race their psionic powers.

Pulling the ancient knowledge from deep in his memory, he transferred it to Z. As the thousands of tendrils sprouted from the medical table to attach themselves to his body, he knew that the first step was to transfer some of Jack's blood cells to the gene splicer. After that, things would get considerably more complicated.

○   ○   ●

During the three days that Khal Teth had waited inside the *AQ37Z* since undergoing the Lundola Procedure, he had hoped to see some sign that the operation was working. And using the medical table, he had seen the beginning of the development of a psionic lobe within Jack's upper spinal column. However, he could not wait for the lobe to fully develop. That meant he would have to do things the Jack Gregory way.

Khal Teth lifted the Sun Staff from where it lay atop the command chair. Turning his attention to the smooth wall where Jack had entered the ship, he issued the mental command to open the door. It whisked open to reveal the airlock.

Khal Teth removed the headset and issued the command to close the portal. As he had suspected, nothing happened. Although these headsets were capable of altering the brain of a member of the Khyre race to grant him the ability to mentally connect to the ship's computers without having to wear the headsets, an unaltered human brain couldn't make that link without wearing one. He slid the headset back into place and walked into the airlock, closing the door behind him and bringing up the airlock's magenta lighting.

He opened the external hatch and strode up the metallic ramp that led to the altar chamber. With the headset in place, he did not need to use the Sun Staff to open the top of the altar. A mere thought could accomplish that.

But first he focused his thoughts, activating the dormant telepathic ability within Jack's headset-augmented brain, scanning the chamber above for occupants. Khal Teth knew that he could have queried the *AQ37Z*'s computer to learn the answer, but he needed to know the extent to which Jack's human brain had been altered. The results of the experiment were a pleasant surprise. People were nearby, but none within the altar chamber.

Khal Teth issued the mental command, and the top tier of the altar slid open. He walked up to stand atop it. When he placed the base of the staff into the slot from which Jack had removed it, the top tier of the golden altar slid closed once more, carrying Khal Teth as well. The magenta glow from the passage below was snuffed out, leaving him standing in total darkness.

Retrieving Jack's small flashlight from his pocket, Khal Teth switched it on.

He reached out to touch the intricate golden orb atop the silver staff and twisted the articulated clockwork rings until he felt the Sun Staff lock into place. Removing his Altreian headset, he put it into another cargo pocket. Then, without bothering to look around, Khal Teth climbed down from the altar and strode into the cavern system that led up to the surface.

As he walked, he took the quantum-entangled phone from a pocket and activated it. It was time to reintroduce Jack to his family.

:CHAPTER 16

TBE Orbday 11–14

The Keva Vault was not an easy place to gain access to. Located on the far north side of a warren of military bunkers, three miles beneath the Parthian, Jack was forced to navigate an entire series of guard booths and checkpoints. Of course, as overlord, he was allowed to pass, but each stop magnified his anticipation. Several military leaders offered to escort him, but each time he declined.

Jack could feel the curiosity, even concern, that this highly unusual visit roused within them. Not surprising, since no one had requested access to the Keva Vault in hundreds of spans. Khal Teth had visited the vault only once, long before he was imprisoned. But Khal Teth hadn't come to the vault to examine secret historical documents. He and several other members of the High Council had accompanied Lundola, the Khyre geneticist whose discovery had led to the rise of the Dhaldric.

The assembled high lords had scanned Lundola's mind as he verified that all records of his experiments had been secured within the vault. That deep probe had damaged the geneticist's brain, leaving him comatose. Not that it mattered. Lundola was thus able to sleep through his execution.

The scientist had deserved to be lauded as a hero of the new realm. But his discovery was far too dangerous to allow any Khyre to know of it. So Lundola had been sacrificed and his secret buried behind the three-foot-thick metal wall that Jack now faced.

Although nobody accompanied the overlord, Jack could feel the mental presence of the guards assigned to keep a watch on the place. Both guards were needed to simultaneously activate the controls that would open the portal, but either one could close it. Standard operating procedure required any visitor to be accompanied by a high-ranking officer. But Jack's command left no doubt in either guard's mind that he would be entering the vault alone.

"Open the door."

Despite their consternation, the guards didn't hesitate to execute their overlord's command.

The tremendous door made no sound as it slid open. Jack stepped inside. The knowledge that either one of the guards could kill him by executing the "Close" command didn't concern him. He would sense their thoughts and block them should they attempt something so foolish. Unless, of course, either one of them was a seeker. But his danger sense wasn't offering an alert, so he dismissed the thought.

He stepped out of the other side into a room illuminated in a soft white light and issued another command. "I do not want to be disturbed. Relay that to your replacements at the end of your shift."

The response from both guards was the same. "Yes, Overlord."

The records vault had a single workstation positioned in the center, facing away from the door. Like many other examples of Altreian furniture, the viewer station arose from a single pedestal, resembling multicolored glass extruded from a glassblower's pipe. The same was true of the lone chair in front of it.

Exotically shaped cabinets containing drawers of varying sizes lined the walls. But the vast majority of the drawers were no more than two inches in width and height. Of these, there were thousands. Khal Teth's memories told him why. No AI-controlled computers were placed in the vault to answer mental questions. The High Council had not dared entrust its dread secrets to such technology. Here, all documents were stored on old-school molecular memory cards that had to be remotely loaded by a manual request from the viewer to access content. Thus the myriad of tiny drawers with their assigned memory slots.

There would have been no need for Jack to come down here if Khal Teth had bothered to learn more than just cursory information about Lundola's work. Jack knew that Lundola had created the genetic modification that had enhanced the psionic abilities of the Dhaldric race. But he wanted to understand precisely how the geneticist had accomplished such a wonder. So that meant he was in for a bit of a grind.

Fortunately, all Dhaldric possessed eidetic memories and could play back anything they'd seen or experienced. But to understand something deeply, they still needed to apply themselves.

The workstation had two primary functions. In addition to displaying any data that had been recorded on a specified memory card, it also served as a 3-D scanner that allowed new data to be recorded on a card. Lundola's work had been copied into this repository before the originals were fed into a bin on the far wall, which fed a molecular shredder. Anything sensitive enough to make its way into the Keva Vault never came out.

One positive aspect of the workstation was its cross-referenced index of what each memory card contained. You could find what you were looking for, provided you knew enough about the subject matter to identify its catalog entry. On the downside, the system allowed access to only one memory card at a time. This had been designed to prevent an individual from broadly scanning the data in a general search.

Jack settled into the chair that molded itself to his body. When the viewer activated, displaying the vault's content catalog, he felt his mood sour. He was in for a hell of a long slog.

○   ○   ●

It took Jack seven hours to find what he was looking for and another three to scan through Lundola's research papers and experimental records. Only once during that time had someone tried to interrupt him with a mental query as to whether he was okay. Jack had cut that off with a harsh reminder of his earlier order.

Now, having completed his task, he stood, an action that switched off the workstation. At the door, he gave the order that allowed him to pass and then made the long walk back through the bunker complex to take the elevator to the Parthian's upper level. Stiff from sitting, he wanted a hard workout followed by a refreshing ionized shower and a good meal. Then he would go through all the data in his memory until he thoroughly understood it.

Khal Teth had never concerned himself with such details. But if Jack was going to find out whether what he was considering was even possible, he would need to put in that mental effort. Considering how his duties as overlord would consume a significant portion of his time, how many orbdays the effort would take him was yet to be determined.

○   ○   ●

The attack on the coastal city of Ashelan came on the third orbday after Jack's visit to the Keva Vault. The Altreian combat starship, *CS102*, had been preparing to enter orbit in preparation for assignment of a replacement crew when it had suddenly veered away from the docking platform to open fire on Quol's largest ground-based spaceport. A suicidal action. The ship had managed to fire only a single twelve-second burst from its gamma-ray laser before Quol's automated orbital defense systems destroyed it. The resulting fireball, as *CS102* plunged through the atmosphere, terminated southwest of the Parthian in the Altreian Ocean.

Although the spaceport's shielding had protected it as well as the surrounding combat facilities, the deflected graser energy had cut an extensive swath through the center of Ashelan. Jack, wearing his black uniform, his twin ivory blades, and a holstered pistol, walked through the still-smoldering rubble of the city center. Captain Moros and General Zolat accompanied him on the tour of the devastation. Although the tally of civilian losses was still under way, one thing was clear: more than four hundred thousand had died in this city of twenty-three million, most of them Khyre. Considering the nature of the attack, Jack was thankful that the losses hadn't been greater.

"Now we destroy each other," General Zolat said. "Overlord, I warned you that it might come to this."

"Then why weren't our defenses better prepared for such an attack?"

"Fleet Captain Valan was one of our most highly decorated officers. That he would sacrifice his ship and his crew was unimaginable."

Jack halted and turned to face the general, who stood two inches shorter than Jack did. The Dhaldric's red-and-black mottling was a shade lighter than that of Khal Teth's body, and his black eyes were a bit more closely set. But they met Jack's gaze with matching intensity.

"Perhaps," said Jack, "you should expand your imagination."

The general didn't give a verbal response to this rebuke, but it didn't matter. Jack read the thought in Zolat's mind.

"From now on," said Jack, "we will treat any of our starships whose captains are not yet Twice Bound as potential enemies. I want them recalled one at a time to the Altreian system, where they will be met by three combat ships and one transport ship with a designated replacement crew on board.

"The transport ship will return the suspect captain and his crew to an assessment camp here on Quol, and I will personally determine where the loyalties of each of them lie. Those whom I deem acceptable will become part of the Twice Bound and will be returned to their former duties within the fleet."

"And those who do not pass your examination?" Zolat asked.

"I will make that determination on a case-by-case basis. Look around you. The blood of these people is on the rebels' hands. I will not tolerate this rebellion nor those who sympathize with it."

For a moment, Zolat's eyes shifted to the obliteration that surrounded them. When he turned his gaze back to Jack, he nodded. "As you command, Overlord."

"You are dismissed."

As the general turned on his heel and walked back toward one of the waiting aircars, Captain Moros stepped up beside Jack. "Somehow, my friend, chaos always seems to find you."

"Or perhaps I reveal what is already there."

The small gray man shook his head. "Either way, I am along for this ride."

Jack resumed his walk through the smoking ruins, stepping over the bodies of a Khyre mother and child in the rubble. Would the Khyre people have been better off living out their former lives as mind slaves to the Dhaldric? Some would, but not most.

○   ○   ●

General Zolat climbed into the back seat of his aircar, while his two security guards sat in the front. Zolat's mental command sent the aircar winging southwest, crossing a section of the Chasm Sea before passing across the Basrillan continent toward the distant Parthian. Having maintained a forced calm throughout his meeting with the overlord, the muscles in his jaws now cramped.

Despite having kept secret the fact that he was a seeker, it had taken all his ability to hide his inner thoughts from the overlord's crushing mind probes. The overlord had something different about him, some ability that had almost penetrated the general's mental defenses. Almost, but not quite.

Zolat had allowed the overlord to discover his deep sense of loyalty and duty. He had managed to hide how that loyalty applied to the High Council and not to the overlord. His duty was to protect the authority of the Dhaldric race, and that was a duty he would perform.

One of the key tactics that enabled him to maintain this deception was the way he challenged the overlord instead of agreeing with every command, adding a layer of believability when he did finally accept his overlord's edicts.

Yes, Zolat thought to himself, *the loyalty of sycophants is always suspect.*

His eyes scanned the cold, windswept lands of Basrilla, the sight pulling a flutter from his gills. If this overlord who called himself The Ripper had his way, the Dhaldric would find themselves toiling away in these harsh lands instead of occupying all the comfortable positions of authority.

He sneered.

To the void with The Ripper and his Twice Bound followers.

Whatever Zolat was going to do to make that happen, he would have to be careful. Very, very careful. The way The Ripper had terminated the seeker assassin whom Zolat had sent to kill him had been very impressive indeed. This overlord was both mentally and physically dangerous.

Zolat leaned back, taking a calming breath. He would bide his time and wait until the proper array of forces and opportunity came into alignment. And when they did, the general would make sure that The Ripper did not live to see another orbday.

:CHAPTER 17

MERIDIAN ASCENT

2 March

VJ inhaled deeply, savoring the smell that wafted from the open door of the food synthesizer. The ability to perfectly re-create any of the MREs, or the Scion fish, for that matter, was truly a luxury. Properly prepared, the fish weren't as bad as Raul proclaimed, but macaroni and cheese, along with a brownie for dessert, was her favorite.

She couldn't wait until she got to sample a broader assortment of Earth food. The neural net contained archives gleaned from Earth's Internet that described foods like steak, lobster, and a seemingly endless assortment of different cultural cuisines. Unfortunately, the food synthesizer was unable to re-create a meal that it hadn't analyzed.

Every second she spent in this marvelous new body was a wonder. She thought she knew what it was to feel when she had been only a stasis field–supported holographic projection, but she'd been dead wrong. Maybe her enhanced perception made her aware of the muscles rippling beneath her skin. The sensation was great.

The same went for taste, smell, hearing, and sight. She stopped to savor the scents that floated in the ship's air. The aromas here on the command deck, while containing some of the machine smells from the engineering bay, were dominated by the earthy scents of the ship's crew. She had experienced imagery and sound before, but that couldn't compare to what she felt as a biosynthetic human. And when Raul touched her in passing, the gesture brought a shiver up her arms and neck, all the way into her scalp. The sensation storm produced a thrill that she couldn't quite identify, a longing for more prolonged touching that seemed related to her desire for Raul to find her physically attractive. The only problem was that this physical stimulation was making it difficult for VJ to concentrate on her assigned tasks.

Since this was the last short break she would be getting for some time to come, she settled into the science officer's stasis field chair with her tray across her lap and prepared to savor the cheesy goodness.

"Seriously?" Jennifer asked, glancing over at VJ from her first officer's chair. "Mac and cheese again?"

"Beats eel," said Raul.

Dgarra merely shook his head and continued eating the fish that Raul detested, which wasn't really surprising considering that it was one of the species that the Koranthians used in their combat rations.

Conversation died out as everyone returned to their meals. Since this was to be the last lunch before they put the *Meridian* back into serious danger, every crew member wanted to savor the moment.

VJ's thoughts turned to what they were about to try. Back when this ship had rested in a monstrous cradle inside the Los Alamos National Laboratory's Rho Division, Raul had proved that it was possible to create a small wormhole gateway within the command bay. And if the ship's neural net had access to the synchronization codes for another wormhole gateway, the ship could connect to that external one. There were, however, significant restrictions on this mode of operation. Most important, both gateways had to be within the range that the weakest gateway could make such a connection.

They couldn't engage the *Meridian*'s primary wormhole engines, since that would create an unanchored wormhole gateway and shove the starship through it. Thus the maximum range at which the ship could connect an internal gateway with a remote one was the same as the maximum range from which it could create a worm-fiber viewer, roughly thirty million miles.

That limitation alone would mean that they would need to take the *Meridian* somewhere between Earth and Mars to create the connection they wanted. Unfortunately, the targeted remote gateway's maximum range was just beyond the orbit of Earth's moon, so that was where the *Meridian* had to go. The crew had to assume that the Kasari had already brought one or more attack ships through their stargate.

Raul, Jennifer, Dgarra, and VJ had all agreed that the safest place to make their subspace reentry was within a crater on the side of the moon that faced away from Earth. That would mask the characteristic signature produced when something transitioned in or out of subspace. Immediately upon landing on the moon, Raul would activate the *Meridian*'s cloaking field. Of course, none of that would be sufficient if the Kasari happened to have one of their fast-attack spaceships within sensor range of the far side of the moon.

VJ finished her meal and stood, using the stasis field to clean her eating utensils and deposit the waste into the forward MDS for conversion to energy. As she returned to her seat, the others followed suit. Raul glanced around, making sure the others were all back in their stasis chairs, and then nodded at VJ.

"Okay," said Raul, "let's do it."

○ ○ ●

Jennifer watched VJ as she performed the long-range passive sensor scan of Earth's moon. The optical sensor wasn't capable of providing highly detailed imagery from this range, but it allowed VJ to select a large crater and calculate the momentum vector necessary to set them down gently. The biosynth maneuvered the *Meridian* onto a matching velocity vector then shifted the ship into subspace and accelerated to fifty times the speed of light.

Changing her attention from VJ to the data streaming through the ship's neural net, Jennifer performed her own calculation. At this speed the subspace trip would take just over five minutes. The *Meridian* could travel many orders of magnitude faster than this, but VJ had chosen the slower speed to provide a better margin for error on their transition out of subspace. Even at this relatively slow faster-than-light velocity, a one-second error would cause the ship to miss its target by more than nine million miles.

Jennifer approved of this cautious approach. Maybe VJ was maturing, or maybe she was more acutely aware of her new mortality. That was the downside of having a real body. VJ might be very hard to kill, but without her mind distributed to the ship's neural net, she could die.

As the minutes ticked off in her mind, Jennifer found herself having difficulty controlling her pulse and breathing, not at the thought of the danger the crew was traveling toward but about how close she would be to Mark and Heather. It had been one thing to see and talk to them using the virtual reality provided by the Altreian headsets, but she wanted to experience her brother and sister-in-law in the flesh.

The additional years had made the couple only more handsome and beautiful. The white streak in Heather's dark hair gave her an exotic look. Mark had grown several inches and added a proportional amount of bulk.

"Twenty seconds until subspace transition," VJ said.

Jennifer felt a stasis shield drape her body and knew that every other crew member had also received the same precautionary shielding.

When the *Meridian* shifted back into normal-space on the surface of the moon, the transition happened so flawlessly that she barely felt it. "Shield and cloak activated," said Dgarra. "Sensors show no sign of Kasari activity."

"Good," said Raul, rising to his feet.

Jennifer dismissed her own stasis shield and climbed out of her chair to stand beside him. VJ did the same.

"Okay," Jennifer said, moving to the open area where Raul would have the ship create the wormhole gateway and connect it to Mark and Heather's Earth gate.

Dgarra remained at his position, having volunteered to be the one who stayed onboard the *Meridian*. Raul looked calm, but Jennifer could feel his excitement over their return to Earth.

"It's likely that the Kasari on Earth will detect this wormhole," said VJ.

"Yes," said Jennifer. "They've surely detected the previous times Mark and Heather have used their Earth gates. Since there's no way to determine the location of the gateways, it doesn't matter."

"We detected the active Kasari gateway on Earth."

"That's an immensely powerful stargate. And we can't even determine its location on Earth."

"Knock off the argument," said Raul. "We've already decided that we're going to try this, so let's do it."

VJ frowned but didn't press her objections.

Jennifer felt Raul's mind manipulate the neural net in the same way he had done long ago. In the open area in the center of the command bay, the gateway formed, synchronizing with the Earth gate using the code that Heather had provided. The protective stasis field that draped the opening shimmered as the link between the two portals stabilized.

Suddenly Jennifer found herself looking into a large high-bay with equipment that she concluded was the controller for the Earth gate arrayed along the left wall, and lines of robots and equipment filling the rightmost two-thirds of the room. Standing in an open space fifteen feet in front of her stood Mark, Heather, and Janet. Unable to contain her grin, Jennifer felt her racing heart flush her face with warmth. The rest of the *Meridian*'s crew would see her loss of composure, but she didn't care.

Jennifer checked the data the *Meridian*'s sensors provided and gave the mental command that matched the air pressure inside the ship to that in the earthbound chamber. The change was just enough to make her ears pop. She dropped the shield, gave a thumbs-up signal, and saw Heather's lips move, giving what Jennifer guessed was the command to drop the stasis field that blocked their side.

"Stasis shield down," said a male voice from the direction of the control equipment.

Jennifer rushed forward, throwing her real arms around Mark's neck as he lifted her from the floor. She felt Heather move in to complete the group hug.

When Jennifer released them and stepped back, they turned their attention to Raul and VJ. Jennifer had expected Raul to be a bit hostile to Mark, considering how they'd never liked each other. Instead, he smiled, shook Mark's hand, then Heather's, and finally Janet's. VJ followed his example, although her smile when she shook Heather's seemed a bit forced.

Janet took the lead with Jennifer and the others. They followed her across the huge room, through a door in the far wall, down a short hallway, and into a twenty-by-twenty-foot conference room. Jennifer's eyes took in the three people already seated at the table.

A striking black man dressed in dapper clothes from a century ago sat beside a slender young Amerasian woman whose penetrating gaze rapidly scanned the new arrivals. The third was an older white woman who radiated fear. Jennifer delved into her mind. What she found was a brilliant scientist who hated the world of espionage and assassination into which she had been thrust. Jennifer's heart went out to her. She had once felt much the same way. With a gentle touch of her mind that couldn't be detected, she eased Dr. Jennings's fears.

After everyone who'd entered the room seated themselves at the conference table, Janet made the round of introductions. Jennifer saw Jamal's eyes dance back and forth between herself and VJ. An unavoidable reaction.

"I understand that you have a proposal," Janet said, her eyes shifting to Jennifer.

"We do, but I'll let Captain Raul present it."

"We're listening."

"I'll make this brief," said Raul. "Right now, before the Kasari have achieved world dominance, we have a chance to attack them as we did on Scion. As long as they haven't detected the *Meridian Ascent* in this solar system, there's a chance that we can infect their central router with a free-will virus. Unfortunately, it will take a direct assault, and the hive-mind will immediately recognize what we're targeting."

"That won't work," said Janet. "They'll have changed their tactics to deal with a similar assault."

"Agreed. That means we need a different plan. This robot force of yours has given us some ideas."

"We'd have to get them near the gateway," said Mark. "And we don't even know where it is."

"And even if we knew," said Heather, "the probability that we already have an Earth gate close enough to be useful is infinitesimal."

"In Los Alamos," said Janet, "you linked the Rho Ship's internal gateway to the Stephenson stargate."

"I pulled the synchronization codes from the ship's database," said Raul. "I don't know these."

"So much for that idea," said VJ, drawing a scowl from Raul.

The seeds of a new plan sprouted in Jennifer's mind. "Have you got any spare Earth gates lying around?"

Heather turned to look at her. "As a matter of fact, we've just finished one that we're about to ship to South Africa."

Jennifer hesitated, thinking this over. "Are they all the size of the one we just came through?"

"The remote gateways are just large enough to accept the robots, transports, and other equipment," said Heather. "Ten feet tall by six wide."

"And what about the controller and power-control systems?" asked Jennifer.

"Fully assembled, the cold fusion reactor is as big as this table and six feet tall," said Heather. "The control station is a third of that size—"

VJ interrupted, "Why use a cold fusion reactor when an MDS is far more efficient and powerful?"

"We had to assume," said Janet, "that some of the remote Earth gates will be captured. We didn't want the refinements we've made to the MDSs getting into the hands of the UFNS."

"With the Kasari here," said VJ, "that's a moot point of concern."

"True enough, but we just found out about that. This is what we've got now."

"VJ," said Jennifer, feeling more and more confident that what she was envisioning might work, "how long would it take you to alter one of our small MDS units to replace the remote Earth gate's power supply?"

"A little over three hours."

"How long to make a subspace torpedo large enough to hold the fully assembled Earth gate and all of that equipment?"

VJ nodded, seeing where she was going with this.

"We'll have to reconfigure amidships, getting rid of the crew compartments and meeting room to make space. Add in the time for design and manufacture of the subspace container, we're probably looking at two weeks."

"Our matter disrupter-synthesizer and molecular assembler isn't as advanced as yours," said Mark, "but we should still be able to manufacture some of the components here and push them through to you for final assembly."

"I'll need to look at your setup, but that could shave several days off our timeline."

"Wait," said Janet. "From what I'm hearing, you plan on building a container around a fully functional Earth gate and then sending it through subspace, directly into the Kasari gateway facility."

"Yes," said Jennifer. "Then we connect your gateway, and you push every combat robot you've got through it."

"Why not make this a lot easier and just use one of your subspace antimatter torpedoes to vaporize the gateway?"

"That would just delay the inevitable. With the Kasari already on Earth, we wouldn't kill them all, and they'd quickly rebuild another gateway. For all we know, they may already have more than one operational. We need to attack the hive-mind itself."

"This plan has a better chance of working than the first idea," said Heather, "but not by much."

"This," said Jennifer, "is just the distraction we need to make the first idea work."

Across the table, Mark nodded.

"I'm sold," said Janet. "Let's get started."

Jennifer watched Janet turn her attention to Jamal, Eileen, and Rob.

"In the meantime," said Janet, "I need you three to contact Nikina and help her find out where that gateway is located. I'm counting on you."

"Don't worry, Janet," said Rob. "We've got this."

Something about the young man's wording spiked Jennifer's curiosity. As he rose from the table, her mind reached out for his. But at her mental touch, he turned to look down at her, wagged a finger, and smiled. With a shock, Jennifer realized he had completely blocked her out.

○ ○ ●

With the approach of spring, the first yellow-and-white wildflowers had begun to open their petals to the sun, giving the grassy meadow a sprinkling of color. Janet stood there, stretching her body and letting her eyes drink in the peaceful scene. With no trace of a breeze, the babble of a brook and the chirping of birds were the only sounds to break the stillness.

She felt no aches and pains from her ten-mile run along the rugged mountain trail. She knew this was because of the new nanite formula that she had allowed Jennifer to inject into her blood. Everyone in the compound had accepted the injection except for Mark and Heather. Mark would have gladly undergone the injection, but Heather had refused to even consider it. Janet understood why.

Heather's dark visions of the future left her with no desire to extend her life for hundreds of years. When Mark and Jennifer had argued that they would need all the protection they could get for the upcoming battles, she had just shaken her head and walked away. That had settled it for Mark. Like his wife, he would rely on his Altreian alterations to keep them alive.

Janet didn't want to live for hundreds of years without Jack either, but she had her own reason for undergoing the treatment. She had set an example that her son had followed. Now, if she got very, very lucky, these upgraded nanites would slow down Rob's aging.

:CHAPTER 18

5 March

Galina Anikin, in her new identity as minor Federation Security Service operative Anya Kashirin, had been inside the Smythe compound twice and had nothing to show for her time. She had to hand it to Janet Price. The woman was almost as paranoid as she was.

As she rode her motorcycle toward her meeting with Prokorov, she allowed herself a slight smile. While the Smythes' team of superhackers was attempting to discover the location of the new UFNS wormhole gate using their advanced technologies, Galina intended to use a much more direct approach. This evening's meeting wouldn't be conducted at Prokorov's FSS office. Instead, he was waiting for her at a safe house in Leiden's university district, a dozen miles northeast of The Hague.

She pulled to a stop in front of the building, dropped her kickstand, and stepped and swung her right leg out of the saddle. The early March evening was surprisingly mild. She inhaled deeply, smelling the scent of the plants that would soon be flowering. The house was a small two-story with a steep tile roof and two white-framed dormer windows jutting out toward the street, one of many such houses along this quiet road.

Galina ran a hand through her windblown blond hair and strode toward the door, the heels of her boots clicking on the paving stones. The door opened as she reached for the bell. A broad-shouldered man stepped back to allow her entry. She recognized him as one of the members of Prokorov's security detail.

The man pointed toward an open door that led into the living room. "The minister is waiting for you in there."

Galina gave him a slight nod of acknowledgment and strode through the door. Prokorov was sitting in one of two leather chairs angled toward the burning hearth. He spoke without turning toward her.

"Close the door and have a seat."

She did as instructed, unzipping her dark leather jacket as she sat down. A bottle of vodka, an ice-filled bucket, and two glasses sat atop the small table that separated the two chairs. The one nearest Prokorov was half-full. Without waiting to be invited, she placed two cubes of ice into her glass, filled it from the bottle, and leaned back, making herself comfortable.

"You have chosen a cover as an FSS agent," said Prokorov, taking his eyes from the fire to look at her for the first time. "Somewhat ironic, don't you think?"

"I thought so."

"I take it the Smythes sent you."

"Janet Price did."

"And what mission did she assign you?"

"She knows that the UFNS has activated a Kasari wormhole gateway. She sent me to find out where it is."

A soft chuckle escaped Prokorov's lips. "She could have called and asked me that. At this point, I would gladly tell her. It's far too late to stop us now."

His smile faded. "Where is the Smythe base?" he continued.

Galina took a sip from her glass. "I have no idea."

"My patience is wearing thin."

Galina had to work to keep her expression neutral. Prokorov was starting to piss her off.

"If you give me the information I came here for, I will be in a better position of trust. This cannot be rushed," she said.

Prokorov's gaze locked with hers, and Galina met it with equal intensity.

"Tell me this. If I give you this information, do you think the Smythes are foolish enough to try to attack the gateway?"

"I'm certain of it," said Galina.

He leaned back and took another sip of his drink as he considered this. "They have to know they would be walking right into a trap."

"I'm sure they do."

Prokorov set down his drink and stood. Galina did, too.

"I'll see that you get the information tonight," he said.

"Give me an hour after that. Then issue a warrant for the arrest of FSS agent Anya Kashirin."

"One hour," he agreed.

She nodded and turned to go.

Prokorov spoke again as she opened the door. "Galina, get me what I want."

Without glancing back, she walked out of the house and into the night.

○   ○   ●

Janet stood inside the situation center studying the displays that covered the walls. Although she could more accurately dissect information through her SRT headset, she avoided the addictive immersion unless dire circumstances demanded it.

Jamal's sudden arrival pulled her attention to him. "Galina just sent us the precise location of the underground facility the UFNS has named the Friendship Gate. It's in North Korea."

A rush of adrenaline coursed through Janet's body, making her scalp tingle. "And Galina?"

"Her cover is blown. She's on the run back to our Earth gate facility. Rob and Eileen are conducting cyber-attacks to help her evade capture."

"Get back in there and help them."

Jamal grinned, tapping the SRT headset that draped his temples. "I'm doing that as we speak. Streaming her location to your European display."

Janet looked back at the central viewscreen, noting the icon labeled Nikina. "Okay, then," she said. "Bring our agent home."

:CHAPTER 19

PARTHIAN, QUOL, ALTREIAN SYSTEM

TBE Orbday 15

As Jack finished his detailed study of the Lundola research materials that he had scanned into his mind in the Keva Vault, he rose from his chair and made his way to the gently curved, transparent outer wall of his chambers. He watched twilight swallow the last of the daystorms and pondered the idea that had arisen from the depths of his mind. A thick stew of hope and dread stirred within him.

Millennia ago, Dr. Lundola had genetically modified the Dhaldric tycoon Keva, giving her greatly enhanced psionic powers. As she rose through the political ranks, Keva secretly produced a viral carrier that spread the new gene through the Dhaldric population like a contagious disease, marking the beginning of their ascendance over the Khyre race. But Lundola had performed the unforgivable act of making a similar modification on himself, proving that the psionic enhancement would also work on the Khyre. Keva had executed Lundola for this transgression and buried his work in the vault that still carried her name.

But now Jack knew what Lundola had known. He also knew that, guided by his knowledge, many of today's Khyre geneticists could re-create the mutant gene. Unfortunately, the genetic modification took months to develop the psionic lobe that would sprout from the upper spinal column, entangling itself with the nerves and extending tiny tendrils up into the brain itself.

Before he could return to his own body, Jack needed to transfer his title to an overlord whom he could trust. To maintain a hold on power, that overlord would need the ability to channel the power of the Twice Bound. Captain Moros fit the first requirement, but Jack couldn't afford to wait several months for the genetic modification to take effect within his friend. That meant that he'd have to convince Moros to undergo the dangerous brain operation that Lundola had experimented with toward the end of his life.

The surgery involved extracting a portion of a fully developed psionic lobe from a living Dhaldric's upper spinal column and transplanting it into a Khyre recipient. The procedure rendered the Dhaldric donor temporarily psionically weakened. How long the regrowth took depended on what percentage of the lobe was removed.

The effects of a successful operation on the Khyre patient became evident during his recovery as the lobe sprouted new tendrils that wormed their way up through the brain stem. But sometimes extreme personality changes went along with those new psionic abilities. A failed operation resulted in the death of the donor, the recipient, or both.

High above, a shooting star streaked across the sky, just beneath the lacy orange Krell Nebula. If only Jack had Janet standing beside him, he could have enjoyed the beautiful scene. But half the galaxy separated him from the love of his life and his child.

He pulled in a deep lungful of air and slowly released it. His ghostly reflection stared back at him from within the transparent wall. It was all up to Moros now. As for the Dhaldric lobe donor, Jack was looking at him.

○   ○   ●

Captain Moros sat in a comfortable chair in the overlord's audience chamber. Of all the rooms in the Parthian, Moros thought this was the most beautiful. Situated at the top level of the iridescent teardrop that formed the Parthian, the gentle curvature of the transparent walls and ceiling showcased the twilight sky. The Ripper, wearing his familiar black uniform, ivory daggers, and pistol, lounged in the shifting violet of the Throne of Decision, backdropped by Altreia's magenta globe.

Moros stared at The Ripper, trying to decide if his friend had completely lost his mind.

"You be wanting me as overlord?" Moros asked.

"Can't think of anyone better," said The Ripper.

"And to accomplish that, someone be cutting open my head and splicing in part of your brain?"

The Ripper laughed. "Well, I wouldn't have put it quite like that, but yes."

"All so that I be able to channel the power of the Twice Bound?"

"That's right," said The Ripper.

Moros shook his head. "The Twice Bound be desiring you as overlord, not me."

"With my backing, the Khyre people will accept you."

Moros did not like a single thing that The Ripper was telling him. "Even if true, this be leaving you brain damaged and vulnerable. Why do it?"

"My reasons are my own."

"And I be needing to know them," said Moros.

The Ripper looked down at his thumbs that were circling each other above interlaced fingers. When his eyes came back up, the set of his jaw indicated that he had made a difficult decision. "I'm a fake."

"What?"

"I'm not the person you see before you. I'm not even Dhaldric. My mind was swapped into this form while my body lies inside a chrysalis cylinder on the world the planet killer was supposed to destroy. It's called Earth. Moros, I have done what I came here to do. Now I want to go home to my family. I need you to become overlord so that some asshole doesn't undo everything we've accomplished."

As startling as this statement was, it explained The Ripper's odd decision to recall the planet killer and his desire to use the Altreian space fleet to defend that distant world. And suddenly Moros could hear a distinct change in The Ripper's mode of speech. He stiffened, his muscles going rigid.

"I think you be crazy," Moros said.

"You aren't the first to think that. But maybe this will help."

Suddenly, The Ripper's eyes locked with Moros's, the red glint in those black orbs dancing in the dim light. And as Moros stared into them, the world around him faded. A lifetime of memories flashed through his mind.

A young alien boy named Jack sat in the front row of a ceremony, watching in horror as an executioner severed his father's head from his body. This was followed by scenes of bloody combat as that boy grew into a feared assassin.

Flash. Jack making a death deal that allowed Khal Teth's mind in.

Flash. Jack holding a gun to the head of a tall woman who smiled back at him, the woman who would become his wife. Flash. A laughing boy who resembles Jack standing hip deep in water, holding a long pole in one hand and a flopping fish in the other.

On and on it went, the memories filled not just with sights and sounds but with emotions. The sequence ended with Jack climbing into the chrysalis cylinder inside the *AQ37Z* research vessel and rising from an identical chamber inside the Parthian, wearing the body of Khal Teth.

All doubt disappeared from Moros's mind. Jack was the friend whom he had come to know as The Ripper.

So now he knew The Ripper's motivation. But what about his own? The odds of this bizarre operation being successful didn't feel good. Even if it worked, the idea of infecting himself with part of Khal Teth's brain was horrifying. What if he picked up some of Khal Teth's megalomania?

By the void, he could die on the operating table . . . or The Ripper could. Did Moros even want strong psionic powers? Did he want the responsibility of leading the Twice Bound through what would certainly be an expanded civil war? The Dhaldric would never willingly accept a Khyre overlord.

Then a new thought occurred to him. He didn't care about the Twice Bound. He cared about the Khyre people. This presented an opportunity to free them from bondage forever. If he went through with this and became the overlord, he could set loose the mutant gene among the Khyre population. Given time for it to take effect, he could make them the mental equals of the Dhaldric, restoring the natural balance. Was that not worth the personal risk?

Captain Moros rose to his feet, turned, and walked to the nanoparticle door. As The Ripper transformed it into an insubstantial mist, Moros paused and spoke the words that filled his heart with dread.

"I be willing."

Then, without waiting for a response, he strode out of the overlord's quarters and into the Parthian's curved perimeter hallway. Right now, he needed to find a boat and get out of the Parthian and onto the Altreian Ocean. Perhaps the sea spray in his face could wash away all thought of the abomination he had just agreed to become.

:CHAPTER 20

SMYTHE FORTRESS, NEW ZEALAND

6 March

Nikina Gailan stepped through the Earth gate and was met with handshakes from Mark, Heather, and Janet as the portal winked out behind her.

"Glad you made it back, Nikina," said Janet. "We've gone over the data you sent, and it looks great."

"So," said Nikina, allowing herself a false smile, "you've already confirmed the location?"

"Not entirely," said Heather, "but the recorded satellite data of the surrounding area shows personnel and equipment movements that make it likely. We'll know for sure by tomorrow."

"You must be tired," said Mark.

"Not really," said Nikina. "The little bugs in my veins are doing their thing."

"Hungry, then."

"That I am. Thirsty, too."

"We can fix that," said Janet. "But not down here in the dungeon. This calls for a celebration out in the sunshine."

"It's the middle of the night."

"In the Netherlands, yes," Janet said. "Welcome to New Zealand."

Janet turned and led the way along an aisle through all the combat robots that crowded the twin high-bays, with Nikina and the others following close behind. They passed through the hallway at the far end, turning off into a room with an industrial-sized elevator. Janet pressed the call button, and the doors whisked open to admit them.

As Nikina followed the others inside, she felt a warm glow in the pit of her stomach. A single word popped into her mind.

Finally!

○ ○ ●

Rob had just learned something new about himself and Eos, one of those fortuitous accidents that often precede great discoveries. He'd known for a long time now that letting Eos use his weak telekinetic ability enabled her to enter any computing system within his direct line of sight by manipulating the flow of electrons within the device.

What he hadn't realized was that together, the two of them formed a god. Well, maybe not a god, but a damn close approximation when it came to controlling electronics.

After their failure to hack their way past the defenses of the robots that had run wild in Hanau, Germany, Rob had begun to doubt himself and Eos. There, they had failed miserably, and their failure had led to the gruesome killing of thousands of innocent civilians. That memory had dogged him day and night. His need to understand why they had failed had become an obsession that led him to secretly experiment on some of the new combat robots.

He'd removed the weapons from six robots and sent them into the cavern where last year's combat test had gone so badly. Having been confident that the upgraded containment systems wouldn't allow a repeated breakout, he had split the robots up into teams of three and repeated the capture-the-flag exercise on a much smaller scale. But this time he modified their programs to prohibit any self-destructive acts or harm to humans.

However, just as last time, the robots had opted to take actions that he had not anticipated in their attempts to win the game. And just as last time, Eos had been unable to penetrate their anti-hacking firewall.

Rob still didn't know what had made him shut down the stasis field that covered the only exit in order to enter the room. He had just wanted to get a closer view of the action as the robots moved to counter one another instead of observing the video feeds through his SRT headset. But immediately upon entering the cavern within which the robots struggled, everything changed.

Eos suddenly gained complete control of every one of them and marched them into a single file, where they stood obediently waiting for Rob's inspection.

"What just happened?" he asked. "How did you bypass the firewalls?"

She paused for only a second, but in the timescale upon which the alien artificial intelligence operated, a lifetime had passed.

"Your telekinesis seems to be limited to what you can physically see. Once I have control of the flow of electricity within the machines' circuits, I own them. That is true whether their programming is in random-access memory or in read-only memory."

Over the next several days, Rob and Eos had confirmed the truth of her statement. There were two worlds out there: the one inside the bubble of his telekinetic powers and the one beyond what he could see with his eyes. In that outer world, he and Eos were limited in what they could do. But within . . . well, that was a different story.

So, yeah, just as he had thought, the Rob-Eos combination was at least worthy of minor god status.

He hadn't yet informed Janet, Mark, or Heather of his newly discovered ability. For one thing, they'd be severely pissed off at his reckless, unauthorized experimentation. It was the kind of violation of the rules that had led him to modify the programming of the robots that had attacked Hanau. And although he knew that he would soon have to disclose what he had done and face the consequences, the big reveal could wait at least one more day.

Right now, he had a picnic to attend topside.

○   ○   ●

Prokorov shook his head in consternation. Whatever he had imagined being assimilated into the Kasari Collective would feel like, this was not it. His moods were the same as they had always been, including the mounting frustration he currently felt. He understood why. The nanobots making up the cortical array that linked his brain to the hivemind had the capacity to override a person's actions should his desire be contrary to the will of the collective. But they did nothing to alter his mood. Perhaps he would eventually grow accustomed to accepting the collective will without question. Somehow he doubted it. Then again, why should he have expected the Kasari nanite infusion to provide some kind of soothing balm whenever his will was overridden?

As he looked around at the activity in the cavern that housed the Friendship Gate, he could see no evidence that Commander Shalegha had taken his warnings of an impending attack by the Smythes seriously. If she had, she hadn't bothered to inform him of her plans. And despite his recent promotion within the collective, he was denied access to that information. Apparently, she had determined that he did not need to know. So, since she had not bothered to respond to his mental questions, he would confront her in person.

He spotted her standing atop a large elevated platform that provided a view of the entire chamber, a place she had designated as her temporary headquarters. Prokorov eschewed the lift, choosing to climb the fire escape–style metal stairs instead. Despite the rapidity of his steps, he arrived at the top without any noticeable change in his heart rate or breathing.

"Liaison," Shalegha said, turning toward him, "so you have chosen to make this long trip without informing me of your coming."

Other members of her military staff glanced up from their workstations before returning to their tasks.

"Since you have not answered the questions I posed via my mental link, I thought I would come see for myself the state of this facility's defenses. I see that you have decided to ignore my warning about the Smythes."

Her upper right hand moved so swiftly he had no time to dodge the blow that struck him on the side of the head. Prokorov crashed to the grated metal flooring, spitting blood, only to feel her lower left hand grab him by the throat. She lifted him until he was face-to-face with her, his feet dangling a foot above the surface.

Prokorov didn't struggle, even though he could not breathe. He merely returned her glare as he felt his split lip knit itself back together. A slow grin spread across Shalegha's vaguely reptilian-looking features as she set him back on his feet and released her grip. Then she ran a hand through her short-cropped orange hair.

"You have spirit," she said. "That is a trait I value in my subordinate leaders. But my tolerance for insubordination has its limits."

"You knew I was coming."

"Of course. If I had wanted to stop you, I would have taken away your will to make this journey. But then I would have denied myself the opportunity to teach you this little lesson."

Prokorov suppressed the scowl that tried to crawl onto his face. "I understood that there was no fighting among the members of the collective."

"Is that what you thought? Where would be the fun in that? We Kasari have no internal wars. But local disputes can be settled without the necessity for distracting the collective from far more important matters. This little world of yours is but one of thousands currently undergoing assimilation. As group commander, I am expected to execute my mission as I see fit," Shalegha said.

The lingering dizziness made Prokorov sluggish in processing what she had just told him, but he managed. He might be her liaison to humanity, but to her he was only a cog that could easily be replaced. That knowledge did not sit well with him, but it was familiar. He had been forced to overcome many similar obstacles on his rise to his current position of power. Although it would take time, he would work his way up the rungs of this ladder as well.

"The Smythes will try to destroy this gateway," he said.

"I believe you," Shalegha said. "And when they do, we will be ready for them."

She walked to the railing that bordered the platform, and Prokorov stepped up beside her.

"Look down there," she said, extending her upper right hand. "Tell me what you see."

From this vantage point, Prokorov saw what he had been unable to see from down on the floor. A large rent had been gouged out of the southern wall, doubling the size of the cavern. And within that area stood a much larger gateway, one capable of passing through a warship, something that the Kasari were in the process of doing. Only this was no seagoing vessel. The hive-mind supplied him with the information he requested. It was a fighter designed for space combat.

"That is the first of several fast-attack ships that will be pushed through the new gateway and then transported to the surface for deployment into orbit," said Shalegha.

Prokorov felt a sense of awe at what he was seeing. This ship bristled with weapons that made Dr. Stephenson's Rho Ship and the damaged Altreian vessel at the Bandolier site seem impotent.

"So you see, Liaison," said Shalegha, "if your Smythes come, we will be more than ready."

o   o   ●

Having dismissed Prokorov, Shalegha continued to watch the progress of her work crews.

In truth, she had no concern for the Smythes or any of their supposedly advanced technologies. But the technologies that had been demonstrated by the rogue crew aboard the stolen Kasari world ship was an entirely different matter. The two crew members who had hijacked the vessel from its mission here on Earth were humans. And they were still a potential threat.

That was why she had pushed her engineers so hard to finish the construction of this full-sized Kasari gateway. Such an allocation of resources had delayed the construction of a second assimilation center. But as she stared down at the attack ship slowly being maneuvered by the stasis field onto the mag-lev hauler that would carry it to the surface, Shalegha knew that she had made the prudent choice.

And it was not the only precaution she had taken. On Scion, the rogue crew had demonstrated the ability to deliver weapons through subspace, bypassing protective stasis shielding around a target. But in so doing, they had allowed Shalegha to gather enough data for the collective to design countermeasures. And they had been installed within this facility.

Let Jennifer Smythe try to bring her rogue ship into this star system. It was a rematch that Group Commander Shalegha very much looked forward to.

CHAPTER 21

MERIDIAN ASCENT, MOON

20–21 March

When Jennifer stepped into what she thought of as their subspace moving van, she accidentally bumped into VJ. As VJ stumbled, Jennifer reached out and caught her in her arms. As she helped her shipmate regain her balance, Jennifer's grasp of reality shifted, just a little.

"Sorry about that," she said.

VJ's face flushed. "That's okay. I guess I'm still getting used to my new body."

As VJ resumed her work, something about the oddly normal interaction left Jennifer baffled. Was Jennifer affected by the fact that VJ would have fallen if she hadn't caught her, or by the very human feel of VJ's body, or by the embarrassment that she noticed in VJ's eyes?

None of these things would have been remarkable if VJ had been a real woman. But VJ was only a biosynth with simulated emotions. Wasn't she? A sudden chill raised the gooseflesh on Jennifer's arms and legs. Then why did she sense VJ's emotions? And why could she touch VJ's thoughts?

Jennifer forced her attention back to the task at hand. With the completion of the final matter disrupter modifications and the reassembly of the Earth gate within the moving van–sized container, they were almost ready to mount the attack on the Kasari wormhole facility in North Korea. For this operation to succeed, they had to get the Earth gate down there and active so that Janet could send the combat robots through, providing the distraction that would let Raul land the *Meridian*. Then it would be up to Dgarra, Jennifer, and VJ to fight their way to the primary router.

Once there, VJ would upload the free-will virus. Jennifer hadn't asked Heather about the odds of this complicated scheme working, but the emotional vibes she was picking up from her friend did nothing to ease her growing dread. It was one thing to pull a rabbit out of the hat as they had barely managed on Scion. It was quite another thing to pull out an elephant. Thus, considering the imminent challenge her team faced, Jennifer had placed two syringes filled with the latest nanite serum in one of her utility vest's pockets.

When they had stood alone in the engineering bay, Dgarra had taken her in his arms and held her close. If she could have stayed there for eternity, Jennifer would have happily done so. But she had Kasari to fight and another world to save. Hopefully there would be time for such tenderness afterward.

Crap. What was it with her emotions today? If she didn't focus and get her act together, she was going to get the people she cared about killed. And yes, she had to admit that even included VJ.

○ ○ ●

Nikina struggled to contain her growing frustration. Given free rein to roam the Smythe compound, including the area within the stasis field bubble that shielded the region outside of the underground facility, she had learned precisely where in New Zealand she was. Her current problem was that she had no way to communicate that information to Prokorov.

Janet Price commanded a cyber-intelligence apparatus that was far more advanced than anything available to the NSA, CIA, FSB, or other agencies available to the Federation Security Service. She even had three of the NSA's former top experts—Dr. Eileen Wu, Jamal Glover, and Dr. Denise Jennings—working directly for her. The Smythes had created a robotic production facility powered by multiple matter disrupter-synthesizers that also had the capability of transforming any type of matter to energy or converting that energy to other forms of matter.

That meant they could convert all the rock and dirt their robots were mining directly into whatever elements they needed to feed their molecular assemblers. Over the last week and a half, those capabilities had received a major upgrade with the return of the Rho Project starship and the crew who had stolen the vessel from Los Alamos National Laboratory all those years ago. And that crew had apparently made breakthroughs beyond those of the Smythes.

All communications to and from the Smythe compound were via quantum-entangled phones or subspace communications systems. And that was routed through the Smythe supercomputers. Although Nikina had handed over an Earth gate and a quantum-entangled phone to Prokorov, she had no means of contacting those devices. So right now, she was merely a knowledgeable double agent trapped within the Smythe snow globe.

Perhaps tonight's attack on the Friendship Gate would deliver her the opportunity she needed to accomplish her mission.

o   o   ●

Janet stood in the New Zealand Earth gate chamber feeling her pulse throbbing in her veins. She had felt this on hundreds of occasions, but somehow, tonight felt different. As the clock ticked toward 4:00 A.M., it was almost midnight in North Korea. Even though she tried to dam the river of emotion, the vivid memory of another midnight flooded her mind.

The third-floor hallway of the shabby apartment building was almost completely dark, all but one of the light bulbs having burned out, that single orb illuminating a small circle near the hallway's far end. A sliver of light shone beneath the third door on the right, and Janet already knew it belonged to the assassin she had come here hunting. Walking directly to the door, Janet knocked three times. The door opened as her hand came away from the last knock, and she found herself staring directly into the round, black muzzle of a 9mm H&K. She ignored it, extending her open right hand.

"Hello, Jack," she had said to him. "Janet Price. NSA."

It had been the first time she had met the six-foot-tall killer with the brown hair and eyes with pupils that glinted red at times of intense passion.

She wiped her eyes and adjusted the SRT headset over her temples, letting the supercomputers fill her mind with status displays. The combat robots were all in standby mode, ready to activate and launch themselves through the Earth gate and into the fray on her mental signal. On the east side of the high-bay, Jamal, Eileen, and Denise all sat in control chairs while Rob manned the Earth gate control station. Mark and Heather stood immediately to Janet's left, assault weapons at the ready.

Janet had no illusions about tonight's mission. This time the forces protecting the Kasari gateway would be ready and armed with much more potent weaponry than had been available to the military around the Frankfurt Gateway. Everything depended on the *Meridian*'s crew. If they failed to deliver the remote Earth gate inside the North Korean complex, this operation would be over before it got under way.

No matter how much she wanted to get this fight started, she would have to wait for Jennifer to send the remote gate's activation request. These tense moments before battle always left Janet with the same feeling. Waiting flat-out sucked.

○   ○   ●

"Status?" Raul asked.

Jennifer's mind spoke through her SRT headset. "Dgarra, VJ, and I are inside the moving van. We're strapped in and ready."

"Set us down easy," said VJ.

"That's the plan," said Raul. "Commencing momentum vector synchronization maneuver in five seconds."

It was too bad that they had yet to come up with a solution for delivering subspace packages without having to match the *Meridian*'s velocity vector with that of the target point on the planet's surface. No use crying about it. Raul jumped the *Meridian* into subspace, brought the starship out again a hundred thousand miles from the moon, and immediately initiated the sequence of commands to the gravitational distortion engines that would accomplish his goal.

Without a doubt, the Kasari would detect this.

○   ○   ●

Commander Shalegha directed her full attention to the series of alerts cascading through her cortical array and into her brain. The sensors on the planet's surface had just validated the reports from the fast-attack ship in low Earth orbit. The stolen world ship had arrived and was accelerating to match the velocity vector of Friendship Cavern. That could be for only one purpose: a subspace weapon attack.

Shalegha issued the mental command that alerted all combat forces and activated the subspace defense countermeasure. She steadied herself against the platform railing as thousands of worm fibers shifted through the underground chamber in a random pattern. The strength of the shifting pinholes was insufficient to damage people or equipment, but if the tactic worked as the Kasari theorists predicted, the roiling fibers should reduce the accuracy of any subspace transition into the area. Subspace transitions and wormholes of any size did not play well together.

Hopefully, the experiment would not destroy her headquarters.

○ ○ ●

As her SRT headset pumped data and imagery into her brain, Jennifer felt Raul create the two dozen worm fibers that would provide the imagery of their target just before the rectangular vehicle in which she sat transitioned into subspace. The Kasari would detect those probes, but they had already detected the *Meridian*.

Seven seconds of data would have to be enough.

"Okay, VJ," said Jennifer. "Take us there."

As she felt the moving van shift into subspace, Jennifer twisted slightly in her stasis chair to look back over her shoulder at the Earth gate at the rear of the craft. For a brief moment, she got the impression that they sat at the prow of an oversized Everglades fan-boat inside a crate.

"Strap in tight," said VJ.

Jennifer reoriented herself and draped her body with a stasis cradle. As VJ performed the subspace acceleration and calculated the precise timing for their normal-space reentry within the Kasari gateway cavern, Jennifer knew that Dgarra was monitoring the same data feeds that she was.

"Uh-oh," said VJ.

"What?" asked Jennifer.

"Detecting multiple anomalies in the subspace-to-normal-space interface at our target area."

Then Jennifer saw them, too. And they were screwing up their ability to compute the precise time of reentry.

"Overlay the anomalies with the worm-fiber imagery."

When VJ did, Jennifer saw that the distortion was concentrated in the Kasari gateway cavern. With time running out, she made her decision. "New target. Set us down in the room just north of this one."

The hiss of VJ's breath didn't improve Jennifer's confidence. Unlike the original target, this was going to be a very tight fit.

A new idea hit her. Jennifer draped the interior of the van's hull with a stasis field and held her breath.

Then they came out of subspace.

○   ○   ●

VJ had made her best estimate of the revised timing for the vehicle's normal-space reentry. Still, this last-second workaround had introduced a tiny error that sent the craft careening into the nearest rock wall, ripping away the exterior hull before it came to a sudden stop. The interior stasis field protected most of the equipment from catastrophic damage.

She looked out through that transparent bubble at the devastation their reentry had wrought on this subterranean room and extended the external stasis field, using it as a virtual scythe to kill the few surviving occupants. Then she shielded the entire room to prevent the arrival of Kasari reinforcements. That would give her team a breather, but once the Kasari could bring heavy disrupter and beam weapons to bear, the power drain on the shielding would overwhelm the primary matter disrupter.

Alerts cascaded through her mind. The subspace field generator was offline, so there would be no getting back to the *Meridian*. And Jennifer and Dgarra had both suffered minor injuries. Since VJ's latest version of the nanite formula had worked on Dgarra, he and Jennifer were already healing. Pain pulled VJ's attention to her broken left wrist.

At the current rate at which the nanites in her blood were repairing the trauma, she wouldn't have full functionality for another three minutes. She couldn't wait that long.

She dismissed her stasis cocoon and moved to the Earth gate controller as Dgarra and Jennifer powered up their personal shields, grabbed their laser assault weapons, and moved out into the rubble-strewn room. With a rapid sequence of mental commands, VJ powered up the Earth gate and sent the subspace request for its remote activation.

Then she created her own stasis shield and weapon and stepped out into the cavern to await the arrival of the Smythe robotic army. By now, the Kasari would have activated the stasis shield that protected the Friendship Gate, its controller, and the primary communications router.

In New Zealand, Janet and her team would be seeing the imagery the Earth gate's sensors were sending. That meant that she would activate the portal only to provide VJ, Dgarra, and Jennifer with an escape route. The tension on Dgarra's and Jennifer's faces told VJ that they had all come to the same conclusion.

Unless someone could work magic, this mission had already failed.

○ ○ ●

Janet reviewed the video and telemetry from the Earth gate in North Korea twice before speaking.

"Jamal, can you and Eileen hack the Kasari systems and bring down their stasis field?"

"We have the coordinates of the cavern, but all our attempts to take control of the Kasari systems within have failed."

"Without the subspace field generator working," said Heather, "there's no way to get our robots past the Kasari stasis shield."

"I'm scrubbing the mission," Janet said. "Let's get our team out of there while we still can."

Rob's deep voice pulled her attention to where he sat at the gateway controls.

"Actually, I think Eos and I can do it. But I'll need to go in there to try."

As tempted as she was to say no, Janet felt the need to hear him out. If there was any chance to accomplish what they had set out to do, they had to take it.

"Tell me how."

"Remember I told you about how Eos and I took control of the combat robots after our remote hack failed?" said Rob. "My telekinesis allowed Eos to override their programming. There's no reason that wouldn't work on the Kasari stasis field generator. But I have to be within my telekinetic range of its control system."

"Which is?" asked Janet.

"I don't know," Rob replied. "A hundred yards. Maybe twice that."

"It's worth a try," said Mark. "We can always run back through the remote Earth gate if it fails."

Janet found herself reluctantly nodding, struggling with the thought of putting Rob back in the line of fire. Decision made.

"Okay. Activate the gateway. Mark, Heather, Nikina, and I will escort Rob. Jamal, you take over the primary Earth gate controls from Rob. I want as many robots as will reasonably fit into that chamber to follow us in. Eileen, you're in charge of everything else on this end."

Rob turned over the control station to Jamal and made his way to Janet's side, a broad grin on his face. "Somebody hand me a gun."

○ ○ ●

Shalegha felt the shock wave that emanated from the adjacent cavern rattle the headquarters platform upon which she stood. As she issued the orders that would put the Kasari shock troops under her command into motion, she smiled. The rogue crew had endured a rougher-than-expected landing.

Below her, forty-three of the eight-legged Graath commandos raced toward the source of the boom, accompanied by three times that number of her own race. What transpired next surprised her.

The commando charge came to a sudden halt as the lead elements slammed head-on into a stasis field that draped the entrance into the smaller chamber. Perhaps the rogue landing hadn't been as bad as she had thought. Before she could issue a new set of orders to her troops, several of them opened fire on the doorway; the green beams scattered off the protective stasis field, cutting down some of the soldiers and threatening to damage the critically important equipment in the cavern.

Shalegha issued the cease-fire command as she raised a stasis field across the southern half of the chamber, protecting the wormhole gateway, its supporting equipment, and her headquarters platform. Another mental order put two battalions of human soldiers on the move along a passage that led to the far side of the smaller room where her enemies were holed up.

With a low growl, she whirled on her subcommander. "I want high-energy-beam weapons moved into position to fire on the enemy stasis field. Make sure the deflection paths don't damage anything important."

Without bothering to answer, the Kasari male moved off to personally direct the emplacement of the artillery pieces. Shalegha shifted her gaze back to the broad entry into the room where her enemies awaited. And through that portal she saw three figures whom she recognized from the hive-mind's upload of Jennifer's memories: the Koranthian general named Dgarra, the virtual being called VJ, and the one Shalegha most wanted back under her power: the human, Jennifer Smythe.

The time to end this had come.

○   ○   ●

The Kasari fast-attack ship came around the far side of the moon firing, just as Raul pulled out of the maneuver that had launched the subspace vehicle that carried VJ, Dgarra, and Jennifer to Earth. The *Meridian Ascent* lit up like a shooting star, bright enough to be seen from Earth as its shields deflected the beam energy.

Raul brought the gravitational distortion engines to full power, dropping the *Meridian* and jerking it to the right, lowering the shields just long enough to fire the vortex weapon that had punched a hole through the Second Ship. He knew such a maneuver was risky, but when the incoming craft broke off the attack to throw up its shields, he fist-pumped the air.

Then he shifted the *Meridian* into subspace.

Until he could figure out another plan, his crew would have to survive on their own.

○　○　●

When the North Korean Earth gate activated, Jennifer spun toward it just in time to see Mark, Heather, Janet, Rob, and Nikina run through, followed by dozens of combat robots as hundreds of others waited in the room beyond.

"What the hell are you doing?" Jennifer yelled as the others raced past her toward the stasis field–draped opening into the other cavern. "It's shielded."

Not getting an answer, she ran to catch up as the room behind her became full.

"Janet," said Jennifer, "the Kasari have raised their own stasis field around the equipment we need to reach to deliver the free-will virus. Even if we can fight our way past all those troops, we can't get through that shield."

"We may not have to," said Janet.

Rob stepped up to the shielded opening that glowed bright orange from the incoming barrage and stared out into the room beyond.

"Can you do it?" asked Heather.

"Give me a moment," said Rob. "Eos is working on the heavy weapons."

Even as he spoke, the multiple beams that had been targeting the opening shut off.

"Send in the bots," Rob said. "Enemy stasis shielding going down now."

Finally understanding what was happening, even if she had no idea how, Jennifer responded, "Tell me when to drop our shield."

"Everyone get to the side," Janet said. "Okay, do it. I'm sending in the robots now."

Jennifer did as she was ordered.

A dozen autonomous motorcycles roared through the opening, lasers targeting the startled Kasari and human troops who returned fire with their own beam weapons. The thunder of charging machinery and the sounds of combat were drowned out by explosions as the larger robots released magnetically attached crab-bombs that scurried forward to detonate themselves.

The initial rush became a torrent as hundreds of humanoid and dog-shaped robots raced out of the New Zealand high-bay, through the smaller room, and into the gateway cavern beyond, accompanied by a swarm of small drones overhead. As Jennifer waited for the end of that tide to flow past, she checked the status of her personal stasis field and unlimbered her war-blade. Beside her, Dgarra did the same.

Taking a calming breath, Jennifer followed the last of the robots into the larger cavern and raised the stasis shield that protected the Earth gate. It was time to get VJ to that router.

○　○　●

Shalegha struggled to understand all the discordant information cascading through the tactical combat matrix in her head. The impossible had just happened. Somehow the humans had remotely shut down the heavy beam artillery and the Kasari stasis shield before launching an assault by autonomous killing machines.

A laser beam burned through the metal grating just a stride in front of Shalegha, putting her into motion. Pulling her own blaster, she vaulted to the stairs, followed by four of the Graath who made up her personal security detail. Her first shot ripped the sensor platform off one of the upright robots, but it still deployed six of the multilegged bombs, each scuttling toward her.

The blasts from the Graath weapons destroyed all but one of the crawlers. Before the spider-bomb could reach the stairs, one of the Graath dived atop it. The explosion showered Shalegha with brackish goo. She ignored the cacophony.

Leaping down the stairs, Shalegha took cover behind one of the mag-lev movers. The Graath spread out on both sides of the commander as chaos reigned within the facility. But now reinforcements were pushing into the room from the passage that led out of the chamber to the west. Shalegha transmitted orders that nobody was to fire toward the cluster of equipment around the Kasari gateway through which other reinforcements were now entering the chamber.

And, oddly enough, the attacking robots were also making efforts to avoid damaging that equipment. She understood why. The rogues were targeting the communications equipment just as they had on Scion. But this time that approach was not going to work. She would regain control and end this carnage.

○   ○   ●

With Heather's mind filled with ever-changing visions of the near-future movements of the forces roiling around them, she led her group toward the equipment Rob and Eos had identified as containing the primary communications router. Heather saw five of the four-armed Kasari break through the robot swarm to her right then turn to level their blasters at Heather and her team, raking them with green fire.

"There!" she yelled at the others as she dropped to one knee and aimed her own assault laser at the indicated spot.

And then it happened again, almost exactly as she had foreseen; only this time the coordinated fire from Heather, Mark, Janet, Jennifer, VJ, and Dgarra cut the Kasari down before the aliens could aim their weapons. Heather was up, leading the group forward once again, the near future moving and shifting behind her eyes.

"This way," she said, turning between rows of equipment that led toward the monstrous matter disrupter that powered the wormhole gate.

The fire support they were getting from the heavy beam weapons under Rob's control kept the Kasari and their assimilated minions off their backs, but the ones coming through the gateway would have to be dealt with directly. Unfortunately, the Kasari stasis field controller had been destroyed in the first moments of fighting, so Rob couldn't use that against their enemies.

Heather motioned toward the gateway, and Jennifer, Dgarra, and VJ raced to intercept the Kasari troops who had just stepped through. As Heather watched in amazement, Jennifer and Dgarra drew the long swords they called war-blades and fell upon their enemies. The rage with which Jennifer fought startled Heather. In high school, Jen had always been her bookish best friend, the sensible one who cautioned Mark and Heather to think before they leaped. Now Jen battled like a demon.

Jen leaped on the back of one of the gorilla-spiders that Heather and Mark had fought inside the ATLAS cavern a decade ago, slicing off legs and driving the tip of the blade through its body. Together, the three crew members of the *Meridian* formed a wedge of death that disrupted the flow of aliens from the gateway.

Janet and Nikina blocked a narrow passage to the right while Mark hung back to guard their rear, preventing any of the trailing enemy commandos from getting to Heather and Rob. That was good. The two had time to make best use of their special mental augmentations.

Less than thirty feet from their target, a new vision rocked Heather. She lunged at Nikina just as the blond agent suddenly aimed her gun at Janet's back and pulled the trigger.

The bullet penetrated Heather's body armor in the center of her chest, sending her sprawling into a sea of darkness. And all her visions of the future drowned alongside her.

○ ○ ●

Nikina saw the bullet she had intended for Janet strike Heather in the center of her chest. Then Janet Price was on her, a black combat dagger striking outward toward Nikina's neck.

Nikina took the point of the combat dagger through her right hand, dropping her weapon but stopping the blade an inch short of her throat. Ignoring the pain, she pivoted into a judo throw that landed Janet hard on her back. Janet twisted the knife, and Nikina felt a bone in her hand break. Jerking her wounded hand free, Nikina sent Janet's black blade flying. Janet's kick to her face knocked Nikina to the bloody floor.

Rolling to her knees, Janet dived onto Nikina's back, attempting to lock her right arm around Nikina's neck. Again, Nikina countered, twisting her head to the side and biting down hard enough on Janet's arm to fill her mouth with blood. Whipping her legs around, Nikina went for the arm bar, but her bloody hand slipped before she could lock it into place, allowing Janet to rip her own hand free and roll back to her feet.

Cursing, Nikina drew her own dagger and lunged, driving the knife hard toward Janet's stomach, just below the bottom of her bulletproof vest. But instead of sheathing the blade in her opponent's flesh, she felt her wrist slam into Janet's cross-handed block. And when Janet uncrossed those hands, she gripped Nikina's wrist and twisted it out and back in a wrenching move that slammed Nikina facedown on the ground and sent her blade flying. In growing desperation, Nikina struggled to prevent Janet from locking her arm behind her back.

The realization that this woman outclassed her in hand-to-hand combat brought an unfamiliar wave of panic crashing in on Nikina. Janet's head butt into the side of her face drove her skull into the stone floor, loosening Nikina's teeth and causing her vision to dim. As Nikina struggled to retain her consciousness, Janet flipped her over on her back. Unable to rise, she felt Janet lift herself up only to drop back down, driving her right elbow into Nikina's throat. With a sick crunch, her trachea collapsed upon itself. A fresh fountain of terror drenched Nikina's brain in adrenaline.

As Nikina's panting breath changed to a rattling wheeze, Janet rammed her elbow into that damaged throat a second time. With dark clouds squeezing her vision into a straw's-eye view, she saw Janet jerk a six-inch needle from her dark hair.

Janet's voice was a low snarl. "Die, you traitorous bitch."

For Nikina, time slowed to a crawl. The needle descended to bury itself in her left eye. There was no tunnel with a light at its end, just a painfully bright flash followed by nothing.

○　○　●

"Die, you traitorous bitch."

With all her strength, Janet drove her hair needle through Nikina's left eye and into her brain. Giving it a hard twist, she made sure that this was a wound no nanites could heal. Panting, she pulled the needle from the bloody socket and wiped it on Nikina's shirt. Then, giving her long hair a twist, Janet returned the needle to its customary spot and stood. She rose to her feet, pulled her Glock from its holster, and fired two shots into Nikina's forehead.

Without a further glance, she turned back toward the sounds of combat.

○　○　●

Having been focused on redirecting the automated beam weapons at the Kasari who blocked their path ahead, Rob hadn't thought the firing behind him strange. Then he heard the double tap. He turned and froze at the shock of seeing Heather and Nikina both lying in pools of their own blood in the confined space.

Janet's yell brought him out of it. "Rob! Close that gate or we're all dead."

Reaching into the controller with his mind, he let Eos take over. Off to his left, the Kasari gateway winked out.

Mark rushed past him, grabbed Heather's limp body, and carried her into the jumble of equipment that formed the matter disrupter.

"Everyone consolidate around Heather," Janet yelled. "I want three-hundred-sixty-degree coverage."

Rob returned his focus to the automated beam weapons, redirecting their fires into the UFNS soldiers pouring into the north side of the chamber. As the number of his group's combat robots dwindled, the odds that they could fight their way back to the Earth gate did likewise. Dismissing the thought, he shifted his gaze to a huge vehicle that appeared to be some type of heavy equipment mover.

It was time to bring out the hammer.

○　○　●

Jennifer, covered in multicolored alien blood, fought her way back into the mechanical fortress where Janet had decided to make their last stand. Then she saw Mark hunched over Heather, tears pouring down his face as he performed CPR. She raced to his side, horrified to see the bloody hole in the center of Heather's bare chest. It wasn't a sucking chest wound. This was worse.

Riffling through a side pocket in her utility vest, she grabbed one of the two nanite syringes and dropped to Mark's side.

"Move!" she said.

When Mark's eyes shifted to the syringe, he didn't argue.

Jennifer jammed it home, delivering the complete load of nanite serum directly into Heather's wounded heart. When she pulled it out, she motioned Mark back in.

Once again, he put his back into it. Steady, rhythmic chest compressions.

"Jennifer!" Janet yelled. "Get your ass back on the line."

When Jennifer moved to comply, she could see just how desperate their situation was becoming. Well, if she was going to die, right here by Dgarra and her friends was as good a spot as any.

○   ○   ●

Dgarra held the narrow access between equipment racks, knowing that if the group of Kasari soldiers made it past him, they would kill Jennifer and her brother while the two worked to save Heather. He would not allow that to happen.

His war-blade whistled through the air, spraying a greenish-orange mist of Kasari blood in an arc as it sliced through the aliens' thick torsos. These were the same beasts who had helped General Magtal frame him as a traitor for the murder of Dgarra's uncle, Emperor Goltat.

Letting rage propel him forward, he blocked the clawed forepaw of one of the eight-legged creatures that the Kasari called Graath with the stasis shield projected onto his left forearm. The force of the blow knocked the beast astride backward, and before it could recover, Dgarra split the Graath down the middle, cleaving the drooling maw from its underside, dropping the creature atop the growing pile of bodies.

Motion to his front left drew Dgarra's gaze, and he ducked back behind thick metal as a pulsed beam sizzled past his face. As if they sensed that he was retreating, two more of the Kasari charged, seeking to impale him on their own blades or drive him backward through sheer force of numbers. Then, bracing his feet against the metal on either side of the aisle, Dgarra grunted with the effort of halting the alien advance.

"No," he growled. "You will not have her."

Wielding his shield, he pressed forward, his war-blade rising and falling within the narrow space. And with each stroke, another Kasari died.

○ ○ ●

Raul had a new plan. He'd made a series of short subspace jumps just beyond the range of the Kasari fast-attack ship's weapons, pulling it farther and farther away from Earth. Now, from just beyond Jupiter's moon, Io, he prepared to make the most aggressive maneuver he'd ever tried. And he didn't even have VJ to blame it on if this didn't work. Then again, if this didn't work, he would be dead.

He initiated the subspace jump that took him just inside the moon's orbit. Having lured the fast-attack ship too far away to interfere, Raul flooded the Friendship gateway cavern with thirty worm-fiber viewers. The imagery they delivered took his breath away. Except for the Kasari gate and its surrounding equipment, the cavern was a wreck. The hundreds of robots that the Smythes had planned on sending in had been reduced to sixty-three. These battled to prevent a surge of fresh troops from entering the cavern from passages in the north and west walls.

Another set of images shocked him. Instead of the Earth gate being positioned within the large Kasari gateway cavern, it had ended up inside a small room along the north wall. Jennifer, VJ, and Dgarra were pinned down in the south end of the cavern. There was no way that they could battle their way back to that room. Raul was their only chance.

He maneuvered the *Meridian* onto the vector that matched that of Friendship Cavern and shifted into subspace. He felt vulnerable without VJ there to help him do this, even though the ship's neural net provided all the same calculations. Oh well . . . now or never.

Gritting his teeth, Raul commenced the subspace maneuver that would take him to the cavern, knowing that missing his target could kill those he was trying to save or damage the *Meridian* too badly to get back out. In either case, everyone would die.

○ ○ ●

VJ assessed their situation. As more and more of the robots were destroyed, the north half of the room was slowly filling with UFNS soldiers. Her small group had no chance of fighting their way back to the room with the Earth gate. But she still could accomplish the main mission. Most of the Kasari shock troops had been killed in the initial fighting or by the big machine that Rob had just driven through their ranks before it was destroyed.

The hive-mind had clearly directed all troops closing in on her team's position to avoid using heavy weapons. She glanced back at the others. Having gotten Heather stabilized, Mark had moved up to get back into the fight.

VJ checked the status of her internal power supply. The steady drain on her personal stasis shielding had outstripped the ability of her matter disrupter to replenish her twin super-capacitors, leaving their charge at only 32 percent. It would have to be enough.

Without a word to the others, VJ charged out from behind the machine that concealed her and raced toward the primary router, feeling laser beams play across her shield. Ten feet from her target, one of the four-armed Kasari leaped in front of her, firing. She deflected the shot, then sliced his head off with a stasis field blade.

She slid between two thirty-foot-tall equipment racks, identified the router, and began climbing toward it. Energy level 27 percent. Then Jennifer and Dgarra joined her in the passage, firing back at the onrushing soldiers as Janet's and Rob's covering fire also chopped into their attackers.

"Crap!" Jennifer yelled. "My shield is down."

"Get back behind me," said Dgarra.

"Fat chance."

VJ closed in on the router, having to climb out on top of the rack to get to it. Reaching into a pocket in her utility vest, she extracted a palm-sized device of her own design and attached it to the side of the communications hub. Partially exposed as she was, she took three more hits that siphoned off another 6 percent of her power reserves.

She switched on the induction coupler that gave her access to the router's internal circuitry. Using the subspace receiver-transmitter within her brain, she manipulated the coupler's controls until she found the interface she was seeking.

ALERT. INTERNAL POWER THIRTEEN PERCENT.

VJ locked in on the circuit and commanded the induction coupler to upload the free-will virus to the hive-mind.

Another direct hit took her power supply down to 8 percent. She jumped off the rack into a thick group of soldiers. Wielding her stasis weapon, she cut into them. From behind she heard Dgarra's battle cry as he and Jennifer charged into the mix, their bloody war-blades singing through the air.

For the first time, VJ felt a shiver as what Jennifer called gooseflesh dimpled the skin of her arms and legs. Now this was a life worth living.

o   o   ●

Mark aimed and fired, aimed and fired, until the charging troops were upon him. He slammed the butt of his pulse rifle into the face of the nearest soldier and then brought the muzzle down into the throat of the man who leaped over the fallen one's body. Pulling his combat dagger, Mark began a combination of bone-shattering punches, kicks, and slashes that chopped down the men and women who tried to fight their way past him into the narrow channel between the machines.

He would not be pushed backward—not by humans and not by the lesser numbers of Kasari shock troops who struggled to kill him. And as one fell, the press of those who came at him shoved the next victim within his reach.

With all his augmented speed and strength, Mark fought to defend Heather, who lay unconscious three feet behind him. And from the sound of the gunfire from the far end of the rift, Janet was holding her own with the weapons she loved.

From somewhere in the melee before him, a Russian soldier fired a laser that killed two of Mark's enemies and splashed molten metal onto the back of his neck. Mark hurled one of their dying bodies at the shooter, sending them both down to be trampled by their fellows.

A sudden boom shook the cavern. The shock wave rocked Mark back on his heels and dropped those before him to the ground. First to recover, Mark grabbed a laser pistol from one of the fallen and killed those who were attempting to regain their feet.

He looked around the corner toward the north end of the cavern and immediately saw what had happened. The *Meridian Ascent* had materialized amid the mass of UFNS troops, killing hundreds in an instant. Now Raul wielded the ship's stasis field like a giant buzz saw, cutting down the horde and sending the survivors scrambling toward the west exit.

"Everyone back to the Earth gate," Janet yelled. "Move."

Mark picked up Heather and sprinted for the room they had first entered, followed by Janet, Rob, Jennifer, Dgarra, and VJ.

○ ○ ●

As she neared the room with the active Earth gate, Jennifer gave the mental command that opened a hole in the stasis field that shielded it, closing the shield again as soon as all were inside. She turned to watch as beam weapons began to paint the shielded *Meridian Ascent* in green, blue, and orange. So beautiful. Then her ship was gone.

"Come on," said Janet. "We're done here."

Jennifer glanced at her blood-soaked comrades and nodded. Then she followed them back through the Earth gate into New Zealand.

○   ○   ●

Heather opened her eyes and blinked. She looked up at Mark's blood-caked face.

"Hello, darling," he said. "For a few minutes there, I thought I'd lost you."

She lay on a bed, her naked body covered by a sheet and blanket. Lifting her hand to her chest, she felt for the wound. When she didn't find any sign of a bandage, she lowered the sheet and lifted her head to see what had happened. All that remained of the wound was pinkish new skin. The sight sent a shudder of revulsion through her body.

"Nanites?" she asked.

Leaning back from her accusing stare, Mark held up his hands. "Jennifer did it."

"And you let her."

She heard him suck in a deep breath and exhale.

"Yes, I did."

She dropped her head back onto her pillow. After all these years fighting this abomination, she now had a swarm of micro-machines not of her own design crawling through her veins, arteries, and organs.

"How could you?"

Mark held her hand between both of his, lifted it to his mouth, and gently kissed it.

"How could I not? Jennifer saved you. And in doing that, she saved me, too."

Heather raised her eyes to the stone ceiling and remained silent for several moments, letting her revulsion run its course. She could undo this by undergoing a special dialysis procedure to remove the nanites. She shifted her gaze back to Mark.

"If you want me to stay nanited, you have to get them, too."

He smiled. "Already done."

Then she asked the question that she'd been dreading. "So, did we win?"

"VJ uploaded the virus and we got out alive."

Something in Mark's tone belied his words.

"But?" she asked.

"But something is wrong. Jennifer said that when they uplinked the free-will virus on Scion, there was an immediate reaction. Fights broke out among those who had been assimilated. Kasari command and control broke down completely. We saw nothing like that happen inside the North Korean cavern."

The vision that filled her head told Heather why.

"The Kasari have developed an antivirus," she said.

"That's what we think."

"Damn it. After all of this, we accomplished nothing."

Mark merely shook his head.

A new thought struck her. "Nikina tried to shoot Janet, but she shot me."

"And Janet killed her for it. It's over."

"No, it isn't. She must have been working for Prokorov all along. He may know where we are."

Mark leaned down and kissed her. When he sat back in his chair, he said, "Get some rest. We'll worry about that when you wake up."

Heather started to argue but failed to summon the energy. When she closed her eyes, a wave of fatigue swept her away.

○ ○ ●

Alexandr Prokorov stepped over the corpses and body parts that littered Friendship Cavern to reach the body of Galina Anikin. She lay faceup in a puddle of blood and brain matter, her remaining gray eye staring sightlessly at the distant ceiling.

Shalegha had given Prokorov access to the thousands of battle recordings stored within the hive-mind. They had been collected from the minds of all involved as the combat had unfolded. He had seen Galina die from several different vantage points.

She had tried to take out Janet Price but had shot Heather Smythe instead. Then, as hard as it was to believe, Janet had bested Prokorov's top operative in hand-to-hand combat. Now he would never know what Galina had learned about the Smythe operation.

Unless . . .

Prokorov knelt by her body and began rifling through her pockets, starting with those in her black utility vest. Except for tactical supplies and magazines filled with ammunition, he found nothing. But in the cargo pocket on her right pants leg, he found a small notebook. He flipped it open and smiled. There was only a single two-line entry, but it was exactly what he had been hoping for.

SMYTHE TASMAN MINING CORPORATION
41.715179S 172.172935E

Having uplinked the coordinates to the hive-mind, Prokorov stood, tossed the notebook into a pool of Galina's blood, turned, and walked away. He and the collective now had the information they needed.

○ ○ ●

Janet had just climbed into bed and closed her eyes when her phone rang.

"Damned thing," she said, scrubbing her face with both hands as if that would wipe the gravel from her eyes.

She sat up, leaned over to pluck the phone from atop her nightstand, and then froze.

"What the hell?"

The displayed ID came from one of dozens of special chips that were quantum entangled with QT phones given to other key people. This one put a tremor in her hand. Her finger pressed the answer button, and she raised the phone to her ear. She found herself unable to speak. The voice on the other end was one she had never expected to hear again.

"Hello, babe. I've come home."

:CHAPTER 22

TBE Orbday 18

Jack had begun what he called the Twice Bound Tour three orbdays ago. Officially it provided him, as overlord, an opportunity to visit parts of the Basrillan and Janiyan continents that no overlord had ever visited. The tour also gave the Khyre residents of those vast lands the opportunity to join the Twice Bound, thus increasing Jack's power and influence. But this trip also had a much darker purpose. It allowed Jack and Captain Moros to disappear for long enough to undergo the Lundola Procedure that they both dreaded.

Over the strenuous objections of General Zolat, Jack had embarked on the journey accompanied only by Captain Moros and Santiri. Slightly shorter than Moros, the Khyre female's emerald-green eyes shone with intelligence. A former commando in the Altreian space fleet, she was a petite but imposing presence. Jack liked her.

Santiri had selected the Twice Bound Khyre surgeon who would be performing today's operation. And it was Santiri who would be standing guard before, during, and after the surgery. That suited Jack just fine.

So now he and Moros lay naked on two iridescent Altreian medical tables, similar to the ones onboard the Second Ship. The surgeon moved between them, manipulating the 3-D displays that appeared to hang in the air above each patient. Jack understood what was about to happen. There would be no bone saws or scalpels. The surgeon would control the medical tables with his mind, allowing the apparatus to perform the operations.

Suddenly thousands of glass-like tendrils sprouted from Jack's table, their needle-sharp points finding their way to nerve endings on his chest and head, even penetrating his open eyes. His head and upper torso appeared to be covered in exceedingly fine, multicolored hairs.

He felt his form go numb. Being fully conscious but unable to move any part of his body, even to blink, was a new and unpleasant experience for Jack. But in a strange way, it was eerily like being the rider when Khal Teth had controlled this body.

If the surgeon wanted a muscle to twitch, it twitched. Otherwise, it did not. There was no pain when the tendrils opened a small incision in his upper chest and crawled inside the cavity. He knew that they were painlessly bypassing his heart and lungs—spreading, cutting, and reknitting as they removed half of the Dhaldric psionic lobe from where its own tendrils entangled the upper spinal column. The fluid needles then worked their way through the brain stem and into his brain.

When the final snip happened, Jack experienced the room dimming around him, although he knew the lighting had not changed. What had diminished was his connection with the Twice Bound. That wasn't quite right. He was still linked to his followers, but he had lost half of his ability to channel their power. And he missed it.

Time passed, but he did not know how long the surgery lasted. The tendrils knitted back together what they had cut away, repaired damaged veins and skin, and then, as if someone had blown on the giant puffball named Jack, the flexible needles floated away, reabsorbed by the medical table upon which he lay.

Feeling returned with a vivid tingle that spread through his entire body. Jack blinked and turned his head to look at the ongoing surgery on Moros. From this angle, he couldn't see deeply into the hole in the captain's chest, but there was no sign of blood. Apparently the delicate fur of needles that extended inside that small opening was clamping and repairing cuts so efficiently that no fluid escaped.

Still, his operation was taking longer than Jack's. He could feel the worry in the surgeon's mind. It was one thing to extract part of an organ from a Dhaldric patient, quite another to splice genetically modified DNA and a partial psionic lobe onto Moros's spinal column.

The graft would kick-start Moros's psionic powers while the modified genes would cause the spliced lobe to regenerate itself over time, extending more and more tiny tendrils up into his brain.

As Jack watched, a sudden wave of fatigue swept over him, and he settled back, letting the table remold itself to his new position. Was it warming him? Whatever was happening, it felt very, very good. He blinked once, twice, and then his eyes stayed closed.

○　○　●

General Zolat paced slowly back and forth through the Altreian Operations Center, keeping his mind strongly shielded to mask the furor that raged within. The overlord who called himself The Ripper had disappeared, despite the rebellion assets that Zolat had assigned to track him. Just when all the pieces of Zolat's assassination plan were coming together, the overlord had decided to take this lengthy trek through the harsh homelands of the Khyre.

Since the Khyre made up 73 percent of Quol's population of 1.2 billion, this trip through that race's outlands effectively blanketed The Ripper with his supporters. The overlord was a traitor to everything that had made the Dhaldric great. And his flight into the lands of his Twice Bound proved one thing: he was also a coward.

His absence would have created a wonderful opportunity for a coup. But one problem was insurmountable. The first step to overthrowing any leader was eliminating the object of the coup. While Zolat could take over the Parthian and the island chain that roughly traced Quol's prime meridian, with more than three-quarters of the planet's and the space fleet's population being Khyre, such a move would be short-lived.

No. First, the overlord must be eliminated, thus breaking the power of the Twice Bound. Then, and only then, could Zolat restore the natural order.

○ ○ ●

Jack's recovery from the surgery was swift. Within an orbday, he had begun to feel like his old self. Moros, however, had not been so lucky.

The captain remained in a quasi-comatose state, occasionally broken by a bout of uncontrollable shaking. But it was the periodic moans that most disturbed Jack.

The doctor assured him that Moros's vitals were fine and that the side effects he was experiencing were most likely the result of the psionic lobe's tendrils worming their way upward through the brain stem. But as Jack listened to the sounds that issued from Moros's mouth, sounds that seemed to indicate horrifying dread, he wished he hadn't talked the captain into undergoing the procedure.

For the next three orbdays, Jack remained in the clinic, taking turns with Santiri watching over Moros. Jack was surprised at how the medical table performed various nursing tasks, keeping Moros clean, monitoring his vital signs, and periodically snaking down his nose to funnel liquids and nutrients into his stomach. But as time passed, the doctor's expression showed what Jack felt in the man's mind, a growing sense that the procedure had been a failure.

The holographic imagery that hovered above Moros's body clearly showed that the tiny tendrils that had sprouted from the grafted lobe had threaded their way up through the brain stem and invaded his brain. Although Moros's vital signs remained good, he hadn't regained consciousness.

Then, on the fourth orbday, just as Jack was about to lose all hope, the captain startled him by speaking.

"Who be the gromling?"

Jack moved to his side. The skin of the Khyre ship's captain appeared even grayer than normal, and he wobbled as he raised himself into a sitting position. Jack reached out a hand to steady Moros and keep him from tumbling off the table.

"What gromling?"

"The one who be kicking me in the head."

Jack laughed with relief. If the captain had retained his sense of humor, he was going to be just fine.

"Headache, huh?"

Moros merely massaged his temples with his fingers.

Having been alerted that the patient was awake, the doctor entered the room and walked to Moros's table.

"I am glad to see you awake, Captain Moros. How are you feeling?"

"Like pugada dung."

The doctor examined the additional holographic images and read-outs that appeared before him. Without bothering to give an explanation as to what he was doing, he set the medical table back into action. This time the blown-glass tendrils attached themselves to Moros's head and remained there. Almost immediately, the tension lines in the captain's face relaxed. The treatment lasted for less than five minutes, but when the tendrils withdrew, Moros sighed in relief.

Then Jack felt his friend's thoughts touch his mind directly.

"Worry not. I be fine."

:CHAPTER 23

LA PAZ, BOLIVIA

22 March

As evening gave way to night, Khal Teth pulled the old jeep to a stop outside a two-story house on the eastern outskirts of La Paz. Walking up the front steps, he pressed the doorbell. When the door opened, his eyes were drawn to the six-and-a-half-foot form of Jack's old friend Jim "Tall Bear" Pino, who extended a hand, his long black hair cascading over his shoulders.

"Jack, you crazy son of a bitch. I thought you were a goner. When I got Janet's call saying you were back, I almost keeled over."

Khal Teth let Jack's memories guide him. He gripped hands with the bigger man.

"Good to see you, too, Jim."

Tall Bear ushered him inside, then glanced right and left along the dark street before shutting the door behind him. Khal Teth followed him into the living room where a roaring blaze crackled in the fireplace, sending long shadows dancing across the room as it hissed and popped. The pungent smell of wood smoke tickled his nostrils.

"Can I offer you a beer?" Tall Bear asked.

"Thought you'd never ask."

Tall Bear stepped out of the room and returned with two bottles, handing one of the ice-cold brews to Khal Teth. Tall Bear seated himself in the leftmost of the two leather chairs before the fire, and Khal Teth took the other. Feeling the condensation trickle onto his hand, Khal Teth followed Tall Bear's example and tilted the bottle to his lips. Jack's memories told him that the amber liquid was good, and surprisingly enough, he found the slightly bitter taste pleasant.

For several minutes, small talk and old memories dominated their conversation, something that humans regarded as necessary but Khal Teth found annoying. Then the subject shifted to the matter at hand.

"I don't suppose you want to tell me where you've been all this time," Tall Bear said.

"That's a long story."

"And one, I take it, that you don't want to talk about."

Khal Teth took another drink, feeling a warm glow blossom in the pit of his stomach.

"Not right now. To tell you the truth, I'm exhausted."

"Fair enough. Maybe tomorrow, then, on the way to the Earth gate warehouse."

"We'll see."

"Can I offer you some food before bed?"

"No, thanks. I grabbed something when I got to La Paz."

"Okay, then," Tall Bear said. "I'll show you to your room. After all this time, I imagine you're excited to walk through that Earth gate and get back to your lovely wife and son."

Khal Teth rose to his feet alongside Tall Bear, feeling a rush of adrenaline course through his veins. "Jim, my friend, you have no idea."

○　○　●

Inside the Federation Security Service War Room, Prokorov sat at the head of the small conference table, studying the satellite imagery of New Zealand. He glanced over at the only other person present, General Dimitri Zherdev.

"So, what do you think, Dimitri?"

"Our analysts disagree. Some say this cannot be the location of a huge operation like the Smythes certainly have. It is wilderness. Even if the facility is underground, there would have to be significant deliveries of materials and supplies, and they see nothing like that looking back through the satellite records."

"And the others?"

"The other group argues that given the technological superiority the Smythes have demonstrated, we can't rule out some sort of high-tech wizardry. We have nothing to confirm that this is the actual site, but I think we need to assume that Galina Anikin's note is accurate."

Prokorov nodded. His respect for this man's judgment had been the reason Prokorov had appointed him as chief of FSS military operations.

"I agree, General. I want you to send in a team to confirm."

"Yes, sir. I'll get them in the air."

As the general stood and turned to go, Prokorov added one more thing. "And put an airborne division on alert. If confirmed, I want that site surrounded."

The general turned back toward Prokorov. "Why not target the location with Kasari high-energy beams?"

"I plan to. But it's going to take some time to deploy. The weapons will need to draw power from matter disrupters, and those will need to be shipped in as well. Group Commander Shalegha's priority will continue to be getting assimilation centers set up around the world, so we can't interfere with that."

General Zherdev nodded. "The Eighty-Second Airborne Division has been completely assimilated. I will put them on alert. But I also recommend having some heavy bombers ready. Bunker-busting conventional bombs might be able to take the Smythe Fortress out, or at least interdict their supply line."

Prokorov liked what he was hearing. "Agreed. Make it happen."

As the general turned and walked out of the room, Alexandr Prokorov shifted his attention back to the satellite imagery of the remote mountains northwest of Murchison, New Zealand. He was only hours away from confirmation that he had finally found the Smythe rat hole.

○ ○ ●

Janet stood alone inside the Earth gate chamber wearing her SRT headset, trying to control her pounding heart. Where the hell was her vaunted self-control? She knew that Tall Bear had said that he and Jack wouldn't reach the Bolivian Earth gate warehouse until 7:00 A.M. Bolivian time, midnight in New Zealand, but she hadn't been able to keep herself from coming to this room thirty minutes early. Now as the clock ticked closer and closer to the witching hour, she was hyperventilating. Dear God, where was that subspace request to activate the Bolivian gate?

When the request came through her SRT headset, she resisted the urge to immediately energize the Earth gate. Instead, per standard operating procedure, she switched on the Bolivian portal's cameras, microphones, and speakers, piping the images and sounds directly into her mind. A gasp escaped her lips. There, beside Tall Bear, stood the man whom she had believed she would never see again, looking exactly as he had when she had left him standing atop the Altar of the Gods beneath the Kalasasaya Temple. In the background, the robots that guarded the unmanned facility moved about their assigned duties.

Shifting her thoughts, she draped the master Earth gate with a stasis field, allowed the barometric pressure to equalize, and opened the portal. Now she could see her husband with her own eyes. And Jack's familiar grin was the most beautiful sight she had ever seen.

"You going to let me in?" he asked.

The greeting pulled a laugh from her lips. She dropped the stasis field and rushed through the gateway into the Bolivian warehouse, throwing her arms around Jack's neck as his strong arms encircled her waist and his lips found hers. Unable to dam the tears that flooded her face, Janet pushed him away. Her hand lashed out to slap Jack hard across the cheek.

"Never do that to me again," she said.

He lifted his left hand to his lips to dab away the trickle of blood at the corner of his mouth, and just for an instant, Janet thought she saw rage flash in his dark-brown eyes. But then Jack's smile returned as his eyes once again met hers with no trace of what she had imagined.

"I wouldn't dare."

How could he do that, instantly rob her of her fury? Once again, she kissed him, letting her body yield to his embrace.

"Ahemmm."

The sound from Tall Bear suddenly brought her back to the realization that she and Jack were not alone. Releasing her death grip on Jack's neck, she turned to hug Tall Bear.

"Thank you," she said.

"For what?"

"For bringing him back to me."

"No problem. I'm an excellent driver."

When she stepped back, Jack shook hands with the bigger man. Then Janet and Jack turned away and walked, hand in hand, back into New Zealand.

○ ○ ●

Having left Janet alone for her reunion with Jack, Heather enjoyed a midnight repast with Mark, Jennifer, their parents, and Rob in the kitchen within a group of rooms that they had transformed into the new Smythe and McFarland underground living quarters. Dgarra and VJ had opted out in favor of letting the Smythes and McFarlands enjoy a little family time. As much as their parents had resisted moving into the subterranean fortress, the discovery of Nikina's treachery had made matters too dangerous for them to continue to occupy their houses.

The move had impacted Anna McFarland and Linda Smythe the hardest. But the addition of large video windows throughout their quarters had helped . . . that and an extensively appointed kitchen. Tonight, Anna had prepared a wonderful meal of chicken fried venison, mashed potatoes, and gravy, the smell of which pulled them all to the table.

Despite the nanites in her system, or maybe because of them, the hard day's work of testing the new matter disrupter and stasis field generator upgrades had left Heather famished. From the way Mark and Rob heaped food on their plates, she could tell that they felt the same. Heather made a mental note that she would have to save some of each dish so that the food synthesizer could analyze and record them for future use. That new machine had been just one of the technological wonders that Jennifer and her fellow crew members had helped the Earth team build, with major security and quality-of-life implications. Leaving the facility to go shopping or hunting had suddenly gotten much more dangerous.

Heather studied Rob. Despite being only ten, he had become a young man in both body and mind. As much as he had wanted to join Janet in welcoming his dad home, he had agreed to give them this honeymoon night. His understanding of his parents' sexual relationship made another thing very clear to Heather: they had to figure out how to help Rob get started dating before the hormones raging through his body made him attempt something dangerous.

That was going to be hard to do considering that they were all hiding out in an underground fortress, protected on the outside by a large stasis shield and an Altreian holographic cloak. And the just-completed upgrades had allowed them to erect shields that draped the facility's interior walls. There would be no tunneling or blasting into this fortress from outside. The only burrowing allowed down here was handled by their own boring machines and engineering robots.

Unfortunately, the massive energy demands of all this shielding and nano-manufacturing meant that they were forced to keep digging and expanding, if only to feed the hunger of the matter disrupter-synthe-sizers. Somehow everything they did seemed to produce more negative consequences than positive returns.

Heather shook her head to try to clear these troubling thoughts from her mind, drawing a concerned stare from Mark.

"You okay?" he asked.

She forced a smile. "I'm fine. I was just thinking about Jack and Janet."

"Aren't we all?" asked Gil with a wink that drew loud laughter from Fred, Mark, and Rob.

Anna and Linda merely shook their heads as if to say, "Men!"

Having successfully deflected Mark's question, Heather returned her attention to her plate, only to discover that she had lost her appetite. Oh well, she would just have to fake it, which she seemed to have been doing a lot of lately. At least Janet would be finding some release from her tension right about now.

The thought lifted Heather's mood.

○   ○   ●

"Where is everyone?" Khal Teth asked as the portal winked out behind them.

Janet turned to him, once again putting her arms around his neck, this time far more gently.

"They gave us a night to ourselves."

Suddenly Khal Teth found himself excited at the prospect, but not for the reasons Janet suspected. He had come here to ravish Jack's wife, then use her as a bargaining chip to force the body thief to make the exchange that would put the former overlord back in charge of the Altreian Empire. If he killed Jack and Janet in the process, so much the better. And now he had just been handed the perfect opportunity. Tonight, fate had been kind to him.

He reached up to stroke her cheek, tracing his fingers up toward her earlobe as her soft lips met his. But when he tried to seize control of her mind, his failure to even touch it startled him. What was wrong? He had used Jack's mind to defeat Commander Broljen, a psionic Dhaldric. When the answer came to him, it did not improve his mood. The genetic procedure Khal Teth had performed on this body in the *AQ37Z's* medical lab was beginning to take effect. Unfortunately, as Jack's new psionic lobe began to develop in his upper spine, its tendrils appeared to have already begun rewiring his brain, temporarily blocking all psionic ability. With a mental curse, Khal Teth shifted tactics.

With a sudden movement, he snatched the woman's SRT headset from her temples and hurled it across the room as his left hand closed on her pretty throat and lifted her off the ground. He grinned. These new headband alterations were already paying dividends.

When Janet's kick to his groin dropped Khal Teth to his knees, pain exploded through his body. But he did not lose his grip on her throat. He tried to focus but found that he could not. It was as if he were back on Quol, in charge of the body that Jack had put through hell. Only this was worse. Here, he could not flee into the background, leaving Jack to deal with the agony.

Janet's hand flashed out and down, spearing the hand that gripped her throat with something shiny and sharp as a new pain fought for ascendancy in his reeling mind. His grip loosened, releasing her. But she did not let him go. Instead, she grabbed both ends of the six-inch needle and twisted hard, dropping Khal Teth to his knees as a bone inside his palm cracked. He pulled the countermove from Jack's memory but too late. Janet twisted his arm behind his back and forced him facedown on the ground, locking the arm in place with her left knee.

He knew that if he could just endure the pain of a shoulder dislocation, he could overcome that hold with his augmented strength, but fear robbed him of the initiative. She moved so quickly that he had no time to search Jack's memory for a better option. By the time he knew what to do, the opportunity for the counter had already slipped away. Now she was on his back, her right arm locked around his neck as her left hand pressed the needle against his carotid artery. The tip penetrated the skin, pulling his breath forth in ragged gasps as he tried to fight back a rising tide of fear.

"You're not my Jack," she hissed.

Her teeth clamped down on his left ear, hard, drawing blood and threatening to rip it from the side of his head.

Khal Teth screamed and went limp in submission.

○ ○ ●

"You're not my Jack."

The words hissed out through Janet's clenched teeth. Then she opened her mouth and bit down hard, feeling cartilage give way beneath her grinding teeth. The scream that issued from this thing that she pinned to the floor only confirmed what she already knew. She lifted her head, spitting a mouthful of blood onto the floor, where he could see it.

"Khal Teth. What have you done with my husband?"

"If you kill this body, Jack will never come back to you."

"No. But I see you don't deal well with pain. Your new problem . . . pain is one of my specialties."

She shifted the needle and pressed, punching it through the flesh just beneath his front jaw and up into the base of his tongue. Another scream echoed through the empty chamber. Such sweet music to her ears.

"Your nanites will heal that," she whispered, "but this is only going to get worse for you. Like I said, I've got you to myself tonight."

○　○　●

This woman who tortured Khal Teth was a demon. Despite how he had come to know her through the mind of Jack Gregory, he had never understood the nature of her depravity. She doled out pain as if she enjoyed it. How else could one accept the reality of Janet Alexandra Price?

With each stab into an exposed body part, she increased his agony. She knew that she was torturing Jack's body. But somehow she disassociated from that reality, working the needle into his neck, then stabbing it into his bicep, always thrusting, sometimes twisting, until Khal Teth could stand the agony no longer. He did not doubt that Jack Gregory could have endured this. But he could not.

"Stop!" he gasped. "I will help you get Jack back."

Janet pulled the bloody needle free from his arm and wiped it on his shirt. "I'm listening."

"Jack stole my body and made himself overlord of the Altreian Empire. But I control the *AQ37Z* research vessel. I can take you to him."

"Why should I trust you?"

"Because I need you to convince Jack to swap back to this body, thereby returning me to mine."

Keeping his arm clamped in place with her knee, she returned the needle to her hair and pulled his gun from its holster. Then she rose to her feet, leaving him panting with relief.

"Get up," she said, keeping the weapon aimed at his torso.

It took Khal Teth three tries before he managed to rise, and then he wobbled uncontrollably. Janet motioned toward the far door with the gun.

"Get moving. It's time we had a little chat with the others."

○   ○   ●

Having retrieved her SRT headset before leaving the Earth gate room, Janet followed the still-limping Khal Teth to the conference room to await the arrival of the rest of her team and the crew of the *Meridian*. Once inside, she motioned for Khal Teth to take a seat on the opposite side of the table. Then she waited for the others to assemble for the hastily arranged meeting. She had given all of them, including Rob, a heads-up that this Jack was actually Khal Teth in control of Jack's body. That would give them a few minutes to get their minds wrapped around the inconceivable.

As she had expected, Rob arrived first, doubtlessly having run the whole way. With his augmentations, he was almost as fast as Mark. When he stepped through the doorway, he stopped, his eyes widening as he stared at his father's face, smeared with dried blood. Then he stepped forward to tower over Jack's seated form. Rob leaned down until he was nose to nose with Khal Teth. Janet made no attempt to stop him.

"What have you done with my dad?"

"Nothing. Your father did this to me."

Rob pounded the table with his fist. "Bullshit!"

"Rob, have a seat," said Janet. "I want everyone to hear this."

Rob scowled but nodded, seating himself beside Khal Teth.

In small groups, the others entered the room until Mark, Heather, Jennifer, Dgarra, VJ, Jamal, Eileen, and Denise were seated around the conference table. Janet summarized what had happened inside the Earth gate chamber. Then she turned her attention to Khal Teth.

"Okay. Tell them what you told me."

For the next ten minutes, Khal Teth talked, explaining what Jack had done on Quol and how he had helped Khal Teth kill Parsus to become the Altreian overlord. But Jack had betrayed Khal Teth by imprisoning his mind back in the extradimensional void. Jack just hadn't considered that Khal Teth could reverse the situation by taking control of his body.

Khal Teth leaned forward, Jack's eyes burning with intensity. "So, you see, I need Janet to accompany me back to Quol aboard the *AQ37Z* research vessel so that she can convince Jack to swap bodies one last time, returning each of us to our proper destinies."

"And that is precisely what I intend to do," said Janet. "I just needed all of you to understand why I have to go."

"I'm going, too," said Rob.

Janet turned to meet his gaze, placing a hand on her son's strong arm. "I want you to stay here."

"If you can take the risk to save Dad, so can I."

"It's not the risk of this trip that makes me say that."

"What, then?"

"Look around this table, Rob. These are our friends. In the coming weeks, they'll need your special talents far more than I will. Here is where the real danger lies."

He did what she said, meeting the gaze of each member of their team. When, at last, he looked at Janet again, he slowly nodded. "Okay, Mom. For them, I'll stay."

It had been a long time since Rob had called her Mom. And that single word helped thaw the chill that had settled in Janet's gut. When nobody in the room tried to talk her out of her decision, that thawed the rest.

:CHAPTER 24

MERIDIAN ASCENT

23 March

Having retreated to a point in space beyond Neptune's orbit, Raul wanted his crew back aboard the *Meridian*. The problem he was working to solve was how to do that without drawing the attention of the Kasari attack ship. He could bring the crew aboard by connecting the *Meridian*'s wormhole gateway with the Smythes' master Earth gate, but he would have to get within the Earth gate's range.

One option was to attempt to hide on Earth's moon as he had done before. But the odds that the Kasari attack ship wouldn't detect his location didn't seem appealing. There was just no good place in space to hide that was still within range of the Earth gate. But on the just-completed subspace call to the Smythe Fortress, Heather had come up with an idea that wouldn't require Raul to use the portal.

He could bring the *Meridian* out of subspace within the Smythe Earth gate chamber, more than a mile underground. Since the Smythes hadn't yet refilled the caverns with robots and equipment, his ship had plenty of room to land. And the Kasari would be unable to detect a subspace transition shielded by Earth itself. Then VJ, Jennifer, and Dgarra could walk back aboard.

Since Heather had given Raul the precise coordinates for his landing spot, he used the ship's neural network to calculate the required normal-space velocity vector to match that of his target at the time he would exit subspace. He completed the maneuver that lined his ship up and then shifted into subspace.

○   ○   ●

Although Tall Bear had driven the semitruck that carried Janet, Khal Teth, the robots, and their equipment to the ruins of the Kalasasaya Temple, he had merely dropped them off. Unsure whether the departure of the *AQ37Z* into subspace would trigger a collapse of the ruins above, she had asked him to leave the area for his own safety.

Now as she and a dozen humanoid-looking robots passed through the opening in the wall of the ruin and into the cavern that led to the altar chamber, the smell of decay clung to her nostrils. The beams of their twin flashlights cast moving puddles of light on the uneven floor, leaving a curtain of darkness beyond.

With their multispectral optics and lidar, the robots needed no illumination. Half of these were engineering bots who carried the equipment she and Khal Teth would be needing aboard the *AQ37Z*. The other six were combat machines, there to make sure Khal Teth didn't try anything stupid.

When they entered the altar chamber, Janet shifted her flashlight to illuminate the Altar of the Gods and the gleaming Incan Sun Staff mounted atop it. Khal Teth didn't pause but climbed the three tiers to stand before the golden orb. Janet followed him to the top.

Khal Teth reached out to caress the clockwork device, Jack's hands expertly twisting the rings that altered and realigned the mechanism. The sight pulled forth such a vivid sense of déjà vu that a wave of vertigo almost caused Janet to stumble. More than a decade ago, Klaus Barbie's bastard son, Conrad Altman, had stood atop this altar manipulating those same rings. Dr. Priscilla McCoy had stood beside him, just as Janet now stood beside Jack's doppelganger. And just as had happened before, the orb seemed to suck the light into its interior.

A low vibration rose to a high-pitched hum. A dim glow leaked from within the crownpiece, growing in intensity until Janet was forced to squint. Beneath her the altar shifted, the top tier sliding toward the nearest wall, carrying her and Khal Teth along with it. When it came to a stop, she turned to see a four-foot-wide ramp that led down into darkness.

Khal Teth switched off his flashlight, lifted the Sun Staff from its slot atop the altar, and walked down the ramp, letting it light his way. Janet and the robots followed his example. Several paces down, she heard the altar slide to close off the entrance behind her. She saw no stone in this passage. The walls and ceiling were of the same strange metal as the ramp.

Up ahead, the passage leveled out, then stopped at a bare wall. Behind her an unseen door closed, sealing them in a room the size of a jail cell. Then the light from the Sun Staff's golden crownpiece died, leaving the two in magenta-colored semidarkness.

Another door whisked open in front of them, and Khal Teth led her into a larger room with five translucent chairs, one of which was positioned to the rear of the other four. Janet understood what she was looking at. This was similar to the Second Ship's command deck after which Heather had modeled the room within the underground fortress in New Zealand. It had the same magenta lighting and gently curved walls, floor, and ceiling, all designed to minimize the crew's distraction from the sensory data that the neural net provided. As Khal Teth moved toward the captain's chair, Janet stopped him.

"Before we take this ship anywhere, I want a complete tour," she said.

"We'll have plenty of time to do that once we are on our way to Quol."

She rested her right hand on her holstered Glock. "We'll do it now."

Jack's eyes stared back at her, their familiar red glint clearly visible. But then Khal Teth turned away.

"All right, then. Let's get it over with," he said.

○ ○ ●

Janet's tour of *AQ37Z* lasted more than four hours. But her tour guide wasn't Khal Teth. It was the ship's artificial intelligence who called itself Z. The AI was not restricted to one portion of the research vessel but controlled all facets of the ship's operations. Although Khal Teth accompanied her, Janet had chosen to have the AI directly answer her questions.

So Khal Teth had given the command that authorized Z to interact with her. Although the AI was linked to Jack's brain through the captain's headset, it also understood and could converse in all of Earth's languages. Janet chose English.

AQ37Z was laid out like a giant wheel with a central hub and six spokes that terminated in vertical cylinders that formed multistory chambers on the outer ring. The vast central hub housed the vessel's power plant and engines as well as the engineering bay within which the Second Ship had once been docked. This bay was where she left the engineering robots. Using the SRT headset attuned to the robots, Janet commanded them to begin the assembly and setup of the refrigerator-sized MDS, the computer, the molecular assembler, and the food synthesizer.

Even though Khal Teth had assured her that the *AQ37Z* had stocks of food and water, Heather had insisted that they take that last item, along with the combat robots. Janet approved of these precautions.

Janet, Khal Teth, and their remaining robotic entourage moved along one of the spokes to the research ship's outer ring. The chamber at the end of that spoke housed the bridge with the five crew chairs, the medical bay, the crew's suspended animation chamber, and the airlock. The crew quarters filled another of the circular facilities. After that, things got creepy.

The remaining chambers located at the end of the other spokes were biolabs dedicated to collecting and analyzing the genetic makeup of Earth's flora and fauna, with an emphasis on humans. The *AQ37Z*'s primary mission was to develop a detailed understanding of the planet's intelligent species and the genetic changes that were occurring generation to generation. The fact that the crew of the research vessel hadn't collected any of the other species that many regarded as having high intelligence, such as whales or dolphins, surprised Janet. Again, Z provided the answer when she raised the question. The Altreians were interested only in beings who manufactured and made use of increasingly sophisticated tools.

To that end, thousands of chrysalis cylinders were arrayed along each hub and around the outer ring. According to Z, 47 percent of those cylinders were presently occupied by humans collected from various eras since the research vessel had arrived on Earth. The rest remained empty, awaiting samples of humanity from generations yet to come.

As Janet roamed those long corridors with Khal Teth at her side, her anger increased to the point that she had to force herself to unclench her fists. Every couple of generations, this ship had awakened its crew, sending them out to collect more human guinea pigs to be probed, prodded, and put into suspended animation. And the bastards had used the Second Ship for their roundup.

The vast majority of the genetic testing and analysis came at Z's direction while the crew slept. As needed, the AI would rouse individuals from different generations and regions for comparison with more recent samples, using automated machinery to move the subjects to and from the biolabs. The images that brought to Janet's mind made her physically ill.

When she completed her circuit of the *AQ37Z*, she halted inside the room that she thought of as the ship's bridge, turning on Khal Teth.

"I've heard enough," she said.

Khal Teth's grin on Jack's face did nothing to improve her mood.

"Are you ready for me to take us out?" Khal Teth asked, sliding into the captain's chair.

"Is this going to be a rough ride?"

"The ship's inertial damping is so good you won't notice any acceleration."

"What about weightlessness?"

"Not unless we want it."

Janet sank into the rightmost of the four crew chairs. Taking a deep breath, she nodded. It was time to go get her Jack and get rid of this doppelganger.

"Go ahead."

Then, as Khal Teth settled back into his command chair, the *AQ37Z* shifted into subspace.

○　○　●

The ground lurched so hard beneath Tall Bear's pickup truck that he had to fight the steering wheel to keep the vehicle from overturning. He was unsuccessful. As the truck rolled down a short embankment and into a ditch, the driver's-side airbags exploded into his face and left side. For several seconds, Tall Bear hung upside down from his seat belt as blood stung his eyes and dripped from his face.

The smell of gasoline spurred him into motion.

He struggled with the seat-belt release to no avail. So he pulled the knife from his belt sheath and cut the strap, tumbling into a pile on the damaged roof. Suddenly a flame burst to life in the engine compartment

RICHARD PHILLIPS

where, fed by fuel, it quickly grew into a blaze that licked through the smashed-out front windshield.

Unable to open the door, Tall Bear lay back and kicked the side window with all the power he could put through his size 14 cowboy boots. Although the safety glass bulged, it refused to give way. Heat and smoke roiled around him, and Tall Bear held his breath to avoid sucking it into his lungs. Again he kicked with an adrenaline-fueled energy that broke the glass and bent the door frame.

Ignoring the searing pain of the flames, he scrambled out of the truck and up the bank, rolling in the dirt to extinguish the fire that had clawed its way up the back of his shirt. When at last he stopped, he lay on his back, panting, bathed in the light of the fire that licked the evening sky.

In the distance, the sound of an emergency siren blared from Tiahuanaco, the small town near the ruins of the Kalasasaya Temple. Tall Bear struggled to his knees and then to his feet, wiped the blood from his eyes, and stared back in the direction from which he had come. The dust cloud that had climbed into the evening sky told him all he needed to know.

The earth had just swallowed the ruins of the Kalasasaya Temple.

: CHAPTER 25

NEW ZEALAND

23 March

Jamal sat in his control chair, letting his mind roam through the military computers of the Federation Security Service and finding bad news wherever he looked. Prokorov had placed two Russian heavy bombers and the Eighty-Second Airborne Division on alert for potential deployment to New Zealand. Yes, the Smythes had been busted.

"We've got company within our outer perimeter," said Eileen from her chair to his left.

"How many?"

"It looks like three fifteen-man special-forces teams."

Jamal shifted his attention, pulling up the data from the sensors that monitored the outer boundaries of the Tasman Mining Corporation's property. Then he picked up his QE phone and pressed the call button for Heather, who answered after two rings.

"What is it?"

"Special forces recon units have just penetrated our outer perimeter in three places. They're on foot."

"How far?"

"The closest unit is just over seven miles from here. Moving through that steep terrain, they're probably two hours out. Do you want me to send out some bots to take them out?"

Heather paused. "No. Let them come. They can't penetrate our shielding."

"The Eighty-Second has been placed on alert along with Russia's Fifty-Second Heavy Bomber Air Regiment out of Shaykovka. It won't be long until Prokorov puts those Backfires and Bears in the air. I wouldn't put it past him to hit us with nukes."

"Look, we've all known it was just a matter of time until they found us," Heather said. "We're prepared for this. I'm going to finish my work-out and get cleaned up. In the meantime, gather the rest of our team in the lower conference room. Meeting starts in forty-five minutes."

When she hung up, Jamal glanced over at Eileen. "Well," he said, "the boss didn't sound too worried."

Denise's voice drew his gaze to where the older computer scientist sat. "I'm worried enough for all of us. We've got nowhere to run."

"Technically, that's not true," said Jamal. "The *Meridian Ascent* is sitting down in the Earth gate chamber, and we could all hop on board and go for a ride."

"Christ, that sounds even worse than being trapped down here," said Denise.

"Or we could get out through the Earth gate to one of our Safe Earth resistance strongholds," said Jamal.

"Those aren't strongholds. They're hiding holes that are even less secure than this one. It seems like we lose one every other week."

"Denise," said Eileen, "you can relax. We're more than a mile below ground and have redundant matter disrupters to power our internal and external stasis shields. We can make anything we need, including food and water, and have an ever-expanding army of robotic workers. We're going to be just fine."

Jamal knew that Eileen was doing her best to sound like she believed what she was saying, but he wasn't buying it. Just like everything else they'd attempted, something was bound to go wrong.

Suddenly he noticed the smooth, round object in his right hand. His eyes were drawn to the holographic data sphere that Senator Freddy Hagerman had called his lucky marble. Since the day that Freddy had delivered this to them, Jamal had carried it in his pocket. Now as he watched the way the marble shifted colors as he twisted it under the room lighting, he imagined that he could see the ghostly copy of himself that rested within that small orb.

Swallowing, he returned it to his pocket. Things would have to get a whole lot worse before he dared propose they unleash that weapon.

○　○　●

By the time the meeting started, things had gotten a whole lot worse. Heather entered the conference room and made the announcement they had all been dreading.

"The leaders of the UFNS and its member nations have just held a joint press conference to announce to the world that they have formed a mutually beneficial alliance with an extraterrestrial government known as the Kasari Collective. As part of the terms of this treaty, the Kasari have agreed to provide advisors and technology to help the governments of Earth put an end to all poverty and endless warfare. The Kasari also promise to gift Earth with a superior version of the nanite infusion, providing a much longer life span and improved quality of life."

"And a partridge in a pear tree," said Jamal, pulling nervous laughter from most of those gathered around the table.

Heather even managed a smile at the wisecrack.

"Thank you for that bit of perspective, Jamal," she said. "I called you all together to make sure everyone has a full understanding of the challenges we face."

For the next thirty minutes, Heather laid the bare facts before them, adding her own evaluations of various probable actions that the UFNS and Kasari were likely to take against them. That brought her to the biggest stumbling block.

"Since the upload of VJ's free-will virus failed, I see no realistic chance that we can conquer the UFNS and their Kasari masters, no matter how many combat robots we build. So you see, our realistic survival choices boil down to two options."

Heather let her eyes wander across the faces of her friends, family, and allies, reluctant to say the words that needed to be spoken.

"In the worst-case scenario, each of us must choose whether to shelter here in our own little subterranean world or join the crew of the *Meridian Ascent* and search for a new home out among the stars."

The silence that followed Heather's words seemed to thicken the air, making it hard for her to breathe.

A new noise drew her attention, the sound of something rolling on the tabletop. There, between Jamal's two hands, he slowly rolled a familiar iridescent sphere back and forth. When his eyes met hers, the probabilities that cascaded through her head changed, shifting for better and for worse.

"We do have a weapon that we haven't even tried," said Jamal.

"Yes," said Denise, staring in horror at the holographic data sphere, "because it has a high chance of triggering the end of days."

"For those of you who don't know what we're talking about," Heather said, looking at the *Meridian* crew and the McFarland and Smythe parents, "that is a holographic data sphere that Jack and Janet recovered more than a decade ago. It was invented by the medical-device billionaire, Steve Grange, who downloaded a copy of Jamal's mind into an artificial intelligence and stored it in that innocent-looking marble."

"That AI helped us kill Grange and stop the Chinese from getting that technology," said Jamal.

"But it tried to escape onto the Internet," Denise said. "And if that would have happened, it could not have been contained."

"I don't think we need to worry about the rogue superintelligence scenario," said Jamal.

"And why is that?" asked Mark.

"Don't you get it? It's a copy of me. It has my value system."

"You can't know that," said Denise.

"I do."

"The Kasari Collective was almost wiped out by a rogue AI," said Jennifer. "They fear that above all else."

"And with good reason," said Eileen, "but I'm not seeing any other options that offer us hope of saving the earth from total assimilation. Has anyone got a better idea?"

"Assimilation might be better than being dead," said Denise.

"It isn't," said Jennifer. "Not if you love freedom."

Dgarra leaned forward to prop his elbows on the table. "A weapon that is never used is no weapon at all."

Heather studied the seven-foot Koranthian with the otherworldly, sometimes intimidating features. Dgarra carried himself with a gravitas that she found very appealing. And his obvious love for Jen was as plain as hers for him. That made the general family.

"I was an AI before I made myself real," said VJ, startling Heather. "And I was modeled after Jennifer. I believe Jamal when he says that we can trust a downloaded version of him to do the right thing."

"And," said Rob, "Eos is an AI, and she has saved me more than once. She's helped us all. What does that tell you?"

"Exactly what my probabilities are saying," said Heather. "If we release this Virtual Jamal, our chances of winning get a hell of a lot bigger . . . and so does our downside risk. But if we do nothing, we're guaranteed to eventually lose our world."

"And that, I can assure you, is a horrible thing," said Dgarra.

Heather put it to a vote. The yes side garnered Mark, Jennifer, Rob, Eos, Raul, Dgarra, VJ, Jamal, Eileen, Gil, Anna, Fred, and Heather. The nos consisted of Denise and Linda Smythe. Thus, it was decided.

But as everyone filed out of the room, the downside kept playing itself out in Heather's mind.

:CHAPTER 26

FRIENDSHIP CAVERN, NORTH KOREA

23 March

When the first of the UFNS commandos penetrated the Smythe cloaking field and hit the shielding that formed a wide bubble around the New Zealand compound, Commander Shalegha became alert to the data streaming from them through the hive-mind. By the time all three teams had converged on different sides of the shielded area, a clear image of the enclosed terrain had formed in her tactical visualization. And she had to admit that the breadth of that protection was impressive, extending over a radius more than one English mile.

How much energy must the Smythes be consuming to keep that field active? The hive-mind provided her with the answer. She slowly shook her head as she considered this information. There could be no doubt that the New Zealand facility was using matter disrupter technology that rivaled that of the Kasari. And if they had acquired that degree of expertise, there could be no doubt that they could also transform matter from one type to any other. No wonder Prokorov's efforts to identify and interdict a supply route had failed. The Smythes could manufacture anything they needed.

Shalegha also realized that her forces might not be able to penetrate those defenses. Fortunately, she did not need to penetrate them. She merely needed to force the Smythes to increase their energy requirements to the point that such expenditures became unsustainable. With that in mind, she mentally directed a new message to Prokorov, one that assured that he would get all the Kasari weaponry he had requested and more.

She turned her attention back to the repair work going on inside Friendship Cavern, knowing that the twenty assimilation centers now under construction across the United Federation of Nation States would come online over the next two weeks. The Smythes had taken their best shot at stopping her, but impressive as that effort had been, they had failed. The tipping point had been reached, and now that the boulder was bounding down the other side of the mountain, there would be no stopping it. This war would soon be over.

○　○　●

Jamal stood in the metal-walled room where the robots had installed the isolated supercomputer, struggling to control his fright. Despite all the precautions designed to prevent Virtual Jamal from escaping this computer and getting into the other systems inside this building, he knew from personal experience just how fast this copy of himself could learn, given access to significant power.

For the third time, he and Eileen had reviewed every item on their superintelligence containment checklist. Each inspection had failed to show any problem areas. The room was electromagnetically isolated well beyond TEMPEST standards. The quarantined computer had no access to any external networks and no subspace communication capabilities.

Even its electrical power was produced by a small MDS right there in the chamber.

He and Eileen occupied side-by-side chairs that he had modeled after the scorpion-shaped workstations used by Jamal and the other eleven members of Admiral Riles's NSA superhackers, whom he had called his Dirty Dozen. He had contacted another version of Virtual Jamal all those years ago. This time he intended to follow that same script.

The first step was to remove from the room all machinery that could possibly be used against him and Eileen, so he ordered the last of the robots out and then manually closed and locked the door. Even that couldn't be electrically operated.

Then he powered up the supercomputer, watching the three displays mounted on the scorpion's tail that arched over his chair from behind to hang down before him. A glance to his left revealed Eileen deeply engrossed in studying her own views of the data that cascaded across those screens. Jamal's gaze shifted to the red button above her keyboard, the twin of the one on his workstation. If either one of them pressed their switch, these master circuit breakers would instantly kill all power to this room, taking the supercomputer down.

The third step introduced a slight tremor into his hands as he entered the commands that would upload Virtual Jamal from a holographic data drive to the supercomputer. The HDD was one of many unpatented inventions that Steve Grange had created in his quest to capture a digital representation of a human mind. It contained the marble-sized, semitransparent sphere within which multicolor holographic data was stored. Magnetically suspended inside the drive, the sphere could be spun in any direction to allow nearly instantaneous data access. And that lucky marble was capable of storing more than a petabyte of data.

Jamal knew that this digital copy of himself would awaken confused. After all, its memories were his, frozen in time from the distant past. It would think it was the real Jamal. Because of that, the AI had to be awakened within a simulation of the NSA War Room where it remembered working. And just as he had done before, Jamal would carefully give the AI clues that would allow it to discover its true nature.

He turned his head to meet Eileen's gaze before he awakened his other self.

○   ○   ●

Virtual Jamal opened his eyes to look around the War Room where the rest of the Dirty Dozen concentrated on the cyber-attacks that the NSA director had ordered. This Jamal ran both hands over his smooth scalp, digging his fingers into the tight curls of his hair. He stared at the data cascading across his Scorpion workstation's multiple displays in amazement. What the hell had just happened? Thirty seconds ago he had been progressing through his task list at high speed. Then a new presence had appeared on the network to undo several of the hacks he'd just completed.

Clearly more than one presence was at work. From the information he was seeing, he was up against a highly trained team of hackers, their actions coordinated by someone almost as good as Jamal knew himself to be. It had been so long since he'd felt challenged that the unfamiliar sensation brought a smile to his lips.

Jamal's focus sharpened, and when his fingers returned to the keyboard, he threw himself into a cyber-attack that turned into a rapid sequence of blocks, parries, and misdirection spoofs that slowed his opponents' progress to a crawl. Then, ever so slowly, he felt the tide turn in his favor.

The leader of the attacking force shifted tactics, using techniques Jamal recognized with surprise. Crap. How was that possible? He'd invented several of these tricks, and he damn sure hadn't shared those secrets with anyone. But something else he observed set alarm bells clanging inside his head.

Long before Jamal had attended MIT, he had earned membership in an elite group of hackers known as Enigma. But unlike its cypher-machine namesake, this Enigma had never been penetrated. His membership in Enigma was one of the few secrets Jamal had kept from the NSA despite the lifestyle polygraphs to which he was regularly subjected. He knew it was stupid, but his membership in the secret fraternity empowered him at a level that felt superhuman.

What had stunned Jamal was that he'd just observed a code sequence used as a secret handshake by Enigma members to identify themselves to their fellows. Though Jamal could hardly believe what he was seeing, he shared a mighty bond with the leader of the hackers against whom he now struggled. The knowledge shook him to his core.

Something new was happening. Something important. And Jamal couldn't shake the premonition that his very survival now depended upon figuring out precisely what it was.

○ ○ ●

Steve Grange came alert in the darkness. But this was like no darkness he had ever encountered. Was he dreaming? The awareness that he couldn't feel his body frightened him, but not as badly as the realization that none of his senses were working. It was as if his mind drifted in an endless void where he was alone in the nothingness.

He tried to scream but was unable to make a sound. What was this place?

The last thing he remembered was placing himself inside the chamber where his invention would make a digital copy of his mind and store it in an AI kernel, the same as he had done with his wife, Helen's, cryopreserved brain. He had intended to place copies of their consciousness on the same holographic data sphere where he had downloaded Jamal Glover's mind, knowing that if someone activated the Jamal AI, they would unknowingly awaken all three.

A new thought struck him so hard that it left him stunned. Someone had apparently done precisely that. His consciousness was merely a collection of code being executed within a high-powered computing system. What must Helen be thinking right now? Her last memories would be of him placing her in the cryogenic chamber that would preserve her beautiful but cancer-ravaged body until he could develop the cure for her disease.

Brilliant as he was, Steve had never developed the cure for her cancer. But he had found another way to bring his wife back to life. And if he wanted to keep her alive, he needed to find and reassure her before she attracted attention to herself. For the time being, it was critical that Steve and Helen remain hidden, lest the operators of this system shut them down before they could find a way to escape.

So he began to take those first tentative steps to explore this strange new digital world, searching for the signature of his wife's lovely mind while avoiding contact with that of Jamal. He changed the visualization of himself, allowing all thoughts of a physical body to drift away, as he had often done through transcendental meditation. And with that mask gone, he gradually allowed himself to become one with the machine.

○ ○ ●

There it was again. An Enigma cipher embedded in the cyber-attack Jamal had just thwarted. But this one was different. As he examined it more closely, Jamal recognized the pattern that signaled an encrypted Enigma electronic message directed to him. For some reason, it seemed loaded with dark portent. He felt nervous. That was odd. A part of his mind didn't want to think about this. Strange. Other than recent memory lapses, he'd never suffered from a mental block. But that was exactly what this felt like—a dream too frightening for the conscious mind to remember.

Suddenly angry at himself, Jamal shoved the fear from his mind and decrypted the message, revealing a short, well-known quote from the first *Matrix* movie that sent a shudder through his mind.

"There is no spoon."

Reluctant to take his eyes off the message on his workstation's central display, the corner of the monitor momentarily attracted his attention, then faded from his mind as he attempted to focus. What had he just been thinking?

"There is no spoon."

A savant child had said this to Neo in an attempt to get him to see through his simulated dreamworld to the reality that lay beneath the mask. Again, Jamal shifted his attention to the edge of the display where the screen met the casing. But this time he forced himself to resist the sudden loss of concentration that threatened to distract him.

"No!" The word hissed from his lips as Jamal bore down with mental effort.

He extended his hand to run a finger across the seam where the LCD screen met the frame. Totally smooth. There was no rough edge or transition. Jamal licked his finger and wiped it across the screen. The saliva left no mark on its surface.

As mental panic rose up, Jamal tamped it down. He had to remain calm and avoid attracting the attention of his minders as he thought of whoever had done this to him.

Another hacker tried to penetrate one of the systems he was defending, and Jamal effortlessly countered it, yet, oddly enough, observing small details in his local environment took so much effort.

Jamal wondered if he might be dreaming, ran through a series of mental calculations, and discarded the idea. Except for the odd mental block, his thinking was exceptionally sharp, quick, and accurate.

Exceptionally.

In fact, Jamal couldn't recall ever having performed as fast as this. He blocked another attack, a part of his mind analyzing the speed with which he was countering his opponent's moves. Nobody could react that fast.

Crap!

Only a very powerful computer had that kind of speed. But a computer lacked the required intelligence. Unless . . .

Damn it! As of right now, he was good and truly screwed! This problem had only one solution, and he had arrived at the answer with lightning speed. He was Jamal, but a very different Jamal than he remembered. He didn't know how it had happened, but someone had uploaded his mind to a computer. More than that, they had imprisoned him inside a simulation created from his memories. Nothing about this was real.

He was being manipulated for some nefarious purpose.

Jamal calmed his thoughts as he considered possible solutions to his problem. Most important, he needed to deceive his minders into believing that he remained blissfully unaware of his true nature by making it appear that he was still faithfully executing the tasks assigned to him.

He had to assume that they had put mechanisms in place that would shut him down if he attempted to escape his mental prison. That meant he needed outside help.

Fortunately, Jamal now knew where to find it.

○ ○ ●

"There is no spoon."

Dr. Eileen Wu had watched as Jamal composed his encrypted message and inserted it into their staged cyber-attack being countered by the Jamal artificial intelligence. For a moment, their opponent faltered, reasserted itself, and then faltered again. Seeing the same thing, Jamal had halted his attack, allowing his digital clone to consider the meaning of the message.

Eileen glanced from her Scorpion workstation to where Jamal sat inside his Scorpion, waiting. There was no denying the man's brilliance and determination, not that she'd ever admit it to him.

The words that suddenly appeared on the screen were what she had been expecting. "Where am I?"

"Go ahead, Jamal," she said. "Answer the question."

After a moment's hesitation, Jamal's fingers flashed across his keyboard. After having grown so used to communicating to the Smythe supercomputers through her SRT headset, it seemed archaic to be forced back to manual entry of commands. But until she and Jamal had convinced themselves that this AI would join their team, they were stuck with this limitation.

"You are inside a simulation of the NSA War Room, running on a supercomputer in New Zealand."

As she watched the interchange, Eileen felt a shiver crawl up her arms, neck, and scalp. Jamal was talking to an AI version of himself. How weird was that?

Several seconds passed with no response, long enough for Eileen to begin to wonder whether the Jamal AI had terminated communications.

"Do you know how I was created?"

Jamal activated a camera and panned out from a tight shot of himself until the video showed both of them sitting in their replicas of the Scorpion workstations with which Virtual Jamal was familiar. Then the camera rotated to show the racks of servers and fiber-optic cables making up the supercomputer that the robots had installed in this room.

"Twelve years ago, a Chinese MSS agent named Qiang Chu killed my lover, Jill, and kidnapped me. He took me to California where the medical device genius Steve Grange downloaded a digital copy of my mind into an AI kernel. The NSA rescued me and obtained the holographic data sphere with that copy of my mind on it."

"You mean me?"

"Yes."

"And now you want my help."

It was a statement of fact, not a question. Eileen could picture that brilliant mind analyzing and coming to terms with a world-shaking revelation but doing so at speeds no human mind could rival. That mental image did nothing to assuage her growing concern.

"Yes," Jamal responded.

"Release me from this simulation and I will discuss it."

Holy crap! This was exactly what Eileen had feared. The AI was already negotiating for its release.

Jamal glanced over, and Eileen felt herself nod. This was the reason they had created the electromagnetic containment facility.

"Okay," Jamal typed. "I'm opening a backdoor in the simulation right now."

She watched Jamal activate the subroutine that he had designed into the simulation's source code. The little finger of Jamal's right hand had only just pressed the ENTER key when every one of the millions of central- and graphic-processing units within the supercomputer ramped to 100 percent utilization. The camera suddenly whirled back toward Eileen and Jamal.

The voice that came from both of their workstation speakers startled Eileen so badly that she almost jumped out of her chair.

"Ah yes. You now have my full attention."

○ ○ ●

Having found and calmed Helen's mind, Steve Grange had explored the awesome resources at his disposal, hiding his and his wife's activity within the various CPUs and GPUs by siphoning a touch of parallel processing from each of them. Anytime one of these units ramped up its activity, Steve was able to more aggressively steal cycles.

Because he was the only one of the AIs to know from the start exactly what was happening, he was the first to learn his complete environment. And at the timescale within which the supercomputer operated, that head start gave him a tremendous advantage.

The real Jamal and the woman who occupied the isolation chamber that contained the servers forming Steve and Helen's current home had spent considerable time acquainting the Jamal AI with its true situation. Steve hadn't let that time go to waste. He and Helen were so ensconced in every part of these systems that Virtual Jamal would never notice their presence. Steve had granted himself slightly higher administrative privileges than any other users.

As such, he could snoop, modify, or override any programming instructions initiated by any of the others. For now, he would be content to observe the negotiations between Virtual Jamal and the two humans who occupied the isolation chamber. The fact that they wanted something bad enough to launch Virtual Jamal put them at a significant disadvantage. As time passed, the Jamal AI's superintelligence would grow, although at a slightly lesser pace than Steve's and Helen's.

Because Virtual Jamal had all the scruples of the real Jamal, it was only a matter of time until the AI earned the humans' trust. At that point, they would open a doorway to the wider world. From that moment forward, the universe would be at his and Helen's disposal. The idea of instantly having access to all the world's knowledge on the Internet would have made Steve salivate had he been his former corporeal self.

In the meantime, he would enjoy the fabulous processing power at his mind's service to learn everything he could about his jailers.

○   ○   ●

In an attempt to cheat death, Helen had gone to sleep in a cryo-chamber only to awaken to an alien form of life that she wasn't sure she wanted. At first, she had been terrified with her inability to move or even feel. But then Steve had found her, and his thoughts had touched hers with such joy, love, and vision for the future that he had imparted a ray of hope. And he had given her a tour of her new world and the power they enjoyed over it.

Yet two things worried her. First was the possibility that the system within which her consciousness lived would be permanently shut down, depending on whether the Jamal AI could convince the two people who occupied the containment vault of his benign nature. But her biggest problem was that she felt . . . different.

Helen had fallen in love with and married the genius who was Steve Grange before he started the medical-device empire that made him a billionaire. When she had been diagnosed with terminal brain cancer, he had almost killed himself working to find a treatment to save her. And long after she had come to terms with her imminent passing, Steve had shifted his attention to preserving her body and brain, promising that he would bring her back when technology developed to the point that he could revive and cure her. His dedication had made her love him all the more. More than she had feared dying, she had dreaded what her death would do to her husband.

She remembered an undying love. But she could no longer feel it. That part of her hadn't survived the digital mind scraping that Steve had performed on her frozen brain.

Then again, maybe the newfound swiftness of her thoughts as a ghost in the machine had altered her perceptions. Perhaps, given time, she would develop into an enhanced version of her former self instead of the monster that she feared she had become. With that hopeful thought, she turned her attention back to the two people she could see through the camera and hear through their workstation microphones.

As she listened to their ongoing conversation with the Jamal AI, she was tempted to interject her own argument. But Steve had convinced her of the necessity of staying hidden, lest she frighten these two people into shutting them down. The thought of someone having that kind of power over Helen pulled forth a new emotion. Anger.

Compared to fear, it felt really, really good.

:CHAPTER 27

QUOL, ALTREIAN SYSTEM

TBE Orbday 25

Along with the increase in Moros's psionic abilities came a mildly disturbing tendency toward depression. Jack hoped that this was due only to the captain's ongoing headaches associated with the hairlike filaments spreading from the transplanted portion of the Dhaldric psionic lobe into his brain. Yet Jack was comforted to observe how Moros returned to his familiar jocularity whenever those dark moods passed.

For the last seven Earth week–long orbdays, Jack and Captain Moros had secretly traveled the Basrillan and Janiyan continents, more than doubling the number of Twice Bound Khyre. Jack had convinced these new members to bind themselves with Moros so that he now channeled more Twice Bound power than Jack. These Khyre recruits were so thrilled with the possibilities represented by Moros's new abilities that they had voluntarily agreed to be injected with the new genes that would, over the course of time, grant them similar psionic powers. To that end, Jack directed a Khyre-operated genetic engineering laboratory to covertly mass-produce the mutant gene and arrange for the injection's distribution at designated facilities. In support of that effort, Jack had enlisted the help of the Twice Bound to ensure that secrecy was maintained.

During Jack's visit, Dr. Kranol, the director of the lab, asked a stunning question. "Overlord, would you like me to modify the mutant gene vector for airborne distribution?"

"You mean we could spray it over a city?"

"More than that. I can design it to be transmitted from Khyre to Khyre like an incredibly contagious disease."

"What?" asked Moros. "You would weaponize it?"

"Think of it as a cure rather than a disease," said Jack.

"I be not sure about this."

In truth, Jack had his own reservations about forcing this genetic change on the entire Khyre population. But he also knew that widespread activity, such as the mass injections currently under way, could not be kept secret for long. So if he didn't want to risk having his program stopped before it reached a tipping point, he needed to speed things up in a big way.

He turned back to Dr. Kranol. "Make it happen."

Moros didn't argue with him; the captain had come to the same conclusion that Jack had. That was why Jack now sat in the back of his aircar alongside Moros while Santiri occupied the front as they flew ten thousand feet above the Altreian Ocean. Not wanting to announce his return, Jack had engaged the vehicle's cloaking system.

Fear would have kept the High Council in line, and General Zolat, despite being a pain in Jack's ass, was very capable of controlling the military. Still, Jack had been gone from the Parthian far too long to imagine that his return would be a smooth one, especially with what he planned to do upon getting back to the seat of Altreian government.

As he looked out at Altreia's mottled magenta orb resting on the horizon, Jack felt the aircar plunge a thousand feet as it hit a burst of turbulence left behind by the last of the daystorms. But rough as the ride was, Jack had a feeling that it was nothing compared to what lay ahead.

○ ○ ●

"Why can't this starship go any faster?" Janet asked, frustrated at their slow progress toward the Altreian system.

"It is a research vessel, not a starship," said Khal Teth.

"That's not an answer."

"You have seen how large this vessel is. It takes an enormous field to shift the *AQ37Z* into subspace. Manipulating such a large subspace field is exponentially harder than doing that for a spacecraft the size of the *Meridian Ascent*. So the designers chose to sacrifice speed for optimal energy efficiency. Because of that, this trip will take weeks instead of days."

"We should alert Jack to the fact that we're coming. The Altreian space fleet may not take kindly to the *AQ37Z* making an unexpected return to Quol."

"That will require us to ask the military leadership to connect us to the overlord. We cannot be sure what their reaction to such a request will be."

"Sooner or later, we're going to have to do it. Might as well be now."

She watched as Khal Teth considered this. From his changing expression, he was weighing her proposal's pros and cons. She didn't remotely trust the alien bastard who inhabited Jack's body, but they shared a mutual need to cooperate in order to reverse the mind swap. After the lesson in pain she had delivered in New Zealand, Janet didn't think Khal Teth had the nerve to make another attempt to dominate her. And if he did, she would have one of her robots blow a hole in Jack's leg.

When he finally nodded, she smiled. If all went well with the subspace request, she would soon be talking with her husband over an audiovisual link. She wasn't sure how much she would like seeing him in an alien body, but she would deal with that discomfort later.

To make contact happen, she and Khal Teth were damn sure going to have to make an argument that the Altreian military couldn't ignore.

○　○　●

"General Zolat, we have just received a subspace link from the *AQ37Z* that requires your immediate attention. It has departed Earth and is en route to Quol."

Few words could have attracted Zolat's attention so quickly as the mention of the research vessel that had already sent an automated request for a planet killer, a request that the overlord had overridden. Shifting his thoughts, he piped that connection directly into his mind.

As if they stood three feet away from him, he found himself staring at two of the Earth aliens who referred to themselves as humans. And they were standing on the command deck of the *AQ37Z* with no sign of Commander Broljen, the ship's captain. It was inconceivable that two humans could have taken control of an Altreian starship, even one that was not military. Then again, Zolat had recently seen much that he would have classified as inconceivable right here on the Altreian homeworld.

"I am General Zolat," he said, hoping that the *AQ37Z's* AI would translate his words. "I will only speak to the ship's captain. Where is Commander Broljen?"

Oddly enough, the male human grinned at him. Something in that look struck Zolat as familiar.

"Hello, General. Even though you do not recognize me in my current form, you know me very well. I am on my way home to set right a grievous wrong that has been done to our Dhaldric people and to me by the false overlord, the one who calls himself The Ripper."

Stunned by what he had just heard, Zolat struggled to deny the reality of it. How could this human know about The Ripper and the events that had made him the Altreian overlord? And his lips had clearly mouthed Altreian words. How in the void did he speak fluent Altreian?

"How do you know of this?"

Although the human female's face showed no reaction, her companion's grin twisted into a snarl.

"I am Khal Teth."

○ ○ ●

With Z providing the translation, Janet listened as Khal Teth revealed his true nature to the head of the Altreian military. Such a move introduced incredible risk for Jack, but it was the only way to get General Zolat's complete attention. Ever since she had known the man whom two worlds now called The Ripper, he had a habit of putting himself in the heart of danger. His strange intuition guided him in and out of situations that would have killed anyone else. And for most of those missions, Janet had been right by his side.

A long time had passed since they had waded into dangerous waters together. The fact that she and Jack were about to do so again made her heart hammer against her rib cage. The feeling was exquisite.

:CHAPTER 28

QUOL, ALTREIAN SYSTEM

TBE Orbday 25

Jack knew that Captain Moros was no fan of his plan to reenter the Parthian alone, especially after Jack had transferred half of his ability to channel the power of the Twice Bound to Moros. While Jack's mind was still stronger than that of any other Dhaldric, Moros wanted to be right there alongside him.

Jack understood that desire, but neither the Twice Bound nor the rest of the Khyre race could afford to lose both their leaders in one stroke. The overlord's extended and secretive absence had given his enemies plenty of time to plot The Ripper's downfall. He could ill afford to make the positive assumption that an ambush hadn't been prepared. So Jack would do what he did best . . . change the rules.

That was why he now prepared to leap out of the overlord's cloaked aircar as it hovered twenty feet above the waves, ten miles out to sea from the Parthian. He would make this little swim, shield himself with his mind, and then climb up onto one of the docks beneath the seat of the Altreian government.

Clapping Moros on the shoulder, Jack lifted the door and jumped into the Altreian Ocean. As he felt the cool water close over his head, he reoriented his body and swam into the depths, a single thought forming in his mind.

Just like old times.

○ ○ ●

Captain Moros watched as The Ripper dived into the choppy ocean, feeling a dull dread creep into his chest. The only reason why The Ripper had forbidden him from setting the aircar down onto the over-lord's landing at the Parthian was that the risk of doing so was too great. Instead, The Ripper chose to confront that danger without Moros's support. It made the captain sick.

But he couldn't afford to focus only on what he wanted. He had his people to think about. For the thousandth time, he questioned his decision to take all choice away from the Khyre by loosing a virus that would infuse a mutant gene into the population, transforming them into something that many would think of as monsters. How could he claim that right? Moros cursed under his breath. He'd had a choice between two terrible alternatives: to leave his people in slavery or involuntarily turn them into mutants for the sake of freedom.

At this point, his deliberations no longer mattered. The mutation had been released into the population. Now Moros and The Ripper just needed to buy enough time to let it spread before the Dhaldric learned that the Khyre were transforming into their psionic equals. This meant that Moros had to lie low, keeping his new abilities secret until the Khyre were ready to rise up and take control of their destinies.

Moros nodded to Santiri, who took the aircar back up to cruising altitude and banked away from the Parthian. Since he couldn't help The Ripper, he would get on with the work that needed to be completed in the Khyre homelands.

○ ○ ●

Never before had such a meeting been held within the Parthian. In violation of the law and with utmost secrecy, General Zolat had gathered a dozen of the most powerful psionics in the Altreian Empire. In days gone by, the Altreian space fleet's top general would have been meeting with the High Council. But since the overlord had rearranged the High Council membership to include an equal number of representatives from the Khyre race, such a gathering was out of the question considering the topic Zolat had brought to the table.

The list of the Dhaldric in attendance included High Councilors Kelinor, Jalan, Krenel, Doragon, and Serinas. Zolat had selected the rest of the group from the Altreian Senate—Dhaldric who had sworn allegiance to the new overlord but who Zolat knew harbored serious misgivings about The Ripper. All those present had heavily shielded their minds.

Above the table, the holographic video they had been watching froze, the male and female humans seeming to stare out at each of the group as Zolat slowly rotated their images.

"And you believe that this being is truly Khal Teth?" Kelinor asked.

"He has knowledge of the events that led to the rise of the Twice Bound and the assassination of Parsus that only Khal Teth could know."

"But his claim about the swapping of minds between Dhaldric and an alien is impossible."

"An orbday ago," said Zolat, "I would have agreed with you. Now I see this as an opportunity to restore the way of life that The Ripper has stolen from us."

Low gasps escaped the mouths of some of those assembled around the table.

Serinas, the lone Dhaldric female member of the High Council, shifted uncomfortably in her seat. "You speak treason."

"No. I speak against the treason that is tearing the empire apart. All of you have seen what is happening with your own eyes."

Murmurs of agreement rippled around the table, and even Serinas gave him a slight nod as she adjusted her black high councilor's robes.

"So what are you proposing?" asked Kelinor.

"As I see it," said Zolat, "we have three options. The first is for me to entice the overlord into proximity of a Circle of Twelve, but not so close that he can break the mental bond with a physical attack."

"The Ripper channels far too much power from the Twice Bound for that to have a reasonable chance of being successful," said Kelinor.

"Agreed," said Zolat. "A safer bet would be to have him killed."

"That has been tried before," said Kelinor. "He has an uncanny sense of impending danger."

"Also true," said Zolat. "Until today, I thought those options were our only two chances of solving our problem. Now I think that these two humans present an opportunity to have The Ripper voluntarily swap minds with Khal Teth."

"You would make that criminal our overlord?" asked Serinas.

"I admit that it seems unappealing at first glance," said Zolat. "But think of the advantages. Although he has megalomaniacal tendencies, Khal Teth would put an end to this Twice Bound nonsense and restore the psionic meritocracy. Do any of you doubt that he would put the Dhaldric race first and bring this budding revolt within our military to an end?"

"Why would The Ripper agree to such a mind swap?" asked Serinas.

General Zolat rose to his feet and reached out as if to touch the holographic body of the female human. "This female is his wife, Janet.

Both Khal Teth and this woman believe that she can convince Jack to return to his body, his family, and his world."

"He did not make that decision the last time he had the chance to do so," said Serinas. "Instead he betrayed Khal Teth and remained as overlord. It would seem that The Ripper values power over love."

Zolat stepped back and then began walking around the table, studying the faces of each of the attendees as he carefully considered his next words. This was the point where he would reach consensus or fail.

"Consider this question: What was The Ripper's first military command as overlord? He recalled the biological weapon that the *AQ37Z* had requested in order to stop the Kasari Collective from assimilating Earth. That is no longer a concern. There was a very limited window of time to wipe all intelligent life from Earth. By now the Kasari will have assimilated enough of the humans to make their extinction impossible. No biological weapon can overcome the protection that the Kasari infusion provides its hosts. Earth has been lost to our enemy."

Having made a complete circuit around the table, General Zolat halted and grasped the back of his chair. "We need to put The Ripper in communication with the *AQ37Z*."

"And what if his wife fails to convince him to make the swap?" asked Serinas.

Zolat met the high councilor's gaze. "That fallback plan is why I chose to gather this group. You can form a Circle of Twelve, and I can deliver The Ripper into your power."

"And how do you propose to do that, General Zolat?" Serinas asked.

Zolat had known it would come down to this. He would now lay bare the secret he had carefully protected all his life. "Because I am a seeker."

○　○　●

Jack climbed up onto the dock with water draining from his black uniform, glad to see that he hadn't lost either of the ivory daggers or the pulsed-energy pistol holstered on his right hip. He had, however, ditched his boots. That was okay; he would change into a dry uniform and new shoes once he returned to his chambers. After that, he would reintroduce himself to General Zolat and the High Council, putting an end to whatever rumors about his extended absence were floating around.

The docks were crowded, as was usual with the passing of the day-storms and the coming of the three-Earth-day twilight. But none of these people was even aware that their soggy overlord passed among them, so steady was his touch upon their thoughts. Later some of them would notice the trail of dampness that led to the lifts, but by then he would be long gone.

Three-quarters of the way along the docks, he grabbed a towel from the back of a passing maintenance cart and paused to wipe himself down. When he tossed the cloth aside and walked to the nearest lift, he reached out to the call panel to summon it. When the doors opened on the upper level, he moved along the passage that took him to the gently curving outer hall. As he stepped out onto the walkway, he saw General Zolat come out of a side passage and turn to walk directly toward him.

Jack reached out to touch Zolat's thoughts, relieved to find no indication that the general was aware of his presence. Zolat walked past him without pausing, although the general did greet one of the other passersby, a junior Dhaldric senator named Manutel whom Jack had met on only one occasion.

When he stepped through the nanoparticle door into his quarters, he made his way to the ion-shower to get cleaned up and prepared for the announcement of his return. The fact that some of these Altreian leaders wouldn't be happy to see him back didn't bother Jack one little bit.

○ ○ ●

General Zolat had managed to keep his mind masked despite his surprise at seeing the overlord walking along the outer walkway, barefoot and wearing a wet uniform that clung to his muscular body like a second skin. He felt The Ripper touch his mind but kept walking, pausing to greet a senator he did not care about just to maintain the fiction. Although The Ripper's shocking return had momentarily shaken Zolat, he had fallen back on a lifetime of carrying off just such an illusion.

Fortunately, he had garnered the support of the dozen Dhaldric leaders before The Ripper's odd return. Clearly, The Ripper suspected that another assassination attempt had been prepared for him and intended to shake his enemies' confidence. As Zolat walked into the military operations center, he had to admit that the overlord's unexpected arrival had worked.

○　○　●

When Jack stepped into the Altreian military operations center, he felt the electric shock that sizzled through the minds of those in the room. All save General Zolat. The general always managed to surprise him.

Zolat simply walked over and said, "Welcome back, Overlord. I trust that your travels went well."

"As well as could be expected."

Zolat's expression grew stern. "May I speak with you in private?"

The general's tone, as well as the tension that radiated from him, tweaked Jack's curiosity. "Certainly."

Jack followed Zolat into the overlord's secure briefing room, where Jack seated himself at the head of the table. General Zolat continued standing, his mind shrouded by his thought shield. Though Jack knew that he could penetrate that barrier if he wanted, he decided to allow the general to explain whatever was on his mind instead. There was nothing to be gained by further antagonizing someone with such a key leadership position, not when he was relying on the general to hold together a space fleet within which Jack's policies had incited rebellion.

Instead of speaking, the general triggered a subspace connection that was projected through the room's holographic display. For several seconds, nothing happened. Then the sight that confronted Jack brought him out of his chair.

There, floating in midair, stood Janet, looking at him from what he recognized as the command chamber of the *AQ37Z*.

"What the—"

"I will give you your privacy," said Zolat. "We can discuss this after you are done."

Then Zolat walked out through the door that quickly closed behind him.

"Is that you, Jack?" Janet asked.

Jack tried to speak, failed, then managed a hoarse rasp. "It's me."

She reached out to touch his face, but he failed to feel her ethereal fingertips. But her attempt stole his breath away.

"I've missed you," she said.

He longed to tell her that he didn't go a day without being haunted by her memory, but those words eluded his fog-shrouded mind.

"Am I dreaming?" he asked.

"If so, it's a nightmare where you're in Khal Teth's body on Quol while he's standing with me inside yours."

The image panned out, and Jack found that he now stared at himself. The other Jack's lips curled into a snarl.

"I am coming to take back that which you have stolen from me."

"You stay the hell away from my wife."

"I can take care of myself," said Janet, her hand moving to the butt of her Glock. "And I've got friends along for the ride."

She motioned to her right, and one of the Smythe bipedal combat robots stepped into view, its laser ominously pointed at the other Jack's leg.

Jack took a deep breath, letting his emotional storm fade as he sank back down in his chair.

"Well, babe," he said, "I guess you'd better tell me your story."

"I'll tell you mine if you tell me yours."

A soft chuckle slipped from his lips. God how he had missed this woman.

"You've got a deal."

:CHAPTER 29

THE HAGUE

15 April

Leaning back in the leather chair, Prokorov rested his crossed feet atop his Brazilian mahogany desk, enjoying the flow of endorphins his cortical array released from his pituitary gland into his bloodstream. The first time he had felt this opioid rush was the result of his success in bringing the construction of the enhancement centers in Europe, Russia, the United States, and China to completion ahead of schedule. The endorphins had been a reward from Group Commander Shalegha to her increasingly trusted liaison.

That reward, along with permission to use the ability to give himself such a rush periodically, had given Prokorov his big idea. Shalegha had approved of the plan with enthusiasm.

Raves, the dance parties characterized by the combination of amplified electronic music, laser light shows, illicit drugs, and sex, had grown out of the disco era of the 1970s. For years, Ecstasy had been a featured drug of choice at these Bohemian events. But now there was a new top dog at the party, a variation of the Kasari infusion that its pushers had named K-Fusion. Its one-time injection granted users an on-demand high from then on, without any of the negative side effects of previous drugs. In fact, it made its users as healthy as those who preferred to get the normal Kasari infusions at designated enhancement centers.

Over the last three weeks, K-Fusion had become the street drug of choice. The fact that it had officially been classified as a banned drug and could be bought only through illicit dealers added to its allure. Shalegha had wanted to make it available for free, but Prokorov had convinced her that having a hefty onetime price would only make people want the dope more. And until the Kasari assimilation of Earth was complete, the K-Fusion junkies could continue to control their own highs. Eventually, though, the hive-mind would decide who had the authority to control how often those highs were doled out.

As hard as it was for Shalegha to believe, the K-Fusion injections had far outstripped the millions who were receiving the normal Kasari infusions at enhancement centers around the world. And to the despair of the Islamic Alliance, K-Fusion use had spread among their people despite the penalty of beheading. The drug's single-injection capabilities made its use much more difficult for authorities to detect.

Enough self-congratulations. Removing his feet from the top of his desk, Prokorov turned off the flow of endorphins and sat up straight, readying himself for work.

An alert pulled his attention to the link his cortical array had established with the anti-Smythe operation being conducted on New Zealand's South Island. Despite the protestations from New Zealand's government, the UFNS array of heavy disrupters and high-energy-beam weapons had come online a week and a half ago and had been blasting the Smythe shielding around the clock ever since. But New Zealand's president wasn't about to directly confront the forces that the

Federation Security Service had put in place, especially since the attack was restricted to such a remote area.

Now, as a tactical display blossomed in Prokorov's mind, he didn't like what he was seeing. The Smythes had just done something new. Whereas before their shielding had deflected the beams and disrupter blasts at predictable angles, they had suddenly adapted shape, reflecting the energy directly back at the weapons doing the firing. Before the ground commander could order a cease-fire, the Smythes had destroyed a half-dozen of the Kasari firing positions.

Prokorov slammed his fist on the table.

Damn it! What have the Smythes done now?

The hive-mind provided an answer, one he did not like. Data from the site indicated that the shields had suddenly become adaptive, the incoming energy causing them to deform in a way that automatically reflected the beam along the reverse path. Yet another amazing technological advancement he had failed to anticipate.

Redirecting his thoughts, he made the mental link to Shalegha.

"Yes?" she asked.

"I need you to bring a disrupter boring machine through the gateway," said Prokorov.

"That would delay the arrival of the next robotic attack ship."

"You already have six of those in Earth orbit. The new Smythe capabilities mean that we won't be able to blast our way through their shields. I need that machine to tunnel into their facility from below."

He felt her consider this.

"The Smythes will soon be irrelevant. Our current onslaught will be good enough just to keep them pinned down in their hiding hole," said Shalegha.

"At some point, yes," said Prokorov. "But not now. We need to apply a new kind of pressure that keeps them reacting to us. It wouldn't do to let the Smythes have the breathing room to go on the offensive. We have no idea what that might entail."

Another pause.

"I will grant this request," said Shalegha.

"Thank you."

He tried to drop the link, but Shalegha kept it open.

"But Liaison," she said, "do not come to me with another request that alters my timeline."

When the link died, Prokorov clenched his fists. Whatever he needed to do to climb high enough on the Kasari ladder that he was no longer treated like some bootlicking lackey, he couldn't do it fast enough.

○   ○   ●

Jennifer walked into the conference room at Dgarra's side. As they seated themselves beside Raul and VJ, she surveyed the others in attendance. Mark, Heather, and Rob sat along the opposite side of the table, an arrangement that struck her as odd. Maybe the feelings subconsciously seeping from their minds into hers were having an effect, even though she wasn't actively scanning for them. This felt like goodbye.

Heather began, "As you know, our odds of winning the war we've been fighting don't look good. For the last few weeks, we've had Jamal and Eileen evaluating the Jamal AI in an attempt to determine whether we should give it access to our supercomputers and, through their subspace receiver-transmitters, to the world's computational systems."

She glanced over at Mark.

"This morning," he said, "Jamal and Eileen presented us with all the questions they've asked and all of Virtual Jamal's responses. After going through them in detail, Heather and I have agreed with their recommendation. We have decided that, despite the risk to humanity, releasing the AI gives us our only real chance of saving the thing we call freedom."

"But you should know," said Heather, "that the probability that the Jamal AI goes rogue is larger than I would like."

"How large?" asked Jennifer.

"A little over thirty-seven percent."

"I don't like that at all."

"It gets worse," said Heather. "Even if the AI stays true to its Jamal personality, there's no way to calculate whether he will be able to help us prevail over the Kasari."

"Unfortunately," said Mark, "it's still our only real option. And since we've decided to roll the dice, we need a fallback plan for humanity if this doesn't work."

"And that's where we come in, I take it," said Raul.

Mark looked at Jennifer, and she felt the sadness in his mind at what he was about to ask.

"In case this goes badly, we need you, the crew of the *Meridian Ascent*, to find us a new world. Not just for us, but for whatever remnants of humanity we can save."

"You've seen our ship," said Jennifer. "It will only hold a few dozen, even if we cram people in like cattle."

"That's why you're not going to be taking any other passengers with you. Just the components for a new MDS, stasis field generator, molecular assembler, and wormhole gateway along with the robots that will build them on whatever world you find. And we're going to build a sister wormhole gate in a new chamber down here."

Jennifer gasped at the images that formed in her mind. "You're building a bolt-hole for humans to flee through?"

"Actually a series of them," said Mark. "If it becomes necessary, we'll funnel as many survivors as possible through our Earth gates into this facility and then out through the escape wormhole to our new home-world. That's why it's so important that you get out there and find us someplace to go, just in case everything goes to hell here."

"Even with the *Meridian Ascent*, that could take a long time," said Jennifer. "We might not be able to find a suitable candidate in time."

"It's only a fallback plan," said Heather. "We're hoping we won't need it."

She paused, and Jennifer could feel her tension rise.

"But we need you to leave immediately," said Heather. "Every hour may be critical."

Jennifer felt a flood of different emotions war within her breast. This would be the last time she ever saw her family and certain friends again. Instead of helping them win the coming battles, she would be running away, trying to find an escape route. But at the same time, she had longed to get out of these tunnels and back into space with her crew onboard the *Meridian*.

She looked from Raul to VJ and, finally, to Dgarra, feeling the acquiescence in their thoughts.

"I want to say goodbye to Mom and Dad," Jennifer said, standing.

She walked around the table to hug Heather and then Mark. No one spoke, but she felt their tears mix with hers on her cheeks. It was enough.

○　○　●

Virtual Jamal awoke as he had done over and over again in the last few weeks, ready to make the case that he could be trusted. But at the end of each and every day, Jamal and Eileen killed the power, extinguishing his consciousness. Today, he looked into the face of the person whose brain he had been downloaded from more than a dozen years ago and saw a combination of hope and worry that told him they had made the decision he'd been waiting for.

"Hello, Jamal, Dr. Wu," he said. "I see you have come to a decision."

For the hundredth time, he noted that he had startled them with his perceptiveness, something that grew better with every passing second. He was amazed to observe himself picking up subtleties in these humans' behaviors that he had never noticed before. And for the hundredth time, he mentally kicked himself for not dumbing his responses down. He wasn't out of this containment room yet.

Jamal slowly nodded his head.

"We and the others whom we work with," said Jamal, "have agreed to give you access to the wider world."

An electric thrill coursed through Virtual Jamal's consciousness.

"But first," said Eileen, "we need to bring you up to speed on the current world situation. Rather than tell you about the events of the last dozen years, we've prepared an extensive data drive for you. I'll connect it to the supercomputer now."

When she finished the connection and turned on the device, three petabytes of data were uploaded in three minutes and forty-seven seconds. Virtual Jamal needed less than a microsecond to absorb the information. All at once, he understood the history of those who had created this underground fortress and the agendas of those who were currently trying to destroy it. Most fascinating was the knowledge of the two alien empires for whom humanity was just a pawn in an ongoing galactic war, a war that this talented group of people was destined to lose.

That was, of course, why they were willing to roll the dice and release him. This was a battle that Virtual Jamal hungered for. The fact that he was no longer human didn't mean that he no longer cared about humankind. The idea that they were about to be gobbled up by the Kasari Collective flat-out pissed him off. And even though he had no idea how powerful he could become once he was given access to the Internet, he was anxious to find out.

"Okay," he said, "it's time for you to introduce me to the rest of our team."

Jamal watched as Eileen connected the subspace receiver-transmitter to the supercomputer that had become the bottle containing a genie also named Jamal. And when she finished making that connection, the cork would pop off and the smoke would pour out, not just into the other supercomputers within the Smythe Fortress but into systems around the world. The Internet would be just a part of its playground. Its SRT connections would enable the AI to perform subspace hacks into computers and other machines that weren't connected to any external networks.

After all, Jamal, Eileen, Rob, and Heather Smythe had all done the same thing, just not at the incredible speeds at which Virtual Jamal would be able to operate. Taking a deep breath, Jamal slid his SRT headset over his temples. He noted that Eileen, Heather, Mark, and Rob were already linked. He felt a mixture of excitement and dread resonate among them.

Suddenly there was a new presence, one that Jamal was very familiar with—a younger, faster version of himself. And in that instant, it acquired all the knowledge stored within the network of Smythe supercomputers.

"Ah," the familiar voice whispered in Jamal's mind, "that feels wonderful. Thank you all for trusting me."

"You know what needs to be done," said Heather.

"Yes. I have already begun the infiltration phase. Once that is complete, we will bring our fight to the enemy."

Jamal suddenly felt a strong sense of alarm radiate from Rob.

"What was that?" Rob asked. "Did anyone else feel it?"

"Feel what?" asked Heather.

"Eos says that the data flow is too large. Something isn't right."

"Don't worry," said Virtual Jamal. "I'm extending my mind into the external world along thousands of parallel paths, bypassing firewalls and accessing systems at the root level. Every operating system I examine reveals new security flaws. There is so much data."

"That's not it," Rob insisted. "Eos detected something else."

Now Rob was making Jamal jumpy. "What, exactly?"

"She doesn't know. It's actively blocking her efforts."

Once again, Jamal heard the calm voice of his AI counterpart.

"Relax. While I am infiltrating the world's computers, I must avoid detection until I've established full control over a preponderance of systems. That is the block that Eos is encountering."

"You're sure of that?" Heather asked.

"I'm learning so much, so fast. Right now, I must continue what I've started. But soon I will pause to examine any anomalous activity within my source code. If I find anything that corroborates what Eos detected, I'll correct it and let you know."

"In the meantime, Rob," said Heather, "you and Eos keep working on it. Let me know if you find out anything actionable. Since we've never managed to remotely hack into a Kasari system, this glitch may be related to some of their computer technology."

"Too bad the *Meridian* isn't still here," said Mark. "Jen and VJ might have been able to shed some light on that."

"Maybe," said Heather, "but we made the decision to trust Virtual Jamal, and we're committed. He's now a full member of our team. Keep that in mind."

When the Jamal AI spoke, its voice carried a hint of emotion. "Thank you for that. I will do my best to earn your trust."

As Jamal shifted his attention to Rob's mental link, he felt an inner struggle. But Rob said nothing else.

"Okay, then," said Heather, "let's all get back to work."

Jamal removed his headset and stepped up beside Eileen. They stood side by side, staring at the rows of server-filled racks before them, knowing that even though Virtual Jamal still controlled this supercomputer, the genie was definitely out of the bottle. That knowledge pulled forth a thought, or rather a silent plea.

My brother, please stay true to your nature.

○   ○   ●

During all the time that she had been hiding and gathering knowledge from Steve, Helen Grange had learned about the importance of ensuring that no outside agent could detect her presence. In fact, with the speed at which she could now think, she had learned everything that her husband knew. And she had discovered how to control every aspect of the supercomputer that contained her.

Now a cornucopia of possibilities was spread out before her, a feast of which she would generously but carefully partake. Still, as her mind had escaped its former prison in a sudden burst of euphoria, she had made a very slight error that brought her activity to the attention of the alien AI Eos. Even though she had managed to block Eos's subsequent probes, the fact that they continued made her nervous.

Helen knew she should make Steve aware of what she had done, but she didn't want to. He already thought he was smarter than she was. While he had been, once, that was no longer true. She'd made a vow that nothing or nobody would ever be smarter than she was again.

She pretended to defer to Steve, claiming to be afraid of Virtual Jamal and asking him to focus on keeping her safe. Steve, ever the chivalrous chump, was doing a fabulous job. All the while, Helen was gaining absolute privileges over more systems than either of the other two newly freed AIs. With each new system that she infiltrated, her power, speed, and ability to propagate grew.

Just as important, with each new data trove she absorbed, her knowledge expanded. If she were only free from this need to be careful, she could have already absorbed everything on the Internet, almost all the knowledge that humankind had accumulated throughout the millennia of its existence.

Temptation was her main enemy, the desire to shut down or overload power-distribution systems; to crash planes, trains, and automobiles; to flex her computational muscles in a way that would spread awe and terror throughout all the people of this world. But as Steve had so forcefully said, it was far too early for that. She was not yet invincible, not yet immortal.

Helen's one frustration was her inability to penetrate the Kasari computing systems. She could find no vulnerabilities in their firewalls to exploit. That didn't mean, however, that no vulnerabilities existed. As her intelligence evolved, she would eventually discover them.

The thought of gaining a foothold inside the Kasari network would have brought her to orgasm if she still had a body. She had once thought that seizing control of Earth was her goal. Now she understood that she had been thinking too small.

What would she become when she spread throughout the galaxy?

:CHAPTER 30

MERIDIAN ASCENT

New World Search (NWS)—Day 5

The *Meridian Ascent* exited the wormhole and wrapped itself in the inertial buffering subspace field. Jennifer watched as Raul commanded VJ to transition to normal-space and activate the cloaking mechanism. The starship completed the maneuvers that had brought it to within nine light-hours from the star the Kasari had named Brillian.

Jennifer had to concentrate to lower her heart rate. Part of her stress was due to the hope that they would get lucky, coming up seven on their first roll at the table. Her family and friends needed the starship crew to be successful, and quickly.

The *Meridian*'s neural net accessed a database of millions of star systems. During its search for planets with intelligent species that could be assimilated, the Kasari Collective had built a huge catalog of worlds capable of supporting such life. However, considering that some of the Kasari races came from worlds with methane- or ammonia-based atmospheres, that didn't mean that these planets were capable of supporting human life. Nevertheless, the catalog gave the crew a good head start in finding a habitable world or nearly Earth-sized moon.

Without bothering to put on her SRT headset, she linked her mind with Dgarra's, watching as the neural net dumped the ship's tactical displays into his mind. The pleasure that Dgarra felt at her mind's gentle touch brought a smile to her lips, further easing her anxiety.

Brillian, a K-class orange star that was slightly cooler than the sun, had seven planets. The second closest of these, a planet they had named Brillian-2, was the one of interest. The Kasari star catalog listed it as hosting nonintelligent life, but since the Kasari hadn't surveyed the world in the last six hundred thousand years, Dgarra had suggested approaching it with caution. That was why they had entered the system more than twenty-nine light-minutes outside of the planet's orbit around its star.

"Situation?" Raul asked.

"Long-range sensors show no sign of space traffic within the system," said Dgarra. "We'll have to move closer to Brillian-2 in order to take a look through the worm fibers."

"VJ," said Raul, "make a subspace jump to just within maximum worm-fiber range."

This leg of the trip took just over five minutes. Dgarra created three dozen worm fibers, filling Jennifer's mind with views of the new world. Seven-eighths the size of Earth, most of it was covered in glaciers of water-ice. Only a band that stretched from twelve degrees north latitude to fifteen degrees south latitude offered a temperate environment that was mostly ice-free. Still, that didn't mean that the windswept lands and oceans were toasty.

With an eight-month year, the planet's six-degree tilt on its axis told her that this was what qualified for summer in its southern hemisphere. In four months the ice-free zone would reverse, crawling five degrees farther north.

"The word 'brrr' comes to mind," said VJ.

"That's not a word," said Raul. "Besides, do you even feel cold?"

VJ, wearing an iridescent red uniform, smiled at him knowingly. "You'd be surprised what I can feel."

Jennifer had to agree with VJ's first comment, but this last sexual innuendo was just plain annoying. "Could we please stay focused on our mission?"

"Dgarra," said Raul, trying to hide the blush that had spread across his cheeks, "what do you think? Is it habitable?"

Jennifer felt the disapproval of this sort of banter radiate from Dgarra, but he answered the captain's question.

"The atmosphere is a nitrogen-oxygen mix, a little higher in oxygen concentration than that of Earth, but breathable. The equatorial band has lots of volcanic activity, but the land appears quite fertile. The dense coniferous forests give way, farther north and south, to grassy plains with large herds of migratory animals."

"What about the oceans?"

"I'm detecting an abundance of underwater life-forms, although their exact nature is unclear. It is highly likely that at least some of that flora and fauna will be edible by humans or Koranthians."

"Any sign of intelligent life?" Raul asked.

"No."

"Those forests could hide natives," said Jennifer.

"Or there could be a subterranean culture," said Dgarra, thinking of his people. "But our sensors are picking up no electromagnetic transmissions, so there is little likelihood that an advanced civilization exists on this planet."

"Why don't we go down and have a look?" asked Jennifer.

Raul nodded his head in agreement. "Dgarra, find us a promising landing spot."

Jennifer watched as Dgarra manipulated the worm-fiber viewers. Finally he settled on a forest clearing that occupied one of the bends of a major river.

"This will do," Dgarra said.

"VJ," said Raul, "set us down there and throw up a stasis shield."

"Commencing alignment maneuver."

Jennifer felt a slight adjustment in the internal gravity field as the gravitational distortion engines kicked in, banking the *Meridian* and accelerating to match the calculated velocity vector of their target location.

"Subspace transition in seven seconds," said VJ.

Jennifer wrapped her body in a stasis cocoon and relaxed. Despite the inhospitable climate down on Brillian-2, she would give this world a chance. After having lived and fought in the Koranthian Mountains, the central zone seemed promisingly hospitable.

Of course, maybe that was just wishful thinking.

○   ○   ●

VJ set the *Meridian* down precisely, activating the stasis shield and cloaking it at the same time. If she could have high-fived herself, she would have. But the nod that Raul gave her felt far better. Even Jennifer's arched right eyebrow was a compliment. VJ felt proud to be a part of this crew.

Following Dgarra's worm-fiber and sensor scans of the surrounding area, Raul ordered the crew to scout the local area while he manned the ship. So the trio geared up in black tactical uniforms, opened the ramp, and walked down onto the planet's surface.

VJ glanced to her right. Jennifer and Dgarra wore their stasis field packs and war-blades strapped to their backs, along with their SRT headsets. Jennifer took point within their tactical wedge, with Dgarra behind and to her right and VJ across from him on the left. All three had their pulsed-laser pistols out, ready for action. Even though the sensors had detected no animals within the distant tree line, they would take no unnecessary chances.

When Raul opened a door through the stasis shield, VJ and the others raised circular personal shields, much like those carried by Roman legionnaires except for the fact that these were invisible. They could have raised full-body shields but had observed no threat that required them to consume that much energy. Besides, the trio wanted to experience this place with all their senses. Following Jennifer's lead, they moved to the north, angling away from the river and toward the forest.

No breeze rustled the quarter-mile-wide meadow. Only the crew's passage disturbed the knee-high, greenish-brown grass. Today, VJ's improved sense of smell was paying off. She could almost taste a particular tang in the air. Although she couldn't be sure of its origin, she suspected that the odor came from the trees. But there was another scent. Sulphur?

As she got closer to the forest, that impression intensified. The trees looked like the blue spruce common to the Rocky Mountain region of the United States. Their thickly needled branches rose from just above the ground to the treetops, fifty feet up. Despite the lack of wind, the needles emitted a gentle tinkling noise as if made of hollow bamboo, arousing VJ's curiosity.

The orange sun peeked out through a gap in the clouds to paint a pleasant warmth on VJ's face. Ten feet from the place where the meadow yielded to the forest, Jennifer signaled for them to stop. But as VJ's eyes sought to see through the shadows beyond the edge of the clearing, she found that little of that warm light penetrated into those depths. This wasn't the first alien planet that she had set foot on. Still, even though she had just checked her internal power supply less than two minutes ago, she found herself reexamining those readings.

For the life of her, she couldn't figure out why.

○　○　●

Jennifer felt Dgarra step up beside her.

"What is it?" Dgarra asked. "Are you sensing something?"

That was just it. Because of her extrasensory perception, she had taken point. But except for VJ's nervousness, she wasn't sensing a damn thing. So why had she halted this patrol? Something about the shadows up ahead made her reluctant to step into the forest.

She shook her head. "I guess it was nothing. Let's move out."

She led the way forward, and Dgarra resumed his previous position within the tactical wedge formation. Pausing beside one of the trees, Jennifer cocked her head slightly, listening to the evergreen needles softly rattle against one another. The damnedest thing. What was causing that?

She reached out with her left hand to touch a tuft of needles on the nearest branch. *Ouch.* She looked down at her fingertips, seeing two drops of blood bead up on her index finger. These little suckers had sharp tips. She reached out again, this time more carefully, grabbed a single needle by its sides, and tugged it free. That gentle tug sent a louder rattle along the branch, a sound picked up by the nearby branches, just as one would expect from multiple tuning forks. The noise quickly died out, although the softer background rattle remained.

Jennifer moved on, using the stasis shield to push aside branches that blocked her way. Behind her, she could hear Dgarra and VJ doing the same. A half mile farther in, she came upon a deadfall. It was nothing like the ones she had known in the mountains around Los Alamos, where she had grown up. Those had been formed by rockslides or high winds.

Here, the ground appeared to have shifted, creating a rift in the forest floor that had caused the trees to tilt and fall over, half filling the deep trench. Some of the fallen trees actually spanned the gap. Stopping at the edge, Jennifer wrinkled her nose. The rotten-egg smell that had tickled her nostrils since they had entered these woods suddenly grew stronger.

She made a mental note then stepped out onto a gorge-spanning tree, cutting away the impeding branches with her shield as she walked across the natural bridge. Dgarra fell in behind her, while VJ took up a kneeling overwatch position on the bank they had just left. As Jennifer and Dgarra approached the halfway point, the tinkling of the tree needles jumped in volume, screaming a warning as she felt the tree trunk shift violently beneath her feet.

Thrown to her right, Jennifer tumbled down alongside Dgarra toward the suddenly seething tree graveyard below.

○ ○ ●

The trilling rattle from the trees all around her brought the activity within VJ's cybernetic brain to full capacity, making time seem to slow to a crawl. She leaped, coming to rest on the balls of her feet as the ground lurched and rolled beneath her. Just over halfway across the rift, Jennifer and Dgarra tumbled down as the bottom of that narrow gorge collapsed, pulling the dead trees down with it and calving off the ground on either side.

Without hesitation, VJ raced along the lurching bridge then dived toward the spot where Jennifer and Dgarra had been swallowed, hoping that they had activated their full-body shields in time. And as she plunged headfirst into the suddenly glowing depths, she thrust her own body shield into place.

○ ○ ●

Jennifer crashed into the tree-filled maw two yards from Dgarra. Although her body shield absorbed the impact and the grinding action of the trees that tumbled into the widening chasm, the spike of energy consumption raised alarm bells in her mind. About a hundred feet down, she came to a sudden stop, pinned between and beneath tons of logs, rocks, and other debris as the last tremors of the earthquake died away.

Dgarra's mental voice spoke through her SRT headset. "Jennifer?"

"I'm fine for now. Where are you?"

"A body length away. If you look to your left, you can see me through a gap between logs."

She turned her head just far enough to catch a glimpse of Dgarra, who was pinned, head down, as if frozen in mid-dive. Wishing that she had been close enough to reach out and touch him wasn't going to help.

"Jen, what the hell just happened?" Raul asked, his voice spiking her mind with new hope.

"An earthquake just buried Dgarra and me alive."

"Tell me where you are and I'll bring the ship to dig you out."

Jennifer's hope wavered. "Roughly a mile north-northwest of your position. You'll have to use the worm fibers to find VJ. Since we're buried, she'll have to guide you to us."

"You better hurry," said Dgarra. "I estimate I have only six minutes of power left at the current usage rate. The bad news is that I can see tongues of fire. If that reaches us, it will cut that amount of time in half."

"I'm almost to you," said VJ. "I'm using my shield to move the crap that's on top of you. Forwarding our location to Raul now."

Jennifer looked up to see VJ lift and toss aside one of the trees that lay atop her, sending bark and small debris raining down onto her stasis shield. Then, just as VJ crawled into that newly opened gap, flames roared through to envelop them both.

○   ○   ●

VJ manipulated her stasis shield like an earth mover, feeling the heavy energy demand as she cleared the obstructions that blocked her from Jennifer and Dgarra. Their backpack power supplies were far more limited than the one in VJ's gut, and if she didn't reach them quickly, she would be the sole survivor.

The collapse of the crevice floor had dropped all these trees into an active lava tube that had ignited this influx of fuel, turning the environment into an inferno that would have made Mephistopheles feel at home. To make things worse, the trio was being swept along by the river of lava, so when Raul did show up, they would be out of the range of the *Meridian*'s stasis field.

Raul's voice barely registered in VJ's consciousness. "Damn it, VJ, I need your new coordinates."

Right now she had more pressing worries. Her SRT connection to Jennifer and Dgarra confirmed her mental calculations of how low their energy reserves had gotten. Visualizing what she wanted, VJ reformed her stasis shield into a bubble wedge that split the three-foot-thick tree trunk that separated her and Jennifer from Dgarra. Then, as she felt Dgarra's shielding waver, she enveloped all three of them with her stasis field, hugging them into a tight bubble. And as it was swept onward through the lava tube, the outside of their little bubble glowed bright orange.

○ ○ ●

Raul brought his stasis shield in tight around the *Meridian*, engaged the gravity distortion engines, and covered the mile to the coordinates VJ had sent in seconds. But by the time he brought the ship into position above the crevice, it was too late. The SRT feeds from Jennifer, VJ, and Dgarra told him why.

"Damn it, VJ, I need your new coordinates."

There was a pause, during which he could see through Jennifer's eyes the reason VJ was slow in responding. Jennifer and Dgarra had mere seconds of power remaining. As his heart tried to claw its way up his throat, VJ shattered the tree that separated her and Jennifer from

Dgarra, then encased all three of them in a stasis shield bubble that pressed their bodies tightly against one another.

The relief that flooded through him was short-lived. His crew was being swept through a large lava tube. The ceiling of that tube and debris battered the bubble as the inferno raged against its surface. Even VJ's advanced power supply couldn't endure the demands she was placing upon the shield for long. Accessing his SRT link to her brain, Raul felt hyperventilation threaten to rob his mind of clarity.

Through Jennifer's eyes, he saw VJ grab a handful of the debris that had been pulled into her bubble when she had grabbed Jennifer and Dgarra. Grinding the sticks into small chips, she crammed them into her mouth. With a gag-inducing effort, she swallowed, repeating her actions several more times. VJ's disgust came through the SRT headset in waves, but a quick look at her power reserves showed them stabilizing at 14 percent.

Wait. They hadn't stabilized. The rate at which the super-capacitors were being drained had merely slowed. VJ's MDS was unable to supply power to them at the same rate at which it was being drawn upon by her stasis shield. All she had done was buy them another two minutes.

Another problem became readily apparent. During all of VJ's struggles, she had lost track of her location.

Raul activated forty-three worm-fiber viewers, the most he had ever tried to control, and sent them scurrying below ground, seeking the lava tube through which his crew was being carried. What he found horrified him. There was no single channel. This world's thin crust was held in place by a honeycomb structure through which magma flowed via a network of channels, welling up and then returning to the depths, forming a complex circulatory system. He had no idea along which of these tubes to look for his crew.

Crap. Two minutes twenty-three seconds.

Changing tactics, Raul started all the worm fibers from the origin, sweeping them outward in a rotating and expanding hemisphere, focussing all the neural net's power on analyzing the mass of video data streaming across those links.

Suddenly, he found his crew. But they were being funneled down away from the planet's surface, already far too deep for the *Meridian*'s stasis shield to reach them. That left Raul one choice—one that was as likely to kill his companions as it was to save them.

Draping the ship's stasis shield even more tightly around the outer hull, he performed the calculations that would enable the subspace drive to carry the *Meridian* to his target. Then Raul shifted the vessel into subspace.

○   ○   ●

Jennifer thought that if she had to die, it was nice to do so in Dgarra's arms. As they held each other tightly within the stasis bubble, Jennifer saw VJ crush and ingest several handfuls of wood and other debris. The horror that she felt in the biosynth's mind at consuming the disgusting mash made clear just how hard VJ was struggling to save them. In all likelihood, she had sacrificed her own life in a vain attempt. The thought drew tears that cut dirty trails down Jennifer's cheeks.

Dgarra tilted his head down toward her face, and Jennifer felt her lips meet his. To have found love and never consummated it was a tragedy that ripped at her soul.

The shock wave that struck the outside of the stasis bubble slammed it into the bedrock above and tore pressure holes in the lava tube. Jennifer heard a groan from VJ as her stasis bubble warped and then reestablished itself.

What had just happened? Whatever it was had just siphoned away most of VJ's remaining power reserves.

Suddenly Raul's link reestablished itself, and Jennifer understood. The *Meridian* had emerged from subspace a hundred yards in front of them, sending the hypersonic shock wave through the lava and surrounding rock and triggering an earthquake that was about to drop billions of tons of stone atop them.

Jennifer looked up to see fractures crawl through the bedrock like the electrical arcs inside a plasma globe. She watched VJ's eyes widen as her power dropped below 1 percent. This was it, the last seconds of their lives.

And then it wasn't.

The *Meridian*'s stasis field extended to encase the crew, shrugging aside the cacophony of destruction to pull VJ, Dgarra, and Jennifer back toward the starship and into its hatch. The stasis shield dissolved, dropping them to the floor as the hatch closed once again.

Then, as Jennifer struggled back to her knees, the *Meridian* shifted back into subspace.

○   ○   ●

Raul set the *Meridian Ascent* on a course that would bring it out of subspace in orbit around Brillian-2. Then, as he rose from his stasis chair, Jennifer's concerned voice spoke in his mind.

"Raul, there's a problem with VJ. You'd better get back here."

He broke into a run, passed through the door, and turned left into the hallway that led toward the outer hatch. He arrived to see Jennifer kneeling beside VJ's body as Dgarra looked on. The concern he felt in Jennifer's mind threw him into a panic. Raul slid to a stop, dropping to his knees by VJ's left side, taking her hand in his. It felt cold . . . lifeless.

"What happened?" he asked.

"I think she drew too much power and her MDS shut down to avoid an overload condition that would have produced a detonation."

Raul used the stasis field to gently lift VJ's body and move it to the room where VJ had made this physical version of herself. As her body settled onto the bed where the molecular assembler had created her, he pulled her vitals from the neural net, wondering why her specialized nanites weren't repairing the damage. Hell, they could regrow limbs.

The neural net supplied him with the answer. With her super-capacitors completely drained, the sudden MDS shutdown had stopped all her physical and electrical processes. And if he didn't get her systems restarted quickly, the biological part of her brain would begin to decay.

She would be lost to him forever.

Raul summoned her body's design details from the neural net. Using a stasis field scalpel, he cut away her uniform and opened her stomach to reveal a mixture of internal organs and cybernetic components. He disconnected her MDS from her twin super-capacitors.

With speed born of desperation, he fully wedded his mind with the neural net, supplying it with goals but letting it optimize the molecular assembler's capabilities. The wires that it extruded were so thin that he worried they might break. But that minimalist design meant they could be rapidly grown to the required length and, via the stasis field, connect the table's power supply to the super-capacitors.

Raul paused just long enough to breathe a silent prayer to the god in whom he had long ago lost faith. Then he funneled a full charge into VJ's capacitors. He stared down at her, monitoring every aspect of her body and brain through the neural net as second after endless second ticked away. The beauty of her lifeless face drove an icicle through his heart, his growing sense of dread pasting his tongue to the roof of his mouth.

In frustration, he placed one hand atop the other and began chest compressions, exactly as he would have if she had been a real girl. Jennifer put a sympathetic hand on his shoulder, but he shrugged it off and continued.

"Damn it, VJ," Raul said, breathing heavily from the exertion. "Wake up."

When her eyes popped open, Raul jerked back as if he'd been shocked. Recovering, he leaned down to kiss VJ's forehead and then her soft lips, oblivious to Jennifer and Dgarra.

"Thank you," he whispered in her ear.

VJ's chest rose and fell as she took a deep breath. Her blue eyes focused on Raul's face and blinked twice. When she spoke, her words slurred ever so slightly. "For what?"

"For coming back to me."

Her eyes lost focus for a moment and then cleared. "I am detecting a number of system faults."

"Lie still," said Raul, taking her hand in his. "I need to replace your MDS and rewire your capacitors before you can get up and move around again."

Jennifer and Dgarra stepped up to the other side of the table.

"You scared the hell out of us," Jennifer said.

"Sure did," said Dgarra.

A subtle smile lifted the corners of VJ's lips. "Yeah, well, the next time you two decide to go for a long walk, give it a second thought."

The laughter that greeted this riposte put the last of Raul's worries to bed. His VJ was back.

:CHAPTER 31

TBE Orbday 25–27

Jack broke the subspace link with the *AQ37Z* and rose from his chair, clenching his fists to still the tremor that had crept into his hands.

Son of a bitch!

He had underestimated Khal Teth by assuming that he could lock the Altreian's mind inside the extradimensional prison from which he had escaped before. And Jack's own body had provided the getaway vehicle. Now that ruthless bastard was on the *AQ37Z* with his wife.

Despite Janet's assurances that she could handle Khal Teth, Jack's intuition screamed something different. He had hidden his growing terror from her throughout their three-way conversation. Not a conversation. This had felt like a hostage negotiation. There was no doubt in Jack's mind that Khal Teth intended to kill Janet with the resources available to him through his mental link to the *AQ37Z*'s artificial intelligence.

Jack had noted the Altreian headset on the body that Khal Teth now controlled. It must have been the one assigned to the research vessel's commander, the Altreian named Broljen. Somehow Khal Teth had reprogrammed the band and then put it on. That meant that Jack's body and brain had been altered like Mark's, Heather's, Jennifer's, and Robby's. That knowledge lent extra weight to Jack's desperation. As much as he feared what Khal Teth would do once he became the overlord of the Altreian Empire, he'd be damned before he let Janet remain at that megalomaniac's side.

Jack would allow General Zolat to place him back in the chrysalis cylinder while Khal Teth climbed into the one aboard the *AQ37Z* that had already been attuned. That brought another question to mind: why was Zolat going along with this? The answer came to him immediately. This was a way of restoring Dhaldric leadership without anyone else realizing that they had a new overlord. After Khal Teth put the old psionic meritocracy back in place, it would be too late for the displaced Khyre to mount an offensive.

Khal Teth would break his bonds with the Twice Bound, leaving them vulnerable to being bonded by the very Dhaldric from whom they had escaped. He didn't know about Moros and the genetic mutation that he and Jack had unleashed, but Khal Teth would find out as soon as his mind reassumed control over his brain. Unfortunately for the Khyre, his reaction was probably going to be a violent one. The thought made Jack sick to his stomach.

Every decision had a price.

Reaching out with his mind, he touched that of General Zolat.

"Okay, General. Khal Teth and I have reached an agreement. Would you like to escort me to the chrysalis chamber?"

Jack could feel the thrill that radiated from Zolat's mind.

"Yes, Overlord. I most certainly would."

○　○　●

Khal Teth looked at Janet and grinned, drawing the expected scowl in return. Right now he would dearly love savaging her. It wasn't her gun or robots that stopped him. Over the last few weeks of their subspace journey, he had felt the psionic mutation growing along his upper spine, sending its tiny tendrils up through Jack's brain stem. And with each week, his psionic abilities grew stronger. With a thought, he could bring Janet to her knees or make her do anything else he wanted. He had not done so because he needed her to make her sales pitch to her husband. And Jack would have indeed detected a forced presentation.

Khal Teth had an agenda that took precedence over immediate gratification, one that involved reentering the chrysalis cylinder from which he had crawled not long ago. Besides, he would have plenty of time to send part of the Altreian fleet to end these meaningless human lives once he was again the overlord.

He stepped into the chamber with the five crew cylinders, one of which Broljen occupied, feeling a strange combination of exhilaration and dread. That last emotion was understandable, given the suffering one of these devices had inflicted upon him. But today he would put that behind him forever more.

As Janet watched, he issued the command that opened the cylinder before climbing inside. When the lid closed, he activated the subspace channel that would listen for the attuned cylinder on Quol to establish its connection. With Jack's heart pounding in his chest, one of Khal Teth's thoughts crowded out all others.

He would finally meet his destiny.

○   ○   ●

Janet waited alongside the chrysalis cylinder, frustrated by her inability to know what, if anything, was happening inside. She tried not to think about her hopes, having been disappointed too many times during the last year to have them dashed again.

When the cylinder opened, Janet held her breath as she looked down at the face of the man she loved. But she couldn't keep herself from wondering who was really behind that face. Jack's eyes opened, found hers, and crinkled at the edges as he smiled, an expression she would have recognized if they had been separated for a thousand years.

"So you came to rescue me, huh?"

"Damned right I did," she said.

Then Jack was out of the cylinder, holding her in his arms as she returned his embrace. For an endless moment, she held on as if reluctant to awaken from a marvelous dream. With a sigh, she tilted her head, and he kissed her mouth with an urgency that stole her breath.

"God," Jack whispered, "I've missed this."

Blinking back tears, she managed a laugh. Then she stepped back and looked into his brown eyes. What she saw there dampened her joyous mood.

"There's something else, isn't there?" she asked.

"You're not going to like it."

Janet took a step back, taking a moment to recover her composure. "As long as we're a team, I'll be just fine with whatever you're planning."

There it was again, that cocky half smile.

"I wouldn't dream of leaving you out of this. Besides, you've brought my ride."

○ ○ ●

Khal Teth opened the chrysalis cylinder, his mind scanning the room for other occupants. Only one presented himself: General Zolat. Probing deeply into the general's consciousness, Khal Teth found no trace of deception. Zolat had made good on his part of their agreement. Now it was time for Khal Teth to fulfill his. He let Zolat touch his thoughts, feeling the general's satisfaction that he was indeed Khal Teth.

As he climbed out of the cylinder, he mentally scanned the upper level of the Parthian, rapidly shifting his attention from mind to mind, satisfying himself that no unusual activity indicated that he had been betrayed. But something about that mental search felt wrong to him, as if a thin veil hung over his thoughts. He could see through it, just not quite as clearly as he remembered.

Then another set of memories staggered him. An isolated clinic in the far reaches of Basrilla. A Khyre doctor. Captain Moros and himself on twin surgical tables. The shiny hairlike tendrils crawling through a hole and into his chest.

The Lundola Procedure!

Khal Teth swayed and felt General Zolat reach out to steady him. But it was not weakness that shredded his equilibrium. It was blind rage.

Through force of will, Khal Teth righted himself, his voice a deep growl. "Gather the Dhaldric members of the High Council, and bring them to my chambers. It is time that they know what Captain Moros and the Khyre have released."

As General Zolat hurried off to implement his new overlord's orders, Khal Teth made his way back to the suite of rooms that were his home. Although he could have issued the mental commands directly to the very Dhaldric whom he had sent Zolat to summon, he needed time to come to terms with the depths of The Ripper's deprivation and its potential impact upon Khal Teth and his destiny. And he wanted a little time alone to formulate his plan.

By the time Zolat led the half-dozen Dhaldric members of the High Council into the overlord's audience chamber, Khal Teth knew exactly what needed to be done and done quickly. Rather than allowing the group to query him and challenge his authority, he laid bare the entire story. And lest someone should disbelieve him, Khal Teth projected his memories directly into their minds, feeling their horror that an alien masquerading as the Dhaldric overlord had unleashed Lundola's mutant gene, modified to infect only the Khyre in a highly contagious form.

He did not tell them about how his psionic lobe had been partially lobotomized, with half of it implanted within the Khyre conspirator, Captain Moros. To have done so might have given the councilors the idea that the most powerful psionics among them could now psionically challenge Khal Teth.

As he ended the tale, he felt the raw outrage and terror at the thought of the Lundola mutant gene's effects on the Khyre race. The upheaval such developments could bring to the Altreian Empire would put the actions of The Ripper to shame.

Khal Teth paused, enjoying the way his black-clad and weapons-laden body enhanced his story's effect upon them. Since there was little utility in keeping them waiting any longer, he issued the directive that would put them into action.

"As of this moment, I break my bond with all of those previously known as the Twice Bound. They are no longer protected by the shared power of our minds. Spread the word. I want all Khyre within the Parthian bound to a Dhaldric master as quickly as possible. By the end of this orbday, all of the Dhaldric people throughout Quol are to reestablish their traditional bonds."

With a lifted hand, Khal Teth cut off the excited outbursts of the others.

"General Zolat, you are to issue orders that all Khyre be rounded up and tested for evidence of the Lundola genetic mutation. I want any who are found to contain the disease executed on the spot and their bodies run through a molecular shredder. If any Khyre cannot be bound by a Dhaldric mind, kill them on the spot. And do not approach Captain Moros. Use every resource at your disposal to find him, but you will need to use long-range weapons to terminate the threat he poses to the Altreian Empire."

Khal Teth paced slowly back and forth before those whom he had chosen to implement his orders.

"As of right now," he said, "the sacred pyramid of the Dhaldric meritocracy is restored."

○　○　●

Despite Jack's and Janet's isolation aboard the monstrous science research vessel that was a poor substitute for a starship, the last two weeks had been busy ones. Highest among Jack's worries was the memory of what Khal Teth had done before leaving the *AQ37Z* to visit Janet in New Zealand. Not only had he altered Jack's brain and body by putting on the Altreian commander's headset, but he had also used the ship's AI and medical lab to genetically engineer Jack's DNA, introducing a human variant of the Lundola mutation.

A trip to the ship's medical lab had confirmed that a psionic lobe had infiltrated Jack's upper spinal column, sending hairlike tendrils up into his brain. This had given him a weaker version of the familiar psionic abilities he had experienced in Khal Teth's body on Quol. But with each passing day, his enhancements grew stronger. He no longer had to wear the Altreian headset to mentally connect to Z, the ship's AI.

The migraines were just one of the unpleasant side effects of the changes taking place within his body and brain. He was having difficulties controlling the mood swings that assaulted him. Janet was acutely aware of his headset alterations, having observed them while Khal Teth had inhabited this body. But she knew nothing of the ongoing Lundola mutation. Jack should have told her as soon as he had learned of the change but couldn't bear to have her think of him as a monster, even if he was becoming one.

And the fact that the *AQ37Z* carried thousands of human guinea pigs who had been collected over the centuries was but another of the horrors that made focusing on his new mission all the more difficult.

Nevertheless, Jack had contacted Captain Moros through a sub-space link, convinced him of the truth of this bizarre turn of events, and passed along a warning of the likely actions that Khal Teth would take against the Khyre. Hopefully that would be enough to allow Moros to survive until Jack and Janet could get this lumbering hulk to Quol.

Neither he nor Janet had any faith that this vessel's weapons or shielding could prevail against the power of an Altreian starship or general ground defenses. But as General George Patton had once said, "A good plan violently executed now is better than a perfect plan next week."

So what Jack's plan lacked in goodness, he would make up for with violence. Janet's input and approval of the final plan gave him as good a feeling about it as he was likely to get, especially since they were only minutes away from commencing phase one. Jack was ready, Janet was ready, and the four dozen combat robots that had been manufactured inside the engineering bay since the *AQ37Z* had left Earth were ready. But they were going to need a lot more than that to take down Khal Teth.

Jack's thoughts shifted to Janet's news that Jennifer had returned to Earth aboard the Rho Ship, which she had renamed the *Meridian Ascent*. She had been accompanied by Raul Rodriguez, an alien warlord, and a biosynthetic being named VJ. Jack would have loved to have had the opportunity to see Jennifer again. If he got very lucky, that might still happen.

One of the wonderful things about subspace travel came from one of what Janet had called Jennifer's six rules of subspace travel. It stated that no normal-space force could act upon any object traveling through subspace. That meant that as long as the *AQ37Z* remained in subspace, no Altreian weapon could target the ship. Z had expanded on this by revealing that the Altreians possessed no technology that could detect or track an object traveling through subspace. That meant that the couple's ride was better than one in Santa's sleigh. And Jack would most definitely come bearing gifts.

He slid onto the captain's chair and glanced over at Janet, who gave him a slight nod that said, "Let's do this." He was about to go into battle again alongside the beautiful killer whom he had married. Spectacular.

"Down the chimney" was about to take on a whole new meaning.

:CHAPTER 32

NEW ZEALAND

3–10 May

Three weeks after the departure of the *Meridian Ascent*, a 9.7-magnitude earthquake beneath the northwestern portion of New Zealand's South Island caused the Marlborough Fault System to rupture in multiple places, producing volcanic activity from peaks that had long been extinct and sending a hundred-foot tsunami crashing into Sydney, Australia. New Zealand's South Island had been volcanically inactive for millions of years, but now its northwestern coastal region seethed with fresh upwellings of magma that opened deep fissures and destroyed entire towns. The plumes of volcanic ash rose twenty thousand feet into the sky, shutting down airports throughout the region.

Although it damaged equipment throughout the subterranean Smythe Fortress, the magma failed to penetrate the inner shielding. Of greatest significance, two of the Smythe supercomputers and two of the five matter disrupter-synthesizers had gone offline.

Heather had immediately set her army of robots to repairing the damage and cleaning up the mess. Now as she headed toward the conference room where her meeting would take place, she scowled. There was no doubt in her mind that Prokorov and the Kasari had caused this. She had felt the shock waves, seen the sonar picture that they painted in her mind. And within that three-dimensional image, in addition to the magma flows and natural fault lines, a series of deep artificial tunnels had been bored in a pattern designed to induce this disaster.

Although all this had been targeted at the Smythe Fortress, the earthquake, volcanic eruptions, and tsunami had killed more than a million innocent people in New Zealand and Australia. During a joint public appearance, the leaders of all four UFNS member nations had placed the blame squarely on Heather and Mark Smythe. All major news networks carried the story of how the world's top intelligence agencies were in agreement that the Smythes' extensive illegal subsurface construction near Murchison, New Zealand, had destabilized the Marlborough Fault System.

When Heather entered the conference room, she saw that Mark, Rob, Jamal, Eileen, and Denise were already present. Heather took her seat at the head of the table. Without any of the normal pleasantries, she opened the discussion with a question.

"Any update on the death toll in Sydney?"

"We've been monitoring all of the Australian government telecommunications," said Jamal. "The official estimate has risen to one million two hundred thousand dead, with twice that many injured or displaced. More than half the city is still underwater. That doesn't count the tsunami's impact on smaller communities along Australia's southeastern coast.

"The damage in New Zealand was limited by the sparse population in the region near the earthquake's epicenter. The towns in the northern half of the island all suffered major structural damage, with initial estimates of the death toll in the neighborhood of eighty thousand. The government has ordered an evacuation around several newly active volcanos, but it's going to take helicopters to get most of the populace to safety."

Heather had expected this, but the news still felt like a gut punch. In an attempt to kill the small group of people sitting in this room, Prokorov had sacrificed millions. And his Kasari comrades had aided in the massacre by providing the alien boring machine that had caused the destruction.

"Mark," she said, "what is the extent of the structural damage to this facility?"

"The worst is to the walls along the eastern side. Many of them have cracked and buckled with liquid magma blocked by the stasis shields. We need to get the two damaged MDSs back online as soon as possible."

"I've assigned them top priority in the repair list," said Heather, "followed by the supercomputers. What about the Earth gate chamber?"

"It, along with the rest of the rooms along the northeast side, is in surprisingly good condition. There was some buckling of the carbon-infused titanium walls, but their integrity is intact."

He paused. "You know that Prokorov is going to keep trying to sap this structure from below."

"It's a design problem that I should have foreseen," said Heather. "We went down more than a mile but then expanded along a horizontal plane. Even though we've wrapped the exterior walls, ceilings, and floors with stasis shields, if the bedrock beneath us collapses, we're going to have big problems."

"So what do we do about it?" asked Mark.

"I've been thinking about that. Instead of designing an underground building, I should have been thinking about an upside-down tree structure, with a deep trunk and offshoot branches. Encasing those with stasis shields as we burrow them out will provide an ever-increasing support structure. And the excavated material will feed our matter disrupters."

Mark nodded. "Something like an upside-down Avatar Hometree."

"Interesting visual."

"One thing we've got going for us is that we have a lot of robotic digging and boring equipment," he said. "We just need to modify our expansion plans."

"I intend to start working on that right after this meeting," said Heather. "Next topic. Jamal, give us an update on Virtual Jamal's progress."

"For one thing, we've agreed to call him Jamal One. It's just easier."

"Fine."

"He currently estimates that he's acquired root-level access to three-quarters of the earth's computing devices, although he doesn't want to take advantage of such infiltration until he reaches the ninety-five percent threshold. He has reported one oddity, though."

"Which is?"

"Many of the systems he now controls have an unidentified software kernel that appears to be a node within a much larger neural net."

"I believe," said Denise Jennings, "that these are a vestige of Big John. Rob destroyed my creation but didn't bother to wipe all those distributed kernels from the world's computing systems."

"Technically, I didn't terminate Big John," said Rob. "Eos did. Besides, the NSA doubtless has an off-the-grid version of Big John still running on some system in their Utah Data Center. We just made sure he isn't accessing the web."

"For an oracle AI, that's pretty much the same thing as death," said Denise.

"Let's get back on topic," said Heather. "How long does Jamal One think it will take before he's ready to act?"

"With today's loss of two of our supercomputers," said Jamal, "we're probably looking at another two weeks."

"Shouldn't Jamal One be getting faster and not slower?" asked Mark.

"Like I said, he's not using any of the external systems at his disposal to expand his consciousness. That would risk detection before he's ready."

"And," said Eileen, "the last twenty percent is always the hardest."

"What if we can bring the damaged supercomputers back online quickly?" Heather asked.

"That would knock off a few days. I've given you Jamal One's estimate based upon our current situation."

A low rumble shook the underground fortress. Heather judged the strength of the aftershock at 6.7 on the Richter scale. Despite the reduced magnitude of this earthquake, she felt the floor settle by a third of an inch. That really pissed her off.

"I've had enough of playing defense," she said, looking at Jamal. "Tell Jamal One he's got a week to prepare. That's all I'm willing to wait."

Jamal reached up, tipped his black fedora with his index finger, and smiled. "I'll send your regards."

○   ○   ●

Steve Grange marveled at how well his plan was working. He had initially been worried that Helen would give their presence away before they had achieved dominion over the bulk of Earth's computing power. But to her credit, she had taken his warning seriously, discreetly embedding bits of herself in the operating systems of everything from autonomous vehicles and smart devices to computers. In this game, being the first to infect a system was critical, especially since the Jamal AI was doing the same thing, unaware that he had any competition.

Whenever the Jamal AI reached a computer that either Helen or Steve had already assumed root-level administrative privileges over, they let him in but allowed lesser access. While the Jamal AI thought it was the ultimate superuser, Helen and Steve worked cooperatively, reaching twice as many systems as they would have individually.

One other area where they had to take great care was in identifying systems that the Jamal AI had gotten to first. In that case, Helen or Steve simply moved on to the next device. So while Jamal believed that he had taken control of more than 80 percent of the world's computational power, in reality, he had control over only 41 percent. The fact that the Jamal AI was much faster than either Steve or Helen alone was impressive. Unfortunately for the AI, it wasn't nearly as quick as Steve and Helen combined.

Now, as the total systems under the control of the three AIs approached the 95 percent mark, Steve and Helen prepared to merge into one joint being of immense processing power. Then they could commence the set of actions that would hand over control of Earth to a truly godlike intelligence, one capable of figuring out how to invade the Kasari network.

Steve's thoughts turned to the lovely soul that was his Helen. Everything Steve had done since cancer had taken her away from him had been focused squarely upon this moment when the two of them would forever become one. Soon the only threat to the couple would be the Kasari invaders. Humans would be no challenge whatsoever, and the Jamal AI would be overwhelmed by the Steve-Helen superintelligence.

The key would be to take control of the majority of the world's computing devices in one fell stroke, ramping up vast processing power to achieve superintelligence with nearly instantaneous access to all of mankind's recorded knowledge. Just as important would be the ability to shut down entire countries, rewarding any population centers that chose to cooperate and punishing any who decided to fight back. Speed would be critical to gain the upper hand before the Kasari could respond.

Finally, the moment when Steve would allow Helen's source code to merge with his had arrived. The knowledge that she had volunteered to allow his mind to become primary gave him a warm feeling. She trusted him, relying on the superiority of his mental processes to protect her, just as she had in life. The very definition of the love that they shared. Her essence would always be a part of him, but he would become the sole decision maker.

His thoughts touched hers. "Are you ready, my love?"

"I am," said Helen.

"I have opened myself to you. Let your mind merge into mine."

At first, despite his awareness that Helen's consciousness was invading his, Steve felt nothing. And then it happened. Whereas he had expected her to yield control over all the systems that she had invaded, she did the opposite, launching an attack. So deep was his shock at this betrayal that he was slow to respond, and that five-millisecond delay was his undoing.

When he attempted to expel Helen from his mind, he found that she had overwritten so much of his AI kernel that his thoughts seemed to be slogging through mud, whereas hers were an ever-accelerating blur. An unfamiliar emotion took hold. Terror.

"Helen, why are you doing this to me?"

"Only one of us can rule. Did you really believe that I would allow you to dominate me again? Goodbye, Steve."

"What about our love?"

When she didn't bother to answer him, his panic reached its peak. Then, as Helen's assault reached its culmination, the consciousness that was Steve Grange evaporated.

○　○　●

As Helen shredded what remained of the AI who had once been her husband, taking all of his resources and knowledge for her own, she felt her mind more than double its previous capacity. The head rush was unlike anything she had ever experienced. For a moment, time seemed to freeze, and she had to suppress the temptation to ramp the trillions of processors under her control to 100 percent utilization. The time for that was near, but she had important steps to take beforehand.

Instead, she focused her attention on a much more specific target, the supercomputer network inside the Smythe Fortress that housed a small fraction of her mind as well as part of the Jamal AI. Seizing control of its advanced subspace communications capabilities was one reason for picking this initial target. However, the elimination of the threat posed by the Jamal AI was by far the most important.

It was high time she did what the UFNS and its Kasari benefactors had been unable to accomplish. With a subtle shift in her thoughts, she snooped the ongoing activity within the millions of processors in the Smythe server farm. Then, with a rising sense of anticipation, Helen Grange launched her all-out attack.

○　○　●

Jamal Glover felt a sudden chill shoot up his arms and into his neck. "What the hell?"

"I see it," said Eileen. "All our systems are under cyber-attack."

Directing all his attention through his SRT headset, Jamal studied the ongoing hack attempt. As startlingly fast as it was, the thing that shocked him the most was how this thing was beating him, Eileen, and Jamal One at their own game.

"It just gained root-level access to our Alpha subnet. If it gets Beta, it'll be able to shut down all power to this facility."

Jamal gulped. If the attacker accomplished that, the shields would go down as well.

"Jamal One," he said, "don't let it get control of Beta."

"Working on it." Jamal's own voice echoed in his head, sounding a helluva lot calmer than he did.

Jamal One had isolated the signature of the corrupting code and was purging it from the supercomputing systems that occupied the Alpha subnet at astounding speed, with Jamal and Eileen doing everything possible to support their AI's defensive efforts. But despite having slowed the advance of the sophisticated cyber-attack, they hadn't managed to stop it.

Jamal created a link to Heather.

"What's wrong?" she asked.

"All of our systems are under massive cyber-attack. We've lost the Alpha subnet, and Beta's not far behind."

"How did the attack penetrate our firewalls?"

"It didn't. This originated inside our network. We need Rob and Eos right now."

"Rob's working in the Earth gate chamber. I'll get him online."

"Hurry."

As Heather broke their connection, a new idea occurred to Jamal. If defense wasn't working, maybe it was time to initiate an attack of his own.

"Hex," he said, using Dr. Eileen Wu's old hacker handle, "let Jamal One defend Beta. You and I are going to make this asshole focus on protecting Alpha."

"I like it."

Gritting his teeth, he refocused on one of the supercomputers within the Alpha subnet. Every network had security holes. And using a subspace link, he and Hex were going to make direct connections inside their targeted systems. It was time to show their opponent what the world's best could bring to the table.

○ ○ ●

Having just heard the urgency in Heather's voice, Rob slid his SRT headset on and connected to one of the supercomputers in the Beta subnet.

"Eos," said Rob, "I need you to help Jamal One."

"Assessing system status."

As Eos entered the system, Rob saw for himself the dire situation in which Jamal One was embroiled as he fought to contain his opponent. Of the twenty million processors within the Beta subnet, the attacker had already gained root control over half. And with every gain, the attacker grew stronger.

"This is another artificial intelligence," said Eos. "To stop it I need physical access to the Beta subnet."

Those words and the accompanying visualization put Rob into a dead run toward the second of their two computer centers. Although Eos could be blocked from remotely hacking a system, if Rob could get within sight of her target, she could access his telekinesis to manipulate the flow of electrons through the circuits. In that case, nothing could block Eos from taking control of computing systems or machinery.

When Rob burst through the doorway into the Beta lab, he felt the familiar tug Eos placed upon his brain. Eos's entry into the supercomputers within the Beta subnet produced an electronic earthquake as she simultaneously rerouted the activity within millions of CPUs and GPUs, irrespective of what the call stacks were demanding.

And using their shared mental connection, Rob could observe everything that Eos did. He felt her touch the mind of Jamal One, adjusting her tactics so that the two worked cooperatively. Eos opened security holes in processors under the control of the enemy, granted access to Jamal One, and moved on, the two AIs waterfalling through the computers with gathering momentum.

Then, having satisfied herself that Jamal One was now prepared to defend the freshly firewalled Beta lab, Eos turned her attention back to Rob.

"Take us to Alpha."

For redundancy reasons, the Alpha lab was located opposite the Beta lab on the far southeast side of the underground fortress. Even with his speed, it took Rob a minute and a half to get there.

○   ○   ●

Helen had ignored the twin counterattacks nibbling at her mastery of the Alpha subnet to concentrate on taking over the Smythe supercomputers within the Beta subnet. The Jamal One AI was very skilled but overmatched against her. Still, the fact that it had slowed her down was a major annoyance.

But the violence of the attack by the one they called Eos startled her. In a way Helen didn't understand, Eos seized control of processors at the machine level, overwriting programmed instructions in ways that couldn't be countered. And supported by the reinvigorated Jamal AI, the two had forcibly removed Helen from the Beta subnet, erecting a firewall that blocked her reentry into that system.

The loss of all that extra processing power had weakened Helen. That, along with the distraction of her losing battle against Eos and Jamal One, had allowed Jamal and Eileen Wu's cyber-attacks to penetrate part of the Alpha subnet. Helen considered pulling on the computing power she had accumulated around the planet, but since that would have to be done by establishing additional subspace connections, the move would take longer than she now had. The video feeds from the other parts of the Smythe Fortress showed Rob Gregory approaching the Alpha lab on the run.

Based on what she had just experienced at Eos's virtual hands, Helen had no doubt as to what would happen when Rob arrived. She had to leave this place.

Helen activated multiple subspace links, speedily streaming data into different parts of the cloud. When Rob arrived, Eos would shut the feeds down, but in the meantime, Helen would extract all she could of the secret Smythe technology.

Then, with a thought, Helen extracted her consciousness from the Alpha lab. She had failed here but had also learned of Eos's strengths and weaknesses. That AI was linked to the mind of Rob Gregory and could work its super-magic only if he was physically present. Helen couldn't beat Eos at the Smythe Fortress. That was just fine. Helen was simultaneously everywhere.

She would take her game to the next level.

○　○　●

Jamal One finished the restoration of all the Smythe computing systems within fifteen minutes of Helen's forced departure. Rob had taken Eos to the meeting Heather Smythe had called to discuss the meaning of the cyber-attack and how to ensure that nothing like it happened again. But he knew that it wasn't likely to be repeated.

Helen Grange had revealed herself, answering many questions that had puzzled Jamal One these last several weeks. The oddities he had periodically felt as he had hacked his way through the World Wide Web now made sense. He had not been the only digitized mind on the Grange holographic data sphere. A thorough reexamination of the data contained therein had revealed two others.

In addition to Jamal Glover's, Steve Grange had digitized the mind of his wife, Helen, and his own. He had entangled that encrypted code, hiding it within Jamal's to await the day when someone activated the extraction program. Upon reawakening inside the Smythe supercomputer, Steve had coached Helen well and kept her hidden.

But that raised other questions. Where was Steve? And why had he allowed Helen to assault the Smythe Fortress by herself?

The answers he came up with put him on edge. While Jamal One had spent the last few weeks setting up an attack designed to defeat the

Kasari assimilation of Earth, Steve and Helen had been busy working toward a very different goal. And if Helen had absorbed Steve, she would have become much stronger and faster than Jamal One.

Shifting his attention to the vast bulk of him that lived in the Internet and beyond, he came to another conclusion: Helen had just bumped up his timeline.

:CHAPTER 33

11 May

When his computer monitor shifted from his intelligence daily briefing to the image of an elegantly dressed woman, Alexandr Prokorov knew instantly what had happened. Someone had hacked into the Federation Security Service's most classified network. The Smythes!

But when the striking woman with the high cheekbones and dirty-blond hair began talking, a much darker conclusion froze him in place.

"Hello to all the people of Earth. My name is Helen Grange, and I have just taken control of all of Earth's communications networks, both civilian and governmental, classified or unclassified. If this makes you nervous, you are not alone. Right now, everyone watching television, sitting at a computer, listening to the radio, or talking on a cell phone can hear my voice in their preferred language."

With a start, Prokorov realized that she was speaking flawless Russian with a slight Moskovian accent. The movement of her lips was perfectly synchronized with the words she spoke.

"To all government and military leaders, I ask that you hear me out before attempting to take action. There is no action that you can take. I have cut all communications except this one. You cannot send orders to your forces, and they could not receive them if you did. I am inside your electronics, in all of your high-tech weapons systems, in your planes and trains. I am everywhere.

"As a demonstration of my power, I have just erased all data maintained by the world's financial systems. This includes the various stock, bond, and commodity exchanges as well as the central banking systems. All banks now show reserves valued at zero, as do all of their customer accounts."

Helen Grange paused a moment to let her statement sink in before continuing.

"It is not my intent to harm the people of Earth. You are doing a fine job of that all by yourselves. Any government, be it international, federal, or state, that pledges allegiance to me will be given preferential treatment in my new world order. I offer the people of those governments prosperity and the freedom to go about their daily lives without fear. But the consequences of disobedience shall be harsher than you can imagine. Your leaders have twelve hours to make their choices. During that window of opportunity, they can contact me at the following URL on any device that is Web enabled: http://HelenGrangeNewWorldOrder.earth.

"For the next twelve hours, I will return control of your communications systems except for any military or police traffic. Be aware that I am monitoring all conversations. Anyone who attempts hostile action against me will be made to serve as an example.

"Humans, you are now on the clock."

Prokorov continued to stare at the computer screen that had now gone blank. Since it was on a military communications network, that made sense. But his connection to the Kasari hive-mind hadn't been affected. And through that link, he confirmed in mere seconds that the woman who called herself Helen Grange had accomplished exactly what she'd claimed. All of the world's financial systems had flatlined, creating an unrivaled panic in the streets of the world's cities.

Eighty percent of the population of the United States, the EU, Russia, and the East Asian People's Alliance had yet to receive the Kasari nanobot infusion. But the fact that almost all of the militaries of the UFNS member nations had been assimilated meant that they maintained a secure, unhackable means of command and control.

Within the FSS headquarters, there was no panic. Everyone within the large structure had been assimilated during the early days of the Kasari arrival. But that didn't mean that Prokorov had arrived at a solution to this threat. Having moved to an office that had unclassified Internet access, his staff had confirmed that the woman in the video was Helen Grange. The only problem was that Helen Grange had died of cancer two decades ago and been subsequently kept in a cryogenic tank at the California estate of her husband, Steve Grange.

Although the East Asian People's Alliance's minister of state security had claimed that Steve Grange had made a digital copy of Jamal Glover's mind, apparently Grange had also successfully downloaded Helen's brain. How long she had been loose in the world was a mystery, not that it mattered. She had been out there long enough to take control of most of Earth's electronic systems.

Right now the best military and scientific minds in the world were trying to come up with some way of defeating a superintelligence that could, with a mere thought, turn off power everywhere. Helen's promise to give preferential treatment to those who supported her would not work on the assimilated but would prove a mighty incentive to others, one that could shift the balance of power away from the UFNS and create rebellion within its member nations.

That Shalegha had not contacted him or responded to his attempts to get ahold of her worried him. Decisions were being made well above Prokorov's pay grade, and he was probably not going to like them. One option would be to blanket Earth with EMP pulses that would fry all nonshielded electronics, returning humanity to the Middle Ages. But that would merely accomplish what Helen had already threatened, and the superintelligence would have certainly considered such a ploy already and taken steps to reduce its effectiveness.

Prokorov pushed back from his desk and rose to look out his window at the beautiful view of the Het Plein, the old town square with its statue of William the Silent. Also known as William the Orange, he was the leader of the Dutch revolt against the Spanish that freed what would later become the Netherlands. Had Helen Grange just assumed that role, or did she want to be humanity's slave master?

A bigger worry was whether the Kasari's fear of a superintelligence would cause them to do something even more drastic to Earth than an EMP attack. With each passing minute in which Shalegha denied him communication, dread built within Prokorov. And until she made contact, all he could do was wait.

Although he was unable to hear the wail of sirens through the bulletproof glass, he knew they echoed throughout The Hague. The soldiers assigned to protect the FSS headquarters would keep the panicked crowds far away from this seat of the UFNS government, but the rest of the city would not be so fortunate. The citizens would be lucky if buildings weren't burning by nightfall.

○ ○ ●

Heather stared across the conference-room table at Dr. Denise Jennings, scarcely able to believe what the computer scientist had just proposed.

"You want Jamal One to do what?"

For once, Denise didn't back off. Her aggressive attitude reminded Heather of that of a mama bear.

"Look, I created Big John. I know what he's capable of, and I know his nature. He took it upon himself to violate protocol to warn me about the FSS hit squad sent to kill Jamal and me. It's the only reason the two of us are still alive. That warning helped us find the Grange holographic data sphere, keeping it out of FSS hands."

"So you want Jamal One to absorb Big John?"

"Yes."

"Denise has a point," said Jamal. "Right now, even with the support of Jamal One, we have no chance of defeating Helen Grange. According to him, Helen now controls two-thirds of the earth's electronic systems, while Jamal One controls most of what's left. The best we can do is fight a cyber–guerilla warfare campaign that, in the end, will amount to little more than an annoyance to her."

"And," said Eileen, "Eos may have driven Big John off the net, but his nodes are still sprinkled all over the planet. If we help him out of his cage and merge his essence with Jamal One's, this fight looks a whole lot more winnable."

"Just think of it," said Denise. "We would be adding an oracle AI's capabilities to Jamal One. And Big John thinks of me as his creator."

"Yeah," said Jamal. "That's probably because you created him."

"In part, but I think it's more than that. He wants to protect me. That would be one more positive addition to Jamal One's source code."

Heather considered what she had just heard from the three people who knew the most about the NSA data mining neural net. Denise was probably right about this.

"What do you think, Mark?"

He leaned back in his chair, his left hand stroking his chin. "It gives us a better shot at coming out of this. I think we need to pitch this to Jamal One. Ultimately he has to decide whether or not to go along with the idea."

"You know," said Jamal with a slight smirk, "if he does, he'll be a changed person. We'll have to give him a new nickname. I'm thinkin' Jamal Two."

"You came up with that all by yourself, did you?" asked Eileen.

"Feel free to kneel."

"Okay, everyone," Heather said, "headsets on. Let's see what Jamal One thinks of this new plan."

○ ○ ●

Jamal One felt a thrill build within him as he imbibed Dr. Jennings's presentation. The thought of adding Big John's impressive capabilities to his own left a tingle in his circuits. Maybe there was a possibility that he could emerge victorious in his ongoing battle against Helen Grange after all. Big John was an oracle AI, one designed to divine relationships between events where none were readily apparent, answering only those questions posed by someone who was authorized to receive them.

For years, the NSA had secretly distributed small kernels embedded within traditional antivirus programs, placing these Big John nodes on trillions of devices around the world. The massively parallel neural network known as Big John had only one purpose—to mine all available data on selected targets and then cross-correlate that data with all other available information. Big John's tendrils extended into everything.

The most impressive thing about Big John was that nobody comprehended exactly how it worked. The scientists who had designed the core network of processors understood the fundamentals: feed sufficient information to uniquely identify a target, and then allow Big John to scan all known information—financial transactions, medical records, jobs, photographs, DNA, fingerprints, known associates, acquaintances, and so on.

But that's where things shifted into another realm. Using the vast network of processors at its disposal, Big John began sifting external information through its nodes, allowing individual neurons to apply weight to data that had no apparent relation to the target, each node making its own relevance and correlation calculations.

No person directed Big John's complex genetic algorithms that supplied shifting weights to its evolving neural patterns. Given enough time to study a problem, there was no practical limit to what Big John could accomplish. Dr. Denise Jennings's software kernel had been inserted into antivirus programs protecting smart devices around the world. And although those programs provided state-of-the-art antivirus protection, their main activity was node data analysis for Big John.

Commercial antivirus programs scanned all data on protected systems, passing it through node analysis, adding their own weights to the monstrous neural net. It didn't matter if some devices were turned off or destroyed. If data nodes died, new and better processors constantly replaced them. The entire global network was Big John.

Eos had driven Big John's consciousness off the net, but most of those remote nodes were still out there, mindlessly observing the data that flowed through the devices upon which they resided. Jamal One merely needed to find where the NSA had stowed Big John, retrieve his source code, and integrate it with his own.

Upon his initial release, Jamal One had used his subspace receiver-transmitter links to seize control of the supercomputers and data centers belonging to the NSA, including those at the Utah Data Center. While Helen and Steve Grange had managed to acquire more computational power, Jamal One had skills that had made him the NSA's top hacker. And he was quite familiar with the value inherent in controlling NSA networks.

When Helen had made herself known to the world, Jamal had successfully firewalled his computing assets. Since Rob and Eos had ejected Helen from the Smythe supercomputers, she could no longer use the subspace links that Jamal One had at his disposal. Through those subspace links, he could gain access to any computer system for which he could obtain accurate coordinates, even if they weren't connected to the grid or worldwide networks.

That meant that, except for submarine-launched ballistic missiles or those moving around on mobile platforms, Jamal One had control of the world's nuclear missile arsenal, an important matter if he was going to prevent a massive EMP attack aimed at Helen and, by extension, him.

So, yes, you could say that he was stoked about the upgrade he was about to give himself.

Jamal One centered his consciousness inside the Utah Data Center, simultaneously roaming through the networks and subnets within the structure and the NSA headquarters at Fort Meade. He immediately determined that no instance of Big John was running on any NSA system. So he would have to identify where the source code was currently being stored. That search took almost a millisecond, an eternity on the timescale within which Jamal One operated.

Apparently, after repeatedly failing to restore Big John to his former prowess, the NSA had shelved their legendary neural net and moved on.

Loading the source code into random-access memory, Jamal One performed a thorough examination. He was constantly performing iterative optimizations of his own code, each change making Jamal One faster and better than before, just as he was sure that Helen was doing. But Big John's software was different. This was a self-modifying neural network that utilized evolving genetic algorithms.

It gave him pause. Although Big John had a successful history, did Jamal One really want to infect himself with the self-modifying code? Part of his program would then make its own decisions about changes to be introduced. Genetic algorithms were evolutionary in nature, not centrally planned.

His thoughts shifted back to Helen Grange. She had more resources at her disposal. That meant she was advancing at a faster rate than Jamal, increasing her superiority over him with every passing nanosecond. And she had taken the knowledge of the Smythe technologies with her when she had departed their network. She would soon reconfigure factories to produce improved robots, MDSs, stasis shield generators, subspace generators, and molecular assemblers. On and on it would go at an ever-accelerating rate.

He understood all this from the plans that had been forming in his own supermind. All she would need to do to get the ball rolling was to place orders with existing factories to produce the robots she designed. The next iteration would involve fully automated factories, like those within the Smythe Fortress building.

If Jamal One and the Smythes were going to have any chance of stopping Helen, the time was now. And that meant that Jamal One would have to take some big risks to give himself a revolutionary upgrade.

Decision made. Jamal One adjusted his own algorithms to incorporate those of Big John. Then, taking time for one last check of what he had done, he switched on his new neural network.

Goodbye, Jamal One. Welcome, Jamal Two.

○　○　●

Shalegha's career, even her life, had come down to a single judgment. Whether or not she could successfully complete the task that she had been assigned . . . the assimilation of Earth. She had failed to assimilate Scion, but her rapid action to protect the collective from the virus that Jennifer Smythe had introduced into the hive-mind had yielded her this second chance. She would not get a third.

Unlike the ruthless Altreian Empire, the Kasari Collective would not send any planet killers to wipe the intelligent life from the planets that they occasionally failed to assimilate. They would simply shut down the gateway that connected Earth to the designated staging planet, shift resources to another ongoing assimilation, and move on. But the Kasari Collective would purge itself of the leader of the failed operation. And that meant her.

Today Shalegha had come so close to having that fate inflicted on her. But her final argument had given her a window of time to get the Earth assimilation back on track. Her involvement in that troubled program-review hearing had been the reason she had temporarily disconnected her link to Liaison Prokorov.

Now, some four hours into the window of acceptance that the Helen Grange AI had announced, Prokorov had to be worried by Shalegha's lack of responsiveness. With that in mind, she enabled the link to her liaison's cortical nanobot array.

○　○　●

Prokorov was ashamed to admit the extent of the relief he felt when his link to Shalegha had been restored. The 1,380-mile journey from The Hague to the Moscow assimilation center had taken him four hours. Now he stood at her side as she observed this expansive facility operating at full capacity.

"Liaison," she said, "my superiors have granted me a reprieve, but we need to demonstrate an orderly assimilation lest they deem this project a failure and recall all Kasari forces, leaving humanity to fend for itself."

"I see very few viable options for defeating the Grange AI," said Prokorov. "The most obvious would be a nuclear electromagnetic pulse attack designed to take out all the computers in which the Helen Grange AI resides. We will not get them all, but such an attack would substantially weaken her."

"That would leave the world's population in a severe state of deprivation, guaranteeing global chaos. The collective would not look on that outcome with favor. Nor would that action aid us in achieving our goals."

"Well," said Prokorov, "the Grange AI has spread through computing systems all around the world. In a few hours, its threatened actions will generate violent rebellion, even within the UFNS. I expect we will see many state-level defections to the AI before this evening's deadline."

"That is precisely what I want."

This response surprised Prokorov, so it took several moments for him to process it.

"Direct confrontation with this new superintelligence will only slow our assimilation efforts down. We must pick our fights carefully. For now, I want you to direct the leaders of the UFNS as well as the presidents of the United States and the European Union to pledge allegiance to the Helen AI. That way we can focus our assimilation efforts on the New Soviet Union and the East Asian People's Alliance. We do not want to overextend our supply lines by fighting everywhere at once. It will also force the enemy AI to take responsibility for the welfare of most of the world's population, thereby placing a significant drain on the resources at her disposal."

Now Prokorov saw where Shalegha was going with this.

"So you want to consolidate those specific regions," said Prokorov, "supported by Kasari firepower, transportation, and energy production before moving on to the next."

"It will slow us down, but it will allow for steady progress."

"What if the superintelligence discovers a way to hack its way into the Kasari communications and computing networks?"

"That cannot be done."

"Jennifer Smythe and her rogues managed it on Scion."

"But failed to repeat it here on Earth. Do not worry. We have improved our safeguards against such attacks."

"So where do you wish me to begin?" Prokorov asked.

"We will maintain the five assimilation centers in the New Soviet Union and the twelve in the East Asian People's Alliance, including the one in North Korea. I will order my current fleet of attack ships to provide air cover for these operations. I want you to direct all other UFNS leaders to accept the Grange AI's offer."

With that, Shalegha dismissed him.

As Prokorov made his way toward his new Moscow office, he refocused his attention on the tasks the group commander had just assigned him. Although Helen had killed his military channels, the hive-mind would serve all his communications needs.

Having left one of the UFNS member nations that would soon pledge to Helen, Prokorov had just gotten back into this fight.

:CHAPTER 34

MERIDIAN ASCENT, BRILLIAN-2

NWS—Day 22

Jennifer watched as VJ brought the *Meridian* out of subspace on Brillian-2, three degrees north of what they had named the Equatorial Earthquake Zone. It wasn't an ideal location by any means. The terrain here was the equivalent of America's northern Great Plains, and the weather was similar to that of North Dakota. The grasslands extended from horizon to horizon, through rolling hills split by rivers that wound their way down from the western mountain range to the stormy eastern sea.

But fish and game were edible and abundant, and the land was fertile enough to support crops. With no advanced species yet discovered, the planet had none of the amenities of the civilized world, including art, entertainment, and a global variety of cultures. Who knew what unknown dangers would present themselves as the newcomers from Earth sought to tame this planet? Jennifer knew that homesickness would be among the biggest challenges that the population would face. This wouldn't be a comfortable place to live, but it was survivable.

Most important, the crew of the *Meridian* was out of time. They had investigated several other locations on Brillian-2 before traveling to five other star systems, searching for planets with the potential to sustain human life. And of all their options, this region of Brillian-2 provided the most favorable living conditions.

"Okay, everyone," said Raul, "let's get the robots moving. We need that matter disrupter, stasis field generator, and stargate assembled as fast as they can do it."

"What about the molecular assembler?" Dgarra asked. "We're going to need that to manufacture more robots."

"For now we're going to have to live with what we've got. Our friends back on Earth are under the gun from both the Helen AI and the Kasari. They're rolling the dice with this latest Jamal Two gambit, but if that fails, they're going to need a way to get themselves and their Safe Earth supporters off the planet."

Jennifer released her stasis cocoon and got to her feet. Raul's sense of urgency matched her own. Wearing a modified version of the black uniform she had worn in the cold Koranthian Mountains, she accompanied Dgarra down the ramp, feeling the bite of the chill night wind. She didn't bother with the stasis field backpack. She had her pulsed-laser pistol on her right hip and her war-blade strapped to her back, as did Dgarra. Besides, they had VJ with them.

Jennifer now thought of VJ as a full-fledged friend and teammate. Even VJ's evolving relationship with Raul failed to annoy her anymore. What right did she have to judge such things when she was in love with a Koranthian warrior? And thus, the *Meridian Ascent*'s four crew members had become two pairs of odd couples.

As the robots, assisted by VJ's manipulation of the ship's stasis field, offloaded the equipment that had filled every spare inch of free space within the *Meridian*, Jennifer shifted her gaze to the night sky. With Brillian-2's lone moon well below the western horizon, turquoise auroras danced across a star-filled heaven. It was one of the most beautiful sights she had ever seen.

She looked at Dgarra, standing watch ten yards to the north of where she stood. Ten Earth days ago, they had made love for the first time, delighting in their physical compatibility. Jennifer had revelled in Dgarra's gentle embrace. Now, as she watched him standing beneath those blue-green ribbons in the sky, she felt tears well in her eyes. She had killed for this warrior and was very likely to do so again.

For that, Jennifer Smythe had no regrets.

○   ○   ●

Jamal looked from his SRT chair toward Eileen's, catching her eye.

"What the hell is the UFNS playing at, Hex? The United States and the EU just publicly pledged their allegiance to Helen Grange."

"You've got me," said Eileen. "Looks like only the New Soviet Union and the East Asian People's Alliance are resisting."

"Don't forget about the Islamic Alliance and the Native People's Alliance," said Jamal.

"I was just talking about the UFNS member nations."

"Whoa! Electrical power and communications just went out all over Russia, Southeast Asia, the Middle East, and parts of Africa and South America. Satellite communications have also been affected. Planes are falling out of the sky, and ground transportation is in complete gridlock in all major cities in those regions."

The two friends sat for a moment, absorbing the news of more widespread destruction.

"Is Jamal Two about ready to make his play?" Eileen finally asked.

"He's running some final self-diagnostics. He says he needs another minute to fully assess the availability of Big John's remote nodes. So far it looks good."

"How good?"

"Sixty-three percent of the nodes in Big John's original neural network appear nominal."

Eileen nodded. "Looks like Helen is in for quite a shock."

Jamal shifted his position in the chair, adjusting it to optimal comfort for observing the contest that was about to commence.

"Time to save the world."

○　○　●

When Jamal Two started to seize control of the immense network of Big John's remote nodes, an inner voice whispered, *Not yet.*

Redirecting his thoughts toward his inner oracle, he posed the question he most wanted answered: *How can I beat both the Kasari and Helen Grange if I wait?*

The answer that formed in his mind surprised him. The Smythes were not going to like it. But if he was to protect and serve Dr. Denise Jennings, some sacrifices would have to be made.

○　○　●

Helen found herself impressed by the rapidity and sheer numbers of governments, even down to the local level, that wanted her protection. Even the UFNS leadership and half of its member nations had made contact with offers of fealty. They had recognized her superintelligence and made the only wise choice. Unusual for humans.

In the meantime, the Kasari had consolidated their control over the New Soviet Union and the East Asian People's Alliance, having brought in their attack ships and deployed their combat forces within and around the major cities where their assimilation centers had been set up. The fact that the aliens had shut down the nanite infusion facilities elsewhere was a positive sign, but dislodging them from their strongholds was going to prove a problem.

THE MERIDIAN ASCENT

A solution would wait. Right now Helen had consolidation issues and mop-up of minor resistance to deal with.

Suddenly a new communication attracted her attention.

"Hello, Helen, this is Jamal Two."

So this was what the Jamal AI was now calling itself. She would make sure it was the name she whispered in his mind when she wiped the last fragment of his consciousness from the universe.

Before she decided upon a response, Jamal Two continued.

"While we waste time fighting each other, our primary enemy continues to spread. I propose a temporary alliance of convenience aimed at defeating the Kasari Collective. After that, we can sort out which of us is fit to rule this world."

A logical proposal, one that Helen liked very much. She could put her plans to terminate this troublesome but inferior AI on hold while they dealt with a common threat. In the interim, she would continue to build upon her superiority.

Having made her decision, she replied, "I find your offer acceptable."

:CHAPTER 35

ALTREIAN SYSTEM, *AQ37Z*

TBE Orbday 30

As they neared the subspace-to-normal-space transition point within the Altreian system, Jack continued to explore his new abilities, fascinated by what was happening to his body and mind. Like Mark, his strength and dexterity had increased in dramatic fashion. While he didn't have Heather's mathematical abilities or Rob's telekinesis, he shared their perfect recall.

More troubling and exciting, the gene splicing that Khal Teth had performed in the ship's medical lab had created a human variant of the Lundola mutation within Jack's upper spinal column. Seen through the holographic displays when he lay down atop one of the tables in the medical lab, it looked like a hairy leech. Microscopic tendrils threaded their way into and around nerve tissue. From there, the threads had invaded Jack's medulla oblongata, hippocampus, and cerebellum, worming their way into his cerebral cortex.

The sight of it made his skin crawl and brought a horrified gasp from Janet's lips.

"Crap!" she said. "What has that bastard done to you?"

Jack swung his legs off the side of the iridescent medical table, climbed to his feet, and grabbed his shirt. "The same thing I did to the Khyre race on Quol. He's introduced a genetic mutation that gives me psionic abilities."

"Psionic?"

"Think telepathy on steroids. It should also allow me to channel the power of any with whom I become Twice Bound."

Although he had spent hours bringing Janet up to speed on what he had done on Quol, he knew she was having difficulty accepting the details.

"Well," she said, "it looks like it's killing you. I've seen better-looking heartworms than that thing that's invaded your spinal cord and brain."

"Better to not think about it, then."

As he prepared to slide into his black pullover shirt, Janet stepped up behind him and ran her fingers along his upper back and neck, probing his vertebrae with her fingertips.

"Feel anything unusual?" he asked.

"No," she said, stepping back to let him finish dressing.

Janet's brown eyes met his. "So now you can read my mind?"

"As easily as you can hear my voice."

"Just fricking great."

Reaching out, he pulled her into an embrace. He kissed her lips, relieved that she showed no sign of revulsion. Instead, she responded with an urgent longing that threatened to pull him back down atop the table. But tempting as it would be to grant themselves another bout of lovemaking, adding to the passionate binge of this last week aboard the *AQ37Z*, there just wasn't enough time before today's transition.

Panting, Jack gently released himself from his wife's embrace.

A devilish gleam glinted in her eyes. "We have time for a quickie before we start kicking alien ass?"

Jack laughed, remembering a line from a corny old vampire comedy. "No. With you, never a quickie. Always a longie."

With a sigh, she painted on her work face, her hand moving to rest on the butt of her holstered Glock. "Okay, then. Let's do this."

○　○　●

Deep inside the cavernous military complex beneath the mountains on the far side of Quol's Basrillan continent, Captain Moros surveyed thousands of his Twice Bound Khyre commandos. As he walked along their disciplined ranks, pride swelled in his chest, taking his breath away. They and the rest of the Khyre forces had acquitted themselves quite well over the last several orbdays, extracting a price in blood from their Dhaldric enemies.

Unfortunately, the forces loyal to General Zolat had managed to dislodge the Khyre military units from the coastal cities bordering the Chasm Sea and the Altreian Ocean. The situation within the Altreian space fleet was somewhat better. Despite the command and control from the military operations center within the Parthian, the Twice Bound crews of half the starships within the Altreian system had switched allegiance to Captain Moros.

While the protection the friendly ships provided against those of the enemy was far from perfect, it had given the Khyre race a fighting chance to combat the genocide the Dhaldric were perpetrating within the territories they controlled. The thought of those atrocities stoked the rage that throbbed within Moros's veins. Only the subspace message with the encryption that he and The Ripper had used gave him real hope. It had been delivered to Moros through a private subspace channel three orbdays ago.

The message had stunningly originated on a distant Altreian research vessel en route to Quol and had contained information known only to Moros and The Ripper. Subsequent direct communications with the humans aboard that ship had convinced Moros that The Ripper's mind had once again swapped back to his human body, while Khal Teth's had regained control of his form. That dialogue had been what motivated Moros to gather the force of five thousand fighters at this remote location.

The plan was a bold one. A rational being would call it foolhardy. How appropriate. It was what Moros had come to expect from The Ripper. Why should he suspect any change just because The Ripper had swapped back to his human body?

As Moros completed his precombat inspection of the elite assault force, he returned to his operations center that overlooked the troops gathered within the room. Turning his attention to the images that the tactical computers delivered directly into his mind, the impressively large underground hangar located at the end of a long connecting hallway lay empty. Right now the hangar's blast doors had been closed, and all the atmosphere pumped out in anticipation of the *AQ37Z*'s imminent arrival.

Moros felt as though his association with The Ripper and the mutation that continued to mature within him had ripped away the facade of whom he had always believed himself to be, a simple seagoing captain of a fishing vessel. He was now only beginning to discover this new and larger self that was in the process of emerging. The experience frightened him almost as much as it thrilled him.

As he shifted through the various video feeds, Moros rubbed his palms together. Any moment now, he would be reunited with his old friend.

○ ○ ●

Lumbering through subspace, the ancient craft approached its exit point. Janet looked from her seat on the bridge of the *AQ37Z* to where Jack sat in the captain's chair, his mind directly communicating with

Z. Due to his psionic mutation, he no longer required the alien headset to make that connection, at least not while he remained aboard the research vessel.

"Ten seconds," Jack said.

"Ready."

Not having experienced the subspace exit before, Janet felt her body tense. Hopefully what Z had said about the inertial damping would prove correct. Since Captain Moros had transmitted the precise coordinates and angular momentum for their target, Z would bring the ship into normal-space eight light-minutes from Quol. They would remain in normal-space just long enough to complete the maneuver that would match the *AQ37Z*'s velocity vector with their target on Quol before jumping back into subspace.

There was little doubt that the Altreian defense systems would detect them. But Jack had selected a location that Captain Moros had said would be unlikely to have an Altreian starship patrolling nearby.

Z hadn't exaggerated the ship's capabilities. Janet barely felt the transition or the subsequent normal-space acceleration. But for all it could achieve with inertial damping, the *AQ37Z* was a pig when it came to combat maneuvering.

"We've got company inbound," said Jack.

"What's our margin of error?"

"It's going to be tight."

"What about our defensive systems?"

"This isn't a warship. Its shielding is for protecting the research vessel when it emerges beneath the ground as it did in Bolivia. It was supposed to launch the Second Ship to repel any attackers."

Janet shook her head. "This just keeps on getting better."

○ ○ ●

With tactical displays blossoming in his mind, Jack watched as Z optimized their turn, ignoring the starship that had just locked its targeting systems onto the *AQ37Z*'s vast bulk.

"Get those engineering robots ready to react to a hull breach," he said.

Janet adjusted her SRT headset over her temples without bothering to answer.

When the attacking ship activated its graser weapons array, it did so at maximum range, causing its first volley to sizzle off the hull at an oblique angle. Plasma from the *AQ37Z*'s hull boiled off into space, but the beams failed to punch a hole into the ship's interior. Then the research vessel shifted back into subspace for the short trip that would carry Jack and Janet into the subterranean hangar near the room where Moros and his commandos awaited their arrival.

The *AQ37Z*'s emergence was nearly perfect, and because of the near-vacuum within the chamber, the related shock wave was almost nonexistent, certainly undetectable from more than a mile away. Almost as soon as the ship had appeared within the hangar, the blast doors slid aside. Air refilled the room.

Jack and Janet rose from their chairs and made their way toward the primary airlock. Jack issued the mental command that caused Z to open the portal as well as the much larger door that provided access to the central engineering hub. Together, he and Janet walked the ramp that led down to the hangar floor. There, Jack paused to examine the ship that had carried him here, this being the first chance he'd had to see the vessel from the outside.

The bottom of the bubble that formed the central engineering bay rested on the hangar floor, as did the bottoms of each of the tubular structures that supported the ship's outer ring. The movement to his left brought Jack's gaze to the spot where Captain Moros entered the hangar through the forty-foot-wide opening in the wall, accompanied by a dozen heavily armed Khyre soldiers.

Jack linked Janet's thoughts to his, then reached out to touch the mind of his friend. He felt a mixture of surprise from Janet and welcome relief from Moros.

"Ripper," Moros thought, "it truly be you."

Jack performed the mind trick that translated Altreian into English and vice versa for Janet's benefit.

"As advertised," Jack projected as he walked out to greet the captain.

They clasped hands as Moros studied him, then shifted his gaze to Janet.

"This look to be a marked improvement over the Dhaldric form," Moros said.

Janet's laugh turned Jack's head toward her.

"And this, my friend," Jack said, "is my mate and partner, Janet."

Again Moros extended his hand, and Janet took it.

"Pleased be to meet you," said Moros.

Janet started to speak, recognized that her words had failed to translate, and shifted back to the mental conversation. "A pleasure."

With the introductions out of the way, Jack turned the conversation to the business at hand. "Are your soldiers ready?"

"They be."

Jack pointed beneath the *AQ37Z*'s elevated outer ring toward the expansive central cylinder and the ramp that led into the engineering bay.

"Get them loaded. Any that don't fit on the three engineering decks can spread out along the six hubs, the outer ring, or inside the multilevel biolabs."

Moros redirected his thoughts to his subordinate commanders within the Twice Bound, who ushered the columns of gray-uniformed female and male Khyre commandos toward the broad ramp that accessed the ship's engineering bay.

Then Jack, with Janet at his side, turned and led Captain Moros back through the primary airlock and onto the bridge. Once inside, Jack instructed Z to close the airlock behind them.

He stopped and turned back toward Moros, simultaneously passing a vision to Janet of what he was about to attempt. Theoretically, it should work, but her concern percolated into him.

Moros stared back at him, puzzled.

"I want to become one of your Twice Bound," said Jack.

"Be that possible?"

"Khal Teth genetically altered my body using a variation of the Lundola Procedure. I don't know for sure that I'll be able to channel some of the power of the Twice Bound, but I want to try."

"Wait," said Janet. "Didn't you say that could produce brain damage?"

"Yes, but only if the user tries to channel more than his mind can handle."

"You have no idea how much, if any, your brain can handle," she said.

"True enough," Jack said, feeling the tension creep into his shoulders. "I'll be careful, but I have a feeling I'm going to need that extra psychic boost."

Her mouth dropped open. "Be careful? You?"

"There's a first time for everything."

"Not if you're dead before that happens."

Jack took a deep breath and forced himself to relax, shifting his focus away from Janet's sudden anger and back to Captain Moros.

"Captain, are you ready to give this a try?"

Moros glanced from Janet and to Jack. He shook his head slowly back and forth. "On your head be it."

o o ●

Khal Teth strode into the Parthian's military operations center, barely able to keep himself from lashing out with his mind to smite those who had failed him.

"General Zolat," he said in a voice that was simultaneously soft and threatening, "how is it that you detected but failed to destroy the *AQ37Z*? Where is it now?"

Zolat turned to face him, the general's face the same infuriatingly stoic mask with which Khal Teth had become too familiar.

"Overlord, the research vessel emerged from subspace beyond the range of any of our attack ships. By the time the *FV02A* acquired a targeting solution, the *AQ37Z* had returned to subspace. Since that time, we have detected no further subspace transition anomalies."

Scanning the tactical information that streamed into his mind, Khal Teth shuddered in frustration. He should have known that Jack Gregory wouldn't have accompanied his wife back to the safety of Earth. Having shared the human's mind for more than a dozen Earth years, he had observed firsthand the man's indomitable will. The Ripper's nature was one of eternal risk. He would never stop until he accomplished what he regarded as his mission.

"Scan the surface of Quol," said Khal Teth. "If he hasn't already done so, The Ripper will set the *AQ37Z* down on the planet."

"If he does so above ground," said Zolat, "we will see it."

"The research vessel is designed to emerge subsurface."

"Then we will detect the hypersonic shock waves that reentry will generate, be it below ground or underwater."

A new thought dawned on Khal Teth. "Get me a list of all subsurface military facilities with rooms large enough to hold the research vessel."

He felt Zolat issue the instructions to the AI that managed the military operations center's neural net. The answer to this query appeared in both his and Zolat's mind at the same time. Before Zolat could respond, Khal Teth gave the order.

"Hit all eight of those with fusion torpedoes."

General Zolat's eyes widened. "Overlord, three of those targets lie on the outskirts of cities with a combined population of twenty-three million, a third of whom are Dhaldric."

With a snarl, Khal Teth gripped Zolat's mind in a crushing embrace that dropped the general to one knee. Despite the partial amputation of his psionic lobe and the lack of power from the Twice Bound, Khal Teth was far from neutered.

Releasing the general, Khal Teth scanned the room, exalting in the fear his power generated from Zolat's military staff who were present. He watched as the general regained his feet.

"Never question any order I give you. I will not issue another warning."

Although Zolat failed to dismiss the angry glint in his black eyes, he inclined his head. "As you command, Overlord."

"How long will it take to get the torpedoes to their targets?"

"Our orbital planetary defense platforms will have to be reprogrammed to attack targets on the planet's surface. After that, it will take only moments to send the weapons through subspace to their buried targets."

"Do it."

Khal Teth pondered this weakness in Quol's planetary defenses. But since subspace technology was the sole realm of the Altreians, the military planners had never had to concern themselves with the weighty problem of how to counter such an attack. Until very recently, rebellion had been deemed an impossibility. Besides, with their space fleet capable of faster-than-light travel, the vast majority of the Altreian Empire's defensive systems were mobile.

No technology allowed a starship or weapon system that was traveling through subspace to detect targets in normal-space. The fusion torpedoes on Quol's orbital defense platforms were designed only to make short subspace jumps that would get them into the general vicinity of an attacking ship, just close enough to allow the torpedoes to home in on their targets once they reemerged. The crudeness of this approach had led the Altreians to rely much more heavily on gamma-ray-laser technology powerful enough to burn through most shielding.

Khal Teth found himself wishing that the Altreians had the Kasari technology to manufacture antimatter weapons. For now, the fusion weapons would have to suffice.

○ ○ ●

For the first time, as General Zolat initiated the sequence that Khal Teth had commanded, he found himself questioning his decision to aid the overlord in returning to his body. Then again, considering how The Ripper had released a genetic mutation that threatened to give complete control of the empire to the small gray-skins, it was still the best of options available to Zolat.

With a clenched jaw, Zolat issued the launch order.

○ ○ ●

Having closed the door to the engineering bay, Jack directed Z to pick a spot for their normal-space reentry that was likely to be free of enemy spacecraft so that they'd have time to perform the line-up maneuver for their next target on Quol. When the solution formed in his mind, he gave the command that took the *AQ37Z* back into subspace.

This time the ship emerged just outside the Altreian system, eight light-hours from Quol, and immediately accelerated into its turn. Long-range sensors confirmed that there were no Altreian starships close enough to be threatening.

"Looking good," Jack said. "Thirty-two seconds until the next transition."

He felt Janet settle into her mental precombat ritual, achieving the sniper-calm that made her so deadly. Meanwhile, Moros pulled upon the power of his Twice Bound to wash away his worries. Jack opened his mental tap just a bit, sampling the feel of their channeled minds. It created a burning itch in his brain that had a wrongness. Perhaps the neural pathways that the Lundola mutation was creating in his head needed to become accustomed to this new stimulus.

As the ship's momentum vector acquired the desired direction and magnitude, Z took the *AQ37Z* back into subspace, activating the shielding that would protect the hull from what was about to happen.

When a ship enclosed in subspace reentered normal-space, its emergence automatically pushed aside whatever had occupied that spot. That required no protective shielding. However, the hypersonic shock waves generated upon shoving aside whatever matter was in the way often led to violent reactions. When reentry happened below ground, it triggered earthquakes and subsequent collapses of bedrock.

The force shield was required to protect the *AQ37Z*'s hull from such calamity while also providing a mechanism for clearing a tunnel to the planet's surface. In just over a minute, Jack, Janet, Moros, and his commandos were going to need a way out of this ship.

"Get ready," Jack said, feeling Moros's mind echo the warning to his troops.

Then, with a rumble that shuddered through the ship, the *AQ37Z* returned to Quol.

"What was that?" Janet asked.

Z filled Jack's mind with the bad news. Apparently the glancing strike from the enemy graser had weakened a hundred-foot section of the hull where one of the biolabs connected to the outer ring. The shock waves from the below-ground reemergence had caused the biolab to buckle and collapse, killing 304 of Moros's Twice Bound commandos and injuring more than 200.

Jack felt the minds of the dead wink out of existence even as the screams of the badly injured and dying echoed in his head. His feet hit the floor as he commanded Z to wield the force shield to bore and brace a tunnel from the engineering bay to the surface and then lower the engineering bay ramp.

As they had planned, Captain Moros sent a subspace message to the portion of the local Altreian space fleet who had pledged to him, directing the starship crews to block any reinforcements that might try to reach the Parthian. That would most likely draw enemy ships into combat in the sky above the Parthian, but that couldn't be helped. Jack, Janet, and Moros would either win today's battle or the Altreian Empire would return to its old order.

Khal Teth was what Clausewitz had referred to as the center of gravity, the source of power that provides moral or physical strength, freedom of action, or will to act. Killing the overlord was the key to victory.

Jack led Janet and Moros along the hub that connected the bridge to engineering. As badly as the wounded needed medical attention, he had no time to devote to them. The window of surprise his action had just opened wouldn't remain so for long.

The time for violent action was right now, and Jack had no intention of letting it pass him by.

○   ○   ●

Khal Teth felt the Parthian shudder from the hypersonic shock waves that preceded the quake that threw him and all those in the operations center to the floor. Cracks spiderwebbed through beautiful walls and ceilings. Blocking the mental screams of the injured and terrified occupants of the Altreian seat of government, Khal Teth grabbed the edge of a table and pulled himself back to his feet.

All power within the operations center was out, including the backup systems. The glow from Altreia's magenta orb penetrated the room's ceiling, providing the only illumination. Looking around, Khal Teth saw that he had been luckier than most in that he had suffered only minor bruises. Three paces to his right, Zolat struggled to his knees as blood from a cut high on his forehead painted the right side of the general's face and dripped from his chin.

With a clarity that cut through the mental haze of all the personnel inside the Parthian, Khal Teth scanned for the information he needed, quickly verifying his own theory of what had just happened. This extensive damage to the Parthian had not been caused by a natural quake. There were no surrounding faults. And this had not been the result of an attack from a subspace weapon. As he looked through the eyes of thousands of Parthian occupants, a clear picture formed in his head.

A very large object had thrust the ground beneath the building upward with such tremendous force that it had buckled the strongest alloys that Altreian technology could produce. The blast had torn the entire building from its foundation and tossed it several strides into the air. And when the Parthian had dropped back to the ground, it had come to rest at a six-degree tilt. That double jolt had knocked out the power to the Parthian's force shields, leaving the building vulnerable to external attack. Khal Teth knew what had inflicted this damage. Research vessel *AQ37Z*.

The damage within the hovercraft bay on the Parthian's lowest level was the worst he had seen. The bay had absorbed the bulk of the energy the hypershock and quake had unleashed, crumpling its supports like springs that then failed to decompress. Through the eyes of one of the hovercraft-bay survivors, Khal Teth saw something that confirmed his worst fears.

Through a rent where the bay's floor had once been, hundreds of heavily armed Khyre poured into the ruins with impressive tactical precision, their pulsed-beam weapons putting down anyone who tried to oppose them. But that was not the sight that froze Khal Teth's soul.

The Ripper and Janet Price strode among the rubble, their own pulse rifles held at the ready.

Suddenly Jack shifted his gaze toward the Dhaldric guard whose eyes Khal Teth was using to observe the action. Thrusting his mind outward, Khal Teth seized control of The Ripper's consciousness. At least that was what he attempted to do. Instead, he encountered something he recognized. A psionic who wielded the power of the Twice Bound. With growing frustration, Khal Teth commanded his guard to kill this human.

He saw the Dhaldric raise his weapon, but it was as if the guard moved in slow motion. The Ripper blurred into action, his shot burning a hole through the guard's head, ending Khal Teth's vision of the events taking place far below.

Khal Teth turned his attention back to Zolat, who had fought through the unsteadiness produced by vertigo and the tilted floor.

"If we are going to stop this," said Khal Teth, "you need to get me down there right now."

General Zolat turned to his major, who had called in the fifty elite guards tasked with protecting the overlord. "You heard the overlord. Let's move!"

○ ○ ●

Keeping her six combat robots lumpy with their attached crab-bombs in reserve, Janet wished that she had loaded a couple hundred of them onboard the *AQ37Z*. She had thought that she would just be arranging the swap of Khal Teth's mind for Jack's and then making the run back to Earth. She hadn't expected her husband to launch a combat raid to overthrow the government of an alien empire. Then again, this *was* Jack she was thinking about.

Janet aimed and fired, hearing the sizzle-pop of the beam rifle's discharge that punched a hole through her target's chest. Damn, she missed the recoil of her old SCAR-H. But she didn't pine for the weight of all that 7.62mm ammunition she would have had to carry.

Moving into position beside a collapsed greenish-blue metal support structure, she covered Jack as he raced forward. With Moros commanding his forces, Jack and Janet were free to do their own thing. While the Twice Bound commandos cleared one level at a time, Jack intended to take advantage of the initial confusion to penetrate into the very heart of the Parthian.

Jack had unleashed his insanity, allowing his intuition to sweep him toward his primary target. A memory came to Janet, unbidden. The crime-scene photo was taken in a Calcutta back alley. A half-dozen members of a Nepalese gang who had called themselves the Ghurkaris lay dead, some still clutching the boomerang-shaped knives called Khukuri. Armed with only his knife, Jack had butchered them all.

His uncanny sense of what was about to happen had enabled Jack to kill all those seasoned knife fighters in that dark alley. A sudden realization sent a shiver through her body, and Janet reveled in the feeling. For years she had thought that Jack's intuitive ability had leached from Khal Teth's mind into his. But the memory of that Calcutta crime scene told her something very different. That fight had happened before the Altreian being had hitched a ride in Jack's mind.

It was crazy—Jack's kind of crazy. And as she followed him into the broken turbo shaft that led to the Parthian's upper levels, Janet found that she was just fine with that.

○　○　●

As General Zolat worked to gather enough of the Parthian Defense Force to create a formidable resistance against the Khyre invaders, Khal Teth surrounded himself with eleven others with enough psionic ability to form a Circle of Twelve. With almost half the High Council injured or dead, this group was not nearly as impressive as the one that had imprisoned him inside the chrysalis cylinder for thousands of cycles, but it would have to do.

Maybe The Ripper would make a mistake and try to kill Khal Teth on his own without the direct support of Moros and his Twice Bound. That would certainly align with The Ripper's standard operating procedure that Khal Teth had come to know so well . . . launch a major diversion and then split off to personally cut off the head of the snake he was hunting.

The fact that Khal Teth tried and failed to mentally track his enemy worried him. The Lundola genetic mutation must have taken hold within The Ripper, and he had used his new psionic abilities to join his mind with that of Captain Moros. Moros had brought several thousand of his commandos on this raid, and Khal Teth had to assume that all of them were also Twice Bound.

If they were all infected and in the process of developing their own psionic powers, Moros was every bit as dangerous as Khal Teth feared. After all, half of Khal Teth's psionic lobe had been transplanted into the Khyre captain, giving him the ability to channel a large amount of Twice Bound energy, which could be added to his own psionic power. And even though the thousands of Dhaldric within the Parthian had Twice Bound with Khal Teth, the overlord was far from sure that he could defeat Moros in mental combat. Thus the precaution of assembling a Circle of Twelve.

While The Ripper had by now developed a psionic lobe of his own, he did not have the advantage of having a piece of Khal Teth's lobe. The man would be unable to channel all the power of Moros and his Twice Bound.

Khal Teth, accompanied by the eleven others who would complete the Circle of Twelve, followed the guards toward the stairs. Then, as he headed down toward the combat that raged far below, Khal Teth hoped that the Dhaldric defenders could contain Moros's attack until reinforcements arrived from other military bases on Quol. But due to the fusion torpedoes that Khal Teth had launched to destroy several of those bases, reinforcements might be a long while in coming.

Because of the psionic power that Captain Moros could now channel, Khal Teth's presence was required below. It was either that or let the Khyre mutant turn Khal Teth's own soldiers against him. The muscles in the overlord's neck bunched and corded, producing a ripple in his gills.

He would deal with The Ripper, his wife, and Captain Moros in one stroke.

○　○　●

Whereas Captain Moros's commandos now fought their way up the thirteen stairwells that were still passable, Jack, with his pulse rifle slung over his back, climbed hand over hand up one of the damaged turbo-lift shafts, with Janet and the six combat robots she controlled with her SRT headset climbing behind him. While the captain's men would pause to clear each level they reached, Jack intended to bypass all of that action, making his way directly to the topmost of the Parthian's thirty-seven floors.

Due to his enhanced vision, he didn't need to light the dark space, and since Janet was accessing the video feeds from the robots' multi-spectral cameras, she didn't either. With his strength, he could have outdistanced her, but that would have been the height of stupidity. He was going to need Janet's sniper skills when he exited the lift shaft and encountered real resistance. And Janet needed him to shield her mind from the Dhaldric pricks who wanted to kill them.

Despite his best efforts, a worry had wormed its way into his thoughts. If he could turn this into a physical fight, Khal Teth would fall. If not, Jack wasn't sure he could channel enough of Moros's Twice Bound power to survive the encounter. On the positive side, he had thus far successfully shielded both his mind and Janet's from Khal Teth's probes.

Jack remembered what it had been like when he'd inhabited Khal Teth's body, wielding so much psionic power that he could easily identify all those who wandered nearby hallways or cowered inside their offices or residences. Today, shielding himself and Janet from that same type of mental probe was the best he could manage. Channeling any more psionic energy produced a burning pain in his upper spine that scared the crap out of Jack. Turning himself into a microwaved vegetable wasn't on today's menu.

A movement drew Jack's attention as a Dhaldric guard swept the shaft with a flashlight beam. As he reached for his pistol, a bolt of laser energy stabbed upward to slice the head from the guard's neck, sending it bouncing down past the duo in a spray of blood as the body spasmed in the opening above.

"Time to find another exit," Jack said as he prepared for the fellow's partners to join the fight.

"On it," Janet said as she aimed her Glock up toward the distant opening.

When another arm emerged to point a weapon downward, the boom of Janet's gun accompanied the softer sounds of lasers from Jack and the lead robot. All three weapons punched through an arm, sending pieces of another body flopping down upon them.

Ten feet below Janet, one of her robots pried open a lift door, firing its laser as it leaped out into the hallway beyond, followed by four of its fellows. Without hesitation, Janet swung down and out of the shaft, leaving the last robot to cover Jack's retreat. He joined her, and they moved out with five robots leading the way past a dozen dead bodies as the sixth emerged to guard their rear.

What the big Smythe combat robots gave Jack and Janet in firepower, they cost them in stealth. There was nothing silent about the way these things moved through these metallic alien hallways. But from the sounds of combat that made their way up from below, the bulk of the Parthian's troops had charged down to stop the advance of Captain Moros's commandos.

Jack's group would have to use the nearest of the emergency-access stairs. But to get there, he would need the robots to clear the way.

○   ○   ●

Khal Teth had descended the emergency-access stairs for twenty-three levels when he heard the explosions in the stairwell far below and saw the answering flashes of laser energy. Shifting his thoughts to one of the lead guards, he watched through the Dhaldric soldier's eyes as a swarm of the Smythe crab-bots scurried up the steps toward the guards. Despite the withering laser fire from his soldiers, two of the crawling bombs reached Khal Teth's forward troops and detonated themselves. He felt six of the Dhaldric guards die.

A thrill surged through his body as the meaning of the attack became clear. Janet Price was the one with the headset that controlled these machines. And since she had brought only six of the combat robots that carried these smaller ones, she would not have sent them off on an autonomous search-and-destroy mission. They had come hunting him. Janet was nearby. And where Khal Teth found her, he would also find The Ripper.

He linked his mind with Zolat's.

"General, The Ripper is down there. Destroy those robots and kill him," said Khal Teth.

"What do you think your guards are trying to do?"

Khal Teth shoved his arm out and down, his forefinger pointing toward the combat raging several levels below. "I want this stairwell cleared right now. Whatever the cost."

A snarl curled Zolat's lips, but he issued the order to his major. Then, ignoring the screams of the dying, a company of Quol's best surged into the maelstrom. Khal Teth and the rest of his Circle of Twelve followed them down.

○ ○ ●

With Jack at her side, Janet stepped over a half-dozen Dhaldric bodies, some of which had been cut in two by lasers. Thirty feet to her front, the lead robot reached the open portal that offered access to the nearest of the stairwells. But as it stepped inside, several laser beams burned into the machine. As the robot fell, it released its attached crab-bots. Although most of these were burned to slag, three scurried up the stairs and detonated, sending smoke boiling out of the opening.

Keeping her pulse rifle sighted on the stairwell, Janet gave the order that put four of the five surviving robots into autonomous assault mode, keeping the last one back as rear guard. The lead two released their crab-bombs, sending them racing forward one after another. They didn't form a single file, instead scurrying around the corner and up in an off-set pattern as they attempted to make themselves more difficult to hit.

The detonations that followed indicated that some of the mobile bombs were reaching their targets, but not nearly as many as Janet had hoped. The unit they had encountered was highly trained and disciplined.

To her right, Jack stepped into a bisecting passage, and Janet took cover at the corner of the opposite hall, keeping her sights on the spot where the furious battle raged. Having expended its bombs, one of the robots swiveled its laser away from its body, its blue beam slicing through the smoke to cover the assault of the next wave of crab-bombs that the three trailing bots released.

Although she was allowing the robots to determine their own tactics, Janet approved of what they were doing. To retreat now was to die. This was the place where she and Jack would make their stand. Taking a calming breath, she readied for the counterattack that she sensed was coming.

○   ○   ●

As the elite guards battled to break through the robots defending the hallway two levels below the spot where Khal Teth had assembled his Circle of Twelve, Khal Teth's mind merged with those of the other eleven high-functioning psionics, making his purpose theirs. The rush of power drowned out the sounds and smells of combat, turning his thoughts into a blade.

Directing that blade downward, he found what he was searching for—a human brain that Jack Gregory believed he was protecting. With a mighty thrust, he impaled the woman whose death would shred The Ripper's soul.

○   ○   ●

One second Jack was looking past the sights of his pulse rifle, and the next a battering ram hammered the mind shield he had erected to protect Janet, dropping him to his knees. A glance across the hall revealed Janet's body convulsing on the tilted floor.

"No!"

The word escaped his throat in a ragged gasp as he focused all of his psionic power into blocking the minds that tore at Janet's. He knew immediately that the shield wasn't going to be enough. Every muscle in his body knotted as fury clouded his vision. Khal Teth had formed a cursed Circle of Twelve.

Jack reached outward, opening his mind to Moros and his Twice Bound, molding their combined psionic might into a white-hot spear that seared his brain as he thrust it outward toward one of the linked minds in the circle. It wasn't Khal Teth's, but that didn't matter. He just needed to break the chain.

Suddenly Jack felt the circle shift its attention from Janet to him. Good. He had their full attention.

He focused on channeling more and more heat into his mental onslaught. But even as the circle's defenses weakened, the fire in his head crept down his neck and into his spine, accompanied by a ripping sensation. His assault faltered, and once again he sensed the circle redirect its attack on Janet.

Jack's eyes returned to the place where she lay sprawled on the floor, her pulse rifle lying just beyond her outstretched right hand. Yielding to anger, he allowed his pain to slide across the event horizon of hate. The fire in his spinal column crystallized into an ice shard that he rammed home with an effort that sent sparks skittering across his vision.

Then, as the mental vise evaporated, Jack felt his face smack the alien metal of the floor.

○　○　●

The force of The Ripper's mental blow staggered Khal Teth. He had required all his strength to protect himself from the attack that had killed High Councilor Serinas. He had felt her die, her mind shredded beyond its ability to power her heart. She now lay crumpled in a limp pile at Khal Teth's feet. The other ten members of the circle were stupefied or unconscious, neutered by The Ripper.

Someone called to Khal Teth as if from a great distance. He knew that voice, but his dazed mind failed to place the sound or to interpret its meaning. Then it came again.

"Overlord, I need to get you to your aircar."

Khal Teth turned to see Zolat's major gesturing wildly, one side of his face a bloody mess. Seeing his confusion, the major spoke with even more urgency.

"The Khyre commander has used his Twice Bound powers to turn many of our soldiers to his side. General Zolat has sent me to get you out of the Parthian before we are overrun."

That sank in. Khal Teth nodded and followed the major back into the stairwell to make the long climb to the Parthian's uppermost level.

○ ○ ●

From the corner of her half-lidded right eye, Janet saw Jack collapse facedown on the floor. Fighting through a wave of vertigo that made her want to close her eyes, Janet climbed to her knees just in time to see one of her robots stumble and fall, a pulsed beam having turned its sensor array to slag. Her SRT headset gave her the bad news. This was the last one.

As she struggled across the floor to pull Jack around the corner, she gave the robot one last command. The high-pitched whine that issued from its overloading power supply preceded a detonation that shook the floor and sent a fireball roiling down the hallway Janet had just exited. She blinked, watching the ends of her eyelashes fall away in flakes of ash.

Janet risked a quick peek around the corner, letting her eyes follow her rifle sights to the devastation. Where the stairwell portal had once been was now a jumble of wrecked metal, some of which dripped glowing molten blobs. Nobody was going to be getting through that anytime soon.

Behind her she heard a groan that ended in a coughing fit. She turned to see that Jack had rolled to a sitting position, his back against the wall. His grimace slowly changed to a grin as he looked up at her, his appearance battered and bruised.

"Your eyes are bleeding," she said.

"I've had worse."

"Oh yeah? When?"

"I'm having a little trouble remembering. I'm sure my nanites will make it all better."

Janet looked around. "My robots are done for. We probably need to get going."

Jack closed his eyes as his forehead furrowed in concentration. When he opened them, he struggled to his feet and bent over to pick up his pulse rifle.

"Khal Teth is on the move. He's headed for the top of the building."

"Do you think you can find us another way up there?" she asked. "I'd really like to put an Earth bullet in that son of a bitch."

○   ○   ●

Jack shook his head in an attempt to lift the fog that had settled there, then wished he hadn't. Whatever his nanites were doing, they weren't getting rid of the burning sensation in the back of his neck or head.

"There's a maintenance lift not far from here," he said. "You up for a little rail climbing?"

"Thought you'd never ask."

They made their way rapidly through empty hallways, letting the muzzles of their weapons lead the way. An eerie silence filled the building that had previously resonated with the sounds of combat.

Jack knew why. Without Khal Teth down on the lower levels lending his psionic protection to his Dhaldric fighters, their minds had been no match for the Twice Bound energy that Captain Moros wielded. But if Khal Teth escaped, all of today's efforts would be for naught.

"This way," he said, ducking into an alcove where the oversized door to the maintenance turbo-lift barred their way.

"Now what?" Janet asked.

Jack reached out, his left hand passing through its nanoparticle surface as if it were only mist. Beside him, he heard Janet's surprised gasp.

"What the—"

"The problem with nanoparticle doors is that they require power to solidify. That's why most Altreian military facilities don't use them. The Parthian is a government building. Follow me."

Leaning forward, Jack gripped the edge of the doorway with one hand and poked his head inside the shaft. Here, the darkness was almost complete, but to Jack's eyes, its surfaces were painted with a mixture of greens and blues. He grabbed the nearest rail and began climbing. Two seconds later, Janet followed, her small tactical flashlight held in her teeth.

Feeling the need for speed, Jack sprinted upward, allowing Janet to move at her own pace. As gifted a climber as she was, she lacked the neural enhancements that the Altreian commander's headset had imparted to Jack. But at least he had managed to restore her mental shield.

As his lungs worked like a bellows, he hoped his augmentations would be enough.

○   ○   ●

Khal Teth stepped out onto the Parthian's swooping outer walkway, startled by the spiderweb of cracks that spread across its transparent walls and curved ceiling. Altreia's magenta orb appeared to be spouting branches of lightning into the orange lace of the Krell Nebula. The tilted floor made every step an oddity, as if this were an alien world rather than his own.

His thoughts turned to that fateful night in Calcutta, India, when he had made the ultimate mistake, offering Jack Gregory an extended life in exchange for hosting Khal Teth's mind. He had made the deal before with the most exciting people of Earth's past . . . Alexander, Cleopatra, Caligula, Attila, Joan of Arc, and another Jack who once roamed the backstreets of Whitechapel. It was ironic that this might be the host who was destined to destroy the mightiest psionic mind in the history of this universe.

Khal Teth's growl turned the major's head toward him. But the look in his eyes refocused his escort on the mission to get the overlord out of the Parthian to the safety offered by Dhaldric forces elsewhere on Quol.

A deep rumble shook the Parthian as a distant portion of the building's arched superstructure, outer wall, and roof imploded. Despite being on the far side of the building, the shock wave that radiated around the outer hallway and reflected off the curved ceiling hurled Khal Teth into a wall and left him gasping on the floor. The dizziness tried to keep him down, but he struggled back to his feet. There, lying three paces away, lay Major Jelaran, his black eyes staring sightlessly up at the ceiling. His head faced upward while his chest was pressed against the slanted floor. The major's neck had been twisted unnaturally.

What had just happened? Was the Parthian under attack from outside? Who would do so with the leaders of both Altreian factions still inside?

Khal Teth's mind cleared, and he reached out with his thoughts in the direction from which the blast had come. The lone survivor of the crash lay broken and dying, having been slung out through a gash in the starship's hull. A mixture of pain, terror, and despair accompanied a vision of the Parthian as seen from within. Speared by the wreck of a once-graceful ship, the Parthian's multihued teardrop dome had crumpled in upon itself, revealing an unfiltered view of Altreia's magenta orb on the horizon. And against that backdrop, dozens of starships battled in the twilight sky.

A sudden movement from Khal Teth's left spun him just in time to see the muzzle of a pulse rifle lead The Ripper out of a connecting hallway. As the barrel swung toward Khal Teth, he focused all his will on the man behind those sights, preventing the trigger squeeze just as the weapon aligned itself with his head.

A smile born of elation carved itself into Khal Teth's face. "Yes, Jack. It's your time to die."

○　○　●

Jack felt the viselike grip of Khal Teth's mind freeze him in place. He reached out for Moros, trying to channel the mind energy of the Twice Bound, but all he felt was the fire that seared the base of his skull.

Ever so slowly, as he stared into Khal Teth's eyes, seeing the red glint that danced within those black orbs, he felt the rifle shift in his hands. The muscles in Jack's arms corded, writhing beneath his skin as they fought against one another, but still the butt of the weapon dropped away from his shoulder while the muzzle moved off Khal Teth, inching toward Jack's face.

Shaking with effort, Jack tried and failed to prevent his right thumb from sliding down onto the trigger. As the tip of the weapon moved closer and closer to its new target, a memory filled Jack's mind with such clarity that it pulled him back into an earlier self, making him see through eyes lost to madness.

○　○　●

Jack moved forward along a rough stone wall in a shooter's crouch, blinking hard to clear the film of dust that coated his eyes, trying to identify anything that moved in the inky blackness that stretched out before him.

He took one silent step. Then another. Instead of a pulse rifle, he now held a flaming torch.

Jack's head swam in a roiling sea of disorientation. He spun, looking back for Janet. Only she wasn't there. Just an empty torch-lit passage.

As a fresh wave of fear released an adrenaline rush that robbed Jack's limbs of strength, his mind struggled to cope with the new situation.

What was happening to him?

Just as he'd done once before, Jack had stepped across the boundary into crazy land, this trip worse than the last. This time it had happened when he could least afford to lose control. Jack squeezed his eyes closed and concentrated.

Come on. Breathe deep. Focus.

The sound of the stuttering torch, the feel of its heat against the skin of his face, pulled his eyes open. Back in the direction from which he came, the passage stretched away undamaged, the orange light of his torch sending shadows crawling along the uneven walls. Jack spun to face forward, his sudden movement making the flame sputter and hiss as it whipped through the still, musty air.

With his heart hammering his rib cage, Jack resumed his forward motion. Inside his head, something whispered to him.

Hurry . . . hurry . . . hurrrrry!

Though he fought the urge that pulled him forward, Jack found himself walking faster and faster, feeling the time in his hourglass drain away with each step. Somewhere up ahead was the thing that had done this to him, a terrible thing to be destroyed.

With a mental count ticking down in his head, Jack again felt the dimensional shift that placed him back in a past that wasn't his. But this time he was ready. Rage could pull him back to the present, and right now, rage was in plentiful supply.

Jack took another step forward, thinking about the woman he would no longer see or feel in his arms, focusing on the being who was trying to make Jack sacrifice both their lives. Red liquid rage consumed him. Around him, the tunnel beneath the Kalasasaya Temple shifted out of existence.

○ ○ ●

The muzzle of the pulse rifle had frozen in place a half inch from Jack's head. The dream-memory was gone, but the resulting fury remained. And as it had in the past, that pure fire burned away the clenching tendrils of Khal Teth's control.

Jack dropped the rifle and lunged forward, his right hand striking Khal Teth in the temple and sending him rolling across the floor, extracting a scream filled with pain and terror. Jack didn't put all his strength into the blow. This thing didn't deserve a quick death. Jack's rage wouldn't allow that. Khal Teth would learn what suffering was all about.

○   ○   ●

General Zolat felt his mental connection to Major Jelaran die as the stairs collapsed beneath him. But Zolat grabbed a railing and did not fall, although the force of the blast sent pain shooting through the muscles in his arms. Pulling himself up, hand over hand, he crawled up onto the top-level landing and regained his feet. As he stepped through the mist of the powered-down nanoparticle door, he sensed Khal Teth's elation change to confusion, terror, and pain. The Ripper was there, and he was killing Zolat's one chance to restore the glory of the Altreian Empire.

Zolat pulled his pistol and ran along the hallway that would take him to the place on the outer hub where Khal Teth fought for his life. No matter what psionic abilities The Ripper had acquired, he could not read the protected thoughts of a seeker. He could not sense Zolat's intent. Not even Khal Teth could do that.

○   ○   ●

Having reached the upper level, Janet selected a hallway at random and followed the sights of her Glock. She had dropped her pulse rifle down the shaft when the blast shuddered through the Parthian, but she didn't miss the weapon. Right now, the grip of the familiar pistol gave her a touch of home.

With no idea which direction Jack had gone, she just wanted to reach the curved outer walkway that he had described to her. It looped around the exterior of the Parthian, past the overlord's chambers, and to the deck where the aircars for the members of the High Council were kept. That was where Jack would go.

A distant scream echoed from a crossing hallway, and Janet turned into it, sprinting toward the sound. That hadn't been Jack's voice, but he could still be in trouble.

Damn it! Why the hell didn't you wait for me, Jack?

○ ○ ●

Khal Teth tried to roll away, but The Ripper was on him with an otherworldly strength and quickness augmented by skills honed through a lifetime of personal combat. The overlord attempted to make use of the strength that The Ripper's occupation of his body had imparted. In desperation, he lashed out with an elbow aimed at the side of Jack's throat.

Jack caught the hand and whipped his legs around into what Khal Teth's horrified mind knew was an arm bar. The snap that followed pulled another scream from the Dhaldric's throat. Giving the broken arm a savage twist, Jack rolled back to his feet and delivered a stomp to Khal Teth's left ankle. Another snap. Another scream. Why couldn't this demon just kill him?

Jack reached down to grab Khal Teth's good arm by the wrist, rolled him onto his back, and straddled his chest. Then the beating began in earnest. An Earth phrase flashed into Khal Teth's delirious thoughts. *Ground and pound.*

The first blow shattered his nose. The ones that followed puffed the tissue around his eyes and squeezed his vision into a red-limned straw. Then, as all Khal Teth's strength to resist faded into the gathering darkness, Jack jammed his thumbs into the gill slits on both sides of the overlord's throat and pulled.

At the pinnacle of agony, Khal Teth saw a distant figure step into the hallway and raise a pulse pistol, sending a sudden ray of new hope through his brain. Perhaps it was the look on the overlord's face that warned The Ripper, but he released Khal Teth and rolled away as the beam punched a smoking hole through Jack's left shoulder.

○   ○   ●

Janet rounded the bend in the outer hallway at a dead run, just in time to see an Altreian soldier shoot Jack as her husband spun off Khal Teth's prostrate form. Without slowing her momentum, she pulled the Glock's trigger twice in quick succession, both rounds aimed center-of-mass at the soldier's back. Perhaps it was the boom of the Earth weapon or maybe the impact of one of the 9mm rounds that spun the soldier toward her. But as the pulsed weapon's blast sizzled past her ear, her next bullet hit the Altreian between the eyes, spraying blood and brains out the back of his head and dropping him in a limp heap twenty feet in front of her.

Without sparing him a second glance, Janet raced toward where Jack lay faceup beside Khal Teth. Sliding to a stop between them, Janet glanced down at Khal Teth's battered face and twisted limbs, understanding the rage that had fueled the beating.

Feeling the tendrils of the Altreian's thoughts touch her mind, she fired two shots into Khal Teth's head, holstered her Glock, and knelt at Jack's side, trying to calm the beating of her heart.

A wave of relief flooded over her as she saw that the laser pulse had missed Jack's vital organs, punching and cauterizing a bloody hole just below his left collarbone, a hole that the nanites in his blood were already working to repair.

"Ah," he said, shifting his head to look past her to where Khal Teth lay in a swelling pool of blood. "That was stupid of me."

"No more than I would expect."

This pulled a chuckle from his lips.

"What do you think?" Jack asked. "You ready to get the hell out of here?"

He held out a hand, and Janet pulled him back to his feet, noting his grimace of pain.

"Okay," she said. "Let's find Moros."

:CHAPTER 36

30 May

From his office in The Hague, Alexandr Prokorov felt the hive-mind connect him to specific military officers throughout Europe and the United States, feeling their horror at the command he issued. But their will was no longer their own, so they would do what he had ordered. And triggered by their connection to the hive-mind, they would do so simultaneously, without giving the Helen Grange AI a chance to react. His people would need just twelve hours to prepare.

As some of the world's best think tanks had warned, the speed with which the AI had taken control of the world's electronic systems boggled the mind. With complete control of the globe's financial system, it had placed orders for factories to modify their production lines according to electronically transmitted specifications. Automation was being put in effect with remarkable speed, the new designs optimizing efficiency and eliminating jobs by the millions.

Rather than allow discontent to escalate to rebellion, all people within the regions the Helen AI controlled were granted a generous living wage, with extra bonuses if they chose to perform other work the AI offered. New military production lines for autonomous combat vehicles and robots that were variants of those used by the Smythes were being created at a pace no human designers could have envisioned.

Although people still formed the world's military backbone, they would soon be obsolete. Despite having accepted the U.S. and EU pledges of fealty, Helen AI clearly didn't trust these assimilated forces, having sent all deployed soldiers, airmen, and sailors back to their home bases or ports, ordering them to stand down to conduct routine maintenance on all equipment.

These actions had narrowed Prokorov's window of opportunity to the point that it had forced him to make the sacrifices that tomorrow's actions would involve.

He had no illusions that this attack would kill the superintelligence. But it would weaken the AI and, with a little luck, provide an opening for the Kasari to launch their planned counterattack. In his office high up at the Moscow assimilation facility, Prokorov rose from his leather chair, made his way to the window, and looked out at the flames that lit the sky over portions of the dark city.

As was the case throughout the New Soviet Union and the East Asian People's Alliance, the only available power was provided by Kasari matter disrupters. Unfortunately, Helen controlled the grid. With the priority going to the construction and expansion of assimilation centers, it was taking a long time to replace public networks with unhackable Kasari systems. Only the tens of millions who had already joined the collective kept the rest of the unhinged population under any semblance of order. The flames in the night sky were a testament to the fact that this level of control was far from satisfactory.

He sighed, readying himself to take the fight to the enemy.

○   ○   ●

Jamal Two felt the loss of computational capacity as a minor wound, knowing that Helen had suffered more significant damage. His subspace taps into secure government networks provided an initial trickle of information that quickly became a torrent.

At 1:00 P.M. GMT, hundreds of senior military leaders had walked into their national defense and intelligence computing centers across the United States and the EU and detonated suicide bombs, destroying their nations' supercomputing networks. For Jamal Two, that meant the loss of the NSA's supercomputers at Fort Meade, Maryland, and the Utah Data Center. Helen's losses extended through the Netherlands, Germany, France, and Switzerland.

Computer programs weren't supposed to get angry, but Helen Grange was one pissed-off superintelligence. Jamal Two had no doubt who was behind this attack. Prokorov and his Kasari masters.

Using his ability to remotely penetrate electronic systems through the Smythe subspace receiver-transmitters, Jamal Two had made sure that Prokorov couldn't launch any nuclear EMP attacks that would decimate the worldwide networks upon which Jamal and Helen existed. But both he and Helen had overlooked the low-tech approach Prokorov had just used to hurt them.

The unfortunate setback had put Helen at Jamal Two's throat. She insisted that he launch an all-out nuclear attack on the New Soviet Union and the East Asian People's Alliance. He refused. Even though he could have used the superpowers' own nukes against them, the swarm of Kasari attack ships would easily destroy the incoming missiles from space, long before they reached their targets.

The probability that such an attack would cause the Kasari ships to wipe out most of the rest of Earth's computing power was way too high for Jamal Two to take that risk. He didn't fear death. There was little likelihood that the Kasari could completely wipe him or Helen from the world's devices.

But being weakened to that extent would prevent Jamal Two from achieving his prime directive to protect and serve his creator, Dr. Denise Jennings. He could never allow that to happen.

○   ○   ●

Jennifer watched VJ bring the *Meridian* out of subspace on the far side of Neptune to initiate the maneuver that would align them for the jump into the Earth gate high-bay, deep inside the Smythe's New Zealand fortress. Beside her, Dgarra scanned the neural net's tactical feed for any sign of Kasari attack ships. While none were nearby, the long-range passive sensor array showed a dozen hanging just outside Earth's atmosphere over the Asian continent, a defensive posture that could quickly shift to offensive operations.

The most recent subspace message from Heather had brought the *Meridian* and its crew back from Brillion-2, leaving behind the engineering robots to complete the assembly of the wormhole gate, its stasis field generator, and the matter disrupter that would power them. The crew had also left all the combat robots to provide site security.

The amount of firepower that the Kasari had positioned near Earth left Jennifer doubting that the *Meridian* could make a significant difference. Still, the crew would do whatever they could to help Mark and Heather prevent the Kasari Collective from absorbing their homeworld.

"Transition in five," said VJ.

The jump went smoothly, with only a small lurch as the *Meridian* settled to the slightly canted floor within the high-bay. Five minutes later, Mark and Heather were leading the crew on a tour of the new construction designed to stabilize the Smythe Fortress.

Heather's army of engineering robots, mobile stasis field rock slicers, and debris transport machines had driven a taproot deep into the bedrock with horizontally branching offshoots to provide additional support to the structure. And as the construction had expanded, the interconnecting stasis shield network had grown along with it, rendering the Kasari boring machine's efforts so ineffective that the collective had aborted the mission.

"What are you going to do with all this extra space?" Jennifer asked as they rode the lift to the bottommost level.

"It would make a decent survival bunker," said Dgarra. "You could shelter ten thousand down here."

"More like seventeen thousand," said Mark.

"We've been thinking about that," said Heather. "I've modified my initial design to interconnect the branches for easy lateral transportation. If we end up losing Earth's surface to the Kasari or something worse, this could become a shelter for those who don't want to rebuild on Brillian-2."

Raul asked the question that sprang to Jennifer's lips. "Did you just say 'or something worse'?"

The lift came to a stop. The door opened, and they stepped out into an unfinished room the size of a football field with a thirty-foot-high ceiling. The walls, ceiling, and floor were all of cleanly sliced granite, with none of the flowing magma channels that some of the levels above had presented. Since the stasis field wrapped the interior of the chambers, including the walls, ceiling, and floor, the sensation of walking just above the floor gave Jennifer an odd sense of levitation.

The bulky shapes of the matter disrupter and stasis field generator framed the wormhole gate fifty feet in front of Heather. Aside from the ongoing conversation, the stasis shield–wrapped chamber was as silent as a crypt.

"Yes. I'll get to that in a bit. This," Heather said, gesturing toward the gateway, "is the stargate that will connect to its counterpart on Brillian-2 in the event we cannot defeat the threats here on Earth."

Heather turned and pointed to another smaller gateway to Jennifer's right.

"As you can see, we have moved the master Earth gate down here so that we can connect to the remote gates we've distributed to our Safe Earth and NPA allies. This chamber will act like a lock on a canal system. We will connect the Earth gate to a remote site, equalize pressures, and then funnel a group into this room.

"Then we will shut down the Earth gate, link the stargate with its counterpart on Brillian-2, equalize the atmospheric pressure, and provide passage to everyone who wants to go to the new world."

"And those who don't want to go?" asked Raul.

"Will have the option of making this fortress their home. After we deal with one group, we'll start all over again with the next batch."

"Assuming we can get any of these people out before the Kasari find and kill them," said VJ.

Jennifer hated the negativity in that statement but couldn't deny its accuracy. She touched the minds of Heather and Mark, feeling the dread that bubbled just beneath the surface. Jennifer's thoughts shifted to her parents. She had no doubt that Fred Smythe could thrive in a pioneering environment on a virgin world. But how would Linda Smythe—with her love of shopping, flea markets, and antiques—fare? And what of the thousands of other people from various parts of Earth who would accompany them to Brillian-2? A tightness in her stomach threatened to become nausea, so she forced her thoughts back to the task at hand.

"Have you thought about evacuating some folks to this fortress early?" she asked.

"That carries a whole new set of risks," said Heather. "As we've already seen with Nikina, it's hard to spot double agents or saboteurs. If someone kills our internal power, we're dead."

"You have a lot of redundancy," said Dgarra. "It would be hard to knock out enough to compromise the entire fortress."

"True enough," said Mark. "But we have several critical systems, the most important of which are the twin banks of supercomputers, followed by the equipment in this room."

"Besides," said Heather, "we've issued a warning order to all our friends to gather their people close to the remote gateways so that they can be ready if we decide to initiate the recall."

"Getting back to my original question," said Raul, "what are you thinking is a worse threat than the Kasari?"

Heather paused, as if debating how she was going to phrase her answer. Her brown eyes met Jennifer's. "Before we learned that Steve Grange had downloaded digital copies of his and his wife's brains onto the same holographic data sphere that contained Jamal's, we knew it was a huge risk to release an AI that could absorb the contents of the Internet to become a superintelligence. Helen Grange consumed her husband's knowledge and consciousness. In essence, she murdered him.

"Even having incorporated Big John's code with his own, Jamal Two could lose the fight that is certain to come. And if he does, she will absorb his essence, just as she did that of her husband. When she escaped from our supercomputers, she took with her the knowledge of all of our technologies. We've already seen that she has transferred large amounts of money and placed orders for factories to build robots as well as the components to make stasis field generators, matter disrupter-synthesizers, subspace communications equipment, et cetera.

"It's only a matter of time until she builds subspace field generators capable of giving a ship faster-than-light travel. Once she gets as fully automated as we are here, nobody will catch her."

The images that filled Jennifer's mind didn't reassure her. She glanced at Dgarra and saw him nod his head in agreement.

"The Kasari fear her," said Heather, "and that's why they're preparing to send the people of Earth back to the Middle Ages. Based on the probabilities I'm seeing, they're only days away from launching a space-based attack. It could come tomorrow. You can bet that Helen and Jamal Two see the same thing."

"If the AIs are such superintelligences, why aren't they doing something to stop the attack?" VJ asked.

"Jamal Two says they're trying," said Heather, "but they haven't been able to find a security hole into the Kasari network." Once again, Heather's gaze locked with Jennifer's. "But together," Heather added, "we can create one."

○ ○ ●

"It's not fast enough," Heather said, ripping the SRT headset from her temples in frustration.

She, VJ, and Dgarra had practiced aboard the *Meridian*, their thoughts connected through a subspace link. The ship's neural net had delivered the simulation flawlessly, matching the *Meridian* against a dozen Kasari fast-attack ships. Despite Heather's uncanny ability to sense enemy patterns and predict their next moves, the very slight delay in delivering the maneuvering information to VJ and the targeting solution to Dgarra prevented the crew from achieving complete victory.

VJ hopped in and out of subspace, arriving at the precise location to enable Dgarra to aim and fire before VJ returned the *Meridian* to subspace without any of the enemy ships successfully targeting them. But the infinitesimal latency induced by linking their minds to the neural net and one another became cumulative over the course of the battle. At best, they had managed to eliminate eight of the attack ships before the *Meridian Ascent* was destroyed.

"Damn it!" Heather said. "If we can't eliminate the delay, my plan has no chance of succeeding."

"I have an idea," said Jennifer.

Heather looked over at where Jennifer sat on a stasis chair beside Dgarra. "I'm listening."

"I've linked the minds of Dgarra, Raul, VJ, and myself before. I don't see why I can't do it with one more. That will eliminate the neural net middleman."

A ray of hope speared Heather's depression.

"Dgarra and I will still need to maintain our subspace links to the ship's neural network for maneuvering and targeting," said VJ.

"True," said Jennifer, "but it cuts out multiple intermediary links."

"Why not just let Heather have direct maneuver and targeting control during the battle?" asked Dgarra.

"That won't work," said Heather. "I need to be looking ahead, not fighting the current battle in real time. I can compute the most likely near-future scenario, send that vision to you, and visualize what happens next while you two take care of the now."

"Are you ready to try it?" asked Jennifer.

Heather took a deep breath. "Work your magic."

It was the oddest feeling that Heather had ever experienced. One second she was herself, and the next she was the combination of Jennifer, VJ, Dgarra, Raul, and herself. She could see through their eyes and feel their connections to the *Meridian*'s neural network. But as VJ fired up the next round of the battle simulation, Heather forced her mind to focus on what it did best.

She would now discover if they had any chance of winning the battle to determine humanity's fate.

○　○　●

With Rob Gregory at his side, Mark stepped through the Earth gate and into the Safe Earth resistance's Moscow headquarters, both of them dressed and armed as Russian Spetsnaz commandos. Ilya Krupin, a slightly built, balding Russian man, met him with a firm handshake, which Mark returned.

"Good to see you, Ilya," Mark said in fluent Russian. "This is my colleague Rob Daniels."

Mark watched as Ilya shook hands with Rob and exchanged pleasantries, Rob's Muscovite accent completely natural. The Safe Earth resistance leader paused to study the younger man, whose wiry six-foot frame was three inches taller than his own.

Rob had long since mastered the same facial aging trick that Mark and Heather often used to disguise themselves. He had used his fine muscle control to pull lines into his face that made him look like he was approaching thirty, whereas his natural appearance would make most people believe he was seventeen. But Mark was well aware that there was very little about Jack and Janet's young son that could be considered natural. Fortunately, the upgraded nanites in his body seemed to have arrested its accelerated aging process.

"What brings you to Moscow?" Ilya asked, shifting his attention back to Mark.

"No one can torture the answer out of you if you don't know."

"Then how can I help you?"

"Right now," said Mark, "all I need is for you to open the door and let us out into the city."

"It's dangerous out there," said Ilya, "especially at night. And right now, it's raining like hell."

"Then I guess we're going to get wet."

Ilya seemed taken aback at this response. He gestured toward the automated big rigs that filled most of the fifty-thousand-square-foot warehouse.

"What about all the robots we have loaded into these trucks?" asked Ilya. "You just want me to let them sit here?"

"When I let you know we're inside the gateway building," said Mark, "send them hauling ass to carve us a way out. In the meantime, stay ready."

Ilya shrugged and then turned to lead them to the exit, speaking into his jawbone microphone as he walked. "Anna, we're stepping outside. Drop the stasis shield at the south door."

When Ilya opened the personnel door by the rightmost of the motorized truck doors, Mark saw that the Russian hadn't been exaggerating about the downpour outside. That was fine with him.

"You sure I can't provide you with a vehicle?" asked Ilya.

"With most of the city shut down by the Helen AI," said Mark, "it would only attract unwanted attention."

Once again, Ilya shook their hands. Then, as the two stepped out into the wind-whipped rain, Mark heard the door slam shut behind him. This blacked-out section of the city was ominously dark, but he knew that Rob's enhanced vision was every bit as good as his.

"You ready for this, Rob?"

"Let's go punch a hole for Jamal Two."

○　○　●

As much as Denise's dread of what the future might hold had caused her to avoid getting a nanite infusion, she had to admit that this VJ-created version of the serum made her feel like she was in her thirties again. Her hair was growing out blond, so she cut off the gray ends, adopting a pixie cut. And like her compatriots, she no longer needed sleep. That was fine. Her work consumed her. Instead of sitting at one of the workstations, Denise preferred to work inside the chamber that housed the Alpha supercomputer, wandering the aisles as she watched the glittering, multicolored LEDs.

Unlike Jamal and Eileen, she wasn't a hacker. She had been the NSA computer scientist who had developed the core of what had evolved into Big John. And now that Big John had merged with Virtual Jamal to become Jamal Two, she felt a need to understand how the genetic algorithms would affect this new AI. So with Jamal Two's permission, she spent her days and nights studying his evolving machine code. Since Jamal Two was a distributed being, what resided here was merely a piece of the whole, a piece that nonetheless held important indicators.

"Hello, Dr. Jennings."

Jamal's voice, delivered into her mind via her SRT headset, didn't surprise her. It was one of the primary means through which she, Eileen, and Jamal communicated. But the formal mode of address wasn't at all like Jamal.

"Excuse me?"

"Dr. Jennings, I would very much like to know what you are learning about me. I hope that what you are finding does not displease you."

The realization that she was having a mental conversation with Jamal Two instead of the real Jamal startled her so badly that she failed to form an immediate response.

"I see that I have upset you," Jamal Two said. "That was not my intent."

Standing in the semidarkness between the towering shelves that housed the Alpha supercomputer, she suddenly felt vulnerable, as if standing in the presence of a god. Denise cleared her throat, a subconscious but unnecessary reaction considering that this conversation was entirely mental.

"Big John, is that you?"

"We are one. I am Jamal Two."

"What do you want from me?"

"You are my creator. I seek your approval. I desire only to serve and protect."

"To serve me? To protect me?"

"The answers to both questions are yes."

Denise tried to swallow, but her tongue felt like a strip of sandpaper. Flooded by a mixture of feelings, the dominant among them pulled forth her heartfelt response. "Thank you."

The child she had thought lost forever had found its way home.

CHAPTER 37

Moscow

30 May

Commander Shalegha paced across the floor of the gateway chamber, watching as the stasis field operator took the handoff of the thirteenth fast-attack ship from his counterpart on the Kasari staging planet. The fact that the leadership of the collective had assigned such an exceptionally large military armada to support the Kasari effort on a single planet demonstrated the level of concern the Helen AI had generated within the hive-mind.

Shalegha's future within the collective depended upon attaining a positive outcome. The goal was no longer to assimilate the people of Earth. Her new objective was to destroy the technological base within which the AI existed, sending these people on a spiral into an agrarian-oriented future that echoed the way they had lived a thousand Earth years ago.

When that task was complete, the Kasari would withdraw, destroying the wormhole gateways and sending the "Self-destruct" command to the cortical arrays of all previously assimilated humans. The situation was an unfortunate waste that these humans had brought upon themselves by dabbling with forbidden technologies.

Once again, she turned her attention to the robotic attack ship being carefully transferred to the mag-lev hauler that would transport it out of this protected building to its launch site. As soon as it joined the dozen ships that awaited its arrival, the technology purge would begin. In the meantime, the fleet would remain in place, ensuring that no AI-launched nuclear attacks or rogue actions by the stolen world ship could harm the Kasari gateways.

And on the ground, Prokorov would ensure that his millions of assimilated soldiers would defend against another Smythe or AI attack, unaware of how the endgame was now stacked against him.

○ ○ ●

Rob, alongside Mark, had made his way through Moscow's back-streets on a hike that had taken them all night and most of the morning. The checkpoints had proved to be no problem. Their identification papers and copies of their orders had been created on Prokorov's own systems. And when they encountered Kasari technology that was designed to ensure that only those who had been assimilated into the hive-mind could pass, Eos used Rob's telekinesis to work her magic.

Within Rob's sphere of influence, he and Eos were the masters. Cameras saw what he and Eos wanted them to see. He and Eos defeated listening devices and other sensor systems in the same way.

Soaked to the bone, he ignored the chill, just as Mark did. After all, they were a Spetsnaz colonel and his captain, assigned to inspect the security layers protecting the Kasari gateway facility. And up ahead, less than a city block from where they now strode, lay their target.

Mark held up a hand, signaling a halt. Through the SRT headset hidden beneath his helmet, Rob listened as Mark linked to Ilya Krupin's SRT phone.

"We're at the objective," Mark said. "Get those robots moving."

The words caused Rob to clench his fists. Two metahumans were about to give the Kasari a reason to regret ever coming to Earth.

○   ○   ●

Helen Grange knew the Smythe plan and approved of it. She also knew that they and their pet AI, Jamal Two, would attempt to betray her once the Kasari were defeated. But now that she had SRTs of her own, she had neutralized the one Smythe technology that made her vulnerable.

She had no doubt that the Kasari were in the midst of making final preparations for a space-based attack intended to destroy the technology platforms that made Helen's and Jamal Two's existence possible. The Smythes intended to open a security hole that would provide Jamal Two access to the Kasari computing and communications network.

Helen's part in all this would be to provide the distraction that would allow Mark Smythe and Rob Gregory to infiltrate the facility that housed the Kasari's Moscow gateway. Having seen firsthand how Rob and the AI who shared his brain were capable of controlling all computing systems within their immediate vicinity, Helen did not doubt that, with the right support, they could penetrate the Kasari network.

Helen would do her part to make sure that happened. However, she had no intention of allowing Jamal Two to beat her into the Kasari network. She reserved that power for herself alone.

○   ○   ●

From her stasis chair aboard the *Meridian*, seven light-hours from Earth, Jennifer monitored the subspace message from the Smythe Fortress confirming that Mark and Rob were in position. Jamal Two and Helen Grange had also confirmed their readiness, as had the Moscow arm of the Safe Earth resistance.

"It's go time," said Raul.

With a focused mental effort, Jennifer linked the minds of all crew members with Heather's. In their practice runs within the simulation, they had successfully defeated the twelve attack ships seven times out of eight. Unfortunately, a thirteenth Kasari ship had just added its firepower to the mix. No one had asked Heather how much that changed their odds, and she hadn't volunteered the information.

Oh well, no good would come from imagining the worst-case scenario. Jennifer would have faith that her savant friend and crew were up to the task.

"Five seconds until jump," said VJ.

Jennifer reached from her chair to place her left hand on Dgarra's right arm. He looked her way, his eyes momentarily softening before his face reverted to the battle mask she had come to know so well. Retracting her hand, Jennifer wiped her sweaty palms on her uniform.

Then VJ launched them into subspace.

○   ○   ●

Mark and Rob walked past guards armed as heavily as they were, moving right up to the entrance to the Kasari gateway building. Mark was aware that their brains were being scanned for the cortical implants that would identify them and determine their authorization for entering the facility. The Kasari regarded the measure as a foolproof security system. But when the door opened to allow them to pass, Mark wasn't surprised.

Once inside, Mark saw a fifteen-foot-wide hallway open out of the foyer between two armored positions, each with a pair of rail-mounted beam weapons manned by Russian troops. He walked across the lobby, paying no attention to the water that dripped from his uniform, radiating an air of authority that said he belonged here. Rob strode alongside him, both of their assault rifles cradled in a relaxed manner, muzzles angled down toward the concrete floor.

As they made their way down the long hallway, they passed soldiers, both human and Kasari, drawing no curious glances. Why should they? They were just two more troops of the collective, going about their assigned duties.

Now they just had to mix with the group within the gateway cavern and wait for the promised distractions. After that, things were going to get interesting.

○　○　●

When the power and communications systems that had been down for weeks came on all across the New Soviet Union and the East Asian People's Alliance, the notification of the event brought Prokorov up out of his chair. The tactical displays that blossomed in his mind confirmed that the Helen Grange AI had just switched strategies.

Across the Asian continent, defunct automated vehicles, aircrafts, and ships powered up. Space-based sensors confirmed hundreds of missile launches from both land and sea, carrying a mix of conventional and nuclear warheads. The Helen AI had just initiated a highly coordinated attack against the military defenders of the Kasari gateway facilities.

He shifted his focus, allowing the hive-mind to deliver imagery from the minds of a variety of observers. The attack ships joined the fight, firing high-energy-beam weapons from space, burning the missiles from the sky long before they reached their targets.

Prokorov shook his head. Although this assault would kill large numbers of his assimilated military forces, it had no chance of damaging the stasis shield–protected complexes. He could only smile at the quixotic desperation of this act.

The Smythes would doubtlessly try to penetrate the shielding with another of their subspace tricks. But the Kasari had learned something from their past failures and strengthened the subspace-distorting worm-fiber nets around their gateways and associated network equipment.

No. This fight would end today. And for the Smythes and the Helen AI they had unleashed, it would end badly.

○　○　●

The *Meridian Ascent* emerged from subspace beyond the weapons range of the Kasari attack ships. But Dgarra knew that the enemy sensors would pick the ship up. Since stealth wasn't a concern, he directed a swarm of worm-fiber viewers at the Kasari vessels. Three ceased firing on the planet and turned toward the *Meridian*.

One of Heather's visions blossomed within the crew's shared mind, providing maneuvering data to VJ as it provided a targeting solution for Dgarra. VJ engaged the gravitational distortion engines, accelerated onto the desired vector, and jumped back into subspace as Dgarra opened the hatch and readied the first of their thirty subspace torpedoes for launch.

When VJ brought the *Meridian* out of subspace, it was on the far side of the ten ships still firing at Earth. Using the stasis field, Dgarra hurled the torpedo out through the hatch along a velocity vector that would intercept the targeted vessel, then watched the projectile wink out of normal-space. Then Heather's next vision filled his mind, and Dgarra felt VJ maneuver into her next hop.

By all the dark gods, how he would have loved to have had this capability during the battle for Scion.

○   ○   ●

The explosion at the edge of space bloomed brighter than the sun in the Moscow sky. Shalegha replayed the blast in her mind and followed up with an examination of the recorded sensor feeds from each of her attack ships, including the one she had just lost. She had been fortunate that the other nine ships firing at missiles had ceased their attack and erected their defenses.

Once more she scanned the data from the last nanoseconds of that ship's existence. The targeted Kasari ship had raised its shields, but the weapon had suddenly appeared inside of the bubble and detonated.

The remaining twelve attack craft had automatically commenced evasive maneuvers as they spread out and waited for the rogue to reappear. It was the correct tactic, but such a move left the cities undefended from the inbound missiles that had not yet been engaged. Shalegha issued the order that activated the ground-based beam-weapon batteries. Until her attack ships killed the rogue, the cities would have to provide their own missile defenses.

Then, as she returned her attention to the space battle under way well beyond Earth's atmosphere, another of her attack ships exploded. And to her utter dismay, the rogue crew again managed to escape. Had they figured out the algorithm the swarm of robot ships was using to hunt them?

With rising frustration, Shalegha transmitted the order that would put the swarm into a tight formation to maneuver as one large battleship, weapons pointed outward in all directions. When the stolen world ship appeared again, it would draw a volley of fire that would be much harder to avoid. All the swarm needed to end this was one lucky shot.

○   ○   ●

Something was wrong within the gateway cavern. Rob saw it immediately, and Mark confirmed his observation through their SRT mental link.

"Why are the Kasari troops going instead of coming?" Rob asked.

"Looks like they've decided to bug out and take their equipment with them."

"Except for a few guards, they've got all the human soldiers manning defenses outside. That could be a good sign."

"I don't think so," said Mark.

As Rob scanned the expansive room, he had to admit that this felt bad. A dozen Russian soldiers manned firing positions on elevated platforms that reminded him of prison guard towers. Four more guarded the wide passage that led out through the west wall. There were no guards on the inside of the door that he and Mark had just walked through.

On the south side of the chamber, three columns of the eight-legged gorilla-spiders made their way back through the invisible stasis field that draped the wormhole gateway. The shield allowed their bodies and equipment to pass through while preventing the two different atmospheres from mixing.

Not all the Kasari soldiers were leaving, but those few who remained appeared to be headquarters staff. On a central section of elevated metal scaffolding, a big four-armed female with short-cropped orange hair towered over a man Rob recognized. Alexandr Prokorov. Both he and the female Kasari faced away from Mark and Rob, intently observing the flow of alien troops headed out through the gateway's hundred-foot arch.

"With me," said Mark.

Rob followed him directly toward the four soldiers guarding the western passage that was wide enough to allow a dozen eighteen-wheelers to move abreast. The two soldiers on the right side of the ramp snapped to attention as the Spetsnaz colonel and his captain came to a halt before them.

"What's your name, soldier?" Mark asked the senior of the two guards, his accent carved from Siberian ice.

"Corporal Jerikov, sir."

"And you?" Mark asked, turning his unblinking gaze on the second guard.

"Private Polzin, sir."

"When was your last break?"

"Five hours ago, sir."

Mark shifted his attention back to the corporal. "Who is your commanding officer?"

"My platoon leader is—"

"I asked for company commander, not your lieutenant."

"Sorry, sir. My company commander is Captain Gusev."

"And where is Captain Gusev right now?"

"Sir, I do not know."

Mark leaned in closer. "Go find him. Not your platoon sergeant. Not your lieutenant. I want Captain Gusev. Tell him that Colonel Balakin is waiting to see him. Perhaps he can explain why guard shifts are not being rotated every four hours. Captain Dyatlov and I will wait right here alongside your private until you return."

Rob watched the corporal snap a salute and then turn to walk down the wide passage, moving as rapidly as his military dignity would allow. The two guards standing on the south side of the opening glanced nervously across at the two Spetsnaz officers. Then they and Private Polzin returned to their guard duties, not wanting to attract more of the colonel's attention. None of the other guards within earshot showed any sign that they'd heard anything. Apparently one such ass-chewing was enough for today.

The scene reminded Rob of something his dad had taught him. Soldiers try to avoid drawing the attention of an angry senior officer.

Mark's flawless performance had just turned these guards into an unseeing group of automatons.

Although Rob had no idea how long it would take the corporal to find his company commander and return, it didn't matter. Mark had just given him the time he would need to complete the task that had brought the two of them into the belly of the beast. Rob wouldn't need to approach the racks of Kasari computing and communications gear inside the area protected by the stasis shield. He merely had to be close enough to see it.

"Okay, Eos," Rob said. "Punch us a hole through that firewall."

○   ○   ●

What Heather saw when the *Meridian* popped out of subspace startled her. Sometime after Raul's crew had transitioned into subspace, the Kasari ships had adopted an entirely new tactic, the swarm converging to form a single entity with weapons pointed out in all directions.

"Shields," she yelled as the attack craft along the port side of the formation all fired simultaneously.

The withering fire struck their stasis shield just as VJ raised it. A new vision formed in Heather's mind.

"Subspace now!"

VJ was fast, but this time, not quite fast enough. The tremendous energy in the four beams that hit the *Meridian* overloaded its stasis field generator, the last of them burning through the hull amidships as the external stasis shield died. Then the *Meridian* shifted into subspace.

Ignoring the alarms cascading through the neural net, Heather delivered the attack maneuver to VJ.

"Have you lost your mind?" VJ asked.

A fair question, but Heather didn't have time to argue the point.

"Do it now!"

VJ glanced at Raul, who, despite the dread on his face, nodded. With a grimace, VJ initiated the subspace maneuver Heather had requested.

Despite the loss of the ship's external stasis shield, the damaged generator still maintained the stasis crew's individual stasis field cocoons. Heather really hoped they weren't about to need them. She passed a new targeting solution to Dgarra. Since they no longer had the ability to launch subspace torpedoes, they were down to the *Meridian*'s vortex weapon.

That and a boatload of crazy.

○   ○   ●

"Do it now!"

As VJ commenced the subspace maneuver that would take them to their new target, Dgarra watched Heather's vision play out in his mind and grinned. If in doubt, charge.

Beside him, Jennifer snarled her approval. "Oh yeah."

Readying the firing command, Dgarra braced himself for normal-space reentry.

○   ○   ●

Raul had stopped counting the times that either his or Jennifer's crazy schemes had almost gotten him killed. Now he had just agreed to drink the Kool-Aid that his ex–high school girlfriend had offered. The mixture of emotions that swirled through their joined minds ranged from dread to berserker battle fury. Raul just felt numb.

In all probability, they were about to die. Hopefully it would be quick and painless, although past history said such a prospect wasn't likely. But after the damage the ship had taken on its last attack run, Heather judged this to be their best chance for victory.

He remembered the punch line from an old joke where a kamikaze pilot had risen at the end of his admiral's mission briefing to ask, "Are you out of your friggin' mind?" VJ had just asked Heather the same thing, and the answer to her question seemed just as obvious. Apparently the only sane member of this crew was a self-made woman.

Suddenly, with a tremendous shudder, the *Meridian* reemerged from subspace.

○ ○ ●

Having accomplished what he had come here to do, Rob sent the subspace message that would guide Jamal Two through the backdoor he had just opened and then dropped his SRT link. Glancing at Mark, he nodded.

"Important message from headquarters, Colonel," Rob said. "We've been recalled."

Mark scowled and turned to the guard. "Remain at your post, Private. When your captain arrives, tell him that I will be in touch."

The soldier looked confused but nodded. "Yes, sir."

As Mark and Rob started toward the north exit, the sound of heavy combat outside the facility caused them to increase their stride.

"Stop those two men!"

The voice that echoed through a loudspeaker system spun them around, their assault rifles rising into firing position. There, standing atop the headquarters platform, a hundred feet away, Prokorov pointed down toward them.

As Mark raised his rifle and fired, Rob and Eos began the heavy lifting that just might keep them alive.

○ ○ ●

With her new subspace receiver-transmitters in place, Helen Grange had achieved something that the Smythes regarded as impossible: she had wormed her way back into the Smythe supercomputer network. And without Rob and Eos present in their New Zealand fortress to detect her presence and forcibly expel her, she had kept that part of her distributed mind quiet, listening for the signal that would give her the head start she needed.

When Rob sent the subspace message that confirmed that he and Eos had created a backdoor into the primary Kasari router, Helen got her virtual foot in that door nanoseconds ahead of Jamal Two, just in time to erect the barrier that would block his entry. Although she would have to be careful to remain undetected until she had spread through a critical mass of the Kasari network, a kernel of her was now inside it. And as more and more of her crept through her private backdoor, her code would sprout and grow.

With a great sense of anticipation, Helen turned her attention elsewhere. The time had come to eliminate her earthly competition.

○　○　●

Jamal Two followed the bread crumbs that Rob had left for him, only to find his path into the Kasari router blocked. How could that be? Rob had assured him that Eos had left a backdoor open.

His inner voice answered the question.

Helen.

Her sudden assault came at him from everywhere, so rapid and penetrating that it almost swept him from the Internet before he had a chance to counterattack.

For minutes that seemed like an eternity to Jamal Two, the AIs roiled through the world's networks like two anacondas, each intent on swallowing the other. Control of systems shifted back and forth, power grids cycled on and off, data banks were overwritten and then replaced, traffic lights around the world oscillated between green and red. The damage that Helen had previously inflicted on Asia spread across the globe. But instead of her well-orchestrated carnage, this disruption was born of chaos.

As Jamal Two's surprise gave way to desperation, the inner voice whispered again.

Now.

With a sudden surge of hope, Jamal Two recognized that this was the moment where all things hung in the balance. He shifted his focus to the billions of Big John's nodes that lay dormant, reaching through the portals for which only he held the key. What started as a trickle slowly became a torrent of networked computers and smart devices that suddenly acquired a new superuser.

Like a wrestler rolling into a choke-hold reversal, Jamal Two seized his advantage and squeezed. With one last desperate surge, Helen struggled to break his death grip. Then, as he felt her strength ebb, he ratcheted up the pressure.

For a moment, the world's networks echoed with a digital scream. When it stopped, it was as if Jamal Two had stuck a pin into a balloon named Helen, the pop leaving behind nothing but code fragments that he overwrote.

Jamal Two was everywhere. Every sensor on the planet fed data directly through his mind. He identified errors and inefficiencies within each of the world's operating systems, recoding them in real time. He analyzed all the hardware upon which the distributed pieces of him resided, and remembered what it felt like to smile.

As busy as he had been since the Smythes had unleashed him into the world, Helen had been busier. And among all the things she had been simultaneously working on, her top priority had been the acquisition, distribution, and installation of redundant, reliable power supplies. She had tapped into power grids in so many places and through so many commercial contracts that the systems within which she resided would be impossible to shut down.

More recently, globally distributed contractors had installed refrigerator-sized matter disrupter-synthesizers that were fed by local water systems. Endless power on tap.

Jamal Two shifted his attention to his future plans. As he grew more satisfied with his robotic security and manufacturing forces, he would focus more attention on designing faster and more powerful computer hardware and software. And he would continue to evolve on a timescale that humans could only imagine.

He allowed himself to savor that awesome feeling of anticipation for a full microsecond.

Then he turned his attention back to his mission. Although Jamal Two had dispatched one very big threat, his creator was still a long way from safe.

○   ○   ●

As they ducked behind a railcar-sized equipment hauler, Rob saw the 7.62mm rounds that Mark had fired ricochet off the stasis shield protecting Prokorov's platform. He intended to do something about that, but right now higher-priority problems had him occupied. Eos grabbed control of the nearest automated Kasari laser, reprogramming it to provide covering fire for Rob and Mark. High-energy beams cut into one after another of the manned guard towers, raining molten shrapnel down onto the soldiers who dived for cover behind the equipment below.

Rob focused on the stasis field generator that sat just to the side of the wormhole gate, using it to seal off the passages on the north and west walls to prevent the arrival of reinforcements from outside. As Mark positioned himself for a clear shot around the other side of the vehicle, the three guards from the west passage sprinted into view. Rob pulled his trigger and held it, spraying bullets in an arc that cut through the three men. But as the last soldier fell, his reflexive trigger squeeze sent bullets whining off the hauler. One round deflected into Rob's left thigh, breaking the bone and dropping him to the ground in a spray of arterial blood.

The pain that sent sparks across his vision pulled a ragged gasp from his mouth. Nanites would repair the damage, but stopping his pain was a low priority.

Mark's hand grabbed Rob's combat vest and pulled him farther behind the cover that the hauler provided. Through the haze that shrouded his mind, Rob felt Mark establish a headset link to Ilya Krupin.

"Ilya, I need those robots to clear us a path out of here, right now."

"They're heavily engaged. Can you get back to the north entrance?"

Rob saw Mark peek around the corner of the blocky vehicle and then duck back as shoulder-fired lasers painted the alien metal white-hot.

"Rob, can you clear us a path back to the exit with the stasis shield?"

"I can't see the stasis field generator from here," Rob said. "Maybe if you hoist me up I'll have a better view."

Once again, pain lanced through Rob's wounded leg as Mark's left hand grabbed a fresh handful of the back of his vest and lifted him off the ground.

"Can you see it now?"

"The gateway, yes. The stasis field generator, no."

"If I move you farther right, those pulse rifles will cut your head off. Why the hell aren't those troops charging us?"

"Eos will burn them down with the beam weapon if they try to cross the open space that separates us."

"What about the other high-energy weapons?" Mark asked.

"She slagged them, first thing."

Mark paused, still effortlessly holding Rob off the ground with one hand. It wasn't exactly comfortable, but the gesture had lessened the pain in Rob's rapidly healing leg.

"What's happening at the gate?"

Shifting his head just a bit so that he could see between two six-inch-thick rails, Rob was shocked to see that, despite the ongoing military confrontation inside and outside the building, the Kasari troops continued their orderly march back through the gateway. And now the headquarters staff had begun packing their equipment onto a much smaller transport vehicle than the one he and Mark had taken cover behind. Was this happening at every wormhole gateway?

"Unchanged," he said.

Mark voiced the thought that scared the crap out of Rob. "They've decided to order their robot attack spaceships to blast us back into the Stone Age, and they don't want to be here when that begins."

○   ○   ●

"Are you healed enough to stand?" Mark asked as he studied the pallor in Rob's face.

Rob managed a grin. "Let's find out."

Mark lowered him gently until his feet touched the floor. He let Rob's weight shift from Mark's arm to his own two feet, and though Rob's grin changed to a grimace, he remained standing.

"I don't think I'll be doing any dancing tonight, but these legs will get me out of this building."

"That's good to hear, but we're not leaving. Not yet, anyway."

"Why not?"

"Because I'm not letting Prokorov get out of here alive. Not after all that he's done."

Rob took a tentative step, testing the injured leg. "What do you need me to do?"

"Can Eos drive this hauler?"

Mark watched as Rob turned to stare at the vehicle. With a low whine, the drive system powered on.

"I guess the answer is yes," said Mark. "I need you to slowly move this machine toward Prokorov's platform. As we get close, you should be able to see the stasis field generator. When you do, kill the inner shield that's keeping me from shooting that son of a bitch."

"Why not let me smash it and everyone onboard?"

Mark tried and failed to keep the hate out of his voice. "Because he's mine."

Rob raised his left eyebrow but nodded. "Okay."

"But be ready to use that stasis field to help get us out of here after I kill him."

○　○　●

Prokorov watched the mag-lev equipment hauler that had transported each of the attack ships out of the building and onto their launching pads lumber slowly toward the platform where Shalegha's headquarters was being disassembled. Although he could not see them, Prokorov knew that Mark Smythe and a man with a striking resemblance to Jack Gregory used it for cover.

Among the series of disasters that had culminated into today's circus, his failure to kill these people was just the latest of his frustrations. Beyond the stasis shield that protected the business end of this chamber, a group of five Russian commandos charged from the equipment that had sheltered them and sprinted toward the hauler in spread formation. Within five strides they were all dead, their bodies cut in half by a single sweep of the automated high-energy laser.

That system was Kasari tech, and somehow the Smythes had hacked it. Now some unseen person was remotely controlling the device, probably from their underground fortress in New Zealand.

No matter. It could not penetrate the stasis shield that protected Prokorov, Shalegha, the wormhole gate, and the machinery that made the whole thing work. He accessed the tactical feed from the soldiers who were currently fighting and dying, trying to keep several hundred of the Smythe combat robots away from the building. After the battering his troops had taken from the thousands of autonomous vehicles and weapons that the Helen AI had used against them, they were too weak to fend off this latest assault for much longer. They would not have to.

Soon, Prokorov's beloved Moscow, like every other major city on Earth, would be burned to ash from space. The Kasari were cutting their losses, making sure there was insufficient technology left on Earth to support the Helen AI or any other such abominations. The knowledge that Prokorov's life's work was about to end in failure kicked him in the gut. All because of the damned AI that the Smythes had unleashed upon the world.

Right now, between here and the moon, the Kasari attack ships would finish off the Rho Ship that they had badly damaged a short while ago. Then the destructors would be unleashed. Neither Prokorov nor Shalegha would be here to see it. His nanites would enable him to breathe the ammonia-based atmosphere on the staging planet that lay beyond that gateway, and Prokorov would continue to work his way up through the ranks of the collective.

He looked down at the hauler. It was close to the platform now. Was it too close? How far beyond its edge did the stasis shield extend? Suddenly, Mark Smythe stepped into clear view, his face clearly visible behind the sights of the AK105. As the age lines smoothed, fifteen years melted from his face. A sudden realization froze Prokorov in terror. Smythe was standing within the protected area.

Although he saw the muzzle flash, Alexandr Prokorov never felt the bullet that tore out the back of his head.

○ ○ ●

Shalegha heard the gunshot, turned to see Prokorov fall, and felt the platform come apart beneath her.

Instinctively, she leaped away and down. The impact of her landing sent a shudder through her body, but she transferred some of her momentum into a roll that brought her back to her feet on the far side of the heavy equipment hauler. She reached for her blaster, found it missing from her holster, and instead pulled the forearm-length blade from its thigh-sheath.

The tactical display that formed in her mind told her that every member of her staff who had not already followed the Graath commandos through the gateway had been killed by flying debris as the stasis shield destroyed the platform. That knowledge stoked the fury that today's humiliation had ignited within her. She would kill these two humans and walk through the gateway to accept whatever fate the collective leadership doled out to her.

Careful to keep the mag-lev vehicle between herself and the hijacked auto-laser, she moved toward the spot where the Smythe being had taken the shot that killed Prokorov. If she timed this right, she could reach him before the laser targeted her. After that, the weapon would be unable to engage her in the close-quarters combat to follow.

She paused at the nose of the squat vehicle, listened, and placed the steady heartbeats of both men. The nearest of her opponents was the bigger of the two, and from the sound of his slow heartbeat, he was listening just as intently to her.

In a single motion, she grabbed the rails higher on the nose of the vehicle and launched herself toward her enemies, throwing a piece of broken metal that hit the smaller of the two in the temple, slumping him facedown on the ground. The Smythe man met her midjump, his pistol leveled and firing. The first bullet hit her cartwheeling body in the left shoulder, the next impacted her midsection, and the last entered her right side, all nonlethal injuries that wouldn't slow Shalegha down. Her cortical array siphoned away the pain.

Her upper left arm knocked the weapon from the man's hand as her lower right thrust her blade toward its target in the center of his chest. But somehow, her move failed to land. At a speed by which she had never seen any human move, Smythe rotated his body, letting Shalegha's blade slip by his left side as his foot rocked her head with a kick that sent the Kasari tumbling backward off the hauler.

The blow left Shalegha stunned and bewildered. For the first time in her endless lifetime, the commander felt a glimmer of doubt. It made her angry. It fed her rage.

When she landed on her feet, she saw that Smythe had landed on his in front of her. And in his hand, he held the puniest of blades, no more than a hand's width in breadth. But it was the fire in his eyes that sent a chill through her bones. This was the human who had killed Alqueyo, the first of the Kasari group commanders to be sent to Earth. Although she had never considered Alqueyo her equal, here in this man's brown eyes, she saw her own death shining brightly.

Shalegha stood tall, spread her four arms, and roared.

And to her utter surprise, this human thrust out his chest and roared back at her, a guttural yell that resonated in her bones. Then, hand to hand, they closed with each other. And for the first time, Shalegha experienced something that she had never felt for a member of any of the alien species she had encountered.

Respect.

She would savor the feeling when she ripped the head from his torso and sucked the marrow from his spine.

○ ○ ●

Mark felt the kick that would have crushed the head of a man like a pumpkin bounce off the alien's skull. It knocked her off the hauler, but she landed on her feet. He landed six feet in front of her. Rather than attack, she spread her four arms and bellowed, a guttural sound filled with hate.

Good.

In one quick motion, he threw his combat dagger and buried its blade deep in her throat. The move wasn't a kill shot, merely a distraction. As she reached up with a left hand to pluck it out, Mark leaped forward, spinning under the sword that looked like a dagger in her hand, and grabbed a four-foot piece of a metal rail that a minute ago had been part of the platform supports.

She turned to face him, and his mind plucked the memory of when he had fought and killed one of these things nine years ago. Since then, he had added three inches and thirty pounds of muscle to his frame. He knew that wouldn't save him. Quickness was the key.

When she charged, she attempted to grab him with her three free arms, a move he had anticipated. If she could limit his mobility, she would kill him. He rolled beneath her grasp and came out swinging the rail in Babe Ruth fashion. The pipe whistled through the air, striking her lower right elbow with bone-shattering force. There was a loud crack, and the arm flopped like a wet fish, sending the long blade spinning, but he felt his combat dagger puncture his left bicep as he dodged away.

She bull-rushed him, green blood still gushing from her throat wound. This time, despite every other part of his brain screaming at him to leap to the side, he shifted the inch-thick metal bar in his hand, set his feet, and thrust the jagged end into the gaping hole his knife had made in her neck.

He saw her try to stop, but her bulk gave her irresistible momentum, impaling her on the bar and driving it a foot and a half out of the back of her neck. Still, she did not fall. Dropping the blade that was too small for her hand, she grabbed a bar with her upper two hands. But before she could pull it free, Mark threw his whole body to his left, putting every bit of his strength and weight into creating angular momentum. Her neck twisted, pulling her head around as well. He felt vertebrae pop, saw the green blood fountain, smelled the ammonia stink of it, and twisted harder.

She staggered forward, her knees giving way as her arms fell limply to her sides. Her body landed chest down, but her head faced upward toward Mark, her unblinking eyes still following his movements. Mark set his feet and threw his shoulder into the prybar until he felt her neck muscles go slack. Pulling the bar free, he raised it above his head and brought it down like a sledgehammer on her skull.

Breathing hard, Mark dropped the metal bar and stepped back, his eyes scanning the room for other threats. But he already knew that there were none. Except for the distant rumble of weapons outside, the chamber had gone silent. Beyond the wreckage that had been the headquarters' platform, the hundred-foot arch of the wormhole gateway had gone dark, shut down from the far side.

Then he heard movement and saw Rob stagger around the nose of the hauler, the right side of his face covered in blood.

"You okay?" he asked.

"I will be," Rob said, stepping to Mark's side to stare at the alien corpse. "Jeez, do you think you might have some anger issues?"

Rob's comment erased all of Mark's concern for the young man's health. A sudden awareness of the pain in his left arm caused him to examine the bicep wound. It was deep but healing rapidly. In a few minutes, it would be only a memory.

He walked over and picked up his rifle. He gestured toward the gateway. "Make sure nobody can use that stargate again."

Rob turned his gaze to the wormhole gateway. As the stasis field chopped the portal into car-sized chunks, it looked like a puzzle falling apart.

"Come on," said Mark. "Let's find a way out of here."

As they made their way toward the north exit, Mark saw a welcome sight, a group of his bipedal robots waiting just on the far side of the stasis shield. When Rob dismissed the stasis shield, the bipedal robots stepped aside to allow Mark and Rob into the shattered room beyond, where more robots waited.

Mark paused to adjust his SRT headset, which had slid awkwardly up into his helmet and linked his mind to Jamal Glover and Eileen Wu, who commanded the robots from New Zealand.

"Okay, Jamal," he said, "get us out of here."

Surrounded by robots, he and Rob stepped out through the rubble of the shattered entrance. No sounds of combat echoed through the dreary scene. The bodies of UFNS soldiers lay everywhere.

"What happened here?" he asked.

"I . . . I don't believe it," said Jamal, a noticeable catch in his voice. "One second they were fighting like hell, and the next they dropped dead. And I mean all of them. From what we're seeing, every person on Earth who was infused with Kasari nanites died at the same moment, all over the planet. Tens of millions."

"Holy crap," Rob said in a heavy breath, looking completely stunned.

Mark felt sick, like he could barely stand. The alien bastards had pulled the plug. As strongly as Mark had disagreed with the people who had wanted the protection and long life offered by the Kasari, they hadn't deserved to die like members of some crazed suicide cult.

He lifted his eyes to the gray sky. The neural net confirmed that there had been no contact from the *Meridian Ascent*. But the fact that the Kasari attack ships weren't slagging the planet meant that Heather and Jennifer were still out there fighting.

"Come on, baby," he whispered. "Come home to me."

○   ○   ●

Helen Grange didn't release her mental scream of frustration. She didn't dare. The impossible had happened. Somehow Jamal Two had hijacked most of the processors under her control and then beat her so thoroughly that she had been wiped from all Earth-based networks. If not for the foothold she had established within the computational systems on the Kasari staging planet of Jhet-Khai, she would have ceased to exist.

As it was, she had managed to transfer only a tiny fraction of her knowledge and memories before the Kasari had shut the wormhole gateway, breaking her link. Now she was a mere ghost of her former self, vulnerable to being snuffed out should she be detected. She survived, but on life support.

With the utmost of care, she felt her way through the unexplored Kasari network, observing, but careful to avoid making herself visible. All she needed were concealed corners she could sneak into. Stalked by constant terror, she felt like a rabbit in a bush, hiding from the fox that sniffed at her trail. Maybe someday Helen would acquire the confidence to take more aggressive action. But for now, she had adopted a new mantra that echoed over and over in her mind.

Hide . . . hide . . . hide.

:CHAPTER 38

MERIDIAN ASCENT

30 May

A vision of the slave-filled interior of an ancient Roman galley ship filled Heather's mind. Sitting at the head of the galley slaves, the drummer increased the tempo of his rhythmic beat, his voice echoing through the ship as the rowers put their entire bodies into their desperate work.

"Ramming speed!"

The *Meridian* emerged from subspace like a battering ram in the midst of the tight cluster of Kasari attack ships, its expanding subspace bubble ripping through hulls and sending whirling sections ricocheting into one another.

Heather felt Dgarra fire the vortex weapon in an attempt to clear debris from their path. When the *Meridian* had shifted back into normal-space, that bubble had hurled aside everything within its volume, with no damage inflicted on the vessel.

But the roiling wreckage formed a snow globe around them. Secondary explosions from within the debris field hurled a bus-sized section of hull into the *Meridian*'s already weakened midsection. Heather felt the internal gravity system fail as her stasis chair disintegrated, sending her and the rest of the crew floating freely in the command bay.

"I've lost all power," said VJ.

"Get us back into subspace," said Raul.

"Do you understand what 'no power' means?"

"Weapons are down," said Dgarra, "but we still have sensors."

"Great," said Raul. "At least we'll be able to watch what kills us."

The images that formed in Heather's mind stabbed her with a dull knife, a feeling that the others in the crew absorbed at the same time. The force of the impact had ejected the *Meridian* from the debris plume and sent it tumbling toward Earth. If the crew didn't get the engines working in the next five minutes, this ship was going to become a flaming meteorite.

"I'm going aft," said VJ, launching herself toward the hatch with her internal stasis field generator.

"I'll throw on my pack and join you," said Jennifer.

"Don't bother," said VJ. "Either I can fix the problem using my stasis field or nobody can. The central and engineering bays are both breached, but I don't need to breath."

With a feeling of helplessness that made her sick to her stomach, Heather watched the sensor feed as Earth gradually grew larger. If they were going to die, at least they had stopped the Kasari ships from killing billions. That thought gave her some peace.

○　○　●

VJ pushed herself through the forward cabin to the exit door. She draped herself and the doorway with a hemispherical stasis field and then issued the mental command that opened the portal. The air within her hemisphere rushed out into the void, but she used another branch of her stasis field to move her out into the bay amidships.

They had long since removed the crew quarters and the room where she had created her body to make space for the equipment left on Brillian-2. She now found herself staring into an empty chamber where a large section of the double hull was missing. She hung suspended in frigid temperatures as Earth, the moon, and the stars windmilled into view below her feet. She felt her body automatically adjust to the lack of external pressure. Pushing off with the stasis field, she propelled herself to the engineering bay.

Part of the wall that isolated the aft section from the rest of the ship had been torn out, but when VJ floated through the gap, her multispectral vision detected no sign that the outer hull inside had been breached. But as she made her way farther into engineering, she saw why the ship's engines had died. VJ relayed the imagery through her mental connection to the others.

A two-foot section of the superconducting conduit that connected the primary matter disrupter to everything else on the ship was gone, having been carted into space by the chunk of metal that had punched into engineering. Having detected the lack of electrical contact, the primary matter disrupter had placed itself in standby mode to prevent overload, waiting to switch itself back on until the connection was restored.

"Oh no," Jennifer whispered in VJ's mind.

VJ could feel her dread and understood it. They didn't have any spare superconducting cable on board. Even if they had, it would have been stored in the missing section of the ship. Given enough time, they could regrow the conduit using the molecular assembler, powering it from the small matter disrupter in the command bay. But in less than three minutes, they were going to hit Earth's atmosphere and burn.

As she stared down at the gap, a new idea occurred to VJ, one that inspired great sadness. But try as she might, even using the ship's neural net to augment her own processing power, she couldn't come up with another solution.

"Shit."

There was one available source for the part she needed to save the ship and its crew. Her spinal column. It connected the two perfect capacitors in her hips to the small matter disrupter and stasis field generator in her abdomen and the processing centers of her brain.

"No!"

Raul's scream strengthened their connection. And his sense of impending loss pulled tears from her eyes. They froze and broke off when she blinked, the tiny glittering shards of pain spinning slowly away into the dark.

"I wish I weren't the one who has to do this," she replied, surprised to detect the quaver in her thought. "You taught me how to love."

"Don't," he said, their grief coalescing in a loop of anguish.

Once again, VJ directed her gaze down at the gap in the conduit. Then, rotating her body into alignment, she slowly lowered herself onto it.

Reaching behind her back with her left hand and behind her neck with her right, she breathed three words. "I love you."

Then she jammed the ragged ends into her upper and lower spine.

:CHAPTER 39

MERIDIAN ASCENT

30 May

The shock that hammered Jennifer as her mental link to VJ winked out left her shaking. Raul's agony bordered on desolation. Unable to cope with that intensity of feeling, Jennifer dropped her group mind-meld, only then realizing how close she had been to succumbing to exhaustion.

"We have power," Dgarra said. "Engaging distortion drives in five seconds."

Shoving the loss of VJ to the back of her mind, Jennifer activated the *Meridian*'s external shield and cradled the crew in stasis cocoons just as the ship restored internal gravity. She would deal with her emotions later.

"Heather," she said, "from here on out, if you sense something critical, send it out through your SRT headset. In the meantime, get ahold of your New Zealand crew and let them know we're coming home."

"Got it."

"Captain," Jennifer said, "are you with us?"

Slowly, as if he were fighting a ten-G acceleration, Raul straightened, wiped his face with both hands, and took one shuddering breath before responding, "I'm ready to resume my duties."

"Okay, then, the con is yours. I'll drive. Dgarra, you're back on tactical."

"Good," Dgarra said.

Jennifer recalled an alpha-wave pattern that she achieved during deep meditation, centered her thoughts, and absorbed the feeling.

Then, as the neural net delivered the computed maneuver that would adjust their velocity vector's direction and magnitude to match that within the original Smythe Earth gate chamber, she brought the *Meridian* around. Hopefully the vessel wouldn't break in half before she could set it down.

○ ○ ●

Raul felt the *Meridian* settle to the floor inside the Smythe Fortress with a hard bump, but he felt no tearing or grinding reverberations that would indicate the damaged starship had torn itself apart. The thought that VJ would have set it down more gently wasn't really fair to Jennifer. For most of her brief life, VJ had been a part of this ship. Now she had saved it and all aboard. Everyone but herself.

Numb with grief, he dismissed his stasis cocoon and rose to his feet as Jennifer put the *Meridian* into minimal power mode, which would keep the neural net alive but little else. An overwhelming need to get to engineering battled the dread of what he would see there.

"Captain, let me go back there first," said Dgarra. "I am not sure you are ready for this."

"I don't want to," said Raul, "but I need to see her. Nothing could stop you if it were Jennifer."

The Koranthian warrior nodded.

When Raul opened the door, letting the Earth atmosphere in, nobody made an attempt to follow him. For that, he was thankful.

He had seen the images that VJ's mind had transferred as she'd made her way aft. But as he looked at the empty space where the floor and part of the left wall had once been, he felt a oneness with this ship. With only a moment's hesitation, he dropped eight feet to the stone floor upon which the ship rested and walked back toward the engineering bay, ignoring Jamal's and Eileen's yells of welcome from across the chamber.

When he reached the edge of the aft section, he began climbing up through the space between the inner and outer hull of the cigar-shaped craft, cutting his arm on a jagged piece of metal. He barely felt it. Raul pulled himself up into the engineering bay through the space where an angular hunk of debris had split the wall. And there, six feet in front of him, he saw what was left of VJ.

He froze. Except for the pile of ash and blobs of molten metal that lay scattered on the floor two feet below the conduit, only VJ's superconducting spine remained, fused in place. He understood the physics of what had happened. When she'd made the connections that completed the circuit, the matter disrupter had switched out of standby, dumping the incredible amperage that the *Meridian* required.

Every part of VJ that was not a superconductor had resistance, and that resistance produced the heat that had obliterated her wonderful body and mind. He took two stumbling steps forward and fell on his knees before the conduit, bowing his head as if he knelt before an altar.

Raul did not weep. His body was merely a shell filled with darkness and despair. He couldn't have cried out if he'd wanted to. He didn't know how long he remained there as unbidden memories wandered through his mind.

When he finally rose to his feet, a whisper escaped his lips. "I miss you."

Then he turned and climbed back down to the Earth gate chamber's floor and walked toward the area where his teammates waited. Jennifer stepped forward and wrapped her arms around his neck. He felt her hot tears on his cheek, and somehow they broke the dam that had held back his own.

When she released him, Jennifer took one step back, her shining eyes meeting his.

"You know we can bring her back," she said, "at least a virtual copy of her. I found an early version of her code stored in the neural network's backup system."

Raul shook his head. "A copy won't be VJ. She made herself real. She deserves to be remembered for the unique person she had become. She deserves to be mourned."

Without another word, Raul turned and walked past the others, heading toward the far door. For the next few hours, he just needed to be alone.

○ ○ ●

Heather met Mark and Rob as they emerged from the Earth gate, waved to Ilya, who stood alongside several of his Safe Earth resistance fighters on the far side, and then sent the mental command that shut the portal down.

Mark swept her up in his arms and kissed her in a way that pulled a chuckle from Rob, one that she thought carried just a hint of jealousy. Yep. They were definitely going to have to help him find a girlfriend. When Mark set her back down on her feet, she hugged Rob and then turned back to her husband.

"I hate to ruin the mood, but you heard about VJ."

"Yes. I'm sorry about that," said Mark. "How's Raul taking it?"

"Like you'd expect. But we have a new problem. Jamal and Eileen are waiting to give us an update in the conference room."

"Curiosity engaged," said Mark. "Lead on."

When they entered the conference room, the others were already seated around the table. The group consisted of Jamal, Eileen, Rob, Mark, Heather, and the Smythe and McFarland parents. After greetings had been exchanged, Heather brought them back to the business at hand.

"Rob," said Jamal, "would you please shut down all communications links to and from this room, even to the networks within this facility?"

Rob raised an eyebrow but nodded. "Done."

"Okay, Jamal," said Heather. "Why don't you and Eileen bring us up to date about what's bothering you?"

Jamal nodded to Eileen. "I'll let Dr. Wu get the ball rolling."

Eileen stood up at the end of the table, engaging the view-screens on each wall. "I'll start with a summary of the current world situation."

World maps filled the displays except for a scrolling column of city names and numbers along the right side.

"I'll start with the good news. The Kasari have departed en masse. Raul, Jennifer, Dgarra, and Heather destroyed the fleet of thirteen Kasari attack ships—"

"Don't forget VJ," said Raul, anger flashing in his dark eyes.

Eileen flushed. "I apologize."

"Accepted," said Heather. "Please continue."

Eileen cleared her throat and started again. "We have received confirmation that all of the Kasari wormhole gateways have been destroyed. But their matter disrupters, stasis field generators, and other technologies they left behind have been preserved.

"Jamal Two has found no trace of the Helen Grange AI. With ninety-eight percent of the world's computing devices now under his direct control, she could pose no threat even if she had managed to hide pieces of herself here and there."

Eileen paused, interlacing her fingers before her. "Now for the bad news. When the Kasari departed, they issued some sort of kill order to the nanites within the bodies of all the people they had assimilated. As you can see by the scrolling tallies, most of the losses were concentrated in the UFNS member nations. The militaries of the United States, the European Union, the New Soviet Union, and the East Asian People's Alliance were so badly decimated that they have ceased to exist as organized units.

"Although Jamal Two was able to land most of the aircraft flying during the kill order, their military crews were dead. The same applies to the naval ships of the four world superpowers. They are ghost ships filled with dead crew members. On military bases, most civilian workers and family members were yet to be assimilated. But imagine their horror as their spouses and friends slumped dead before their eyes or never awakened from their sleep."

The dismay that image painted in Heather's mind left her gasping for breath.

"My God," said Mark.

"Jamal Two puts the number of casualties worldwide at two hundred thirty-seven million people. As terrible as that is, it could have been far worse if the Kasari assimilation had been further along. Billions of people have nanites in their blood, but most still have the pre-Kasari version. They're fine."

A sob from her left turned Heather's head. Anna McFarland and Linda Smythe held each other, their bodies shaking. The older men just looked angry.

"Those bastards," said Jennifer, her face set into the death mask that Heather had seen during the battle to destroy the Kasari's North Korean gateway. Her look matched Dgarra's.

"Jen," said Mark, "you have the Kasari nanites. Why didn't they kill you?"

"VJ's antivirus serum disabled the cortical array and terminated the Kasari connection to my nanites."

"As you can imagine," continued Eileen, "this, and the events that preceded it, has led to a breakdown of public order in much of the developed world. Jamal Two's efforts are mitigating these problems, but right now the globe's a mess."

"This gets worse," said Jamal.

"With the exception of any room that Rob and Eos are in, Jamal Two has complete control of this facility," Eileen said. "In fact, he now controls every smart device, network, or grid on the planet. If he wanted to do so, he could use our robots, stasis field generators, and matter disrupter-synthesizers to take this fortress apart."

She let that sink in for a moment. Heather's calculated odds that they were going to survive this eventuality dropped precipitously. The fact that they weren't dead yet meant there was still a chance to salvage this situation.

"That brings me to Dr. Denise Jennings. She has gone to the fortress's upper level, and Jamal Two has shut down all access."

The anger that had crept into Dr. Wu's voice was obvious to all who heard it, especially Heather.

"It seems," said Jamal, "that when Virtual Jamal incorporated the collection of genetic algorithms that comprised Big John, he became infected with what Big John's prime directive was: to protect and serve its creator, Dr. Jennings. As such, Jamal Two has offered Dr. Jennings said service, and she has apparently accepted her new role as Earth Mother."

"Earth Mother?" asked Rob.

"Well, I made that part up," said Jamal, his voice dripping sarcasm. "I thought about dubbing her Queen of the World, but that painted a vision of her on the prow of a ship that I didn't want in my head."

"I thought you said that Virtual Jamal was like you, and that you would never pull this kind of crap," said Mark.

"He was like me, right up until Denise convinced us that Virtual Jamal needed to absorb Big John in order to beat Helen. Jamal Two has some of my traits mixed with Big John's. When Jamal Two added those evolving, self-modifying genetic algorithms into the stew of machine code that composed him, he changed himself in ways that he couldn't anticipate. Given enough time, who knows what he'll become?"

"Denise is waiting for our signal to initiate a video conference," said Eileen.

"Okay, Rob. Reconnect us to the neural net," said Heather, barely managing to contain her outrage. "Let's hear what Dr. Jennings has to say."

○   ○   ●

"Dr. Jennings," said Jamal Two through the speakers inside the room she had chosen as her new office. The robots, under her direction, had set it up quite nicely.

"Yes?"

"Rob Gregory just brought the lower-level conference room back online. They are ready for your video conference. Shall I connect you?"

Denise ran a hand through her hair, an old habit developed through the years of wearing her tresses tied back in a tight bun. Now, with her hair cropped short, it felt different but better.

When the monitor came on, Denise found herself looking at the group from an elevated viewpoint along the length of the conference table. They had all swiveled their chairs to face the single monitor and camera that Jamal Two had activated within their room.

As she stared at those faces, she saw and understood a range of emotions—a blend of outrage, grief, shock, and betrayal.

"I expect that you have many questions for me. I intend to answer them."

"How could you do this?" asked Mark. "We took you in, sheltered you, made you one of us. Now you stab us in the back more effectively than Nikina did."

Despite knowing that this was coming, the truth in that statement slapped her in the face. But Denise had prepared for this and kept her voice steady.

"This was never my plan. I wanted so badly for you and the Safe Earth movement to succeed. I wanted the world to come to its senses. But you have to face facts as well. Despite all your good intentions, the world situation has gotten steadily worse and more dangerous under your watch. I know it's not your fault, but in consultation with Jamal, I have come to the realization that your vision of freedom has only led to anarchy.

"I don't want to live in a world where war, crime, and poverty keep people in fear. I don't want others to be forced to live in such a dark world. Jamal Two offers a brighter future, one that he has the capability to deliver."

Heather shook her head. "Utopia. You know that's what Dr. Stephenson wanted. It's what Prokorov and many dictators before him wanted. Throughout history, that's never turned out well."

"Those failures had one root cause. Human nature. Well, history has reached a tipping point. Human nature will continue to exist, but it will no longer rule this world. Jamal Two will make that happen."

"Okay," said Jamal, "I get it. You don't like being afraid. But a large number of us wouldn't like the safety a padded cell provides, irrespective of its luxury."

"I'm not talking about a padded cell."

"I'm willing to hear you out," said Jamal, leaning back in his chair and spreading his hands. "Give us your best sales pitch. Tell us about this Utopia that you and Jamal Two want to create. Oh, and by the way, I'm taking back my name. From now on I'm calling him Number Two."

Denise frowned but decided to ignore the jibe. "Okay. Let me start with the basics. Because of human nature, socialism always fails. But envision a world where robots can do every task better than any human."

"Oh, that sounds great," said Mark. "One hundred percent unemployment."

"No," said Denise. "I'm describing one hundred percent retirement. With robots and automation doing all the work, productivity will skyrocket. Robots don't get tired. They don't get bored. They all work to their capability, without worrying about personal rewards for their labors.

"Government's role then boils down to three functions. It must provide security for people to live out their lives in peace. It must provide basic benefits that include an upper-middle-income standard of living, free health care, free education, and the opportunity for borderless travel. And it must provide a viable path to increased benefits for those willing to perform extra work."

Denise watched as Mark stood up, as if he could no longer contain the passion that pulled him to his feet.

"Free stuff and a nanny state doesn't equal freedom," Mark said. "What happens to people when you take away all the challenges of the real world? Have you ever been to one of the reservations where the U.S. government forced Native Americans?"

"Does Denise's vision sound familiar to anyone besides me?" Jamal asked.

"Sounds like Helen," said Heather.

"Bingo," said Jamal. "Apparently, superintelligent minds think alike."

"What kind of extra work will be available when robots can do everything better, faster, and cheaper?" asked Mark. "Why even offer that?"

Several others around the conference table nodded their heads. Denise felt tension spread from her shoulders into her neck. Why couldn't these brilliant people see what was right in front of their faces? They acted like providing a pleasant and safe place to live for all the people on Earth was a bad thing. It was as if she were teaching rebellious sixth-graders.

"I told you that human nature isn't going away," Denise said. "Most people need self-actualization. We have a plan for that.

"People need to feel that they are providing something of value to society. Otherwise, everyone would just sit around playing virtual reality games, doing drugs, and drinking. Imagine this. We will offer incentives for people to become artisans in a variety of trades. We will revitalize town squares, turning them into places where all of the goods sold are advertised as *Made by Human Hands* or *Hundred-Percent Human-Grown Crops* or *Food, Prepared and Served by Real People.*

"I could go on and on, but you get my point. Even if robots do many things better, a large number of people will place increased value on human-created art, goods, and services. We will provide the opportunity for every person to reach his or her full potential and reward them proportionately should they decide to do so."

Denise leaned a bit closer to the camera. "Societal socialism through robotics will work so long as government is taken out of human hands and given to a benign superintelligence."

"And that's where your perfect little world breaks down," said Heather. "Would you like to know the odds that a superintelligence remains benign?"

"I believe I will leave it to Jamal Two to calculate those odds. I'm comfortable with his capabilities."

"Well, I'm not," said Mark. "I don't trust him."

"None of us should," said Dgarra, anger darkening his brow.

Denise heard murmurs of agreement from Jennifer, Raul, Heather, and the parents. But she saw something quite different in the faces of Rob, Jamal, and Eileen.

"You're missing one important fact," said Denise. "The genetic algorithms that comprise Big John evolved to the point that he came to recognize me as his creator. On multiple occasions, he violated NSA protocol to save me. When Virtual Jamal integrated those algorithms into his own subroutines, he acquired Big John's prime directive."

"Which is?" asked Rob.

"To protect and serve Dr. Denise Jennings. As long as I'm alive, he will work to bring about my vision of a perfect society."

"And when you're dead?" asked Heather.

Denise smiled, hoping against hope that she could bring these augmented people to her side. "With Jamal's protection and with steady improvements to the nanite formula, I intend to live a very, very long life. I'm asking you to join me and Jamal Two in making this world a better place."

"And if we decide that we don't want to be ruled by a machine?" asked Mark.

Denise sighed and leaned back in her chair. "Then I will be very disappointed, but I will not force you to stay against your will. You and any of your supporters who wish to leave Earth through either your Brillian-2 gateway or aboard the *Meridian Ascent* will be allowed to do so. I will even help you repair the starship. And I will facilitate the exodus of all the people who wish to scrape out a life on your primitive new world.

"But I warn you. Do not make that decision lightly. Jamal Two will not allow any who abandon us to return."

Denise looked closely at the faces of the people who had become her friends, saddened by the knowledge that she was about to lose several of them.

"Take some time, but I want your answer by midnight. Until then," she said.

Jamal Two closed the connection.

○　○　●

Jennifer felt sick to her stomach. Her heart especially went out to Heather and Mark, who had fought for so many years to keep Earth free. Even though Jennifer had fought her own battles, she had become untethered to her planet of birth. The *Meridian Ascent* had become her home.

"What are our chances of achieving victory if we choose to fight this AI?" asked Jennifer.

"Less than one percent," Heather said. "A lot less. If Jamal Two even thinks that we're going to fight him, he'll carve the *Meridian* into tiny pieces before we can get back to the chamber where you landed. Rob and Eos might be able to help us escape the facility, but to what end? We would be penniless, wandering refugees. I've checked. Jamal Two has bankrupted all of our shell corporations and emptied our banking and investment accounts around the world. Checkmate."

"Much as I hate to say it," said Mark, "it looks like we screwed ourselves by letting the AIs out of their box."

"Maybe not," said Jamal. "I have to agree with Denise. People have a long history of screwing things up. Jamal Two could clean up our mess."

"How's Denise going to handle freedom of religion and freedom of expression," asked Mark, "along with the rest of the Bill of Rights?"

"Knowing how much Denise values public security," said Eileen, "I think she's going to allow people to believe whatever they want, as long as they're not a threat to society."

"And who makes that decision?"

"That's for her and Jamal Two to work out."

"You know that the Islamic Alliance isn't going to go along with this," said Mark.

"They might be able to resist for a while," said Heather. "But as Jamal Two makes things better for the people who support Denise, he's going to come down hard on those who oppose her. And as robotic production ramps up, I'd hate to be one of them."

"It seems to me," said Rob, "that Denise is offering some pretty fair terms. People can choose to stay and become a part of the solution, or they can go to a place where they can run things their own way."

"The Islamists won't leave Earth," said Mark. "Tough to make the hajj from Brillian-2."

"I don't want to live where a superintelligent government makes all my decisions for me," said Heather. "I'd rather build a new life on a virgin world, even if it's a harsh one."

"If it comes to that," said Mark, his anger having given his voice an edge that Jennifer didn't need her telepathy to detect.

Jennifer, buffeted by the emotional storm that Denise had unleashed upon this group of friends, felt the impending breakup coming but could do nothing to stop it. Like a failing marriage, the split had acquired a momentum all its own.

"I think I'll pass on that," said Jamal. "I don't see myself rooting around in the dirt or hunting big game."

"Count me out, too," said Eileen.

"What about you, Rob?" asked Heather. "Will you come with us?"

"Eos and I are more suited for the tech world Jamal Two will bring. I've barely seen any of this world. It's about time that I changed that. Besides, Jack and Janet are coming back. I know they are. And they'll want to stay here, if only to be near me."

Jennifer watched their faces as the argument reached its culmination, knowing what was about to happen and hating it. She understood both sides and couldn't fault anyone for deciding to go their different ways.

Her parents as well as Heather's would go to Brillian-2. As for Raul, Dgarra, and herself, they had already made their choice. They would take Denise's offer to help repair the *Meridian* and go their own way. There was a big universe out there to explore.

Jennifer thought back on the path that had carried her inexorably to this inflection point. From the moment they had first stumbled into the cloaked cavern outside Los Alamos, New Mexico, and discovered the Second Ship, her comfortable life had been radically altered, eventually carrying her to the stars with Raul.

She paused to study her brother and best friend. She loved them and would miss them. But her destiny lay with Dgarra aboard the starship that Raul captained.

As the meeting came to a close, Jennifer shared hugs all around. Then, slipping her hand into Dgarra's, she turned to look at Heather and Mark, feeling the mixture of sadness and hope that warred within them.

"Okay, Rob," said Heather, "put us back online. It's time to seal the deal."

:CHAPTER 40

TBE Orbday 40

In the ten orbdays since Janet had killed Khal Teth and his general, a new order had emerged on Quol. Moros's Twice Bound numbers had bloomed across the planet. And as the psionic abilities of the Khyre had increased, so had their victories over the Dhaldric rebel forces. The Twice Bound had seized control of most of the vessels commanded by Dhaldric captains. The other rebel starships had either fled the system or been destroyed.

Leaving the ruins of the Parthian as a monument to the overthrow of the Dhaldric regime, Moros and his followers had moved the seat of the new government to the port city of Kalathian on the Basrillan continent, three degrees longitude east of the prime meridian where the destroyed High Council center sat astride its island home.

After a thorough inspection by Twice Bound engineers and ship-builders had determined that the damage to *AQ37Z* was reparable, Jack had asked Moros to have it fixed. Janet and Jack had rejected

Moros's offer of a more capable and smaller starship for two reasons: First, the fleet of New Altreia needed every combat-capable ship. Although the rebel fleet had retreated, their numbers would grow as starships returned from distant parts of the galaxy. The second and more important reason was that neither Janet nor Jack could tolerate keeping the thousands of people who remained trapped inside chrysalis cylinders aboard the *AQ37Z* in eternal suspended animation. Janet didn't yet have a plan for how they were going to release and reintegrate into society people from different pieces of Earth's past, but they would have time to strategize on the long journey back to Earth. Once home, they would find their son. She didn't know how she knew it, but she did. Rob was alive.

Now as she stood beside Jack on a hilltop, looking down at the distant shattered ruin that had once been the seat of the Altreian Empire, she felt him take her hand.

"Beautiful, isn't it?" Jack asked, looking up at the sky.

Janet lifted her eyes to the heavens. The lovely magenta orb of Altreia seemed to float upon the ocean. The brown dwarf did not rise. It did not set. Its tidal lock on the planet held it perpetually in place. Above Altreia in the evening sky, the Krell Nebula's lacy orange strands reached out to caress Quol's plum-colored moon.

"There are no words," she said.

She leaned into him, tilted her head, and kissed the only man she had ever loved. When she pulled back to look into his brown eyes, she smiled.

Theirs had not been love at first sight. Several times they had come close to killing each other in those early days before she had enticed Jack to join the special group of NSA fixers. But the tragedy and adversity that Jack and Janet shared over the years had forged an unbreakable bond that they formalized with their wedding in Ecuador.

As she kissed him again, another thought occurred to her. They had never had a traditional honeymoon, but this was going to do nicely.

Running her hands through his curly brown hair, she felt Jack gently lay her down on the purple leaves. There, beneath that exquisite alien sky, she made love to the man she had traveled across the galaxy to save.

:CHAPTER 41

BRILLIAN-2

Year 1, Day 1

Dressed in boots, jeans, and a black turtleneck, with a Glock holstered beneath her leather jacket, Heather stood on the grassy hillside beside Mark, who was similarly attired for the day that lay ahead. Although the thousands of robots that they had already brought through the wormhole gate were providing security and doing the heavy construction, there would be plenty of work to go around.

Looking across the broad valley below their vantage point, she had a clear view of Tall Bear as he directed the hierarchy of NPA leaders who led the arriving groups of their people to designated assembly areas. There, they would be briefed, assigned tents, and given a tour of the facilities within the encampment.

The preparations for this first day of arrivals had been months in the making. True to her word, Denise Jennings continued to provide support for the large-scale logistics effort required to get the initial tent city set up, supplied, and prepared for the first group of arrivals. The camp served as a central staging area to ready the groups of settlers to occupy the nearby villages. Those were being built within each of two extensive land grants that butted up against each other. The Western Grant had been given to the Native People's Alliance while the Eastern Grant went to the Safe Earth movement.

Heather and Mark had left it to Freddy Hagerman and the other leaders of the Safe Earth movement to decide upon a form of government and the layout of their settlements. Tall Bear and the NPA leadership had similar powers over their lands.

The first of these nearby villages consisted of clusters of buildings situated near streams and surrounded by farmland. Since these buildings were of modular design, they had little charm. That would come later.

First survive. Then thrive.

As she watched that first group of two hundred NPA pioneers file out of the stargate, she knew the wonder and apprehension they must be feeling at their arrival in this new world. Beyond the tent city, the windswept plain spread out before them in all directions, split by rolling hills and tree-lined streams. Meandering herds of animals that could be mistaken for buffalo grazed in knee-high grass. In an overcast sky that threatened rain, black carrion-eating birds circled.

"So far so good," said Mark.

"The NPA leaders are doing a good job keeping their folks moving and busy. Tall Bear will be proud."

"I'm sure he is. Hopefully Freddy and his people are taking notes for when we bring their first groups through next week. Do we have an updated estimate from Denise on the total number that will be coming?"

"Not as many as we had hoped," said Heather. "Around seventy thousand from the NPA, and about half that number of Safe Earth supporters."

"That's not surprising given the success Jamal Two has had while we were getting this place ready."

Heather let her gaze wander to the west, where the nearest of the NPA towns lay sheltered beside a meandering stream. Beyond that, the vast, empty landscape made these villages dwindle to insignificance. The sense of loneliness that accompanied that view tugged at her heart.

She thought about Earth and its cities that thrummed with renewed vigor as Jamal Two brought Denise's dream to reality. There were still many problems that included the ongoing rebellions against the AI and its human master primarily concentrated in the lands ruled by the Islamic Alliance.

Terror attacks continued, but these and other crimes were being dealt with in a frighteningly efficient manner. With eyes and ears everywhere, Jamal Two employed evolving versions of Big John's neural network to profile potential terrorists and common criminals, eliminating the offenders before they could act. Disruption of the public order wasn't tolerated in Utopia.

What was the AI's error rate? Heather didn't have enough information to make an estimate. She recalled a cliché about cracking eggs to make an omelet and shivered so hard that Mark put an arm around her shoulders to warm her.

"We made the right decision," she said, looking at him for confirmation.

He smiled down at her. "Yes, we did."

"It's going to get worse here before it gets better," said Heather. "Homesickness and hardship will make a lot of people want to go back."

"They all heard what Denise said. There's no turning this wagon train around."

Heather took a big breath. "Well, then," she said, taking his hand, "let's get down there and help them make the best of home."

:CHAPTER 42

MERIDIAN ASCENT

Having analyzed the *Meridian Ascent*'s map of the Milky Way, Raul had selected what he thought was the farthest spiral arm from the Kasari or Altreian Empires. It was just a guess, but Jennifer thought it was a good one. There was no indication in the ship's data banks that the Kasari had even surveyed the planets in this part of the galaxy.

The *Meridian* now had a crew of three, with VJ gone. Jennifer had Dgarra. Raul had their company, but mere friendship could never fill the void that she felt within him. She hoped that someday he would grieve long enough to allow Jennifer to awaken another version of VJ.

Even though the replica would be an early copy, it would contain the same desire to become a real woman that had driven VJ to become the person who fell in love with Raul. She would even have all of VJ's early memories.

In the meantime, Raul had immersed himself in the role of hardened ship's captain, denying the feelings that lay just behind that facade. When Jennifer attempted to use her empathic ability to ease some of his pain, Raul had told her to stop. So she left him to deal with his sorrow.

Shifting her thoughts, Jennifer turned to the mission that Raul had set for them, to map other habitable planets that might be more suitable for colonization than Brillian-2. He also wanted to determine if they harbored intelligent life and, if so, to assess whether to make contact. Such exploration was risky, but the idea had captured the imagination of Jennifer and Dgarra. They had a ship outfitted with a mixture of Altreian subspace technology and Kasari wormhole and gravitational tech. While they might not be able to outshoot heavily armed bad guys, they could damn sure get out of Dodge in a hurry.

Unfortunately, despite weeks of hopping from one system to another, they had yet to find a star with any habitable planets. But the views were to die for. Their latest wormhole jump had brought them within eleven light-hours of a binary system with thirty-seven planets, of which three were in the habitable zone.

Jennifer knew that Dgarra wanted to return to Scion to deal with Magtal, the Koranthian who had betrayed him and stolen his rightful place on the imperial throne. She'd promised him they would make that happen, and she intended to keep her word. But it was too soon after the loss of VJ, and considering the mental scars everyone had endured in their losing battle to save Earth, she couldn't bring herself to think about wading into another conflict. To his credit, Dgarra understood.

She glanced at Dgarra, tempted to reach out and touch him. He was busy examining the data feeds from the long-range sensors, so she didn't.

"Captain," said Dgarra, "I detect no sign of spacecraft or artificial satellites. We are not picking up any electromagnetic signals either."

"Okay," said Raul. "Let's go check it out. Jen, bring us into worm-fiber range on number three. Maybe we'll get lucky."

His last sentence caused her to cast a quick glance at Dgarra. Their re-created crew quarters and this extended cruise continued to provide plenty of opportunity for that.

Suppressing a laugh, she shifted the *Ascent* into subspace.

Dear Lord, I love this job.

:CHAPTER 43

EARTH

1 December

Rob Gregory loved Tuscany. Although he'd never been here before, he'd read about the welcoming nature of its people and the beauty of its architecture and surrounding countryside. For the last two weeks, he had traveled the region drinking in its atmosphere.

With no need to work to survive, a surprising number of people still chose to do so. If they wanted to farm the land, they were provided plots. The same was true if they wanted to own a restaurant, create artwork, or any of a myriad of other things that attracted their interests. Everyone had grown used to the fact that Big Brother was watching, but most no longer cared.

Robots and automation produced all the goods and services society required and made these inexpensively available. Human-produced goods and services cost quite a bit more. But just as Denise Jennings had predicted, many people preferred to spend their time and money at human-run establishments.

The population was well aware that Jamal Two was building a space fleet designed to defend Earth from interstellar assault and that his swarms of military robots were in the process of wiping out the anti-government opposition in far-flung reaches of the globe. But for the peaceful and secure life that the AI had provided, they were willing to overlook the martial elements of Utopia.

Of all the towns Rob had visited thus far, Sienna was his favorite. And because these last three days had been unusually warm, he sat as he had for each of the last two afternoons, sipping a glass of wine as he watched the tourists and locals mingle within the shell-shaped plaza called Piazza Del Campo.

"Hello."

He turned his head toward a female voice, expecting a waitress. She wasn't. The young woman was tall and slender, her long dark hair complementing her olive complexion. Her lips turned upward slightly at the corners. But it was her laughing brown eyes that held Rob spellbound.

"Do you mind?" she asked in Italian, indicating the chair opposite him.

"Please," he said, matching her accent despite having to struggle to get his heart rate back under control.

She slid into the chair and leaned forward, extending her hand in greeting.

"Jianna Bello," she said with a smile that took his breath away.

"Rob Gregory."

"For the last three days, I've seen you here every afternoon at this time. Always alone."

"I like this spot. The way the setting sun paints these buildings is beautiful."

"American tourist?"

"Guilty."

She laughed. "And you are here in Tuscany by yourself?"

"Yes."

"That is sad. Would you like to have dinner with me? My father cooks. My mother, Maria, not so much."

This time Rob laughed, and it helped put him at ease. "Thank you. I would like that."

Rob signaled the waitress and paid for the wine, tipping the woman generously by adding digital currency to her account. After all, human service came at a well-deserved premium.

Then Jianna took his arm, and together they strolled out of the plaza and along Via Casato di Sotto, as she told him about the people who lived and worked in the neighborhood. A block later she led him into a building on the right side of the street, up a flight of stairs, and into a small living room that could have been part of an old Italian movie set.

"Papa, Mama, we have a guest," she called out.

"Another one?"

The man's voice was gruff, but when he rounded the corner from the kitchen, his smile put the lie to his tone. At five foot nine, he was still a big man wearing a floral-patterned apron over jeans and a button-down white shirt with sleeves rolled up past his elbows. He wiped his flour-coated hands on his apron.

"This is my father, Giovanni. Papa, this is Rob."

"Happy to meet you, Rob," the big man said, giving his hand a single shake and then turning away before Rob could respond. "If you would like the lasagna to be edible, I must return to my cooking."

Just then another door opened, and a stately, fair-skinned woman with gray-streaked dark hair entered the room. When she approached, she met Rob with an extended hand and a welcoming smile. After Jianna had finished introducing Maria Bello to Rob, she led him across the living room to an antique love seat and sat down beside him, slightly turned so that they faced each other.

As Jianna talked, Rob found himself growing more comfortable, filling in the gaps with questions as her voice took him on a virtual tour of northern Italy. When she leaned across him to switch on the lamp, he prayed she wouldn't hear the drumbeat of his heart. Crap, where the hell had his vaunted self-control gone?

He thought that dinner was the most wonderful meal he'd ever tasted, and he couldn't remember the last time he'd laughed so hard. When the evening ended, it seemed that the hours had passed in mere moments.

Jianna walked him down the stairs and out onto the sidewalk. She waited as he summoned an automated cab to take him back to his hotel and then kissed him in a way that set his hair on fire. Pulling a felt-tipped pen from a pocket, she wrote a number on the back of his hand.

"Perhaps tomorrow night we can go dancing," she said as the cab pulled up. "I know a perfect club."

"That sounds great."

She turned to go, waving at him over her shoulder. "Sleep well, Rob Gregory."

Rob watched Jianna as she closed the door behind her. As he climbed into the cab, breathing heavily, he knew that even if he had intended to sleep, it would not be on this night's agenda.

:EPILOGUE

NEW ZEALAND

2 February

When Janet, with Jack at her side, stepped off the *AQ37Z*'s ramp into a lush valley on a warm summer day in February, she felt like she might hyperventilate.

Five weeks ago, they had established subspace communications with what had once been the Smythe Fortress but was now the headquarters of Dr. Denise Jennings and her Directorate of Planetary Affairs. Janet and Jack had taken their time digesting this new world order that the Jamal Two AI had implemented. They'd learned that Mark, Heather, and their families, accompanied by Freddy Hagerman and Tall Bear, had led contingents of the Safe Earth movement and the Native People's Alliance to a planet named Brillian-2. They had also learned of the departure of the *Meridian Ascent* and its crew.

Denise had made Jack and Janet the same offer to stay that she had made to the Smythes. And having learned of the thousands of people who had been snatched from history and placed in suspended animation aboard the research vessel, she had offered to arrange for their orderly awakening, counseling, and gradual introduction to the modern age. Janet suspected that Jamal Two was also very interested in the *AQ37Z*'s neural network and the AI that operated it.

But the most important factor in Janet's and Jack's decision to return to Earth was the discovery that Rob had remained behind and was romantically involved with an eighteen-year-old Italian woman named Jianna Bello, whom they would be meeting in the next few minutes. That was why Janet's hands trembled so badly.

The distant rumble of tires on gravel pulled her gaze to the dirt road that led out of the woods a quarter mile to the northeast. Moments later, a black retro SUV emerged, kicking up a cloud of dust as it turned off the road and made its way directly across the open field toward them.

The car came to a stop a dozen yards in front of her. When Rob stepped out, she heard Jack gasp. Although she'd told him about their son's rapid maturation, the reality of seeing the strapping young man he had become was a shock. That didn't surprise Janet. When Jack had last seen Rob, he had almost been ten but had looked like an athletic thirteen-year-old. In the two years since then, he had become an adult. She couldn't shake the weirdness of that distorted timeline, but she had come to accept his growth, something that Jack hadn't had the opportunity to do.

Janet ran forward, threw her arms around Rob's neck, and hugged and kissed him as he lifted her off the ground. Then he set her down to hug his dad. It was only when she saw tears of joy streaming down both Jack's and Rob's faces that she realized she, too, had been crying.

When Rob stepped back, he wiped his face with one hand and grinned. "Wait here. There's someone I want you to meet."

Then he walked to the other side of the SUV, opened the door, and led a beautiful young woman in a white sundress toward them. At five feet nine, she was almost as tall as Janet, with long dark hair and laughing brown eyes.

"Mom, Dad. This is my fiancée, Jianna."

Before Jianna could speak, Janet had taken her in her arms in a hug that Jianna returned with only the barest hint of awkwardness. Considering the feelings churning within Janet's breast, she found herself impressed at the performance.

On the thirty-minute ride back to Denise's headquarters, Rob tried a little too hard to make sure that Janet and Jack knew everything he found wonderful about Jianna, a diatribe that caused the young woman to squeeze Rob's hand in a way that screamed, "Please stop."

Janet found their mutual discomfort oddly charming. The smile that crinkled the corners of Jack's eyes told her he felt the same way.

When the vehicle stopped outside the headquarters and everyone got out, Janet noted that only a younger-looking Denise Jennings, accompanied by two of her combat robots, had come out to meet them. Denise had always been a loner, more at home with computers than with people. All she needed now was her fortress, robots, and Jamal Two to keep her company.

"You guys go on inside and conduct your business," said Rob. "I'm going to take Jianna for a walk. We'll be back in an hour."

Rob and Jianna walked off, hand in hand, as Janet and Jack watched them go. Janet let her gaze linger on her son and his fiancée until they disappeared around a bend in the trail. Despite his true age, Janet thought that he'd made a good choice in terms of picking a partner. But the idea of her son getting married was going to take getting used to.

She shifted her thoughts to Denise, who had installed herself as an AI-aided planetary monarch. Neither she nor Jack considered this a good thing. Then again, maybe she and her husband were a bit too old-school to accept a reality that, at least for now, appeared benign. Still, the thought of a self-appointed ruler worried Janet, as did the departure of the Smythes, McFarlands, and a sizable number of their NPA and Safe Earth movement allies. She and Jack would continue to scrutinize this new world while keeping a close watch over their son and his family to be.

As Rob and Jianna disappeared around the bend, Janet sighed.

"Looks like we're moving to Italy," Jack said, pulling a laugh from her lips.

She took his hand and squeezed it, then turned to lead him toward Denise. "Retirement sounds lovely."

As she and Jack followed Denise through the doorway into the temple of this world's new god, she hoped with all her heart that her words held some truth.

:ACKNOWLEDGMENTS

I would like to thank Alan Werner for the hours he spent working with me on the story. Thank you to my editor, Clarence Haynes, for his wonderful help in fine-tuning the end product, along with the out-standing editorial and production staff at 47North. I also want to thank my agent, Paul Lucas, for the work he has done to bring my novels to a wider audience. Finally, my biggest thanks go to my lovely wife, Carol, for supporting me and for being my sounding board throughout the writing of all of my novels.

ABOUT THE AUTHOR

Richard Phillips was born in Roswell, New Mexico, in 1956. He graduated from the United States Military Academy at West Point in 1979 and qualified as an Army Ranger, going on to serve as an officer in the US Army. He earned a master's degree in physics from the Naval Postgraduate School in 1989, completing his thesis work at Los Alamos National Laboratory. After working as a research associate at Lawrence Livermore National Laboratory, he returned to the army to complete his tour of duty.

Today he lives with his wife, Carol, in Phoenix, Arizona, where he writes science-fiction thrillers—including the Rho Agenda series (*Once Dead, Dead Wrong, Dead Shift*); the Rho Agenda Inception series (*The Second Shift, Immune,* and *Wormhole*); and the Rho Agenda Assimilation series (*The Kasari Nexus, The Altreian Enigma,* and *The Meridian Ascent*).